Praise for Frances Osbor

"For those who can't ever get enough of the frolics and affairs of the British upper class in the '20s and '30s, *this* is the book for you. . . . Brilliant and utterly divine. . . . It's a breath of fresh air from a vanished world."
—Michael Korda, *The Daily Beast*

"Wonderfully engaging. . . . [It] combines the tingling immediacy of the best kind of history with the stay-up-till-3-a.m.-to-finish-it urgency of a bestseller."
—Allison Pearson, *Daily Mail*

"Intoxicating."
—*People*

"Idina Sackville . . . could have stepped out of an Evelyn Waugh satire about the bright young things who partied away their days in the '20s and '30s, and later crashed and burned. . . . Frances Osborne . . . conjure[s] a vanished world with novelistic detail and flair."
—*The New York Times*

"Beautifully written . . . it catches a social group and the madcap lives they led—so luxurious, so wasted. . . . Superb."
—Barbara Goldsmith, author of
Obsessive Genius and *Little Gloria . . . Happy at Last*

"Passionate and headstrong, Lady Idina was determined to be free even if the cost was scandal and ruin. Frances Osborne has brilliantly captured not only one woman's life but an entire lost society."
—Amanda Foreman, author of
Georgiana: Duchess of Devonshire

"Engaging. . . . A revealing portrait of a remarkable woman. . . . Ms. Osborne has succeeded in her stated aim, to write a book that 'has in a way brought Idina back to life.' And what a life it was."
—*The Wall Street Journal*

Frances Osborne

PARK LANE

Frances Osborne was born in London and studied philosophy and modern languages at Oxford University. She is the author of *Lilla's Feast* and *The Bolter*. Her articles have appeared in *The Daily Telegraph*, *The Times*, *The Independent*, the *Daily Mail*, and *Vogue*. She lives in London with her husband, George Osborne, and their two children.

www.francesosborne.com

ALSO BY FRANCES OSBORNE

Lilla's Feast

The Bolter

Park Lane

Park Lane

A NOVEL

Frances Osborne

Vintage Books
A Division of Random House, Inc.
New York

A VINTAGE BOOKS ORIGINAL, JUNE 2012

Library of Congress Cataloging-in-Publication Data
Osborne, Frances.
Park Lane : a novel / by Frances Osborne.
p. cm.
ISBN 978-0-345-80328-3
1. Women—England—London—Fiction. I. Title.
PR6115.S33P37 2012
813'.6—dc23
2012013545

www.vintagebooks.com

Printed in the United States of America
10 9 8 7 6 5 4 3 2 1

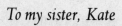

To my sister, Kate

Peace

1914

KEEP CALM *And* HAVE A COCKTAIL

I

GRACE CAN JUST SEE THE BEDROOM DOOR HANDLE ahead of her. In daylight it'd be so bright her face would stare back from the brass. But it's not dawn yet and barely February, so there's just the night-city glow coming through the glass roof. Size of a schoolyard, it is, all that glass. There's as much empty space in the hall of this house as there is in a church.

She's almost there now, made it along the passageway all quiet, and with a dead weight in her grasp. She's not a big girl, either, is Grace.

The handle is night-cold and turnip-big, fingers only just getting a turn. Slowly, Grace Campbell, for it'll come, and Lord knows when. If you go quick through it the noise is quicker, though it'll be a screech.

A foot open the door is when it squeaks, but don't you stop still, Grace Campbell, for the dead light's coming in with you. Another couple of inches, that's all. There it is, and still the bed's quiet.

She's in; pull the door to or the draught'll gush. A week she's been here and she's learning fast, though what could get through those shutters and weigh-a-ton curtains is beyond her. The door closed, it's pitch, and damp from a night's sleep. Let go the handle slowly now, oh Lord, what's she in for, the latch might as well be a hoof on stone.

There's a noise to her left, a starched-sheet rustle. Grace stops and it comes again, a slide, a pat of a pillow.

A light comes on, and Grace is in a room of heavy red and green creeper wallpaper. The room smells of dried roses, and she's facing a wall of red velvet curtain that has seen better days. Lying in the curtained bed, blankets up to her nose, is a young woman hardly older than Grace. Her face, thinks Grace, is so dainty pale that you'd barely see it on the pillow if there wasn't that hair all round, thick and brown and shining as though it is brushed all day and night. Grace's own dark hair is pulled back and into her mob cap, so's you can't see it matches her eyes; they're not like the pair looking at her from the bed, blue that could be ice or sky, who's to know which. Puts a fear into Grace, not knowing.

The scuttle's near pulling her arm out now, worse when you're still, even with how her arms are hardening. She can't put it down, not on the carpet, ever, though there's not a trace of coal dust left on the bottom. Though she can't hold it for much longer and not put it down, she'll drop it soon enough, and imagine the mess with that. Not to mention the riot she'd be read downstairs. Out it would be, almost as soon as she'd arrived.

The worry's enough to make her angry. Drop the scuttle why don't you, Grace Campbell, tidy the sheets with your coal-smeared hands, and tell Miss Beatrice that if she'd went to bed at a reasonable hour she wouldn't mind being woken now.

'Good morning?'

The very mildness of the words is water on her heat, almost so she forgets to bob, as well as she can, what with the scuttle and turning. 'Ever so sorry, Miss Beatrice. It won't happen again, the door.'

Miss Beatrice sits up and her dark hair falls on to her nightdress, all white like an angel's gown. She moves her head, hair like rain as it comes down.

'The door squeaks. You can't help it. Well, hardly anyone can. There is a trick to it but, but, I'm not quite up to leaping out of bed and giving a demonstration.'

'Yes, Miss Beatrice. Would you like me to get it seen to?' Grace almost has it now, talking all respectful as she's supposed to.

'No, I meant . . . Oh, don't worry. I suspect it is an idea of Mother's so that she can hear when I come in, and she'll just find some other way.'

There's no waiting-up here, thinks Grace, not like Ma and Da'd do. Mind you, it wasn't as if Grace was ever out at those hours. Three or four in the morning for Master Edward, she'd heard from the footmen, who'd be half gone having to wait by the door until he came in. You wouldn't have thought that was proper, or that Lady Masters would have any of it.

It's Grace who's waiting now, poker-straight, even if the coals are trying to bend her.

'Please.' Miss Beatrice tilts her head towards the fireplace.

'Thank you, miss, I mean Miss Beatrice, miss.'

Get it right, Grace Campbell, she tells herself and attempts another bob, a rickety one, though, but to the grate, quick. On your knees and reach right to the back, sweep like you're icing a cake. If she doesn't look like she's just out the mine it's a miracle then. Speck in her eye, and a big one, eye's a river but shut it tight, for you can't stop.

Fire's lit, and Miss Beatrice's head is back on the pillow, eyes tight though the lamp's still on. Scuttle half the weight now, it's back to the door, tiptoe now.

'What's your name?'

'Grace, miss.'

'Grace.'

'Yes, Miss Beatrice.'

'I like that name.'

'Thank you, miss.'

'Where are you from, Grace?'

'Carlisle.' Somewhere Miss Beatrice has never been, Grace's sure of that. At least not to Grace's part of Carlisle. Not grand, her street isn't, though the houses only joined to one other, and all new, even if the fresh red brick darkened almost as soon as it went up. And they'd had a maid once. Well, a tweeny. Then Ma said it was an extravagance, in the circumstances. Grace likes to think the girl has gone on to better luck.

'Long way. Almost Scotland.'

Grace nods, mouth shut in case her thoughts come out. Your impulses, Grace, Ma says. Hold them in and you'll go far, we'll be right proud of you.

'Don't worry about the door. I don't usually wake. Maybe it's because I hadn't heard your step before.'

Grace waits; she can't walk on, not while Miss Beatrice is talking to her, not until she's been told she can. That's the rule she's been given, even if Miss Beatrice has stopped talking and is just looking at her.

Then Miss Beatrice says thank you, sweetly, as though she means it. Of a sudden there's a warmth in Grace, the tip of a smile spreading on her and pride that is the first since she came to Number Thirty-Five last week. Out it comes, before the words are through her head even, 'Cup o' tea, Miss Beatrice?'

'Is anyone in the kitchen yet?'

What to say to that? If the kitchen maids aren't in there by now, it'll be their last day. She's out of the room and back along the gallery, where she treads careful and quiet down the middle of the carpet, thick and red enough for a palace. A palace can't be much grander than this house, with all the drawing rooms and saloons, they call them, opening into one another with doors near the size of the front of a house in those side streets Ma always told her to avoid. There's a ballroom at the back, too, whole width of the house, and at the front there's five windows, overlooking Hyde Park. Inside could do with a lick of paint, take a year to do it, it would, Grace's guess, more even. Wallpaper needs doing too, only so much as you can hide behind paintings, and some of those paintings, well . . . Grace can feel herself blush. There's a dozen of them where the people aren't wearing any clothes at all.

Grace hurries. There's Lady Masters' room to do, and her lady's maid's, and Master Edward's. Mary is putting her hand to the big rooms. The large rooms suit Mary, she's a big girl. In their bed at night Grace is hard pushed not to find herself up against all that thick blonde hair and a chest that the rest of her follows behind. Mary knows how men look at her, she does, and sometimes wiggles a little as she walks, as though her heart's on her sleeve for the taking, which in a way it is, even for Grace. Let's be sisters, Mary says to her in their bed at night, like there were no division between them, and Mary not second housemaid to Grace's third and Grace doing the chamber pots.

Pots! She's forgotten the pot in Miss Beatrice's room. Will she now have to do it in front of her, holding a vinegar rag stinking worse that what's in the pot itself? Perhaps Miss Beatrice walks to the bathroom at the back, the younger ones, they surely do that. What an idea, putting Grace into the bedrooms when she is so new. Years of practice it must take to do it quiet, and there wasn't a chance of that. Grace has to be up and running fast.

So why's she gone and offered tea to Miss Beatrice when she shouldn't be doing tea now and it'll make her late? She was soft, wasn't she, after what Mary told her. Miss Beatrice, Mary said when they lay talking at night, had her heart right broken. Just the other day.

Stories that Mary's told, Grace shouldn't believe half of them, but she's a way of making things sound true, pushes any questions there are right aside. Even about the tall one, that she'd swum from her da's dock – well, not his, but where his work is – right across the Thames and back again. In the East End, too, where the river's wider, for that's where she's from, Mary. East End might as well be on the Continent for the distance it sounds away. Yes, says Mary, it's another place, and lose yourself in it you do, before you can blink.

It's still night in the kitchen, downstairs under the street. All freezing grey cavern it is, ceiling only just above ground along the north side of the house. The windows are on the top half, being the only place that overlooks the pavement, and even that's only on to a high-walled, not-so-wide street at the side that sees little light. Why it's painted grey in here is beyond Grace. The rest of the floor, the housekeeper's and butler's rooms, the servants' hall, even the passageways, are brown and yellow, and the colour gives a bit of brightness, yellow, warm, too. The kitchen is all black ovens and pots, the only softening the long bare wood table running the length of it. Seat thirty, it would, but the kitchen only crowd around one end of it, rest of it is piled high with choppings and stirrings.

The oven's heated an hour now, still coal dust in the air, though that could just be Grace's own fingers, the smell stuck to them. Water's already on, tiny bubbles there too. Grace and the kitchen maids are over the top, three frilly mob caps in a row.

'There's bubbles, that means it's done,' says Grace.

'Hardly see them.'

'It's hot enough.'

'Stew-tea, that's all you'll get. But it ain't my job.'

'No,' says Grace, looking at the slag heap of greased plates.

Fire or sink, Grace wonders as she climbs the stairs with Miss Beatrice's tea on a tray, which is the better? Better she says, not good, for better was simply better than worse.

2

BEA GLANCES AT THE CARRIAGE CLOCK BESIDE HER bed. Not much after six thirty, no wonder it feels like the middle of the night. Her head is pounding. My God, it must have been three before she put her book down. Serves her right for picking it up when she came in, but it was sitting there, all navy and gilt, waiting for her as she reached for the light. Though you can hardly switch to sleep straight from the gramophone screeching and being flung around a drawing room. The chairs and sofas had been pushed to the side but, even then, it was too small for the crowd. They were all having a go at the foxtrot, which promises, if you get it right, to be a good deal more elegant than the turkey trot or the grizzly. And Bea likes to get it right, she likes the way she draws attention when she dances well. She knows that the men's gazes are with her as she moves around the room, and she's learnt to sashay as she walks, hips swinging, shoulders back and chest out. She's good at biting her lips, too, to make them pink and slightly swollen. If she can still draw men, she reckons, she can withstand any hail of arrows.

Three and a half hours' sleep, however, is not enough. Bea closes her eyes again. She should not have said yes to tea. She had said yes, in that way of simply accepting something because it is the easiest thing to do without properly considering whether you want it. Bea resolves, equally weakly, not to do it again.

Poor girl, all pale mob cap and cotton frills wavering in front of those curtains that really belong in a theatre. Although perhaps not a girl, for eyes all dark and eyebrows slightly too thick for a slip of a chin, and she had a curiously steady gaze for someone in the first week of a new job. It was a rather striking combination, or could be. 'Unrealised' looks, that's the phrase. Maybe Bea would take her under her wing, and stir things up a little by making a swan of a maid. Funny accent, though, and her body's tiny. But that's not strange. 'Lack of nutrition' Mother proclaimed. 'Appalling, but all that ends when they come to my house.' Then she complains at the bill for food in the servants' hall. At some stage in life, thinks Bea, you seem to be able hold completely contradictory opinions.

Grace – all the way from Carlisle and her inevitable half-dozen siblings crammed into a small terraced house. Bea had scared her; damn, she hadn't meant to do that. She shouldn't have spoken to her. Bea can imagine all too clearly Clemmie's reprimand in her profoundly irksome older-sister way. 'They're trying *not* to be noticed, Bea.'

Bea's head still hurts. Yesterday evening did not begin well. Mother insisted on accompanying her over to Edie's. Rather a fuss, and a waste of time on everybody's part as Bea is almost twenty-one, coming up for her fourth season, for God's sake, and she quite wanted to drive herself. There is something about the thrill of a throttle that would have set her up for the evening. Though as Edie's is barely a few hundred yards away, Bea would have had to pound up and down Park Lane a couple of times to pick up a decent speed. The side streets at night need to be taken at rather a snail's pace, for people seem to step out in front of her at random. She could swear that there are more people crossing the street in the evenings, and that they do so far more carelessly than at other times of day.

She had met Edie on the black and white tiled steps of Miss Wolffe's, about to be 'finished' and coached in the art of debutanteship. The languorous Edie, half-opened eyes and full lips, had cracked a line about being readied for market, and Bea had fallen for her on the spot.

Until then Bea had spent most of her childhood being governessed down at Beauhurst with its cacophony of garish red-brick towers. Edward, her darling just younger brother Edward, was her only companion, while Clemmie looked down upon them from her self-aggrandised position of eldest. Bea and Edward were allowed to run around the beech woods, crawling inside the rhododendron bushes to sit in the tangle of their branches, from where they held council of their secret societies. They were always running: chasing each other through the bamboo maze and down the gravel paths of the high-walled nursery garden. When it rained they plucked the vast rhubarb leaves and used them as umbrellas as they rushed back to the house, where they chased each other yet more, along the endless yards of passageways.

The only other people of Bea's own age she had met were Mother's friends' offspring and by the end of the first week at Miss Wolffe's, Bea felt she had known Edie all her life. However, at a party the very evening after they had both been presented at Court, the floppy-haired Tony de Clancy asked Edie to dance. He placed his pale cheek next to hers and Edie was gone – for a while. Then slightly to Bea's surprise, Tony had drifted back to his clubs and Edie to Bea. However, it is, quite frankly, jolly convenient, for, being married, Edie counts as a chaperone.

Still, there was the question of reaching Edie's, and last night Mother argued, or rather pronounced, for arguing suggests allowing room for another person's opinion, that going about alone in the daytime is one thing, but alone when dressed up for the evening is quite another.

Thus, the small tidal wave that is Mother rushed into the car beside Bea, bearing the flotsam and jetsam of enough jewellery for a duchess's ball.

'You must look happy, Beatrice.'

'I am happy, Mother.' Bea's fingers dug into the cushioned leather.

'Well, you don't look it.'

'I will when we arrive.'

'I would be lying to you if I didn't say that you will be being' – Mother hesitated – 'observed. If you appear to be moping, people might think you will never recover and marry.'

You can't say I didn't try, Bea thought. Good God, even after a lifetime, Mother's hypocrisies don't fail to irritate her. 'What about the beliefs of your suffrage cause, that women should be independent?'

'*Our* suffrage cause. And independence is relative, Beatrice. Once you have a husband, you are at least independent of the need to find one.'

'Yes, Mother,' Bea said, failing to muster any enthusiasm. However much she wanted to declare that she was now jolly well going to lead an independent life, agreeing was the swiftest way to put an end to this conversation.

'And, Beatrice, marrying is the only way in which you will escape me.'

Bea bit her tongue to stifle its reply. She kept it bitten until, after ten eternal minutes in Edie's drawing room, during which Edie assured Mother that she, personally, would drive Bea home at the end of the evening, Mother at last left, near jangling her way down the stairs even though she had not admitted to any plans other than returning to dine alone. But Mother is an evangelist for keeping up an appearance.

Bea wraps around her a silk dressing gown as thick as her curtains and pads barefoot over to the windows where she heaves down on the curtain pull. The shutters, too, might as well be lead. The bar's low enough, but it's only because she's learnt how to swing them open that she can push them out.

Outside it's still pigeon grey, even over the park, but people are already standing on the top of the omnibuses that float up the avenue between Bea and the trees and grass beyond. Bea presses her cheek against the glass; it is cold. Pulling her hair back from her eyes, she wonders whether 'Grace' could do her hair for her, but it's not a good time of day to waylay the servants. They'll bob and smile in the passage but still be bursting to get to wherever they're taking their broom, or whatever they're carrying. Damn, she really should not have said yes to the tea.

Look, a taxi, they're all but invisible at this hour, nearly all of those who can afford to take them are asleep. The delight of a curving street, however, is that she can see almost the length of it from inside the house. It's stopping at Bleasdale House, home to a pair of eligible young men towards whom Bea is too often thrust. Now, that's not an elegant exit from either of them. Her mind races as to where they might have been. Damned unfair sometimes, being a girl. Not that she'd want to do any of that, but being stuck in people's drawing rooms is so, well, limiting.

Bea walks back to the side of the bed, slips her feet into a pair of velvet slippers and, tightening her dressing gown, walks out into the gallery; she will have the tea when she returns. Light is beginning to come in through the glass dome at the top of the atrium and she leans out over the balustrades. Two floors, forty foot below, a pale cotton and mob-capped figure scuttles noiselessly across the marble floor. Bea treads carefully on the thick carpet, quite deliberately like a servant. It is not 'done' to worry about being heard and she enjoys this oh-so-silent rebellion against convention. Looking down from her perfectly pinned and willowy height, her elder sister Clemmie, chin as ever raised, tells Bea that it is common to behave in this manner. But we are common, Clemmie, Bea teases back, all that railway money, however little may be left, is 'trade'. This is the twentieth century, Clem, things are about to change.

Bea tiptoes on through an archway and down a set of stairs hidden in a gap in the wall of gilded bedroom doors. Looking down the wide carpeted steps she feels a wave of temptation to clatter down them and swing around the corner like her eight-year-old self. But she resists, and descends noiselessly.

At the back of the first-floor gallery is a pair of doors taller than the windows in Bea's bedroom. Bea takes a breath, stiffens her stomach and pushes them open to enter a room far higher than it is wide. The ceiling is two storeys above her and the shuttered windows on either side are sixty foot tall. The room is dark. There's not yet enough light outside to make its way through the shutters, and it's the only room in the house with no electricity, though you'd've thought it was the one that needed it most. When there's a crush in here, there are more silk stoles flapping about below the candles than in a flock of, of . . . seagulls.

It reeks of beeswax, as if the next dance were tonight, not more than a month away. Bea's twenty-first birthday that isn't her twenty-first birthday because one hardly wants, says Mother, to draw attention to the fact. Would look like we've given up on you having a wedding – it's a little unfortunate that your birthday is such an appropriate date to have a dance. Before Easter, before the Season, it's not just the fashionable crowd, Mother pointed out, but more interesting people are likely to come. But there's only one thing Mother means by interesting: the people who can make things happen, so that she can tell them what to change. Someone, she says, has to bring this country up to date.

At the far side of the room is another pair of double doors. Bea glides across the waxed floor towards them and swings them open to stand in semi-darkness, surrounded by barely gleaming ghosts of marble faces and torsos. She walks to the side of the room and runs her fingers across the panels to find a curtain cord and then pulls down with all her weight. A box of daylight appears above her head, brightening the walls and revealing a large table of topographical lumps and bumps in the middle of the room. She pulls down again and winds the cord around a thick brass double hook then puts her hands on her hips and breathes in deeply. Seven more blinds to go. Must be as good as an exercise machine.

The museum is awake. Aristotle, Plato, a Venus or two stare from the tops of their wooden pillars. Spreading along the walls, each one a good three or four yards long, oil panoramas of cactus-strewn deserts, bubbling swamps and mountain ranges, are all waking up. Tiny figures of men bent double with pickaxes, or over ladders of iron being laid on to the ground, wriggling into life just in time. For in every case an engine, steam puffing, is somewhat improbably tearing in from the edge of the frame.

Above the fireplace is a portrait of a bushy-eyed man towards the end of his life, a half-smile on his lips. He's a listener who never frowns or butts in but sits there patiently until Bea has talked herself to conclusion. On the table in the centre sits a map of his world, covering Australia to the Arctic Circle, but the mountains have always been Bea's favourites. It's a close call as to which she likes the most. Really it should be the Rockies or the Andes, for those are the ones she can at least reach to run her fingers over, but Bea likes the Carpathians. Not just because they're out of reach, but because people so often forget them.

Might she have gone there with John? John and his dreaming porcelain face had offered Bea a life beyond the drawing-room limits. No prison of a rural manor – that was his elder brother's – no ties to anywhere at all. She and John had talked of life among artists and writers, and of travel. Not just of Paris and Venice, Vienna and Prague, but the vast open spaces of North America, Africa, Siberia even. They would climb mountains and camp. He would draw animals rarely seen, she would write accounts of their travels and become a new Isabella Bird. However, they had not gone. Or rather, Bea hadn't gone.

She wonders for a minute whether it is these thoughts that are giving her a headache, rather than the lateness of last night. She turns back to the map, and runs her fingers over the lines that cross it, the lines that make it different to any other map. Thick, black, they are so out of scale that the width of each single one swallows whole cities in its path. They cross swamp and desert, tunnel through mountains and cross vast countries. Australia, America, India and even China, there is not a continent left across which her great-grandfather, the man looking down from the fireplace, did not build a railway. And then he, William Masters, came to London, and built this mansion in which his dynasty would live according to the social rules of the wealthy – whom he had joined. It is curious, Bea often thinks, that he founded an empire by breaking great boundaries of nature, then came here and willingly let his family be bound by a set of small-minded conventions – from which it does not appear very easy to escape.

3

IT IS SUNDAY, GRACE'S SECOND AT PARK LANE. SHE has been to church with the other servants and now she's sitting a foot away from Michael on a wet wooden park bench. They are looking at muddied grass that stretches for yards and yards, as far as the lake. In front pass families, couples and even the odd person alone, all bundled up to their chins against the chill and damp.

Grace's calves are cold. The air is coming in through the bottom of her skirts and she envies Michael's trousers, even though he's jiggling his legs away in them. Maybe Grace should turn up in a pair. And what would he say to that? Michael, with all his wanting to change the world, might just be impressed.

In a minute or two he'll turn his face to hers, all dark eyebrows and jawbone, that dimple on his chin and skin already browning in the winter sun. They're both dark. Where'd that come from, others asked back home, the Campbells look a family of gypsies.

'My hands are freezing,' says Michael. His hips go forward and he's slouching back on the bench, hands in his pockets. Then he fixes his black eyes on Grace's with a stare. He wasn't angry when they were small. He'd tease her, my Gracie, tie her plaits into one, then persuade her to run round the corner and down one of the small streets to peer into Mrs Biggs' backyard. They'd climb up the wall to look over at the privy with the door falling off, and they'd laugh almost too much for their feet to carry them home. Grace doesn't like to think of that laughter as gone. She'll get it back; if she can get anything, she can get Michael's sweetness back. She'd like to knot all that resentment into a cloth and throw it away. Mind you, there's a lot more she wants to get, besides.

'Look at you, in your gloves. Quite the lady. Proud of you, I am.'

Michael pulls his mouth back, lips stretched but it's not really a smile. He glances down, away from her. He seems, as ever, so torn this way and that that sometimes Grace thinks he looks as if he might burst into tears, though she knows he won't. More likely to punch someone, is Michael. She wants to reach out and put an arm around him, but he's not one for being touched any more. He does love her, though, she knows that. She's only been in London a month but he spends every Sunday with her. Grace pulls her gloves down over her wrists. Underneath, her hands are red and sore.

'You'll be looking after me soon,' Michael continues, softening with it.

'But not with you in the law, Michael.' She's quick back.

'No, Grace, I'm just a clerk in barristers' chambers. There's no going higher than that for the likes of me.' He turns to her, and for a moment it's almost the old Michael. 'But you'll show them, Grace.'

And as he nods back over his shoulder to the edge of the park, Grace thinks, Yes, I'll show them.

The park looks different on Sundays. Not that Grace gets much time in it during the week; still, she sees it out the window. On Sunday the weekday walkers and all their frills and silks and canes are at some country house and it is the people who work who come to the park. The men wear long tweed coats and bowler hats, the women in bonnets. Grace wears a blue one she came down to London in.

'Is that new?' Michael asks.

Grace hesitates. She's tempted to say yes to impress him. One more tiny lie wouldn't make much difference. But she shakes her head.

'Well, there's no money to waste,' he says.

They reach the Serpentine, as Michael tells her the lake is called, and he walks ahead of her on the path around it, eyes forward, a horse pulling at its reins. Grace's shoes are beginning to rub and she hobbles a little, almost as if she were in one of those skirts that Miss Beatrice wears. Michael doesn't notice. That revolution, Grace thinks, the battle's taken up all his head.

'Penny for your thoughts,' she tries, for that'll start him talking again.

He doesn't reply, so she tries another question.

'What are you up to in the evenings?' She always tries to nose around, check there's no woman's got her claws into him. That's not in her plan, some woman who will take him away. In her plan, she and Michael will share a house and, not married, Grace can go on working in the office she wants to be in. Then think of all they could send home. Grace's chest puffs out just at the thought of it.

But if Michael gets a sweetheart, Grace, well, she'd . . . she'd push her into the Thames. Grace's heart lifts for an instant. Then she holds her breath, can't believe she's had thoughts like that. On a Sunday, too. Is that Hell for her? Grace turns her head away from Michael. It's not as if she's being straight with him either. It's hardly as though there's nobody to look at in Number Thirty-Five. Then she stops herself. She can't think that.

'You know I study in the evenings,' he says.

'Trying to change the world?' she teases. 'You sound like the sermon this morning.'

'Brief and to the point?'

'Michael!' How can he say such a thing, straight after church on a Sunday? Then it occurs to her that he might not have gone, the thought of it a weight in her stomach, and she can't not ask.

'How was yours?'

'Non-existent.'

'Ma will have a fit,' says Grace, thinking that the number of things that Ma mustn't know is growing.

'Then don't tell her.'

'I mind.' No church is the beginning of a slide. That's every family's fear, falling towards rags. What she and Michael are doing in London, part of it, is working so that they don't all fall down into one of those dirty terraces. And when a family starts falling there's none that dares come near it for fear of falling too.

'Oh, I was out looking for God in my own way.'

'Say your prayers, Michael, promise me that.'

As he tells her, 'Off then now, sister,' he reaches over to squeeze her hand.

The pressure of his fingers pushes the wool of her gloves into the cracks in her skin and she flinches. If he notices he doesn't say anything at all.

Next morning, the rain's coming down and Grace is by the tradesmen's entrance, trying to get the floor clear of muck. Third time today, and Mrs Wainwright, her salt and pepper hair pulled back from her wide face so tightly that it's a wonder she can speak at all, said to get up from dinner and finish by one o'clock just as though Grace hadn't done it at all. Mrs Wainwright being housekeeper, Grace has to up and to it, lickety-split. Weather like this, just one pair of shoes and there it is again, wet city filth and spreading in every direction. You'd've thought the others were doing it on purpose, walking over it again and again, trying to prove Grace is not up to it. They're still at it, too, about the way she speaks. Not that they have dainty voices themselves, but Susan, who thinks herself Queen Mary even if she's only first housemaid, holds her spike of a nose to 'talk like Grace', and even Mary, friend that she's supposed to be, has to stifle her giggles. Changing to speak like they do, though, would be giving in; Grace is not going to give in any further than she has done already, just by being here.

Mary and she are working it out all right, even though Grace is below her. Grace is still two years older, and they can all tell that. Mrs Wainwright likes Grace, Mary says. Not that Grace would know it for Mrs Wainwright is always over Grace's shoulder, asking why she isn't doing the next thing, and it's as hard as getting something done proper, remembering what she's to be doing after. The morning fires, Grace has the measure of now. It's nerves that make the clatter. The silver, that's something else altogether. Grace had never held a piece of silver before she came here. Their only silver spoon sits in a box on the mantelshelf. To sell it, Ma says, would be selling the fact that my ma was lady enough to own a silver spoon. Now Grace has to worry about all the cutlery you can imagine, not to mention the bowls and serving dishes, and pots and shakers, and the photograph frames. You don't even have to touch them for them to dullen black and need as much elbow as a loom worker.

Grace laughs to herself at this. None of them are doing that, Ma says, not after it was her mother's family who had *owned* a mill. There's a thousand places to sink to before being trapped at the looms.

But at least the looms do as they're asked, more or less, thinks Grace, as she works away at the floor. There's none of this who's saying what to whom, and not knowing what's around each corner. Who'd've thought that men and women in service would have such a high opinion of themselves. It is almost as though, wherever you've come from, if it earns wages then service is a Step Up, and don't you forget. They all know, there's not much hiding it, that Grace hasn't been in service before. Grace wonders if they assume that her family has fallen already, which Ma would say was true. Lord, let them not find out where she thinks she can go, or about her lessons with Miss Sand. Then it'd be all about Grace's hoity-toity ways, no matter that they're as keen as anyone on their manners and who hands what to whom when. More than once, Susan has said that it's not some charity, being in service. Particularly not here, at Thirty-Five Park Lane, and working for a family that's a household name. How Grace has persuaded Mrs Wainwright to take her on is beyond any of them.

The only other servant that's down from the table is the one Grace would like to see. Who wouldn't want to look at Joseph, all six foot that he is, just like one of those statues in the museum of a room at the back of the house, except he's all in the black and gold braid of his livery. Though underneath he must be almost as white as the marble itself . . . Grace Campbell, what are you thinking? She's shocked herself and feels herself redden. You finish your mopping now, Grace, and keep your mind on his sandy hair and green-brown eyes, bits you can see.

Second footman, he is, Joseph, but as calm and steady as if he were the butler himself. At least he's calm and steady with Grace, makes her feel that if she tripped he'd catch her before she fell. He smiles at her as though he's pleased she's come to the house and Grace hopes that she'll find herself alone by the piano in the servants' hall with him again. Last time he relaxed into his Somerset accent and it made Grace feel less of an outsider. 'I'm just a farm boy,' he whispered to her, and Grace giggled.

Now she knows he's up in the dining room. Three for luncheon, even though Lady Masters isn't due back until that evening. It's Master Edward's guests, that's all they know, and Master Edward was in late last night, Joseph told her when they were doing the china that morning. Those large platters are hard to hold with one hand while she scrubs with the other and she doesn't know which is worse, bacon fat or egg. When she's talking to Joseph, it's that much harder to keep her mind on the job and hold on tight to the plates.

'I let him in at five o'clock in the morning,' Joseph told her, his blond hair bobbing above Grace, leaving her eyes level with the shadow of roughening on his chin. She can never quite bring her eyes to his, and he has teased her for this. 'You won't turn to stone, you know, Grace,' but that just makes it worse.

Five o'clock in the morning, though, Grace doesn't want to

think where he's been, and on a Sunday. What's more, a gentleman, as even Grace knows, shouldn't be spending a Sunday in London.

Joseph comes down from the dining room. All in a rush he is. She can't not look up as he passes, and he calls to her.

'There's a cart. It's stuck. In the rain. It's blocking the road. You can see it from the dining room.'

'You'll be caught,' she wants to shout after him but it is too late, he is gone.

His footprints cut a trail over Grace's neatly scrubbed flagstones, but she doesn't turn a hair. She washes them away and reaches for a dustpan and brush to take up to the dining room. Crumbs from breakfast, she can say for a reason to be up there, even though she'll be asked why she hadn't cleared them before.

Grace is on her way upstairs when the doorbell rings. Half past noon, she thinks, maybe a quarter to one, servants' dinner will be finishing downstairs and they'll all be about. Grace listens closely. If Mr Bellows is already in the butler's pantry then she'll have to pass, and he'll ask to see where the crumbs are. Not a sound, and she's quick into the dining room. Even before she allows herself to look out of the window she kneels down to beat some dust out of the rug to put in her pan. Now she looks, and outside she can see Joseph fill the gap between two men who've already wedged their shoulders against the rear of the cart. The water's falling out of the sky as though there's taps up there, and it becomes hard to see anything but a row of white cotton sleeves on wet white arms straining as if they might burst.

Is he sweet on her too? Grace heaves the thought out of her mind. No, Grace, you can't think like that, you need to keep working, and send money home. Sweethearts are for other people.

4

EVEN BY MONDAY LUNCHTIME, THE WHOLE CITY SEEMS to have ground to a halt in the rain, as though it's some rare event, and it's ten to one and she'll have to change before lunch. Her gloves, plain winter grey, look like a zebra's coat, and she's bound to have traces of soot on her face, no doubt even in her nostrils. It has been worth it, though, for travelling by train with the window open had added to the sense of escape. Clemmie and Tom's small house party at their echoing house Gowden, consisting of Tom's ruddy-faced friends 'Bertie' and 'Flipper', had certainly needed fleeing from.

Yesterday morning when, after an unauthorised walk alone across the fields after church, Bea returned to the relentless damp of her sister's house, an already changed Clemmie had been standing half frozen in the cavern of the hall, the telegraph in her hand. She looked her sister up and down, her gaze resting on the mud and leaves on Bea's boots before she reluctantly handed over the brown envelope.

Bea tore it open. Any news, anything at all, meant a possible opportunity to leave early. It would have to be jolly bad news to be worse than another four days of hunting, shooting and school stories. Clemmie gave Bea at most half a dozen seconds before snatching the message from Bea's hands. She stared at the paper as though it were an insult.

DARLINGEST SIS, it read. *AM RESCUING YOU. BE UP HERE ONE SHARP TOMORROW. PROMISE A GRAND SURPRISE. EDWARD*

Clemmie tore the paper in half and threw it on to the floor, the words rattling out of her, 'I am going to so much trouble, Bea, all on your behalf. I give up. Enjoy life as a single woman. I mean, no wonder . . . ' she breaks off, and Bea feels a sharp jab in her ribcage.

'No wonder what, Clemmie?' she challenges her. 'That John behaved as he did?'

Clemmie takes a breath and looks away.

'Oh, for God's sake get changed out of that walking dress. We're all starving. And being late drives the servants mad. Anyway I suppose that maybe this means Edward may at last have found something to do.'

'Clemmie, he's barely been out of school for a year.' Defending Edward is a reflex for Bea, even if she's pushing out of her head thoughts of how he may be spending his time.

'Yes, and he's barely been home since then. A few hours between dawn and noon, and half an hour to change for the evening. He should join the cavalry. It would transform his life.'

'How can you say that? What if the war comes?'

'Everyone is always waiting for some war to come.' And Clemmie turned to walk out of the hall.

'Cavalry officers dance every night too, Clem.'

'If only it was just dancing, and at least he would be doing something during the day He's hardly going to listen to one of us,' Clem shouted back, over her shoulder.

Bea, alone in the cold front hall, bristled. Edward, dear Edward, would surely listen to her, once she had brought herself to broach the conversation.

The taxi turns into Curzon Street bringing Bea within spitting distance of Park Lane. She can even see the walls of Number Thirty-Five when the taxi stops. In front, blocking the width of the road, is a coal cart which should have finished its rounds hours ago. For God's sake, hurry up.

Bea pulls down a window and leans out into the rain. The cart's horse has turned, or has been turned, more like it, at too sharp an angle and the wheels are slipping on the cobbles. It can't be just because they're wet. Must be oil. Whatever fool left that behind will find his engine conks out jolly quick.

The end of the coalman's whip is reaching right up to the beast's shoulder but the rear wheels of the cart keep slipping back into a rut between the stones. The horse whinnies, and the coalman lashes more. The rain is coming down hard now, the cobbles darkening. If Bea walks she'll be drenched. She'll have to dry off as well as change and that will take yet more time, and then she will have let Edward down. Oh, bother it.

The taxi rattles and Bea's driver grunts with displeasure alongside his engine, but he is not getting out to help. Not in this weather. However, as she waits, from the mews on her left appear a small group of men in shirtsleeves, clearly ready to be soaked and blackened.

The men glue themselves to the back of the cart and begin to push. The motor behind Bea's taxi is less patient, and hoots. Bea's driver grinds his foot down on the accelerator in response. As the taxi shakes, the smell of petrol rises and Bea begins to feel nauseous. She decides to find a point, or a line of points, on which to fix her gaze to steady herself. From here she can see the north wall of the house, as far as the main bedroom floor and, across it, she notices a jagged crack pushing up and down right across the house. It is the first time it has caught her attention, yet it is already wide enough to see at fifty foot off.

The coal cart has been pushed forwards several times and each time it has slid back, but the man counting down to the heave is again punching the air in front of him, and they are going at it once more. Another motor, maybe two, has joined both the block of traffic behind and the chorus of horns. Bea looks at her watch:

five to one. Edward is quite capable of teasing her with a day's silence if she is late, and Bea is not altogether relaxed as to what his surprise might be.

Bea decides to walk the few yards she has left to go. She asks the driver if she can borrow his umbrella, saying he can pick it up at the front when he drops her case. She climbs out into the rain. Taking a step at a time on the wet cobbles, she steadies herself on her heels. As she passes the cart it moves up, out of the rut and on. The men behind it, dappled black from forehead to waist, turn around and slap each other on the back, then, noticing Bea, dip their foreheads in her direction.

Bellows opens the door solemn-faced, no doubt appalled at Bea's arrival on foot. He has a curious knack of acting as though your behaviour has let him down. Bea smiles, but obtains no reaction. Thank God Edward doesn't play poker with the man, he'd lose the house.

By the time Bea descends from her room washed and brushed, the door to the yellow drawing room – the morning room, Mother likes to call it, even though they all point out to her that it faces the afternoon sun to the west – is open. It has stopped raining, and from the gallery Bea can hear the sound of Edward's voice. When she turns into the room she sees, beyond Edward, a long lean frame in chiffon and wool, one elbow on the chimney piece and a cigarette in her hand. Her father's sister, Celeste, is standing there as if her elbow had never left its marble perch – even though Mother banned her from the house a decade ago.

Bea doesn't see Celeste often. Celeste's circle is, Clemmie whispers disapprovingly, 'Bohemian'. Still, Bea knocks into her at the odd dance and, perhaps once or twice a year, indeed barely a couple of months ago, meets her for a rather excitingly surreptitious lunch. To be fascinating, Bea thinks, a woman needs to have secrets, and her lunches with Celeste are at least one. So please, Bea says to herself, be damn careful, Celeste, and don't let on.

Celeste has her gaze upon Edward, who has pulled himself fully upright. Of course he has, thinks Bea, for Celeste has a disarming way of looking at you intently that makes the rest of the world vanish. Celeste blows a smoke ring as though she is inhaling both him and the whole room into her possession. The web of Celeste's spell is almost visible, and it seems somehow churlish to break it, but Bea can't spend all afternoon in the doorway. She coughs, and the two of them turn towards her. A Cheshire Cat grin stretches the dark circles under Edward's eyes.

'See, Bea darling,' he declares, 'a terribly grand surprise, and a delightfully wicked one, too.'

'You make me sound like a piano, Eddie. Can't I be a, well, delicious surprise instead?' Celeste replies. She turns to Bea. 'Darling, glorious to see you. It feels like years.'

Bea must learn, she thinks, to lie as effortlessly as Celeste.

Celeste blows another smoke ring and leans her shoulders back in a near-coquettish way. She beckons Bea across the room. Bea doesn't move; she is hardly going to leap into her aunt's arms in front of Edward.

'Celeste, how perfectly glorious to see you. You haven't changed a bit.'

Bellows coughs. It is his turn to be standing in the doorway.

'We'd better go in,' Bea continues. 'Monsieur Fouret—'

'Heavens, is he still with you? I am surprised your mother hasn't returned him to sender on account of some transgression or another. Or simply for being French.'

Celeste takes a final puff of her cigarette and throws it on the fire. The three of them walk out along the gallery and into a dark green-walled dining room peppered with views of Venice. 'Copies,' Edward periodically says to Mother, who bristles at the word. 'It's true,' Edward insists to Bea. 'How else do you think Father is supporting the casinos of Europe?'

They sit down, Bellows, James and Joseph pushing the chairs in behind them. Celeste runs an eye around the room. 'It is certainly a trip back in time.'

After the game terrine has been cleared, Celeste leans across the table. 'So, Eddie darling. Who, or what, is the subject of your attentions?'

'Oh, Celeste,' he laughs. 'The world, but not his wife. Good God, they've killed a cow for us. Ladies, you cannot leave until it has all been eaten.'

'Well, we'd better stretch the conversation out,' replies Bea. Monsieur Fouret, she thinks, is waging war upon my waistline. She takes a large helping of cabbage which, miraculously, is steamed not buttered.

'All right then, Sweet Bea. Let me fill Celeste in on our various diversions.'

'Diverting I hope they are,' says Celeste.

'Well I, of course, am seriously considering rising at dawn with the cavalry, instead of staying up until dawn at the card tables.' Bea does not find this as amusing as her brother does. 'Clemmie and Tom,' he continues, 'are squeezing the family into Gowden.' Ha, thinks Bea. 'Sweet Bea is being an ardent huntress of husbands.' Less funny again.

'Don't tell me,' replies Celeste, who has eaten nothing. 'Your mother is giving a series of lectures on how women must resort to violence in order to remain at home and avoid the responsibilities of having a voice.'

They all laugh. Bea doesn't want to laugh but she does, downright cheek on Celeste's part, sitting in Mother's house, but on the nail. Mother could, quite possibly, surrender a limb rather than follow Celeste's Mrs Pankhurst, and burn down a building for the vote.

Then a stroke of sadness crosses Celeste's face; she's looking around at the room again. 'I wish,' she says, 'it hadn't been so long.'

'But,' replies Edward, 'doesn't that make it all the more fun to be here?'

'No, funnily enough, it doesn't. I just remember all the things that won't happen again. Let's scram. I've always found this dining room a morbid haunt.' Quietened, Celeste leads them back to the yellow drawing room.

Edward vanishes at the door and Celeste's mood shifts as though she levered into reverse for a few moments and is now motoring forwards to make up lost time. She sits down on a slightly worn dark green velvet sofa, pats the seat beside her, leans back and looks at Bea expectantly. And Bea does just as Celeste expects, feeling the sofa sag as she sits into it, as though it will not let her get up again until Celeste has quite finished.

'Heard you needed some cheering up, old girl, something to distract you.'

Celeste has crossed her legs away from Bea, and is talking to her slightly over her shoulder in a voice that, as ever, sounds as if Celeste has spent the past two days as the town crier.

'Me? Oh no, I'm fine, utterly fine.' Bea glances at the clock.

'Poppycock,' replies Celeste. 'And eyes on me, darling. Edward assures me that your Mother will not be back until this evening. Something about a horse, or the garden. Or maybe just another ineffectual pamphlet.'

'That's harsh, Celeste. Think who she manages to talk to.'

Bea pulls herself back up and walks over to the chimney piece where she finds a blue enamelled cigarette box and starts fiddling with the lid, flicking it open and closed. It is, she thinks, my mother you are talking about, Celeste, however unreasonable she can be.

Celeste continues. 'Oh, I know, she speaks to every member of the Cabinet. But what good has just talking done?'

'They're nearly there, Celeste.' Bea opens and closes the cigarette box again. 'They just have to put a suffrage bill through Parliament.'

Celeste has taken a cigarette out of her own case, and waves the hand holding it, sending up a spiral of smoke.

'And for how long have they been saying that? They've been "nearly there" for a decade, darling, and each time they come close, Irish Home Rule inevitably raises its head and pushes the vote off the agenda. And now we've got the Cat and Mouse Act to contend with. It's ridiculous, Beatrice, you know it is.' She slightly angrily flicks her ash to the side, where it misses the ashtray and falls on to the Turkish rug at her feet.

'Don't look so horrified, Beatrice. Your father sold the original as soon as he turned twenty-one. Anyhow, listen. You know jolly well that you can't release a hunger-striker when she's about to pop her clogs and then, just as a bit of colour is coming into her cheeks, take her back inside. It is inhuman, and if you saw what they look like after force-feeding, the poor lambs.' Celeste leans back and upright, fist raised, come-with-me-in-anger. 'But according to the law of this land, of course, we women are barely human. And "talk", bah! As if talk is enough. It's real action that counts, you know that. It's exciting, Beatrice. Little feels more alive than being out there.'

Out there. Bea has a vision of Celeste in the middle of a riot, bearing down on a policeman with an Indian club held above her head by an arm in a flowing silk sleeve.

Bea walks towards the window and stares at the traffic now moving freely down Park Lane.

'I'm not sure that hurting people is the way forward.' Bea's more than not sure. Peaceful protest has been dripped into her by her mother for as long as she can remember. That ends do not always justify means. That there can be no progress through destruction. That being hauled off in handcuffs does not advance the argument that women should play a role in governing the country. It sticks. What mothers say always does.

'You can't worry,' Celeste replies to her back, 'about using aggression. It is the only currency men understand. We don't set out to hurt anyone. The churches, buildings, they're all empty. When any blood is spilled, it's self-defence. If they will try to arrest us—'

Bea turns around. 'What rot, Celeste. The exploding letters? Sulphuric acid, phosphorus? Those hurt.'

'Nobody has been hurt by them.'

'That is chance. And this time last year, you all planted a bomb . . . '

'Lloyd George's house was a building site . . . ' It is Celeste's turn to stand up from the sofa, and she sashays over to Bea and puts a hand on her shoulder. Bea doesn't flinch. 'At night it was as dead as a doornail. Beatrice, it is the only way, and you have to do something with your life. Do you want to become one of those people who exhales hot air and achieves nothing?'

Celeste is looking Bea in the eye almost imploringly, but Bea looks away. Celeste removes her hand and strides back towards the chimney piece, where her elbow resumes its earlier position on the marble.

'She is too damn stubborn, your mother,' she continues, 'to admit that she will not succeed. She was jolly stubborn right from the first. She came down to Sussex and walked into the dining room at Beauhurst on her father's arm with a look of "Don't think you'll make me withdraw with the ladies" written over her, top to toe. I blame it on her mother. Too jolly confident, these Americans. No wholly English girl would be so bold at that age.'

But, thinks Beatrice, I rather admire Mother for that, and Celeste can hardly talk.

Celeste lifts a cigarette out of the enamel box on the chimney piece and lights it with a silver lighter abandoned there. 'She was only nineteen, and already as political as they come. Still, a politician's daughter . . . but I am that, too . . . Christ alive' – Celeste grimaces, and blows the smoke out sharply – 'where does she find these cigarettes? They are quite ghastly.' She throws the cigarette on to the fire and walks back to the small crocodile-skin bag, sitting upright at one end of the sofa, and pulls her own cigarette case out. 'Yet look how different we are. Anyhow, by the end of dinner, she'd bagged my brother. All those dollars and he was so happy to go along with it. And the one time anyone's pulled the wool over your mother's eyes was letting her believe there was much railway money left.' Celeste returns to the fireplace and lighter. As she exhales, she blows the sweet smoke down towards the fire, eyes and mind in some other place.

Well, whatever money there is, thinks Bea, Mother is being rather obscure about what there is left to give. Bea wouldn't have put it past her to have given the lot to Clemmie.

'Politics is in your blood, dear Beatrice,' says Celeste, turning back to look straight at Bea, and waving her cigarette in her direction. 'And you cannot avoid wanting to make things happen, however hard you are pretending not to. I know you don't believe that all that talking is going to get us anywhere.'

Celeste finds the vein. Straight in there, needle sharp. Bea's been going to rallies with Mother for four years or more and they engage her up to a point. The crowds are huge, impressive. Hundreds of banners above thousands of hats. Some of the speakers are rousing; Bea's pulse rises a beat or two ready to leap in. But when they stop, the applause fades, the mood dampens, the crowds wander off and Bea, pulse still fast, feels quite alone.

As Bea is thinking of this, Celeste, seeing her waver, offers her the address of Mrs Pankhurst's HQ.

'The headquarters on Kingsway have been raided so often that the whole operation is now in hiding. We keep moving,' says Celeste, as she starts to pace the room. 'It's war, and it's not just Parliament we're fighting but the Home Secretary, too. Don't tell me he's a friend of your mother's, please, Beatrice,' Celeste is looking straight at her again. 'He kept our mail back, tried to have the telephones cut. The police raided Lincoln's Inn House again and again. It's *The Suffragette* they're after.' Her voice grows more emphatic. 'He's gone and banned printers from taking it on. It's perfectly bloody to find one, and then we have to hide every trace or we'll be back to square one. Go along when you've decided you're up to it. If you need more persuading,' she continues, 'come to Emmeline's rally tomorrow.'

'Mrs Pankhurst, here?' Bea wakes up at this. Mrs Pankhurst is said to be in Paris, evading rearrest. The very rarity of the appearance has a certain appeal. Despite all that Bea believes, Mrs Pankhurst is said to be electrifying. And, blast it, Bea has let out enough of a flicker of interest for Celeste to spot a kill.

'Who else? Coming back from Paris tonight and straight into Mouse Castle in Campden Hill Square.' Celeste looks at Bea, eyes half closed, a smile spreading across her face. 'Eight thirty in the evening,' she continues. 'You'll see the crowd in the right spot. It will be announced in the press tomorrow.'

'Isn't that begging for a fight?'

'Indeed. Come on, Beatrice, think where you've just been. There must have been some buffoons at Clemmie's. Beatrice, they can vote, my dear. You can't. Doesn't that make you angry?'

These last words Celeste speaks almost tenderly, as if she is caressing Bea with them.

'It's not just for the cause, Beatrice. It's for you, too. I think of you as my daughter. Listen, darling, you need something to distract you. In any case, you're a Masters, we break the rules. Doing so is simply part of us.'

Bea is lying in the bath before changing for dinner, the water up to her chin. She lifts her toes out to see them lobster-pink and looks down at the rest of her body, which appears near broiled. She should perhaps not have added quite so much hot water to the bath Susan drew for her but there is something quite delicious about the headiness of a truly warm bath.

Bea looks down at her body with dismay. Her breasts are too small. At least she has the shoulders to balance the width of her lower half, but she is nonetheless out of proportion, making it hard to look slender. Even if her waist does look considerably slimmer than her hips.

Annoyingly, it is definitely her legs that are her greatest asset, for which she has her height to thank. However, they remain hidden – unless she is swimming, which is, of course, rare. She wonders how the order of attractiveness would change if women's legs were bared, though fashion after fashion would inevitably be devised in order to make women's legs look more attractive than they really are.

She begins to feel a little too hot. Good God, how long has she been in here: she'll look like a prune tonight. What's more, she has somehow, perhaps from her conversation with Celeste, found the determination to collar Edward this evening before he goes out and she must seize the moment. She pulls herself out of the bath, grabs one of the towels on the rail beside her and more or less dries herself before, dressing-gowned, she pads back along the gallery to her bedroom. Maybe she should still have the bath filled in her room, but it requires such a trail of buckets of water that she inevitably tells the servants to stop when it is only a few inches deep.

Susan has pulled a selection of clothes out on to Bea's bed. Bea surveys the options and considers raiding her wardrobe for more. No, for God's sake, there are half a dozen outfits here, one of them must do. As ever, there are two pale blue. Pale blue is deemed to be Bea's colour, as it matches her eyes. However, it does make her look rather chilly, and tonight, for what will certainly be a gramophone evening, she does not want to look cool. It is not very conducive to being asked to dance. Maybe she should go for the pale green. Its beads, which almost dangle from it, and the great folds and puffs of chiffon that wind around her upper arms, give it a somewhat oriental air. If she adds the rather ornate topaz and silver pendant brought back from India by a travelling Masters, she will look distinctly exotic. She has enough of a clear line to her chin and nose to pass as some Eastern offering, but for her ice-white skin. Perhaps she could look like one of those women kept in a harem and barely allowed to see the light of day. Bea considers trying to shock Mother by declaring that is her intention. She might at least stop implying that Bea should get a move on and find someone else to marry.

Thinking of bad behaviour, she must hurry if she wants to have a chance to dig Edward out of wherever he is in the house before each of them has to leave for dinner. She rings the bell, hoping that it will be the new girl, Grace, who comes up to fix her hair. She can somehow get the wave just right.

Edward has not been as swift as Bea and is still in his room, being dressed by Joseph who, in his braided livery, looks considerably smarter than her brother and who is the first to see her enter.

'Evening, Miss Beatrice,' and he gives her a deep nod, apparently genuinely pleased to see her. He has, she reflects, an easy charm to him, that perhaps comes from being a couple of inches over six foot and having a decidedly classically good-looking face. Footmen are, of course, supposed to be good-looking, but even Bea's girlfriends have joked about Joseph.

Edward swivels around from the mirror in which he is making an attempt at straightening his collar himself.

'Whoa, Sweet Bea. Doesn't my sister look grand, Joseph?'

'Turn every eye in the room, sir,' and the footman nods, or rather bows, forward from the waist.

Bea feels herself blush a little, and almost blushes again at the thought of it, so turns quickly away.

'Thank you, Joseph.'

'A pleasure, Miss Beatrice.'

Edward breaks in. 'That's all, my man. Off with you. My sis can show her skills at the rest.'

As Joseph nods to them both then turns to leave, it occurs to Bea that any man in uniform, whether cavalry or livery, really cannot help but be at least a little attractive.

'You had Joseph, not James?' asks Bea as, after Joseph has left, she finishes Edward's collar and checks his studs.

'I like the fellow. By the looks of it, so do you.'

Bea pinches her brother.

'Hey, sis, we're not six years old any more.'

'I still know how to pinch my brother when he is teasing me. I am not yet desperate enough to marry the footman.'

'You don't have to marry him.'

'Edward! Be quiet.'

And he falls into silence.

When Bea has finished the studs, she looks up at Edward to read the expression on his face. This is her moment to talk to him, however little she may want to hear the answers. Still fired up enough to keep her gaze on the dark circles under his eyes, she begins.

'Edward.'

'Yes.'

'Are you all right?' He doesn't look all right. He's pale, his hands are not altogether steady and, is she imagining it, but is there the tiniest nervous tic to his smile? But he opens his arms.

'Darling sis, I am on capital form.'

'Or on form,' she says, and this is what she should have said half a year ago, 'all over the capital.' Edward looks at her with a 'How can you not believe me' expression on his face, then he slumps down into the armchair behind him. The bravado has vanished, his arms flop along the sides of the chair, wrists and hands hanging off the end. He is half the size he was.

'Listen, Bea darling, I am trying to be good, but it is hard to give up such a roar of a time. Or rather, what was a roar of a time, and now it's more a case of things not being jolly unless I've a fan of cards in my hands. Or a stack of counters.'

There they are, the words that Bea has been avoiding for months. How long will it be before Edward, like their father, vanishes to the Continent to be occasionally sighted at the tables in Biarritz or Baden-Baden? Bea feels her stomach turn. The idea comes to her of running over to the door, turning the key and removing it, telling Edward that he is never going anywhere without her again. If she could, she'd move him back into her room, take from him some favourite toy and refuse to return it until he has mended his ways.

'Edward,' Bea says, 'my darling, darling Edward, you must stop. You are the man of this house,' she tries.

'To all intents and purposes, it is Mother who is the steam engine.'

'Steamroller, more like,' mutters Bea.

'Yet she always stops,' replies Edward, 'before knocking me down.'

'Edward?'

'Yes.'

'How much have you lost?'

'How much have I won, do you mean?'

How can he joke now, how can he treat this, what he is doing, even the conversation they are having now, so lightly? Bea feels a degree of anger rising inside her.

'And where does all this take you?'

'I don't know, Bea, I don't know.'

'You do know, Edward, you know perfectly well, and you must stop.'

His head is low again, as though there is a puzzle stretched across his knees.

'I am trying, Bea, truly I am.'

'You must succeed, and if –' yes, she'll say it, and mean it too – 'if you do not, I shall tell Mother.' But Edward isn't looking at her. How odd, a maid – Grace it is – has slipped in without knocking and Edward is watching her move across the room holding a tray as if it were a cushion with a crown on it. The girl lifts her head and Edward beams at her as though he is the sun itself, and the maid blushes. Bea feels a jab of annoyance.

'You're not listening to me,' she continues, but he doesn't move.

'Edward,' she growls at him.

'Yes, Bea-Bea, but if I do succeed, then what on earth do I do with myself? I haven't the patience for fishing. Despite Mother's misfounded beliefs, I am a poor horseman, and in any case, like you, feel saddened by those foxes; they're rather elegant, don't you think? As for shooting, well, if I didn't miss anyhow, I'd only try to. And I can hardly become a suffragette. All that's left to me, it seems, are the vices.'

'Well, find another vice, then. And not alcohol. Why, why . . .' She's hesitating about what she's going to say, shocking herself with the very words, but if it will save Edward, then, Beatrice, you cannot be such a prude. 'How about a married woman, Edward? I thought all you young bucks did that sort of thing.'

As a look of astonishment grows on his face it breaks into laughter, and so does Bea. As she laughs she continues, 'I mean it, Edward. It's a better place to pass your time.'

'Edward!'

Oh God, thinks Bea, and the two of them spin around to face the door to see the petite figure that is Mother, all the more formidable for being immaculately dressed even though she has just come up from the country.

'My dearest boy, what a lovely surprise. Oh, how I missed you at Beauhurst. Now, I want you to tell me and your sister everything you've been up to. It is always such an unmitigated pleasure to hear.'

Mother is unfailingly predictable in her bias. This, too, is what Bea has always told Edward: don't worry about the fact that she adores you and simply does what she must with me, she's straight out of Dickens. He laughs at this and, no doubt, if she catches his eye now, he will laugh again. Bea is careful. If they roar together, Mother will suspect that they have been up to something and will not let it rest until she has extracted an answer, and Edward does not look on good enough form to deceive well under the pressure of Mother. So Bea keeps her eyes away as her brother proceeds to nurture their mother's mistaken belief that he could not, in a thousand years, do anything to upset her.

5

ALL OF DOWNSTAIRS EXCEPT THE KITCHEN MAIDS AND the boot boy are lined up, as usual, for breakfast on either side of the long table. Mr Bellows, and what's left of his red hair, is at the top. To his right is Mussyur Fouray, chef's hat still on even though he's at table, and taking up a good two seats with the size of him. Then there's Summers in his two rows of chauffeur's brass buttons, though his chest could fit three, and James and Joseph: James first, because he's first footman, then Joseph as second. James is as dark as Joseph is fair and their gold-braided tailcoats are as dark as their breeches are pale, though how they keep them clean is beyond Grace.

To Mr Bellows' right is Mrs Wainwright, all grey hair and cheekbones, and not an ounce spare on her. Next is Miss Suthers, mouth as ever locked in her lady's-maid pinch. Then come the three little maids in a row: Susan, Mary and Grace, all dressed for the morning in their flower-print frocks and mob caps. That puts Susan staring at the gap between Summers and James, and Mary between James and Joseph, and Mary can't see a man but look at him in that way of hers. This makes Grace feel uncomfortable, and Joseph's the only man she has to look at. Though how she's to look at him is beyond her, for he'll sneak a wink the moment he reckons nobody is watching and she'll blush all over. Thank the Lord it's not often that nobody's casting an eye around, for meals are times to work out what everybody's up to, the top of the table all speaking with such plums in their mouths there's no telling where any of them were born. Even lower down the table, growing closer to Grace, everybody has their Park Lane voice, which might as well be a different language to the one they grew up speaking. Some evenings, especially on Saturdays, if Mary's been out with Lord-knows-who she goes out with, she falls back into the voice she grew up with. I don't have a care in the world when I talk like this, Grace. But Mary also makes out she's in good spirits.

Today, as usual, they're talking of upstairs, the boot boy and the kitchen maids on their separate table at the far end of the room trying to listen as best they can over the clatter of knives and forks. And a din it is, for they eat quick as they can to get something inside before the bells start ringing. Bea keeps glancing up at the bell board on the wall above Mr Bellows' head.

'Deaf now?' says Susan who has seen her looking up. 'A housemaid who can't hear, that's all we need.'

Susan's tongue's as sharp as her face and she's taken against Grace. Not right from the start, a few days in. Mary explained: first housemaids must always be wanting to go up to lady's maid or housekeeper. The only person upstairs who might be needing a lady's maid of her own is Miss Beatrice, though for now, whoever hears the bell goes to her. But sometimes Miss Beatrice does ask for one or the other of them, and Grace can't say she's not pleased when it's her, even if she's surprised at herself with the thought. Keep your head down, Mary tells her, and your mouth shut. If Susan has a whiff that you've a decent head on your shoulders she'll be trying even harder to knock it off.

Always the most dangerous, them that's near the top but not quite there.

Mrs Wainwright silences Susan. 'Grace, you'll hear the bell, I'd stick to your plate.' There's silence again for a second then James, who, even though he's above Joseph and should have some dignity about him, can never keep his mouth shut when he should, leans forward and goes back to yesterday.

'I'm sure she noticed.'

'It's Lady Masters to you, or you'll find yourself changing places with Joseph.'

James drops his eyes. 'Yes, Mr Bellows.'

Joseph's not saying a word. He had a right dressing down yesterday for the state he was in when he came back from the cart. Grace wants to rub his cheeks, put some colour back into them. There's more not said around this table than's spoken out loud. Still, now Grace wants to know something and the question rushes up on her and out of her mouth before she's had a chance to hold it back.

'How'd sh— her ladyship know it?

'Those cigarettes of Miss Celeste's. From Turkey, or wherever's you'll have it. Stink like a public house where no one's opened the window for a week.'

'James . . . '

'Yes, Mr Bellows.' And James quickly glances up at Summers and his buttons and back again, as if he's expecting to be told off by him, too.

'That's daft!' Susan cuts in again. 'There'll be hundreds who smoke them.'

Mrs Wainwright is looking very hard at Miss Suthers and Miss Suthers is looking straight back across at Mrs Wainwright. A lady's maid is as close as you can get to upstairs but there's not a word on Miss Suther's lips, it's all in her eyes, saying it clear. Don't forget what's said while I am doing her ladyship's hair, and a dozen other things beside. Then Miss Beatrice's bell snaps the silence, and the table lets their breath out. 'Earlier than usual,' mutters Susan, two mouthfuls into her toast, but she is up to brush the crumbs off her pinny quick as a hare. 'For me, I think.'

Grace feels resentment rising in her, then checks herself. Is that what's become of her ambitions, and so quick? She can't let herself be jealous of a maid's work. Not when she's supposed to be a secretary. And not with what her family need her to send home.

Grace started with answering the advertisements in *The Times* in her best handwriting, learnt with Miss Sand, and paid for by Ma's sister, Aunt Ethel. She was a schoolteacher, and so mindful of reading and writing, said Ma, that you'd've thought there wasn't any other talent in the world. Aunt Ethel, not being married herself, had always helped Ma with the five of them. Bit of money as she could, here and there.

Five is the sign of a happy marriage, Ma used to say, eyes pale above the dark circles under them, but she didn't want the same for her daughters. Don't you do this, Grace. Waste it all in some man's kitchen, she'd say, while she went at the mixing bowl, her arm a mill wheel, pasting the eggs and flour. My daughters are going to see better than the inside of an oven. Even though back then there was still a maid to rattle the coal into it.

So Grace and Michael sat side by side in Miss Sand's parlour, willing the fire to burn higher, though with a half-dozen of them in that tiny parlour they might as well have been sitting around the funnel of one of Da's engines.

Miss Sand's, where they went when they grew out of school at twelve. The rest of the class were half a dozen girls, with fathers in the professions, who'd been told not to mix with Grace and Michael. When they were all let outside, the girls just turned their backs. Not good enough, railwayman's children, even if Da was an engineer and hardly a navvy – and it was at Miss Sand's that Michael started to change.

Michael was the only boy. Some days there'd be a crowd of lads his age on the street a few doors down from Miss Sand's. The jeering didn't bother him, he just walked straight on the same side of the road as the crowd to shield Grace from it. More of a reader than a talker, he was, and Miss Sand found the books to lend him from her friends.

While Michael learnt Latin, Grace learnt shorthand and typing. Miss Sand worked through the book with her and, after Michael went to London, she blindfolded Grace as she sat down to type and timed her. First-class secretary, she said, any man would be lucky to have you in his office.

My hope's with you, said Ma as she put Grace on the bus to the railway station, the day after the New Year. By which Ma meant send back all you can of that good salary you should have in an office. My investment, said Ma, for even though Michael was clerking – now that, Da said, is a career – it would be a while before he was making good money.

Where he was boarding, women weren't allowed. Not that you should be in the same building as men, said Ma, even if they are gentlemen. If there is such a thing as a gentleman, because in the railways she's not sure of that. She stopped as she said this and looked hard across the room at somewhere altogether different for a moment or two, then was quiet. So Grace went to another boarding house, three to a room and ladies only, though Grace soon saw that what was meant by ladies was broad as a river. Ma didn't know that. All right and proper, she had said to Grace as she put her on the train. You two keep an eye on each other down there, promise me that.

Grace sent off Miss Sand's reference with the letters. Invitations to interview came by return. She'd turned up the next day, scrubbed clean and shining, in gloves and a hat. The interviewers smiled as she came into the room. Their faces fell as she started to speak.

'We'll write if we need you to come back.'

In one interview a gentleman looked her gently in the eye and spoke slowly, as if she didn't understand English.

Grace had a month in hand if she eked out the pennies, holding on until the boarding-house meal in the evening. Before each interview just a slice of bread to stop the stomach hollering. Halfway through the third week she moved on to another section in the newspaper. No letter this time about her typing skills, instead the character-only reference Miss Sand had given her. It wasn't what she'd come here for, nor where she wanted to end up. Grace knows there's more to her than service, for all those back home who said she had a nerve to set her mind further than Carlisle.

She had been too nervous to notice the size of the house on Park Lane. She was so focused on finding the tradesmen's entrance, she can't even remember now who it was who let her in, just the sitting in Mrs Wainwright's housekeeper's office. Mrs, but no ring on her finger, and kind as she was in the interview, since Grace started Mrs Wainwright has become a wall with no door.

Were the servants fed here, Grace wondered, but it was Mrs Wainwright who was doing the asking.

'You're old for a junior housemaid.'

'I can learn quick, mam.'

'That is extremely clear, but have you ever scrubbed a floor? Laid a grate?'

'Yes.' Grace thought of Ma – You'll do better than this, but best know how – and kept her smile up. Not quite three weeks and she missed home. Missed the rain, the chill, even her little sisters. Even now she still wakes in the night thinking she can hear them all those hundreds of miles away.

'I don't know who this Miss Sand is,' said Mrs Wainwright, 'but she writes a good letter. Mary will show you your room and you'll share with her. Even though she's younger I am afraid she'll be above you, for she's been here a good while. I'd give her the sense of that if I were you.'

'Thank you, mam, thank you.'

'Don't gush. Thank me if we keep you on. And, Grace . . . '

'Yes?'

'You'll have to learn to speak more clearly. However, keep quiet and you'll do well. When you're a housekeeper you can raise your voice.'

Grace bought a single sheet of notepaper, an envelope and a stamp on the way back to the boarding house to pack her bags. The dining room was empty and she sat down at the table to write a letter to her parents. It wasn't long. All that needed to be said could fit in a sentence or two, any more and she might get herself in a muddle. She folded the paper, fiddled it into the envelope and stamped it. She was paid up until the end of the week and she wasn't going to be seeing a penny back, not after they'd ordered her food, she'd been told, or could have let the bed out to another young woman. Grace didn't bother pointing out that there were two beds empty on the top floor. There were no goodbyes – all the boarders were out at work – so she left her door key on the sideboard and closed the front door behind her. She passed a pillar box on her way back to Mrs Wainwright.

It's three in the afternoon and they've only an hour off today, too much to do for any longer. The dance is a month away but the invitations have just gone out and so they must, says Mrs Wainwright, start to prepare. Grace doesn't point out that the house is spotless enough for royalty every day of the week.

Mary wants to go for a walk. She'd rather, she says, that Grace came with her, good for Grace, too. 'That's living like a princess to see all that green across the road, asking for a visit.' Grace doesn't want to go out. She sits on her bed where the mattress dips, snug between the mounds on either side. Boots off, feet on the edge of the mattress, her fists are on her knees. Her thumbs press into the sides of her forefingers, twisting the near-translucent paper that she is squeezing between them. A neat script is inked across the page. Not a smudge, Ma never smudges, never let Grace either, one blob spread in the wrong page and she'd send Grace back to the kitchen table to do her lessons again, whatever the cost of the paper.

After Grace had finished her homework, Ma would give her an apron and a pair of old leather gloves to wear – you don't want skivvy's hands, Grace, you won't get into an office like that. That's my life's work, Grace, Ma'd say. She has a funny smile, Ma, all bright and shiny so's you can't tell whether she's teasing.

The letter came two days ago and Grace slipped it straight into her pocket. For two days it's been in her drawer, burning a hole in her clothes. How can you not read a letter somebody has written you?

When you're only going to make the lie worse.

5th February, 1914

Dear Grace,

How happy your letter made us. It is wonderful news and makes everything worthwhile. A private secretary is grand. Is board still taken out if you are living with the family? Still, it's certainty, isn't it. How much can you send home? Twenty-five shillings a month I expect, with what you must be earning! Or thirty, if you're careful. If we can we'll put it by up here.

My Grace, what sort of man is he you are working for? If he bothers you in any way, you must leave, promise me that. It'll all be fine if your name's still good and a girl can lose her name by being bothered. Does he have a wife and children in the house? A housemaid, too? You mustn't let them ask you to do even light dusting. Or that will be the start of it.

Don't go out after dark unless you must. Miss Sand says she can send you some books for the evenings.

Your father and I are glad you go to church with Michael on Sundays.

With my love,
Your Mother

I'm proud of you, girl. Best love, Da.

Thirty shillings a month. That's as much as she earns and half again.

Grace pushes so hard on her thumbs that the paper begins to tear.

6

BEA IS LYING ON HER BED WITH JOHN'S VOICE FILLING the room. She didn't hit her head, he is saying, just slumped . . . shaken . . . carried her back . . . I'm so sorry.

'Sorry for what, John? You've been a hero,' says a female voice.

'Oh, I can't imagine being that.'

More female voices are saying that what she needs is rest, and she wonders how many of them are in the room. Thank God you found her, John . . . But until she's better . . . She's fine . . . Thought you said earlier you had to go back up to town . . . Don't get into trouble . . . We'll cable you. A few minutes later she hears his footsteps leave the room, in that oh so measured pace.

Only they're not John's footsteps, it's a servant knocking at the door, and she's not down in the country at Beauhurst, she's in Park Lane. Her room is empty; she must have fallen asleep again after ringing the bell, if it can be called sleep when your dreams are memories, not good ones at that. Oh, Beatrice, it's February, she tells herself. That's two months, and you still can't get that man out of your head.

They'd been down at Beauhurst, Bea had invited a crowd for a few days and they were in the drawing room with the dregs of coffee after lunch. Bea was sitting on one of the window seats with John, looking over his shoulder as he made cartoons of their friends around the room. Halfway through one of Edie, he put his pencil down and turned around to look at Bea. Let's go for a walk, he whispered, his eyes full of something he wanted to say. Yes, she replied, her heart in her mouth. She stood up, excused herself from the room on the grounds of needing a nap, and near dashed upstairs to change into a walking dress. She pulled a couple out on to the bed but they looked such passion-killers, so she took a coat better suited to Mayfair than the country, but at least she looked like the girl of someone's dreams.

She met him at the gate to the walled nursery garden and he led her away up into the woods and pine air, their feet sinking into the dead leaves underneath as they walked. For five beautiful minutes they walked hand in hand until they came to the curved white lovers' seat by the little waterfall. They sat on either side of the bench, leaning across the divider so that their noses were almost brushing. John took her hand again, and squeezed it.

'Beatrice,' he said, 'I've something I want to say to you.'

'Yes,' she replied, wondering why he was saying and not asking.

'Beatrice, I can't marry you.'

She remembers feeling as though she were a stone that would sink into the earth if she didn't stand. So she did, and moved away from him, she thinks, and then she fell.

It is Susan who comes into Bea's room in Park Lane. Good Lord, Bea isn't sure she's up to Susan this early. Right now she'd like a tender hand, not one that looks as though it would sooner whip your face.

She has pointed this out to Mother, who pooh-poohed her. 'She's first housemaid. If anyone should help you dress it should be her. At least she's honest; it's such a bore when servants steal. You feel you never know where you've put something and that you must be going insane. Then there's the residue of guilt for God knows what becomes of them without a reference. Really, I don't mind a rocky countenance if you can find things where you set them down last.'

It isn't, thinks Bea, Mother who has to have her scalp jabbed by the Woman with Iron Fingers. Mind you, with Suthers as a benchmark, Mother would be unlikely to notice.

Susan is fast. Bea will give her that, and Bea is still ahead of the others when she comes down to breakfast. She noses her way along the sideboard of poached eggs, kidneys and half a dozen other offerings. She takes nothing. At the end the newspapers lie folded like fallen dominoes. She takes one and makes for a chair, not seeing Joseph until he slides it in behind her.

'Miss Beatrice?'

'Oh, coffee, please. And maybe toast.'

He nods, and vanishes.

The usual silversmith's window of sugar shakers and coffee pots squat on the white tablecloth in front of her. She pushes both them and the empty place settings next to her out to the side and spreads the newspaper flat.

The announcement is easy to find:

> Mrs Pankhurst, who has returned to England in order to resume her work for the vote, has taken up residence at Campden Hill Square, where she will address a public open-air meeting tonight, at 8.30.

Bea glances over her shoulder. There's nobody to see her. The box around the notice and the letters themselves seem to thicken and darken before her eyes. Keep away from it, she tells herself. You'll only find yourself caught up in something and everyone will think all that business with John has gone straight to your head. At least, that is no doubt how Mother would present it, as the only explanation why her daughter could have joined 'a bunch of half-crazed lunatics'.

It was hardly an invitation to a riot, though. 'Address a public open-air meeting . . . ' It is, on the face of it, no different to the summons to Mother's meetings and it's not as though Bea would be taking a bat with her.

The alternative is another dinner in another hotel, another show, and the familiar recipe of whiskies and the gramophone after, all of which suddenly sound dull.

The person she wants to talk to, perhaps even reveal her plans to – for he is always on her side – is Edward. But he will not emerge until noon. Mother is, in the circumstances, perhaps not the best conversational foil. That leaves Clemmie, who was back in the house last night. Tom has stayed down in the country and, in a surprising gesture of sentimentality, Clemmie declared she didn't want to hear her voice echo around her and Tom's London home and she would prefer to stay at Park Lane, in her old room.

Clemmie must be awake, should jolly well be awake and ready for talking, if, Bea pauses, if she is speaking to Bea yet. She could go around to Edie's but Edie won't be up for hours. She has recently joined the ranks of those who don't see the morning sun. Bea starts to push back her chair and it is now Bellows who gently moves it out of her way as she pulls herself up and her skirts down, and strides out of the room taking the newspaper with her.

Clemmie is sitting at her old dressing table, silver-topped glass jars opened, cream thick on her face, wrestling a hairbrush through her waves. Bea flops down across her sister's bed. Clemmie's room is lighter and brighter than Bea's and decorated in a rather gloriously feminine lilac and white. Bea is more than a teeny bit envious of this, especially since, if Clemmie keeps returning to claim it, Bea will never be able to move in, which is jolly unfair because Clemmie rather owes her the room now she is married. After all, it was Bea who orchestrated the 'inexplicable' flood in one of the bathrooms above so that Clem's room would be redecorated for the first time in half a century. Short of a house fire, Bea's room will remain looking as if Queen Victoria still had decades to reign.

Bea speaks to the back of her sister's head. 'I'm sorry about Sunday.'

'It's all right, but don't blame me if you're still living here at fifty.'

'It won't be here, Clem.'

'Then where would it be?'

'Oh, New York.'

'Do you still miss it, Bea, America? Even after living there only a year?'

'It was rather exciting leaving so suddenly, on some whim of Mother's.'

Clemmie hesitates. 'Yes,' she replies. 'On some whim of Mother's.'

'Once we were there, it felt as though we could do what we liked, rather than being locked in by all these silly rules. We just ran wild on the banks of that river. Life's different there, Clem. There's more, more' – Bea searches for the word – 'possibility.'

'You talk about it as if it is some sort of Promised Land.'

Bea pauses.

'In a way, Clem, I think it is.'

Clemmie turns around to face her. 'Why don't you go over? You could have a glorious dance.'

'On the Hudson? Only our neighbours would make it that far. It's in the sticks, Clem. That was the heaven of it.'

'Not bad neighbours, Bea. But I meant in Manhattan, silly.'

'Yes,' says Bea, 'in Manhattan.'

John is there, she is thinking. Maybe she could so dazzle him with a dance in her mother's family house on Madison Avenue that he would come running back to her. She imagines herself dressed up, flowers all over the hall, her standing at the foot of the wide wooden staircase, John approaching her with a pleading expression on his face.

However, that is exactly why she cannot go. You can't chase a man across the Atlantic. In fact Bea can't go there until he is back. Damn you, John Vinnicks, why couldn't you have gone to Africa instead of heiress-hunting . . . and as this last thought comes into her head, Bea feels slightly sick.

Clemmie's voice is back in Bea's ears. 'Now, Bea-Bea, help me choose what to wear tonight.'

Beside her on the bed are two dresses: one black and white satin, with a jacket designed to tie around the waist. The other, a pale grey net tunic embroidered with a vast beaded butterfly that must be nearly a foot across.

'You'll take off with those wings. Are you dancing?'

'Just dinner.' Clemmie twists to look at Bea. 'It is being given for me. And Tom. He's coming up this afternoon.' She quickly turns back to her dressing table, her eyes away from Bea as she clips out, 'Sorry, don't mean to brag.'

Brag, thinks Bea, brag? She rolls on her back and studies the pale lace canopy strung over Clemmie's bed. Brag about the dinner, or the husband? She envies neither. She can think of little she would like less to do this evening. Was that what her life was to be, dinners, shows and gramophones, and then, then what? A ruddy-faced sportsman with a decaying house in the country?

'Wear either.'

'But I've hardly been in town since Freddy was born. Rural hibernation really, and one is so *examined* when one reappears. Is she still attractive, did she hook above her weight, et cetera? Whether it was just for the money.'

Bea sits up and swivels around.

'Clemmie, you don't think that?'

'Not on the dresses . . . '

'Clemmie, please. Do you think that Tom married you for your money?'

'No, no, of course not. He's mad about me.' Clemmie pauses. 'But, you know, it could happen to any of us.'

'There's not much money. Not for us girls.'

'That's not what people think, unless they dig around.'

'Because of the railways?'

'And because of Mother's mother being American. Countless pots of gold, people reckon. I mean look at . . . ' Bea feels as though a vice is tightening around her stomach, and decides that she will not spend this evening with the people who must have been examining her.

Celeste responds to Bea's note, her maid addressing the envelope, as ever, to disguise it from Mother. She says that she will come by in a taxi, and be waiting in it just to the right of the front door at half past seven. Bea has told Mother she's going with Edie to a musical recital at the Bechstein Hall, which leaves her with a niggling uncertainty as to whether Mother's and Edie's paths might cross elsewhere that evening. Mother at least does not come downstairs to notice that Bea is heading out for the evening in a public taxi.

Avoiding Joseph's eye as she leaves alone, Bea walks straight out of the door and climbs blindly into the taxi waiting outside, which, to her relief, does contain Celeste, who is immaculately dressed for battle. She is wearing a high-collared coat buttoned up to her chin and is carrying a walking stick. Bea thinks at first, how odd, she doesn't need it, and shortly afterwards starts to wonder what she does need it for. Bea looks down at her own clothes. On the off-chance that she saw Mother on her way out, Bea has dressed for a musical recital. However, at least her overcoat is heavy, though whether it will protect her silk petticoat during whatever evening lies ahead, is in the lap of the gods. She feels a shiver of fear, and enjoys the sensation.

Campden Hill Square is dark. It is not well lit, and between the houses on either side a railed garden falls down the hill to the thoroughfare of Holland Park Avenue. The trees in front of the houses meld into those growing over the fence of the garden's iron rails, forming a leafless canopy.

Bea feels the crowd before she is in its infectious mass of hot breath and expectation. Hundreds of people are jam-packed up the narrow slope of a road on the east side of the square and rise up the hill in a dark swarm. Bea's heart quickens as it engulfs her and she and Celeste are swept down Holland Park Avenue by a tide of new arrivals. The two of them are bobbing about excitedly in the centre, which is moving quickly enough to keep them there. Bea is pushed in the back and tries to look around, but is knocked forward again as she does so. She is surprised by this roughness and lets out a small gasp. Buck up, old girl, she tells herself, these are the suffragettes.

The crowd carries them on and past the eastern side of the square, where the mass is densest. Celeste makes an effort at pushing her way back to the edge but the steady movement forward keeps her locked in line. 'Dammit and blast it,' says Celeste. 'Just go with it, Beatrice, we'll go up the far side of the square with this lot and then make it down from the top. Aim for the third tree from the bottom.'

Bea is not as certain as Celeste. She can't see who's at the top of the square, but she doubts it's empty. Or that they have much choice as to where they are going. The crowd turns up the far side of the square towards the grand terrace at the top, carrying them along with its burble of clipped 'Hold on theres' and thick miaows of 'Oi, that's my foot yer on'. Bea shuts her eyes for an instant. It will hardly make any difference to the direction in which she is travelling.

God, the smell. Bea has never smelt perspiration like this. Some of it smells as though it has settled indelibly not just on the skin, but on the medley of both stiff and worn serges, tweeds, fine wools, the odd mackintosh that Bea is being knocked against. Or rather squeezed against, for the stream feels as if it is tightening around her, and sticks are digging into her sides.

Bea is now frightened by this. If the crowd goes on tightening how will she breathe, how will any of them breathe, how will any of them get away from here? But all that they can do, any of the hundreds of people jammed around her and Celeste, is move wherever they are taken. The crowd surges forward in stops and starts, each jolt throwing Bea against her neighbours. She may have escaped Park Lane this evening, but she is again in a place where she cannot make an independent decision as to where she is going. At least she decided to come here. Yet is it inevitable that, however many decisions you make, at some point you find yourself again being swept along by events? Thank God she's not here alone; if she could, she'd stitch her coat to Celeste's, which is drifting in and out of reach. On they are pushed, right along the terrace to the corner, and back down the hill, where the weight of the crowd descending behind her becomes worryingly heavy. Then they stop. She and Celeste have reached a wall of bodies so densely packed that they cannot be pushed any further.

Below them spread the darkened curves and corners of ladies' hats and gentlemen's bowlers, nearly all pointing in the direction of a single lit window on the first floor of a house near the bottom. Celeste starts to pick her way down towards it, moving into gaps ahead of her invisible to Bea. Instead Bea moves sideways down the hill, 'sorry' by 'sorry', and sharp-elbowed hiss by hiss. She stumbles, they're bloody well sticking their feet out, maybe Mother is right that they are lunatics. Bea is losing Celeste and fluttering a little, the light is jolly poor and the crowd is heaving and pushing and she's struggling to keep upright. Celeste, unhampered by manners, is moving far faster. Bea tries to track what she thinks is her aunt's hat through the jostling ahead but the wall of bodies tightens. That's it, no further, she's done rather well, though Celeste's 'third tree' is still twenty yards out of reach. For the first time in her life, Bea is alone at night and in a crowd of strangers, her heart is racing and she feels breathless with the excited fear of riding towards a high hedge with a complete lack of control. She tries to push again, caring less about whom she knocks on her way – the lesser evil to being seen, or even being, on her own – but the shoulders in front respond by rising more firmly against her. This at last fires some push into Bea herself. Well, damn them, she's jolly well going to get through.

'Not a chance,' says an overly cut-glass female voice behind her. 'You won't get any closer. But you can see the house from here.

Well, some of it. Don't I know you? I'm sure I do.' Bea stiffens. Good God, who is it, one of Mother's friends? But one of Mother's friends would not be here, and it is a voice that means well. Right now that is worth the risk of being discovered. Bea can always say she is engaged in some kind of espionage, just here to find out what the other side is up to. The woman behind this voice might be able to help her. Besides, there's a limit to how long you can stand practically in somebody's arms and ignore them.

So Bea turns, or rather twists her head until she feels she has the neck of a giraffe. The woman is using her umbrella to steady herself as she stands on tiptoe – she is wearing make-up, and a little too much of it. What a relief; not a chance that Bea knows a woman like that.

'No, I don't think so.'

'First time?'

'No,' lies Bea. She doesn't want this stranger to latch on to her in sympathy.

'A thousand here, I should say,' the woman continues, nodding back up the hill. 'Hours ago, some of us came. It's so pleasing to have a good position, isn't it?'

Bea does not feel as though she has a good position. She has failed to reach the tree, and she has lost Celeste, which makes her position, if anything, precarious. She has a sudden dread that this is going to be one of those evenings when the police come rushing out. That would be more that Bea bargained for, she's heard about what can happen then; now nervous, she starts to count the number of walking sticks she has seen. But surely, surely, nothing bad can happen to her on her first time.

'Are the police here?' she asks.

'Oh, I couldn't be sure. I haven't seen any uniforms. Maybe they've popped into the bushes. What a lark!' The woman lowers her voice and leans over to whisper into Bea's ear. 'But of course as long as she's in the house they can't lay a finger on her.'

The crowd has become suffocating. Bea has survived more than her fair share of crushes in houses too small for the numbers invited. This, however, is both more threatening and, well, dammit, more thrilling, even though – or perhaps because – there is no sign of Celeste. The night air is setting in and people are moving from foot to foot as the sway of the crowd pushes them to and fro, shaking the wet-dog smell of damp wool into Bea's nostrils. She has another go at moving towards the tree but the shoulders in front of her tighten further and a voice growls back, 'Should have come ealier if you wanted to be up front.'

Closer to the house, a group of women are starting to chant: 'Em-mel-ine, Em-mel-ine.' In front of Bea is a small figure dressed in pale grey, an expensive pale grey. This is not the place to dress up, thinks Bea, and she's tiny, can't be more than a girl who should be in bed by now. Christ, she's getting old to have thoughts like these. Bea, Celeste is right, you really do need to do something with your life. The figure turns to glance behind her and Bea sees, to her astonishment, a flash of pearl earrings, a face that has seen seven decades and a grey gloved hand gripping the handle of an umbrella. What, Bea asks herself, makes all these women come?

On the dot of eight thirty, a silhouette appears at the lit window and the crowd roars. A small dark figure climbs between the open panes and on to a delicate wrought-iron balcony. It can be barely wide enough for her feet, thinks Bea. The woman stands up, a feathered hat black against the light, like a potentate's, and extends her hands. The crowd rustles into silence and in the minutes that follow Bea forgets she has lost Celeste, forgets she is alone, and forgets she is surrounded by strangers.

'Bravo! Bravo!' She hears the sounds coming from her own lips.

'God bless you, Mrs Pankhurst.' A man's voice. Well, there are enough of them here, though half of them probably plain-clothes policemen. That is how, Celeste has warned her, some of the police come.

Then Mrs Pankhurst speaks. A thousand people stare at the

silhouette moving above them, their heads tilted back, chins up. Mrs Pankhurst raises her arms until her hands are level with her shoulders, palms facing her congregation. She will, she says, come down to join them, but first she must tell them what needs to be done. Her voice is clear. It carries over the dark swell of bodies as it declares that, by fighting, women can 'show to the manhood of this world the kind of stuff we are made of'.

'If,' Mrs Pankhurst continues, 'our violence is wrong then the violence of Christ is wrong.' Then she lists a stream of violent New Testament references. Bea feels herself listening with a single, collective ear that is the crowd drawing in every word of this Christ-like figure who is feeding them, the one thousand, with encouragement alone. 'Nothing,' she says, 'can put down this movement. They may kill us, but they cannot crush this movement.'

Celeste has told Bea that in prison Mrs Pankhurst hunger-strikes so that she has to be released until she is well enough to be re-arrested, then she moves constantly, her whereabouts secret. It is only when she is out of the country that she can spend more than one night in a single place. Now she is 'manifesting herself', thinks Bea, to her disciples. As Mrs Pankhurst speaks of hope and right, and struggle that must shy from no act, whatever the price it takes, exhilaration emanates out through the crowd, passing from touching shoulder to touching shoulder. When it reaches Bea, she finds her lips tingling.

'When your forefathers fought for their liberty, they took lives . . . ' And then a heckle, another man's voice, pushed loud. 'But you are only a woman.' This is immediately followed by half a dozen other voices telling him to be quiet. Bea feels her shoulders tighten, he has made a direct shot, this voice, and the comment grates under her skin. 'Only a woman.' Bea thought of Tom's friends at Gowden. How was she 'only' compared to people like that? What did 'only' a woman 'only' do? After all, she goes to lectures, she is here, too, out in a crowd, alone, surrounded by strangers, listening. But 'do'? Listening could not be stretched to doing. If she were not to exist, thinks Bea, what acts would be undone? She has lived for twenty, almost twenty-one, years without making a mark. Her embarrassment curdles into anger against the heckler, against his little pack of chums, against every single person who thinks a woman is an 'only'.

Mrs Pankhurst does not fear that she has done nothing. She turns the comment back.

'That is what we are fighting, my friends. We women are fighting not as women, but as human beings, for human rights.' She defies the police to arrest her again, and taunts them for cowardice in not keeping her in jail. Cowardice for force-feeding her, head pulled back, strapping her down. They stick a tube through her mouth or nose, and push it right down to her stomach. All the women scream, Celeste has told Bea, in detail, and over lunch, which somewhat stalled Bea's appetite. The warders pour in a liquid. 'All futile, really,' said Celeste. 'They only vomit it back up with the blood from their gums.' Last time Emmeline had had enough and when the warders came in, she held a clay jug above her head and threatened to hit them, and they'd released her before she had died from starvation. 'A martyr ain't good for politics. They're just going to take her back when she's well enough. Ruddy Parliament and their Cat and Mouse Act.'

And now, thinks Bea, the police, the Cat, want their Mouse back and here she is, standing right above their noses, mocking them, and untouchable, even if she is 'only a woman'. Ha, thinks Bea.

Mrs Pankhurst is exhorting her listeners to lay down their own lives, for what, she asks, 'is life? At best it is very short. Would it not be well, when we leave this life, as leave it we must, to leave it having struck a blow for what is truer life; having struck a blow for the freedom of our sex; having struck a blow against subjection; having struck a blow against the vicious conditions into which the majority of our sex is born; having struck a blow against the disease and degradation of the masses of our country? Can you,' asks Mrs Pankhurst, 'keep your self-respect any longer?' And Bea, standing there, wonders at her own life, its lunches and dinners and dances. Mrs Pankhurst, Bea realises, makes her tremble.

Mother calls herself a suffragist, and Mrs Pankhurst 'a proponent of lunacy'. Mother believes that every step Mrs Pankhurst takes makes women appear less suitable to be given the vote. She is far from alone. There are middle-class men who don't believe women should vote, working-class men who fear that women may be given the vote instead of them, and women like Mother who are quite convinced that only their approach can succeed. She expects Bea and Clemmie to fall in line with her point of view, and upon the very first meeting of the National Union branch down near Beauhurst – which she co-founded – dragooned the pair of them to come along. Clemmie begged Mother not to put her name on the list.

'This is ridiculous, Mother, it is simply embarrassing for us all, don't you see that?'

'That's not a wise comment, Clementine, from a young lady who is supposed to be about to come out into society. You need my help to find a husband.'

'Aunt Celeste escaped without a husband,' Bea interrupted.

'She was asked to leave. It became inappropriate to have her with us any longer. Anyhow, there's little joy in being the spinster sister in the attic. Or anywhere.'

'Surely,' returned Clemmie, 'I'm hardly going to find a husband if I appear to be some ranting banner-waver.'

That was a little unfair, for Mother's National Union protests are peaceful and efficient – if ineffective, thinks Bea. After last June's Derby and Emily Davison's miserable death that followed it, the National Union had rallies rippling up and down the country for weeks. The climax was a great march into Hyde Park, a blistering day and an ocean of a hundred thousand men and women marching from almost every town you could put a name to. Bea stood by Mother at the drawing-room window, the field glasses printing rings on her cheeks. Below streamed an armada of boaters and the odd bowler, sails of banners above them. The two of them went down into the sea of people, and floated along with the fluid, almost graceful, movement. The march was magnificent, yet almost a year later appeared to have achieved nothing at all.

The crowd here in Campden Hill Square is very different to those marchers – there's a hardness and an urgency to them. And they are jam-packed into a narrow street, ready to explode.

Mrs Pankhurst vanishes and the balcony is empty, though the crowd is still shouting and cheering. In a minute she'll return, she must return, for the encore. Instead Mrs Pankhurst comes out of the front door. One advantage of being this distance off is that Bea is far enough up the hill to have a view. At least Bea thinks Mrs Pankhurst comes out of the front door, because all she can see is Mrs Pankhurst's infamous 'bodyguard', a dozen battleaxes of women brandishing Indian clubs as if they were swords. No, there's a black feather in there, poking up between the clubs. Behind Bea, a band starts up and the crowd in front of her pushes back to make space for their leader and her bodyguard. The hat of the lady in grey is against Bea's chest, brim digging in. Bea in turn is pushing into the people behind her and gasping for air and she wonders whether this will stop before she can no longer breathe. She is pushed forward again as the crowd surges towards the house with the balcony, taking Bea with it. Umbrellas, walking sticks, there's a forest of them around her ankles and Bea is tripping with every other step, her arms are pushed into her sides and her breasts are being squashed flat against whosoever is in front of her. Bea finds herself swallowing again and again, as though she is trying to keep down the fear rising inside her.

Now there's a whistling and shouting, a new sort of shouting. Police! My God, they're here. What has Bea done, coming here? Blast Aunt Celeste, she must have realised this would happen; what's she trying to achieve – Bea in handcuffs? Mother devastated? For a moment, Bea is upright and can see down the hill to where, closer to Holland Park Avenue, a cohort of arched helmets and raised thin batons are slowly but steadily pushing their way through the crowd towards the Indian clubs. A helmet sinks into the crowd to a cheer.

Something hard and round-ended is digging into Bea's back and she twists around. God almighty, it's a club, and the woman holding it is lifting it high in the air as she tries to push past Bea. Bea lets her squeeze past, almost pulling Bea's coat off her in the process. Let her go forward, Bea mutters, please keep that as far away as possible. But there's another club, and another, there's no keeping away from them, even umbrellas are being raised. Oh, God, some of the women around Bea are being pulled back by what must be police, and it's not just pulled back but pulled right down for they are on the floor, thick-coated men standing over them. A woman has her arms twisted behind her as she is being held down by one man while another wrestles to fit what must be a pair of handcuffs. In front of her another woman is shoved towards the ground, her body falls first against a neighbour's and rests there for a short moment until a pair of thick tweed arms reaches out again and she is pulled down flat, as if ready for the world around to trample on her.

Bea feels an urge to grab at the coat of the man in front to bring him down too so that he knows what it feels like, so that he shares the same bruises as the woman he has, well, manhandled. Do you understand, Bea wants to shout, that it hurts?

Then Bea is moving again, the crowd at the top is pushing towards the house and she's off downhill. She staggers and regains her balance as the wave of movement stops, leaving her crammed so tightly between strange coats that she can't fall. However, the crowd is not going to be motionless for long and God knows where the next push will come from. Where is Celeste? Bea is both furious with her aunt and quite desperate to see her.

As Bea struggles to hold her place, she realises that she is no longer terrified, instead she is wide awake, buzzing almost. It is now as if she is in a new motor, rattling along flat out, knowing the road will suddenly vanish into a bend ahead. Her breath shortens. She can no longer see the small figure in pale grey in front. No, there she is, her umbrella is up. My God, they're trying to pull even her away. Bea tightens her hand around her own umbrella and pushes forward against the person in front – who steps away suddenly, and Bea is falling.

She braces herself for the pain of the impact, but instead a thick hand is tightening itself around her right arm, dragging her up and back. That's it, then, she is being arrested; will he wait for both hands before the cuffs go on, or is it just one at a time? Then there will be a cell and bars, though it will be Celeste's turn to be impressed if she knows Bea is there. But, God, how on earth will Celeste have a clue, and if she doesn't fish Bea out of jail, then . . . what if the police keep her there all night? Bea starts to struggle.

'Don't be a fool.' It's more of a bark than a sentence, and the accent is thick.

The hand clamps tighter. Second charge against her, she thinks, resisting arrest.

'Do you want me to let you go?'

Bea is now upright enough to twist her head around in the direction of her captor but only sees that there are no stripes on the cuff. Plain-clothes police, then. She does want him to let go, and she nods but he doesn't relax his grip. So she shouts, perhaps more of a scream, though as she can't face him, it is probably lost in the chaos around her. 'At once! Let me go. Do you hear?'

The fist releases suddenly, and Bea trips but pulls herself upright. She is facing uphill and sees the crowd that is now a mob descending towards her at speed, behind them, a row of uniformed policemen.

'Take my hand.'

Bea doesn't move.

'Take my hand.' His voice is angrier, more urgent. Bea finds herself obeying and puts her hand in his, which envelops it, dwarfing her own.

He's tugging her sideways, that's all the space there is to squeeze through, and Bea twists her head up in his direction. The policeman is wearing a mackintosh and, even in the dark and the hurry, she can see that it looks as if it's been slightly too pressed, perhaps starched by mistake, and then crumpled in parts. It's February, he must be frozen, even his neck is bare, as are his hands. His grip tightens and she couldn't escape even if she wanted to. He will surely arrest her when they reach the bottom of the square. There is a high-pitched scream to their right and Bea's policeman glances in its direction. As he does so, Bea sees the shadow of a jaw straight as a girder. A fist would break on that.

Then they're out at the bottom and he pulls her towards the garden square railings where he lets go of her hand and leans back against the iron. After a moment or two he nods towards the railings next to him. Then, head straight up, he turns to look at her, holding himself dead still. Now for the handcuffs, and if one is going to be arrested, it may as well be suffered with as much style as can be mustered. Bea pulls her chest up, pushes forward what her corsetière has managed to make the most of, and turns her face away, to look as uninterested as she can.

No handcuffs emerge. It occurs to Bea that he is perhaps not a policeman. She cannot see a great deal of him: his face isn't shining in the lamplight and his eyes are hidden by the shadow of his bowler hat. Yet he somehow has a sense of, well, strength to him, and it is making Bea feel more than a little protected in this bedlam. Even if, dammit, his hands are in his pockets and he's looking across the road, his interest elsewhere. How can he be so rude – and what is he looking at that is so much more interesting than her? Even given, she reflects, the state she must now be in.

Bea turns to follow the man's gaze across Holland Park Avenue and then she's back against the railings like lightning, putting herself right next to him and leaning as far back as she can to avoid a tornado of fists, legs and batons. At the front two or three policemen are carrying a small, inert figure wearing a black hat with a large feather, and heavily veiled. For disguise, Bea guesses, little good that it did her. Bea blinks to keep away the tears. My God, she thinks, just one speech by this woman, a woman whom Bea has been brought up to believe is crazed, and Bea has fallen for her. Perhaps it was that Bea expected so little that it was easy to be impressed, or was she simply infected by the crowd around her? Even without all that, it is sad. To see any frail, brave person lose a fight is, well, sad.

The tornado is still whirling, Mrs Pankhurst's bodyguard, and any others who might be caught in there, have not given up. One of the policemen at the front has lost his helmet and both police and women keep falling and hauling themselves up again. Another policeman staggers out of the fight towards Bea, one side of his face dripping with blood. She recoils further, into something soft, and jumps. It's the man. She's leant right against him and Bea feels her cheeks grow hot. What sort of woman will he think she is? Particularly as he wasn't paying her a blind bit of notice beforehand. She may want his attention, indeed now that he has feigned indifference she needs it, but she would never behave like that, pushing herself up against a man. She's forward again, quicker than she went back and now she's standing two feet in front of the railings, her elbows squeezing her waist. She can't turn around again now, not ever. Beatrice, my God, you've been embarrassed into being coy.

The whirligig has moved on down Holland Park Avenue.

'Ladbroke Grove police station.' He has at last spoken. How awkward. Does that mean she needs to reply? But he continues. 'A couple of hundred yards down that road there.' His voice is strange, not an accent she hears often but she does know it, or maybe it is him she knows. That would explain . . . but how, and where? She tries to think through her visits to friends' houses, but really, her mind is too addled at present. In any case, this man is not a servant. Indeed, there is nothing whatsoever subservient about him.

Bea replies, 'Do you think she can escape now?'

No answer comes. He's looking straight across the road again, simply not bothering to speak. It was a silly question, but you can at least damn well give me an answer, she thinks. He really is ill mannered and blast being embarrassed, he may have dragged her out of a stampede but who does he think she is? Bea has never been shown so little respect before, well, perhaps a jostle in a street, being shouted at by a cart driver when she has rushed across his path, but not by someone she knows.

But she doesn't know him, she doesn't know him from Adam. It is the first time in her life that she has found herself standing with a man to whom she has not been introduced and, of course, out at night unchaperoned – if she is seen here, like this, then she will be assumed to . . . Good God, the thought of it. Thankfully, she will not ever have to see him again. She should go, she really should, but where is Celeste, and how is either of them ever to find the other in this mayhem? However, if Bea walks away from this man then she is obviously alone, and perhaps that is worse than being seen with him. At least she has some sort of explanation for standing here, in that she has been rescued, and if she waits just a little more, Celeste should emerge, Celeste must emerge, or even that woman wearing too much make-up. There is also, Bea thinks to herself, quite sharply, a chance that this man might at some point address me in reply.

People are dispersing, some hurrying away, others plodding a little, heads bowed with the loss of their leader. Bea looks around for Celeste. Those who remain are brushing themselves and others down or they are carrying bowls of water out of the house and washing the blood from faces. The street is littered with hats and helmets, umbrellas, batons, shreds of fabric, but no Celeste. With the realisation that she has been abandoned, Bea feels herself shrink to the size of that woman in grey. The lure of Mrs Pankhurst dulls; it has not been the perfect introduction to her aunt's cause, and the sooner she's at home the better. But how is she to take her leave of this man? She should thank him but it needs to be short and brusque, and it would help if he were paying a jot of attention to her. She considers stepping on his foot – he'd have to turn towards her then.

Bea is coming to a decision that the foot-stepping is a viable way forward when a woman runs back into Holland Park Avenue from Ladbroke Grove and crosses the road to the remnants of the crowd. Her hat is gone, the pins have been pushed and pulled out of her hair and her clothes are torn and bloodstained.

'It's not her,' she cries.

The reply comes back from the front of the house.

'It was a decoy. Mrs Pankhurst left through the rear.'

'Yes!' Bea's heart is knocking at her windpipe. Her cheeks are burning quite properly now. 'Isn't that capital news!'

Bea waits for a reply. If he doesn't speak now then she's off without another word. She'll give him five, no, ten seconds.

'Yes.' Not an iota of excitement in it, just deadpan matter-of-fact as though what's done is done and why should he, in particular, care? Barely audible, too, above the whoops and cheers of those still standing around embracing their neighbours. 'I'm going home,' she says.

'Why?' Bea hasn't turned around and his voice is in her ear. 'How'd'you come here?'

'Sorry?'

'Where,' he pauses, 'from?'

Bea hesitates. There is something about the way he is speaking that is deliberate, as though whatever she is thinking, he is one step ahead of her. She smiles to herself. If they lived in other, or rather, similar worlds, this man would be a challenge. However, in the circumstances, she can at least salvage her pride.

'Find me, please,' she says, holding her voice as steady as she can, 'a taxi.'

He nods, looking ahead still, walks forward and reaches into the road, one broad shoulder leaning over the tarmac. As the headlights swing into the side, Bea can see more of his face: he is younger than she expected, and his skin is a little darker, too. She's seen that face before, she knows she has, but struggles to think where, and it occurs to her that perhaps it was drawn in a newspaper and stories of men who follow ladies after dark fill her mind. Oh God, Bea, get away as quick as you can.

'You got all the fare?' he asks.

Bea nods. Even if she had to beg for it in the street outside her house, she would have said yes. The taxi pulls up and he opens the door for her. She steps in, sitting deep into the far side of the rear seat. His hand is on the door and he leans in. Bea presses a smile across her face and pushes out a 'Thank you.'

He looks straight at her, at last.

'It's not some form of entertainment,' he says, and closes the door. Well really, blast him, and blast him again. What does he think she is, some spoilt little rich girl? She'll show him. But she won't, will she, for he's fifty yards behind her now, and she'll never see him again

And, just for an instant, Bea feels a little sinking of regret.

7

VALENTINE'S DAY, TODAY, AND THEY'RE ALL IN A FLUSTER this morning. Well, the women are. Susan and Mary are a-scuttling up and down the stairs like they were juniors, not first and second housemaid who should have a bit of dignity about them. It's the excitement, though, with Susan's plan. Susan told Grace about it yesterday, or rather asked her to join in, and by that she meant pay money. Grace has been here almost a month now, and it was the first time Susan's done more than order her around. Yet Susan was pleasant as anything to Grace yesterday asking for the ha'penny for the card, only a ha'penny, but Grace is counting them. Anyways, she's not out of sorts over it, a ha'penny is the price of being accepted down here, and this morning she's all brisk with the secrecy, being on the inside of matters rather than out.

There's no first post until Mrs Wainwright is satisfied, says Mr Bellows, and they're hard at it. Slow and careful today, just brush, brush, brush and get it done. Make sure there's no spots for Mrs Wainwright, she's looking at them all as though she knows they're scattered in the head this morning, but the work still needs doing up to the standard it always is. The first floor's easy as pie, a large pie, mind, but everything in its place. There's been no cigars in here, only two armchairs sat on, in the red drawing room, and the sofas are still as puffed up as she and Mary left them yesterday.

Besides, when Grace opens the shutters, all the early morning sends in is a wall of cold. In this half-light there is not much dust to see. Pray that Mrs Wainwright checks it sooner rather than later.

Downstairs, though, well, Grace has never seen anything like it. She's smelt it, though, opened the door to the billiards and if she'd a lit a match it'd've burnt high. Like a public house, no, worse, it's the spirits in here, the glasses are still half full, most of them, and imagine the waste with that.

It's not just the smell, either; you'd cough on the smoke if you weren't choking on the brandy all around. The fire is still going; it can't be more than an hour or two gone since Master Edward's friends left. What time was poor Joseph up until, waiting to let them out?

Joseph. Yesterday, they'd passed on the stairs, Grace looking to the wall because she was too shy to meet his eye.

'Grace?'

'Yes.' She had to stop, didn't she? It would've looked too strange if she didn't, and then she wanted to, wanted to pause.

'Grace, you look nice today.'

Grace near gasped. You can't say it's anything but a pleasure, to be told that by a man you like, and she'd admitted it to herself now, hadn't she? But you can't let yourself have feelings like that, Grace Campbell, so shut them away.

He was waiting for an answer though, so she said, 'Thank you, Joseph', and he flushed from his collar to his forehead. Then he stood back to let her pass, which she did, eyes on the wall.

There are coals all around the grate, shovel's on the edge of the carpet too. Look at that, it'll be black underneath and it'll take something to get that out. How's she to clear this room up quick? Susan will be a razor with her, but Grace will take it in the right way today. Susan just wants what she thinks is in the post. And Grace wants the post, too, for he's hardly going to hand it to her across the table.

They did the other rooms too quick. Mrs Wainwright knew what would happen, she's making a round at half past seven, just as it lightens outside. The sun is coming in now and the light shows dust that you couldn't see a half-hour before, or so Grace guesses when Mrs Wainwright comes down to call her back for it.

At morning break Mr Bellows says that the post won't be until noon, that being the earliest Mrs Wainwright can now be sure that all will be finished. In any case, the second post will have arrived by then. 'That's cruelty,' whispers Mary. 'Then all of us at table will see who has a card and who hasn't one. Not that we don't know it already, but handing out the letters like that, in front of everyone, is rubbing it in.'

Grace is standing at her place near the far end of the table when Mr Bellows leads in the Pugs' Parade, she's learnt to call it, all the senior servants together. Grace, as usual opposite Joseph, stands behind her chair looking at the floor, unsure of how she's to go right through dinner without looking at him. Mr Bellows pulls back his chair and a grind it makes on the stone, but that's the signal for the rest of them to sit and watch him carve the joint into fine pink slices. Rump it is, not the fillet they have upstairs, but Grace has never had meat so many times a week. Every day it is, twice most days, and even though she's rushing around heaving, stretching, elbows pumping, she's already having to lace her corsets looser, and that skirt waist'll keep the breath out of her soon. Grace'll have to eat less as how's she to buy a new one? Then Joseph brings the plates down the table and Grace moves her eyes straight ahead. Just murmur a thank you, now. She doesn't want to be too friendly in front of the other servants.

The treacle dumplings steam up the room on their own account, so it seems, or maybe it's all of them at the table puffing away with the wait. Too many in here and not able to relax just the slightest today; they're as heated up as kettles about to whistle.

Grace can see a small bunch of envelopes in Mr Bellows' hand. He lifts one towards his monocle and says the name right out before passing it down. Grace glances around; the necks she can glimpse have come out in blotches.

Susan has a card; she has a suitor to send it. She can expect a visit and a posy too, once he finishes at the bank at lunchtime, being Saturday. Susan's not shy about this but, Grace'll give it her, not too flashy either. Still, Susan slips the card only part back into the envelope, and they can all see it, pale white card against cream.

Mary is less careful with hers. She giggles and blushes and near as swings her shoulders.

'How do you know,' Grace whispers to her, 'that it's from someone you'd like it to be?'

'Any of them is fine by me,' Mary replies.

Mr Bellows opens his. Susan said they'd be safe, he'll never admit it, not let go his dignity as butler. Mr Bellows doesn't pinken. He quietly slips the card back into its envelope, looks down the table and asks for the teapot just as though he receives a nameless Valentine every day.

Grace has a card, too, at least she thinks it's a card. She hasn't seen the writing before, but it looks how she'd expect it to be, not a good hand, but that's not what she likes him for. She pushes it into her apron pocket – she's not opening it in front of the others, and it is only when Joseph vanishes down the passageway to clear the kitchen staff's dinner that Grace looks up.

Grace is going out tonight with Mary. It's her first night out since she arrived. It's Valentine's Day, Saturday, Mary said, you can't sit in by yourself. Grace has spent all day hoping Joseph would ask her instead, after the card. Just a question mark it had in it, but when she caught his eye in the servants' hall that afternoon, his neck reddened. But he says nothing to her. Maybe he doesn't like it that she's still going out with Mary and her sorts. More fool Grace for accepting; not that Mary gave her much choice. Mary's been building up to this for more than a week and she needs Grace, she begged, he's bringing a friend and four's a good number. Grace couldn't let Mary down now. Still, all day Grace has been thinking of the countryside and Joseph's farm in Somerset. Well, his da's farm, and then it'll be his brother's, that's why Joseph's in service, to make a better life, he'd told her. But Grace can't think of much better than a farm, all fresh grass and milk, golden-brown cows and a whitewashed square of a farmhouse, smoke coming out of the chimney, smell of fresh roast ham, too, from the door. But where's she to use her shorthand there? Grace pushes the thought out of her mind, and goes on dreaming, for that's as close as she'll get. Another letter from Ma and she'll be popped like a string drawn too tight.

Mary found Grace a dress from a friend. You can't go out in those, she'd said as she turned through Grace's drawer of the office clothes Grace and Ma had stitched; looks like you're going to church. Grace couldn't go near a church in the dress she's been pulled into. She's not worn a showy colour like this before. It's a shade of dark pink, not that there's much of it at the front; she wants to cover her chest with her hands. Mary's wearing rouge too. Come on, Grace, don't you want to look your best? Paint my face! Grace is shocked at the thought of it. Not that she needs to paint her face to shock herself this evening. When she looks in the mirror she sees another person. Let's be out of here before Joseph sees, she thinks. The night out won't cost you a penny, Mary tells her, real gents, they are. But Grace has Ma's words in her head, Never go anywhere you can't get home. Grace turns to her drawer and reaches into her purse for a bus fare. She stills, then takes a deep breath and lifts out all she hasn't yet sent home, just in case.

It's Mrs Wainwright that calls her in as she and Mary are leaving. Oh, Grace, moans Mary, can't it wait? Not up to me, thinks Grace.

Mrs Wainwright is all honey and sweet and tells Grace to sit down so that Grace thinks there's some terrible news coming and it runs through her head, from Michael to Ma. Only address they have is here, or rather the mews at the back, but it's all the same.

'Grace,' says Mrs Wainwright. Maybe, thinks Grace, maybe it's just the dress I'm wearing, and her cheeks feel as though they are pinkening to match the colour of it.

'Grace, we all, from time to time, have feelings.' Here Mrs Wainwright pauses, and Grace looks over her shoulder at a photograph she's not seen down here before. A handsome man, not young, Grace'd have him at near forty, but military. You can imagine the buttons shining, even just from looking at the picture. 'But,' Mrs Wainwright continues, 'you're a heady young girl, and these feelings may somehow overcome you.' My word, what does Mrs W. think Grace and Mary are up to tonight, and why isn't Mary in here too? 'However, it is not always,' Mrs Wainwright hesitates again, 'appropriate to show them.'

Mrs Wainwright's hands move down to her desk. Grace follows them. There's a card, there, a Valentine's card. So Mrs W. has an admirer, too. She's picking up the card, taking a breath to speak again. 'Mr Bellows,' she continues, 'is a widower. He is old enough to be your . . . ' And Grace tries to shut out what's coming, it's ever so much worse than a scolding and she can feel shivers of embarrassment as though she's stuck in this dress till Kingdom Come. Grace has had her card in her apron pocket all day, touching it from time to time like a lucky charm, but right now, she never wants to think about a Valentine again.

'And there's the question of the order of things down here. I don't imagine it's a joke, Grace; that would not be particularly pleasant.' Either Mr Bellows thinks she loves him, or he thinks she's making fun of him. Oh, Grace Campbell, oh. If Susan can do this when Grace has done nought to her, then the thought of what she might do if Grace tells on her makes Grace shiver. However, Grace can't work in a house where she can't look the butler in the eye without going crimson, and she needs the position. It may not give her thirty shillings a month, but it gives her a good deal more than nothing. Nor does she want Joseph's smiles to vanish.

'It wasn't me.' When Mrs Wainwright asks her if she knows who it was, Grace shakes her head so as it might fall off.

Grace isn't drinking, which puts her out between Mary and the two men, and they're in a dance hall, all red velvet and smoke and a smell to the crowd that isn't a smell but makes Grace think that dancing is not what it's about here. Still, the band is playing the latest tunes, all animal dances they are, and Mary made Grace practise in their room, with the footsteps from the newspaper. Now Mary has danced off with her fellow and Grace has been left with Mr Pointer.

Call me Will, he'd said, but the familiarity sticks in her throat. He's not a tall man but his limbs are steel wire and he has sharp narrow eyes that were darting from side to side at the beginning of the evening, but are lolling a bit now as the middle of his moustache dampens with beer. Grace can't hear a word of what he's saying, not with the band, and now he's his arm tight around her shoulder and walking her on to the dance floor. It's not one of the dances she knows. 'I don't know how to do this, Mr Pointer,' she says, not knowing if he can hear her or not, but he keeps moving her on.

The couples around them are dancing closer than she'd like and Mr Pointer's body's near against hers. Grace tries to draw back, but he's holding her tight as a trap, and coming in close so that there's hot beer in her ear. It feels as though there's a barrel-band across her chest and her lungs are only moving a little now, panting she is, and Mr Pointer goes 'Oh' and moves closer. Lord knows what she'll feel of him next. 'Come on,' he says, but the thick air, the bodies, Mr Pointer's locked-stiff arms are all making her feel ill. The dance floor's so crowded there's not a chance of keeping your distance, not that anybody on it looks like they want to. You'd've thought someone would put an end to it, in public, but it's too dark, isn't it, for anyone to see if they don't want to. It's the new dances, too, pushing you towards each other every few steps.

Grace puts her heel on the toe of Mr Pointer's boot. The edge, quite careful, so as all her weight's on just that tiny bit, and he steps back. She smiles, mouths 'Pardon', then 'Excuse me'. He nods to the bar, with 'I'll see you there'. Grace wriggles into the crowd fast as she can, knocking through the elbows, she's fetched her coat in a flash, then out the door into the strange street. They came here in a taxicab and what bus, or where the stop is, she doesn't want to spend the time looking for. A taxi draws up and a group of men fall out, with one lady screeching with laughter. Good Lord, Grace thinks, the extravagance, what she earns in . . . but Grace looks back over her shoulder and thinks she can see Mr Pointer coming out the door. It is him, and he's walking towards her. Grace's heart is pounding and she knocks on the taxi's front window a flutter of times in a second, until the driver looks at her as if she's half crazed. Park Lane, she says, and he raises his eyebrows. Then she's on that empty seat quick as she can, grabbing the leather strap inside and pulling the door shut. Once she's moving, she looks back at Mr Pointer and waves at him. At least he might tell Mary she's gone, if Mary'll notice anything.

The cab is shaking from side to side as though the ground's rumbling underneath, and each time it comes up behind a horse Grace is thrown forward as the driver brakes. Once she's back in her seat, her eyes are fixed on the taxi meter as it clicks higher and higher. This is her sending-home money and she's trying to think what else she can do without. It's a while before she knows where she is, then she's by Victoria Station, that's ten minutes' walk, and she knows the way. Grace leans forward and asks the driver to stop. 'Thought you said Park Lane,' he grumbles. 'Remembered where you really live?'

Sunday again. Michael takes Grace to the far side of the park. The damp chill of the last few weeks is fading and the freshness of the air begins to take her mind away from last night. Every minute she sat in church she was wondering if God forgives girls who encourage men. It must have been her fault that Mr Pointer behaved liked that. Is that what London has done to her, and so quick? The thought comes to her that Joseph may be seeing that too and it makes her feel slightly ill, so she fixes her eyes on the building ahead, dark red brick and windows the size of small trees.

'Looks like a palace, Michael.'

'It is a palace.'

'Who lives there?'

He doesn't reply.

'There must be dozens of them.'

'Only dozens of servants, and thought little of. The rich keep their eyes shut and their hearts empty, Grace. They don't give a damn about us. I'd do away with the lot of them.'

Grace jolts back with this, almost as if he's been speaking about her, which he is, in a way. When you're in service it feels as though what happens to the family you work for is happening to you, too. She thinks of Miss Beatrice, and Lady Masters; would Michael want to do away with them? Surely they care about Grace and the rest of them downstairs, what with the questions they ask. She feels a little hollow. No, she thinks, this mustn't be true; she's not going to let Michael make all that friendliness untrue. There's enough bad thoughts she's had this morning and she's not having him take away the good ones she might have left.

'No, Michael,' she says. 'I don't think that's fair.'

'Turning your head, is it? Mayfair and all that money? You'll be on their side, soon . . . If I had my way I'd never give them a civil word. Some day I won't have to.'

'No, Michael, it's simply not fair to say all of them are like that.'

He grunts.

She continues. 'Some of them have the money not to be,' and as she smiles at this wry comment of hers, Michael laughs out loud.

'But it's true,' he says, 'you have to be able to afford to be kind. Remember that: what you can afford to do and what you can't. Not just money either, Grace. Don't give anything away lightly.'

They hover by the Round Pond, watching the miniature yachts trying to make their way across. A few feet from them a man so wide that he looks as if he would be better bouncing along rather than walking, struggles to lean over to launch his wooden boat.

'He's going to go,' says Grace, 'right over.' And Michael laughs again. There it is: she knew the old Michael was there. Whatever she's said to him, it's working and, slowly, the wrongs of yesterday begin to right themselves.

'They're feeding you, sister.'

Grace blushes. She looks across at him. He's drawn, not eating what she is. She'd thought of him when she saw the leftovers in the pantry were turning.

'That's not a thought even to have,' Mary had said. 'It'll set Mrs Wainwright on your tail. She'll say that Lady Masters can't be feeding half of London.'

'I thought she did?'

'Did?'

'The dockworkers. When they were on strike.'

'Who told you that?'

'Oh, no one.'

'Message from God?'

'Joseph.'

'Oh.' Mary's oh was long drawn out. She looked at Grace sideways. 'That was before his time. Best not to know it.'

'Got all you need, Grace? I worry about you.' Really, Michael is on gentle form today, Grace is beginning to feel that this is her moment to tell him any one of those things burning inside her. She needs someone to tell her that nobody will think she really sent the card to Mr Bellows, that it is usual to feel funny after last night, that that is not why Joseph likes her, and how to find thirty shillings a month. He could do all these things, could Michael.

But instead she answers, 'Yes, I have all I need.'

'Sure of that, Grace?' Michael can tell that all's not as it should be. Reassure him, Grace Campbell. She pulls her gloves higher up over her wrists.

'I'm all right, Michael.'

Now he's looking at her and catches her eye and makes her look back him and hold his gaze. He raises his eyebrows.

'If you say so, Grace.'

It's Grace's turn to worry, at the tone of his voice. He knows she's lying, she thinks.

'What are you needing then, Michael?'

'Grace, can you type something out for me?'

Her breath stops in her.

'On the machines, Grace. At your office.'

Her reply comes quickly now, too quickly.

'It's not allowed, spending work time on a personal matter.'

'You could go in early.'

What's she to say to that? This is it, thinks Grace, I've told a lie and I'll burn for it even before I'm in my grave. But something comes to her.

'There's the paper,' she says, 'and the ribbon to pay for.'

'I'll give you those,' he says.

Grace sticks to it, she has to. No, not for personal use, she says, there was another girl, she's been told, as took in her own ribbon and was given the sack on the spot. Out on her ear and not even that week's pay. 'It's the rules, Michael.'

Michael doesn't believe her, but Michael doesn't believe in rules, or rather, he doesn't like them. The corners of his mouth are down and his eyes are half closed, looking at her sideways. He thinks she's shirking, she's sure of it. He turns away and hangs his head.

'I would have thought,' he says, 'that you would do this for me.'

At that moment she has a fear that it mightn't take Michael finding out for Grace to lose him, and that there are other ways in which she can disappoint him. He may be her brother, but he's all too ready to turn his back on a person and never talk to them again.

'Oh, Michael. I'll do anything I can for you. You know that. Just not *that.*' What can she do, she thinks, what can I give my brother that he might need?

'Can,' he snorts, 'can? If we only do what we "can" nothing in this cursed world will change.'

He is silent now.

'What about where you work, Michael, in chambers?'

'You can't come in there.'

'No, I mean you do the typing.'

He looks at her as though she's simple.

'I'm not a typist, Grace.'

She's too flustered, though she's hiding it, to ask him what needs typing, and she can't now. Any case, she wants to talk about anything but typing. In a minute she may trip over her tongue.

Michael is continuing. 'Besides, I have reading to do in order to know what to write. That's if I can find the books.'

'What books?'

Michael rattles out a few names. Philosophy, Grace, Michael tells her. Call it politics if you must, you should know about that. Grace knows about politics, she reads the *Daily Express* once the others have finished with it, and of course Miss Sand told them about the government. Why, a young woman like Grace, even if she is working as a maid at present, should be thinking about politics too, she tells herself.

Mrs Wainwright knows that Grace likes doing the library. Grace has told her she enjoys her elbow pushing into the wood and bringing the shine back up, that smell of polish everywhere. Grace spends as much time as she can there, breathing in old paper and leather. Today being a Monday she's more time to enjoy it, for the family is still in the country and there are no bedroom fires to be lit.

It's on the ground floor, tucked away in a corner and only the double doors tell you it's a place to go into. They're plain dark wood, none of that white and gold of upstairs. Grace likes the plainness: it adds to the surprise when you walk inside.

There's not much light from the side window. It's lamps they use to make the room glow, all wood and leather book spines lining the walls. There's enough of them in red and green to give it a feel of Christmas year round. This morning, as she's standing and looking, polishing a spine or two, Joseph comes in and stands beside her. It's just one man who collected all these, he tells her, the first Sir William Masters. He's the man who built this house fifty years ago. He travelled all over the world. Grace could tell that herself of course from the titles when they're in languages she doesn't understand, and she tells Joseph this. Joseph tells her that Sir William couldn't read them either, not a word that wasn't English. They were for his wife. She could speak all the languages for him.

Then Joseph says, 'Look, Grace, look what's in here.' He opens a cupboard and takes out a long leather tube. 'See the paper inside, Grace? That's plans for the railways he built before he became Sir William and built this house. He didn't start off Sir William,' Joseph says, 'he was a builder; maybe I'll become a builder, Grace.' Joseph is standing right next to her, so as she can feel the heat from his body, and he reaches an arm out for a book but when it brushes past her shoulder, he pulls it back. Grace feels a flush rising through her collar and she holds herself in at the waist, her shoulders back, even though it makes her chest go forward, pushing it closer to him.

Joseph's fixing his eyes straight ahead, poker-necked but full-lipped, and pretending not to look. Grace is sure he knows how close he is and it feels as though he is drawing her towards him, and she has an impulse to kiss him. Her body starts to move, and before she knows it her face is right by his; then, just as suddenly, a fear comes over her, and she sees her life going one way, rather than the other. She stops and holds her breath in, for it's going tell-tale fast, and says, 'I must get on.'

He gasps; at least she thinks it's a gasp she hears. His mouth is half open and his eyes look as though he's been pinched.

He is still for a moment, and looks at the far wall. Then, eyes to the floor, he says, 'See you, Grace,' as though it's the last thing he wants to do. As the door clicks shut behind him it feels like it's cut a piece of her in two.

Her impulses: Grace can control them but look what good that does her. She has an urge to swear out loud but Grace can't swear, she's had it so drummed into her that swearing is the beginning of the end, though what she's about to do now is going to lead her straight there, in one leap. 'Jesus Christ,' she says, in not much more than a whisper but it's out there nonetheless. Then Grace looks over her shoulder to check that nobody has slipped in behind her, double reason to check that.

The library steps are heavy – the trick is to roll them forward rather than try to swing them to the side. They've been left at the end by Z, at the window, giving the impression that someone has read their way through the lot. The wheels rumble on the floorboards, and Grace starts at the noise. What if Mrs Wainwright . . . But she should be moving them to sweep underneath. Though perhaps not so far all at once for there's folding steps she can use to reach the books from, with the feather duster she's left leaning against the side. She'd think of something though, she's always been quick at that, and she's grown quicker recently, had to, lips tight as they can be every Sunday. Now she's stopping and starting, searching the letters. Fr, Fl, Fe . . . Grace likes the orderliness of the library, nothing unexpected can happen here. Fa . . . Ew, there was an E, wasn't there, one of the books Michael told her the name of. E, there you are, Grace, ladder into the side and up she goes, clutching a dusting cloth in case anyone comes in, and searching the Es for a name that rings true.

As she climbs her head grows lighter and by the time she's at the top she feels as though she is flying, not quite herself. She finds it up there, the book she's after. Engels, Friedrich. *The Condition of the Working Class in England*, that's the one Michael said, and how can you forget a name like that?

The books are packed tight as six in a bed up here, takes all of a tug, and not easy with the duster too, and she's near tipped off, and with her hovering ten foot up what would she have broken first? They wouldn't keep her here then, not all crippled, when she's as good as just arrived. And if she said she was dusting behind the book, just that one, nobody would believe her.

Once she's down she lifts up her skirt, pulls her stomach in and squeezes the book up above her waistband. She'd left her apron loose especially: now she ties it as tight as she can and still breathe.

She's moving the steps on to A to make it look as though she's gone right round with the duster. She hurries, worrying that someone'll start wondering why she isn't in the saloon yet, and moves the ladder too quick. There's a thundering from the wheels, enough to make her jump. In the silence she can hear pointy-heeled steps ringing towards the room.

'What in God's name?'

'Ever so sorry, Mrs Wainwright,' and Grace bobs.

'You could have shaken the devil awake. What were you doing?'

'Just saw a bit more and nipped back to catch it.'

'Well, you should've caught it the first time. And don't try nipping anywhere with those steps. That feather duster can reach from the folding ones, if I'm not mistaken.'

Please go, thinks Grace. Go, so I don't have to walk past you with this book under my pinny.

'Is it all done, now?'

'Yes, Mrs Wainwright.'

'Well, then, straighten the steps and into the saloon.'

From behind the ladder, Grace bobs another curtsey, clutching her stomach as though there's a baby in there, hoping Mrs Wainwright doesn't think that, that's just the sort of trouble she'd be on the lookout for. But anyone who knows Grace . . . but they don't, do they?

The service stairs are on the far side of the hall. She walks fast, wants to trot, but the book'll be banging around the bottom of her bloomers. She goes up the stairs, her hand pressed against her. When she's in her room, she loosens her apron and lifts her skirt and petticoat before easing the book out. As she holds it out in front of her, her head empties and she feels as if she's going to fall. If she had any breakfast in her, it'd be on the floor. Where's she to put it, this book, and keep it, all week too? If she had any sense, she'd've waited until Saturday. If she had any sense . . . Well, too late now, Grace Campbell.

The chest of drawers. There's Mary, though. The first week Grace was here she came in to find Mary going through her drawers. Without a flush of embarrassment, Mary had come out with Oh, my drawers are at the top now, easy to forget. Grace imagines finding Mary holding up the book and her stomach turns again – and she needs to be back downstairs, minutes ago. There's her suitcase, the edge of it coming out from under her bed, no lock on it, but if Mary's already looked in it, she'll think it's empty still. Grace takes an armful of clothes from her drawers and burrows the book inside them and into the case.

She's out of the door when she turns back to check the case. She can see it as though it reads *Open Me* across the front. She rushes back to her drawers and pulls out her woollen shawl. She'll be cold without it but it's the thickest thing she has. Her mattress is so thin a child could lift it, and up it comes. Grace wraps the book in her shawl to protect it from the wire netting underneath, and slips it under the pillow end.

As she comes downstairs again, Grace jumps. Mrs Wainwright is standing to the side of the staircase as though she's been waiting for Grace, and Grace's chest tightens. Imagine, just imagine if she'd seen Grace going up with the book. She feels white, and red, and

Lord knows what else, her face must look like a convict's already. Smile, Grace Campbell, she tells herself, take that look away.

'Where have you been, Grace?'

'Upstairs, Mrs Wainwright.'

'Upstairs?'

Grace folds her hands over her belly and dips her head.

Mrs Wainwright pauses.

'Well, we all have to get on, you know. I can't have every one of you off for a couple of days each month. Anyhow, keeping moving will take your mind off it. Into the saloon; you can take a hot water bottle after luncheon. And, Grace . . . '

'Yes, Mrs Wainwright.'

'I expect more of you, Grace. You know that.'

8

BEA'S EYES OPEN EARLY. SHE RINGS THE BELL BESIDE HER BED and, when Grace arrives, asks her for coffee and toast. She is certainly hiding by having breakfast upstairs. Rightly so, for Mother can scent subterfuge at fifty paces, and the thought of it sets Bea's mind abuzz. Not a chance she can sit still enough for breakfast in bed. She slithers out from between the sheets before even reaching for her dressing gown and feels the chill of the morning; then, silk-wrapped, she walks over to the dressing table. The triptych looking-glass sends back three Beatrices. I am legion, she thinks, a demonstration of suffragettes in myself. If that's what I have now become, converted in a single evening by a woman whom I have spent every hour since yearning to follow. Though not, of course, all the way.

Bea searches her features for some sign of metamorphosis, wondering what a suffragette should look like. Her recollections turn from the made-up woman next to her, the slight lady in expensive grey, to the bodyguard and Mrs Pankhurst herself, black and feathered. Then there is Celeste and her sartorial perfection. However, and bother her for vanishing last night, Celeste is a long way from Bea in suffragette hierarchy. Nonetheless, there is a limit to how plain Bea can bring herself to look. Not too detailed, fine. A wide, gathered 'practical' skirt, no.

Bea looks down at the pots on her dressing table. Compared to Clemmie's, or even Mother's spread, they are few. Cold cream, powder. She is not sure whether she should powder for a daytime's work but her nose is already shining and she's not a child. Yes, powder, and decent hair; when Grace comes back with breakfast Bea will ask her to do it. Bea looks back down at her pots and sees the toast already beside her. She didn't see or hear Grace come in. She takes a piece from the rack and tears off a corner, before letting it drop, mangled, on to the plate. Her stomach is too tight to do any more than pick. She reaches for a comb, and starts to pin her own hair.

At a quarter past nine Bea is ready to leave. She's taken an umbrella from the stand – a near guarantee that it will not rain, but gripping the handle makes her feel a little empowered. Joseph opens the door for her, and the stench of engine oil and horse pushes into her nose as she waits for the footman to find her a taxi. Once Joseph has brought one to the door, Bea manoeuvres herself and hobble skirt inside. It is not until he has closed the cab door behind her that she gives the driver the address she has memorised.

The taxi circles the block before turning north. In Curzon Street Bea glances back and looks up for the crack in the side of the house. It seems longer than it was two days ago and she wonders how far it will go. Perhaps it will lengthen until the exterior wall crumbles away, exposing the dining room below to the world outside, rubble sitting on the chairs, the dark green walls and Venetian and pastoral scenes veiled in pale powder. She finds the image somehow both sad and, in a strange way, liberating.

The taxi turns up on to Park Lane and heads north past the shuttered windows of the many who, at this time in the morning, are not even halfway through their night's sleep. The other side of the road is a river of square boxes of motors and teetering omnibuses and beyond them, half a dozen riders are cantering along the sand track inside the park, just as Bea should perhaps be doing. But Bea's taxi draws her away. At Marble Arch the pavement fills. A dozen bus routes are emptying their passengers into a quivering skein of dark, tailored wool moving in search of the next bus, or the steps down into the Underground station. Bea glances west along the north edge of the park towards Campden Hill Square. Flashes of recollection keep coming back to her – of all parts of the evening. Though not, she tells herself, in the correct order of importance, and she tries to put them back to where they should belong. It takes no small effort, for the word 'entertainment' is still driving her teeth together.

It's further than Bea thinks to Maida Vale, and the further she goes the more she wonders what she is doing, going to join these half-mad, club-wielding women. She could still turn back. There's a lunch she could go to, and she really should see about a dress for her dance. No, Beatrice, she tells herself, she must stick with it. Surely, if you have learnt anything over this year, it is not to assume anything at all until you have seen or heard it.

The new red bricks and white pillars of Lauderdale Mansions spread right along the street, broken every few yards by an identical doorway. The taxi has passed along through a dozen similar streets and avenues of red-brick mansion blocks. Bea's heart is now shaking her ribcage as she wonders which is the right door. The number has vanished from her head.

The note of apology came from Celeste yesterday morning, the envelope again written by her maid. Celeste had been called to the back of the house to help with Emmeline's exit. Not a chance of finding Bea again. The invitation was still there, though, to come along. Tomorrow would be good, for the paper goes to press on Thursday afternoons and it's all hands on deck. Celeste will send her name round, in any case. Here's the address.

She's just going to look, she tells herself, just for a few hours. She wants to see what it's like, and it is certainly a glimpse into another world. If anybody offers her a brick, she'll simply decline. I will be tough, she thinks. The world, as she has recently learnt, belongs to the tough.

Bea pulls Celeste's note out of her purse, asks the taxi to stop and steps out into air clearer than that of Park Lane. There is less traffic here, less everything, the road is a valley of seamless red-brick walls and so quiet. Bea is careful; they could be being watched, Celeste said. Don't dawdle, thinks Bea, but don't make a dash for it either – head down, and the brim'll hide half my face. My God, she's behaving as though she's in a John Buchan novel. Stay calm, Beatrice, and try to think of what a lark it is. She is not sure whether it is excitement or fear that she is feeling. It occurs to her that there may be all too little difference between the two.

There's no doorman at the bottom of each staircase in these new blocks of flats. In any case, Lauderdale Road is not that sort of street. Instead there is a brass button next to the flat number outside. It's not a straight ring that she's to do, there's a code to be followed. Memorise, then destroy this, Celeste had written. Bea hasn't, thank God, for her head's a sieve this morning.

The bell button glides into its brass surround. Three short sharp buzzes, a pause then two long ones. Another pause and three short sharp ones again. Then she waits, nose to a pair of thick wooden double doors, firmly locked. She wonders what might happen if they can tell she is only looking. Will they, she wonders, ask her to smash a window to prove her loyalty, or march her straight out?

The door is opened by a starkly dark-haired and white-skinned young woman in a wide-collared blouse and a full, practical navy skirt and when Bea notices this her heart sinks a little. The woman beckons Bea to come in quickly.

'Oh,' says the woman. 'I don't know you.'

'I'm here to help.'

The woman looks Bea up and down. As she does, the heels on Bea's boots feel too high, her narrow skirt too tight. The woman's eyes fix on Bea's pale blue coat, her eyes move down to the embroidered hems and her eyebrows rise as though Bea has come riding in a ball dress.

'Help with what?'

'With, well. With the cause.'

'What cause?'

'I'm sorry, I've made some mistake.'

Bea turns towards the door and takes Celeste's letter out again. No, she's read it right, but after all that Celeste has given her the wrong address. What a fool Bea has been, shows that she shouldn't have come, should have left well alone.

The white-faced woman speaks. 'Who sent you?'

'Celeste Masters.' Bea is speaking to the door.

'And your name?'

'Beatrice.'

'Beatrice what?'

'Masters. She's my aunt.'

'Let me check. Wait here.'

The hallway smells of wood polish and the faint dust left by dozens of footsteps. On the side, at shoulder level, are rows of wooden pigeon holes for post. Bea scans the numbers and names next to them. Morgan, Holmes, Black, Clark. Beside the number of the buzzer she has rung: Hall.

The woman must be a gymnast, she's back so quickly. She nods her head towards the stairs.

'Well, I guess Celeste's entitled to slide her relations into the top drawer. I suppose you must have something to offer. Bring your umbrella. Best not to let on how many of us are up there.' Ignoring the lift, the woman runs back up the wide stairs. Bea, surprised into obeisance, follows as best she can, nearly splitting the hem of her skirt with each step, wondering whether 'top drawer' is better or worse than 'entertainment'. Well, Beatrice, she tells herself, whatever it is about you that prompts people to say these things, it must change.

When Bea walks into the pale narrow hallway of the apartment a woman, clutching papers in one hand and brandishing a pen in the other, scurries across it ahead of her. Someone else appears from one unseen door and disappears into another. Both move quickly and both, Bea notices, are wearing practical skirts.

The door guardian turns to her.

'Celeste's not here. Coat on peg. Boots off.'

'Boots off?'

'Keeps the noise down.'

Bea finds herself, again, doing exactly what she is told. She hangs her coat then sits down on a chair obviously provided for the purpose, and adds her boots to a long line along the hallway. In stockinged feet, she follows her guide through the first door on the left, anticipating the next instruction which she expects she will, again, obey.

The room is painted a pale mauve, with a window almost the length of the far side. In the centre is a large dining table surrounded by five women, fingers glued to typewriter keys and piles of writing paper and newspaper spread around them. They are older than Bea, more gaunt than matronly, and their collars are buttoned up to their necks, as their hands peck at the keyboards and papers. Papers are being straightened in short sharp jabs, fingers licked and pages leafed through so quickly that Bea fancies she should be able to hear them burr, but the cacophony of clattering keys drowns all other sound out.

Bea thought she was early, but these women have been here some time. The pins are coming out of their hair and the room is stuffy with breath and concentration. There is something comic to the scene, as though she's in a coop of flustered hens.

There are no introductions.

'Can you type?' asks the woman who let Bea in.

Bea is almost too surprised to reply. She had not imagined being asked to work as a secretary, but rather to be selecting content, proofreading, discussing views to be held. Celeste, however, is not here yet to sort this out, and it would be churlish of Bea to refuse the first task she is invited to do. She'll just sit down and get on with it until Celeste arrives. Bea's tried a typewriter a couple of times beforehand and it can't be that hard to pick it up.

'Slowly,' Bea replies, a trifle optimistically.

'There's a machine here.'

Bea looks at the other women and copies them, removing her jacket and hanging it over the back of her chair. She sits down and pulls herself in; at least her embarrassingly out-of-place skirt is now hidden under the table.

The woman has vanished and immediately Bea's neighbour to her left leans across. She's in her thirties and there are a few neat waves in what's still pinned up of her hair. Her cheeks are flushed, which is unsurprising given the temperature in here. She passes Bea a bundle of newspaper cuttings with ribbon-ink-stained fingers. Stories here and there are circled, part-crossed out and then apparently rewritten in a scrawl across the columns next door.

'Knock these up. Use a carbon. I'll have both copies. It's going out this afternoon, so you'll need to be quick.'

The carbon paper doesn't want to lie still on the sheet Bea has laid out on the table beside her. She positions it but, as she brings the second sheet of white paper over it, the featherweight carbon flutters out of place. After this has happened three times, an arm reaches out from Bea's left and moves the unused paperweight sitting by her onto the carbon. The arm disappears again. This time, Bea succeeds in sandwiching the dark sheet between the white ones. She picks them up. A black fingerprint appears on the top.

At last she is ready to type. She leans over to the papers she was given and has put to the right of the machine, and flinches. Her elongated steels are digging into both her armpits and the flesh around her hips. Oh, vanity. If she'd worn something shorter, then . . . but she needed the longer corset for the blasted skirt. Anyhow, on with the job, only, in order to decipher the scrawl on the sheets, she really does have to lean forward to look closely. Headline, it says here, with a large circle around a couple of short sentences, *Mr Churchill*, Bea reads, *compelled to listen. Car held up by Suffragettes* . . . All right, here goes. At least she knows how to type capital letters. It would have jolly well blown her cover to have to ask that . . . *w-h-o f-o-r-m-e-d a b-a-r-r-i-c-a-d-e a-c-r-o-s-s t-h-e r-o-a-d w-i-t-h t-h-e-i-r b-i-c-y-c-l-e-s* . . . Aim, drop, aim, drop. Or rather, thwack. It needs a hell of a push to get the letter right across to the paper, let alone make an imprint on it, and how on earth are you supposed to hit the keys any faster without missing and slipping to the one at the side? *g-r-e-a-t a-g-i-t-a-t-u* Blast, she'll have to start all over again. She winds in the third clutch of new sheets in what must be fifteen minutes.

'Good God, what are you doing?' That neighbour again. 'If you're not up to it, just come out with it. This is not the day to dawdle.'

Not up to it? Bea's never not been up to anything. 'Not my usual machine, just warming up,' she replies as she feels herself pinken. I'll show her, she thinks. I'll show the lot of them. The words 'top drawer' are still irritating her, 'entertainment' not far behind them.

'Well, cross those out and keep at it, the typesetters will decipher. And double-space.'

Bea turns to stare at the woman but her neighbour's eyes are fixed on Bea's emerging sheet of paper and are held so strainingly wide that they look as though they might pop out of her head. Gorgon, thinks Bea. What is it with the women here? She speeds up, but the mistakes come thicker and faster; if a key sticks, her finger seems to slide to the side. But back a space, cross it out, and on. Engine oil is what this machine needs and the smell might be a good deal better than it is in here at the moment. Nobody, it appears, has thought of opening a window.

It slowly comes to her that what she is typing is good: a sort of compendium of the week's activities. Well, it will be a compendium when she has finished, if she finishes. No, Bea, you jolly well will. Not up to it? Bea is no longer embarrassed but beginning to seethe and it makes her type faster. *Scene at a Glasgow theatre. Speech from a box . . . At the end of the first act of 'A Little Damozel', . . . addressed the audience . . . banners were unfurled . . . Let Scotland protest against torture in English prisons . . .* I'll bet, thinks Bea, that the Scots enjoyed that. On it goes, forcible feeding the issue of the day, disruptions at the Garrick Theatre, St James's Theatre, Liverpool Picture Palace, Bristol Cinema. Of course Bea has known this for a while; it's not possible to go to a show without wondering whether a side act will rise from a seat in the dress circle and scatter leaflets over those sitting below. It happens in restaurants, too. Even the most stylishly dressed woman can stand up at a table and begin to speak as a small swarm of purple, white and green-sashed women appear from every corner brandishing leaflets. Would she ever do that?

An hour and a half later Bea's forefingers feel bruised and little of the compendium is typed. Her shoulders are stuck around her ears and her stomach, where the steels have been digging in, has gone from painful to numb. She has forgotten to double-space. She wants to slide her chair back (silently), retrieve her coat and umbrella and hail the first taxi she sees, and find Edward, whose path she hasn't crossed since Monday. She could bury her head in his shoulder, confess all, and never come back. Nobody, she is sure, would notice.

'Cup of tea?' The words wake her. Her neighbour is talking to her again. Cup of tea, oh yes, thinks Bea, that would be a godsend.

'Yes, please.'

'End of the passage on the right. Mine's strong, black, sugar. Plenty of it.'

Bea doesn't move. She's not here to make tea, she doesn't make tea, she can't remember ever doing so. And the tone, my God, Bea wouldn't speak to a servant like that and expect her to do anything well. What's more, it is Bea's first morning, and you would have thought they could damn well be civil.

Bea looks around her. Heads are down, keys thumping. No time to be civil. After the emotion of Campden Hill Square, Bea imagined they would be in a state of near-constant embrace, but open affection or warmth appears not to be done. To hell with them, Bea's not going to put up with it. If this is what they are like, then she's off. The options of where she could go instead run through her mind. That lunch party again, then perhaps a ride in the park . . . Bea hesitates for a moment, then decides upon tea.

Bea did not realise a kitchen could be so small. There's barely a yard to pass between the table and the stove, and that has a couple of kettles almost rattling off the top of it. The way is blocked by an older woman, a few streaks of grey in her chignon that match the walls, leaning across the table to empty a large brown teapot into some incongruously dainty pale pink china cups. Without looking up, she tells Bea that there is a queue. A queue? Where? There's not another soul in here.

'A queue for what?'

'Hot water, tea, cups. But they come in all the time. I'd grab a couple, dash them under the tap then go for the tea. Hurry, though, it will be filling up in here soon when the sandwiches arrive. We're all so starving by noon that we have a workers' lunch. Dinner, we should call it.' She looks up at Bea, and smiles, the first Bea has had all morning. Bea could almost kiss her. 'You're new here.'

Bea nods.

'Welcome to the madhouse. Josephine Meldon. No hands free, I'm afraid.'

Bea finds that balancing teacups on saucers while you're walking in a skirt that pins your knees together is not easy. She pauses to steady herself outside a closed door that she didn't notice on her way in. She can hear voices coming from the other side and is tempted to stop and listen but years of a nanny's strictures stall her. As she treads carefully back along the passage, hoping that nobody bursts out of a doorway, a grey-haired woman slides past and knocks on the closed door. Bea turns, tea lapping onto the saucer and scalding her thumb. Better have that cup for herself, or no doubt she'll be sent back again. The woman grasps the knob and puts an ear to the door; there's clearly no problem with eavesdropping for her, if listening before you go in is still eavesdropping. The door opens and Bea can see a wing chair in front of the window, a slip of a woman in it, and the door is shut again so fast that it bangs. Beatrice, she tells herself, back to the typing room. She turns and finds the passage is blocked by a tall, well-built woman, who is standing as though she's been waiting for Bea. Below the woman's thick black hair are thick black eyebrows to match, which arch sharply. Vaguely, thinks Bea, satanic. The woman looks Bea up and down, pausing at the tight skirt around Bea's ankles.

'What are you doing?'

'Tea.' She feels her cheeks redden.

'You're new here, aren't you?'

This is clearly the refrain for the day. Bea nods carefully, mustn't spill any more tea, even though she now feels so hot she'd barely notice.

'Where are you working?'

Her mind is jelly. What's the room called – the room where nobody has a smile?

'Typewriters,' she hazards.

'The engine room of this battleship. Get on with it then, it's Thursday. And this is not a place to stand around.'

Bea nods again.

As she returns to her seat Bea can see an empty teacup between the piles of paper. She replaces it with the full one she has not yet spilt.

'You can leave the old one. Someone will come scavenging for a spare. Meant to tell you to have the same, if I were you. Strength and sugar. You'll need it.' She pauses. 'If you stay the course.' Bea chooses to ignore this, forcing herself to try to invent some excuses for her tormentor. There must be something to pity her for. But the thought that she might not prove her wrong pulls Bea upright sharply, and now the numbness in her fingers is lessening they hurt more, but she pounds away. At least double-spacing takes you down a page faster.

Bea is not sure how much later it is when she looks up again. The chairs around her are empty and pushed back from the table. She did not hear the machines stop and she wonders whether it is already lunchtime, teatime even. Maybe she's been here all day. She fumbles with her cuff to find her wristwatch. Quarter to one, and as she looks back up the others are returning. They sit themselves down slowly, draw their chairs in quietly, shake the papers beside them into neat piles; they are calmer now. Sated by sandwiches, Bea suspects, and servants' lunch indeed, to be finished as early as this. Uncertain as to whether she should now go along to the kitchen herself, or whether she is even hungry, Bea stays put.

She smells the cigarette smoke behind her. Celeste's voice is a throaty whisper in her ear. 'The sandwiches are nearly all gone. You'd better get a move on or you'll be left with paste. Revolting.' Thank God, thinks Bea, and she's up and out of her chair, just stopping herself short of embracing Celeste, who is standing there in a flowing cream silk blouse, cigarette in her hand. She is looking at Bea as though she is sizing up a challenge and just as Bea starts to worry, Celeste breaks into a grin. 'Why, you're beetroot, my dear.' She walks Bea back down to the kitchen and as they pass the closed door, she catches Celeste's eye. Celeste shakes her head gently from side to side.

The kitchen is empty, save a handful of small triangles of sandwiches. Celeste is right, they are paste, and they are revolting. Bea manages four of them.

Celeste has 'gathered' that typing isn't Bea's thing. Hell, thinks Bea, they're going to turf me out already, but Celeste isn't saying this. It would be good, her aunt continues, if she practised. She can't occupy a machine unless she can get the words down fast enough; there's no time to waste, especially today. On reflection, Thursday might not have been the best day to start, although there's never any time, not just in getting the newspaper out every week, but every day another prisoner starves a little more. Bea doesn't want to be taken for a girl who cares only about her fingernails, Celeste tells her. She needs to do her bit until she is known a little. Then … How, thinks Bea, am I to be known a little when nobody either gives me their name or asks mine? In the meantime, continues Celeste, there is plenty more to do. 'I'm afraid that the bottom of it, old chap, is that if you have a leg-up, then you have to work at least twice as hard to prove yourself.'

They turn into a faded pink room next to the dining room. A handful of velvet armchairs and a couple of sofas are pushed back against the wall. Half a dozen card tables have been carried in, put up and set side by side to make a single large central platform. Some of the women in here are older, perhaps in their fifties or sixties. It's not some fad of youth, is it, being a suffragette, and Bea wonders whether, the older a woman grows, the more she cares about the vote. Maybe each year of minding adds up.

The women here have perfectly pinned hair, their buttoned-up shirts pale. In front of them, beside them and in piles by their feet are cascades of large brown envelopes. The window beyond them is wide open. It feels several degrees cooler in here than in the typewriter room, and Bea shivers.

'It's not that hot in here since Mrs Montague chiselled that open yesterday,' says Celeste. 'Block heating, you see. Nobody has an iota of control over it. Fetch your coat if you like but I'd stick in your shirtsleeves, it's easier to move your arms, and you will heat up as you go along. There's a space on the table just over there, you'll want the draught. I'll bring you a pile, and stamps. You'll need a pen. Oh, and the list.'

Bea's shuffling her knees and hobble skirt under the table when Celeste returns.

'We're up to "N",' says Celeste. 'You need to be fast but do write the addresses clearly. Smudges are definitely off. Causes a terrible stink when it goes to the neighbours by mistake. Stamp first, address next, tick it off and into the box at your feet. Well, ideally. But we can scrabble up from the floor later.'

On the table in front of Bea is a pile of leaflets printed on thin, off-white paper. The type is in columns and as dense as a newspaper. Headlined across the top are the words SELF-DENIAL WEEK. Bea reads on.

> This is a crucial period for the Union, and more funds are urgently needed. We therefore propose to repeat the success of our SELF-DENIAL WEEK. This will run from Saturday 7th March to 14th. Members and their sympathetic friends are invited to abstain from luxuries, for example, tea, coffee and cocoa, and submit the funds saved to the above address, clearly marked inside as to how they have been raised. Alternatives to self-denial might be performing EXTRA WORK, and any OTHER FUNDRAISING ACTIVITIES that can be thought of. The results will be announced in a Rally at the Albert Hall on Saturday 25th April at 7.30pm. Tickets, at 6d., are available from the same address. In the meantime please see the newspapers for announcements of meetings to be held.

Self-denial, how appropriately Lenten and fitting for this time of year. Mrs Pankhurst is indeed the new Messiah. It is, Bea thinks, quite brilliant; there is something rather rousing about hundreds, perhaps thousands, of women willingly suffering for a belief, and one week is an imaginable target, though Bea is slightly stumped by the coffee and tea budget. All Bea's purchases are on accounts billed to home and picked up by Mother and it is hardly as if she will ever in her life buy food. She has no idea who buys the tea, although without it the house would probably grind to a halt. However, this is not the moment to ponder, or she will be on permanent tea duty. At best.

Bea watches the other women. No clatter but still little chat in here as tongues move from envelope seal to envelope seal, in between, pens flying across the envelope fronts far faster than Bea can write. Well, faster than Bea can write on the first, second, third envelope – thank God she can sit upright as she does this . . . Speed up and, miraculously, she does. By the time she's passed a dozen, she's going as well as any of them and still picking up speed. Fold, stuff, lick. Write, wave dry, tick the list. Soon she's done her lot, fetched another pile. She's even been brought a cup of tea. These women soak up tea and so, now, does Bea. Keep on, she tells herself, heads are turning, watching her at the speed she is going. Maybe it could be written on her tombstone, *She Could Fill an Envelope Well.*

The paper-cuts on Bea's fingers are mounting up but she doesn't stop, reckoning that it's fine so long as there's no blood on the envelopes – and perhaps such battle scars are the thing to have. At some point Celeste, apparition that she has become, materialises, telling her to slow down, Bea old girl, it's not a race, before vanishing again.

Bea can't slow down, she's on fire. Her heart is pumping and her eyes are wide open, now she's doing this there's no going back to plodding along, she's lost any desire to stop. Each envelope, she tells herself, is a few shillings more to stop a woman having tubes stuck down her throat. It's more than that: as the pile on the floor beside her turns into a pool, the elation rises in her. This is more like it: look what's she done, what she's doing. It's only a moment, a minute, or feels like it, until she glances at her list and there are no more names there. She has finished. Bea draws breath; she leans back, stretches her arms and rolls her head from side to side. Then she examines the reddening lines on her fingers before looking down at the floor. Envelopes are scattered around; has she done a lot, too many, can you do too many? God, what a mess, though. She climbs down on to her hands and knees and the room pauses.

Bea flushes. Not again. Good Lord, she's a rose-tinted lighthouse this morning. There must be a rip in the back of her skirt. What humiliation, given what they must think of her already. Serves her right to be so fixed on fashion – 'frippery', some of these women here must think it. Thinking of what some of them look like, though, they shouldn't be missing out on its favours. Watch it, Beatrice, don't be a cat. She wonders where the rip is, she can't feel the skirt give anywhere, nor, come to think of it, did she hear anything go. Blast her skirt, that's it, she gives in, she'll have a couple of rather more practical old ones altered.

There's a voice in the hall. Not one of the voices in here, all cut-glass or making a good effort at it, but a flat-vowelled voice, pushing the sounds out. Bea raises her head to look in its direction, and sees that the rest of the room is looking in that direction, too. Thank God, it's not her skirt they are staring at after all.

'I've burnt two and I'll burn ten more. I'd do anything for her, I would. Carry one of those bombs in me case to John O'Groats and back . . .'

Bea lets the handful of envelopes she is holding fall to the floor.

'Hssh, now. Not in the hallway.'

The figures pass the doorway quickly. It's the woman with arched eyebrows, speaking far more tenderly than she spoke to Bea. Bea can't see the woman on the other side. Just glimpses a plain brown wool dress. The footsteps and protests go along the passage towards the kitchen, and then vanish.

9

THE MAN WHO IS SUPPOSED TO BE SITTING BETWEEN Edie and Bea that night is late. The dining room is filling up with silk and fur stoles, and there's a mumbling from the far side of the table that they should put their orders in. As good as the Ritz is, the service can slow down and they'll be late for the Adelphi. Not that it will matter much if they skip the first act. The show's been on for months and they must have all seen it at least twice. Even Bea has.

Edie leans across the gap and tells Bea she can see something different about her. What is it? A new admirer? Already? Edie's eyes light up with the suggestion. So she holds the same view, thinks Bea, as Mother. For a moment Bea wonders whether she should tell Edie, but before she has had time to think any more of it a well-fed man not much older than Bea is sitting down between them.

'Sorry, chaps,' he says to the table. 'Those damn women blocking the road.'

Bea feels a flutter of pride, then her stomach tightens. My God, the thought that any of them might find out. They'd think she'd lost her mind, at best. Even worse, they would think it was all caused by John. Which it is not, she tells herself quite firmly, it is because of Mrs Pankhurst and, well, because she wants more to her life than sitting around a table at the Ritz, even if her hands are so worn out they feel as though they're made of wood. It is harder work than she'd have thought, doing the same task over and over again. She fumbles a little with her knife and fork as she eats and blames it on playing the piano, praying that none of them register that they have never seen her near the keys. 'Seamstress's fingers,' says a girl on the other side of the table. They all laugh, and Bea wishes Edward were here to smile across the table at her.

The chorus holds its last note a little longer than the rest. The first act is coming to an end and Bea looks up from the stalls to the circle and boxes, hoping to see a woman stand up and leaflets flutter down. There is no one. What a pity, she thinks.

She ducks out of dancing afterwards, it's the last thing she feels like; she's done quite enough for the day. There's a couple sloping off early with her and they offer to drive her home. Is she all right, they ask over the rattle of the motor, not blue? Bea cringes at the question. It is as though she is thought of not only as heartbroken, but as some kind of invalid as a result. Then the couple fall into a complicit silence. Bea senses them continuing to talk to each other, a thread connecting the two, and she tries to remember whether she ever did this with John.

It's almost midnight when Bea patters into the house. The hall is still, as though the place is deserted. The buzz of the day vanishes from her and Bea feels quite alone. She takes the steps one at a time, her head full of pictures of carbon paper and piles of envelopes she can barely see over, the voice of that woman in brown vowing to raze the country to the ground still vibrating in her ears and she wonders whether, if she goes back to Lauderdale Mansions again and again, she will end up like that. Bea checks herself. There is a clear line to be drawn and, dammit, Beatrice, you are jolly well going to do so.

As Bea reaches the first floor she sees the lights are on in the red drawing room. She walks around the gallery to turn them off but when she enters the room she is met by a waft of cigar-smoke and brandy. Mother is sitting at one end of the green sofa with her back to the door, staring at the drawn curtains.

'Who's that?' Mother doesn't turn around. 'Come in here.'

Bea obeys. She walks around the sofa until she is standing in front of her mother.

'Beatrice.' On the side table is a decanter half full, and a tumbler half empty. 'Sit down, come and talk to me.'

'Are you all right, Mother?'

'Sit down, Beatrice.'

'Actually, I was feeling a bit—'

Mother reaches forward and grabs Bea's arm. 'Don't go.' Her grip is tight, almost pulling Bea down, and she gives way. Next to her Bea sees another tumbler, full, on the side table at the far end. Mother has had a visitor. But that, thinks Bea, is not strange. Mother often has visitors at this time of night. Politicians leave Parliament late.

'What's wrong, Mother?'

'Oh, nothing. Everything.'

'Come, Mother—'

'No, I'll not come, come. For forty-five years, since I first drew breath, I've put my all into everything I've done. I am the engine, Beatrice, of everything that happens around me, inside this house and out. I make people be heard, all those men with causes and ideas and not a chance, without me, of airing their views in the right rooms.'

Mother is not even looking at Bea, just at the fireplace, as though the flames will provide an answer to her woes.

'And one by one they leave me. I can't even persuade' – she looks down towards the full tumbler – 'that our way is the only way, the only way, Bea, to make things change. And that we must stick with it. We just have to be patient. It matters so much to me, Bea, so, so much. These half-crazed harpies will push us back years, of that I am sure, I've been told it quite directly – and more than once. Why do people either give up or lose control? It always seems to be one or the other. You would have thought that holding firm wasn't that hard a task, staying loyal to a person you care about, or at least professed to care about. But what sort of fool am I?' She reaches for the tumbler beside her. 'Sentimentality is ruin. And then there's all of you. Everyone gone, or going. Edward will crack off on some adventure soon, and where will I be then? Clemmie appears now and then, but, rather thanklessly, is paddling as fast as she can in the opposite direction. In any case, she's hardly been a supporter. You have been, though, my darling Beatrice. Thank God you're not going yet.'

Mother's grip has moved to Bea's hand which, even though it seems she could hardly be holding tighter, she now squeezes. Bea thinks she can hear her mother's voice tremble. She can count on her fingers the number of times she has heard this and she is struggling to remember the last time Mother was so emotional towards her. How much she has wanted this but, now, when at last it comes, Bea is betraying her. A lump rises in her throat. Mother releases her hand to reach for the tumbler beside her and Bea has a sudden, visceral fear that Mother, Mother whose iron will has dictated Bea's entire passage through life, is in tears.

Bea draws herself in. If Mother can fall, well, anybody can. She sees her mother lift a handkerchief to her eyes and it feels as though the certainty that Bea has always relied upon is crumbling in front of her.

'Don't desert me, Beatrice. Promise. I need you with me.'

The words hover on Bea's lips: 'Of course, Mother.' She believes both that she will never, can never, desert her mother, and that she may be lying through her teeth. As she prepares herself for the deceit, footsteps come up behind them, and both of them are engulfed in a waft of alcohol. The back of the sofa dips under the weight of a pair of arms and a shadow falls over Bea. Edward's voice, slurring slightly, deepens behind her.

'My two favourite ladies.'

Bea steels herself for the gush of praise from Mother but what comes next is quite the opposite, for Mother is standing up and shaking as she speaks.

'Good God, Edward, you're half cut.'

'Mother dearest, that is slander. I am fully cut.'

'You, too, Edward. You whom I least thought would let me down. Your life is a mess, Edward. You are out at all hours, the friends you bring back wreck the billiard room, and Lord knows where you've been beforehand. You should be down at Beauhurst, or anywhere in the country, getting some fresh air on a horse. Hunt, shoot, fish, Edward, isn't that what you're supposed to be doing? Frankly, I'd rather see you in the cavalry, or going off on some expedition. I shan't miss this new Edward, if the one I used to know has vanished. God knows what your father would have thought if he were still alive.'

Even Bea feels knocked about by this tirade, but the phrase that is ringing around her head is the last, 'if he were still alive . . . if he were still alive . . . ' Mother is talking about Father as if he were dead. Then, of course, he is as good as dead to Mother, if not to all of them. Perhaps it is the thought of why that has made Edward so inflame her.

Bea passes the next few days with her mind a jumble of stuffed envelopes, Mother and the question of whether she can go back to Lauderdale Mansions. Christ, she spends half of her waking time railing to herself about Mother, and then a few tears and Bea is back at the apron-strings. She could give up on it, do her dutiful round of dances and branch meetings of comparatively docile suffragists, recover from the hideousness of the John business and marry somebody her family actually liked. Part of this, to be frank, doesn't sound so unappealing.

However, Celeste has held out the proverbial apple and Bea has sunk her teeth in. She's not betraying Mother for some idle thrill but for a belief that will achieve precisely what Mother is struggling for. Mother, if you knew what I was doing, she reasons, then you would respect me more, you'd be damned proud of me, that I am doing something.

Mrs Pankhurst's words are still in Bea's head – Can you keep your self-respect any longer? – and Bea feels a tingling from her chest to her cheeks. Mrs Pankhurst, she thinks, and in her rises a swirl of desires to hit back where she is being hit, and giddy herself up to yesterday's high. If Bea believes, and she does, then things will change and she, Beatrice, will leave her mark on the world. She will have made something of her life, rather than have drifted through it.

She can't not go back to Lauderdale Mansions. That single bite of enthusiasm has made her feel as though she would wither away without it. Mother, well, Mother simply must not find out.

By nine o'clock on Tuesday Bea's walking in through the door at Lauderdale Mansions and she's clearly not the first. Maybe none of these women here sleeps. She passes the typing room, which is already exhaling muggy air, and reaches the door of the room-of-the-satisfying-envelopes. It is empty and she pauses in the doorway.

'Go!' The voice behind her is hard and angry, as though she has done something terribly, terribly wrong. My God, it occurs to her that it's not a question of Mother knowing about Bea, but of these women knowing about Mother, and if they know she is Celeste's niece, they must surely have realised. They must think her either a traitor or a spy, and what do they do with spies here? Bea feels slightly sick. Whoever it is speaking to her is about to tell her, at the very best, that she never wants to see Bea here again.

Bea has to turn round. She really doesn't want to, but she has at some point to face the door. Or walk out backwards. Which is not, right now, so terrible a proposition.

It is the woman with the devilish eyebrows. Bea looks down at the floor, waiting for the next words '. . . and never come back . . . '

They don't come. Instead the woman sighs, her whole chest heaving up and down as though she's expelling the spirits from her.

'. . . into the typewriter room . . . We're doing the advertisements today.'

Bea pulls herself up, whispers 'Thank you', then 'Good morning', and quicksteps along the passageway and into the mauve room, where she drops into an empty seat in front of a typewriter with a feeling of relief. There is something rather reassuring about being told how to go against the grain instead of having to think it up for yourself at every turn.

The relief does not last long. Advertisements; Bea is staring at her hell on paper. For a start, she has to decipher some handwritten scrawl, and then even these personal requests have rows of capitals that appear in the middle of sentences, and after yesterday's exertions she needs two fingers to hold down the shift key. Even then she's pushing down hard to keep it in place. She needs to build up the strength in, of all things, her fingers, and finds some respite from the morning in imagining binding miniature Indian exercise clubs to each digit.

It is eleven o'clock. Bea is longing for a cup of tea, but is not up to ferrying back the inevitable half-dozen. She's parched, though, and starts to count the number of tea-drinkers in the room, but as she does so her typewriter darkens and there's somebody leaning over her. Bea feels the warmth of another face, and then a whisper blowing into her ear.

'Come with me.' It is Celeste.

Bea, hoping this will involve a detour via the kitchen, follows Celeste, who walks down the passageway towards the end but stops short of the kitchen. She can see the kettles boiling through the door ahead and considers stepping past her aunt. Celeste, however, is turning towards the closed door on their right. Without pausing to knock, she opens it and walks straight in, beckoning Bea to follow.

Bea finds herself in a floral-papered bedroom, at most twelve foot square, still containing a pair of twin beds. In front of the window is a small table with a chair behind, occupied by a woman of around fifty years old. Her greying hair has been set around her face, her white silk blouse fastened by a large pearl brooch. Celeste steers Bea ahead.

'A new recruit. My niece, Beatrice Masters. Tight lips. I'll vouch for her.'

The woman nods and Celeste moves back towards a space on one of the beds. There are perhaps a dozen women in here, their faces a disturbing mix of the radiantly healthy and others just twigs of women, some not more than thirty yet their faces already sagging skin and bone. If a window were opened, thinks Bea, it would blow them away. Their heads, however, are held high, the heads held highest of all sporting purple cheekbones and jaws.

'From the force-feeding,' Celeste whispers as Bea sits down where her aunt pats the counterpane.

Bea is at the pillow end of a bed and she peers forward through the trees of necks topped by waves of pinned hair: some are emaciated, others thick trunks of flesh.

'Bodyguard,' Celeste breathes into her ear.

To the left of the woman behind the table, just to the side of the window, is an incongruously red velvet tasselled wing chair. In it sits another small woman with high cheekbones and a square jaw. Her hair is greying, too, and she looks about the same age as the woman sitting behind the table. Bea thinks back to the evening in Campden Hill Square. She can remember the hat, of course, the straight shoulders, and a flash of jawline. However, the dark and distance had kept the detail of the face from her. Now she can see that it is thinner than it should be. The skin is tired, there are the traces of dark circles under the eyes, but the eyes themselves glow as they survey this small crowd jostling for space, each woman leaning forward towards her. Of course, Bea has seen the photograph more times than she can remember, but here, glimmering in the flesh, almost close enough for Bea to reach out and touch her skin, is Emmeline Pankhurst.

It is not Mrs Pankhurst who speaks first, but a younger woman, aged around thirty, who emerges from a corner.

'I should start by thanking Mrs Hall for lending us her flat. Thank you, Pattie. I hope we are all aware that this arrangement will only work for as long as it is kept secret. Nobody needs reminding of what happened at Lincoln's Inn House.'

The woman's cheeks are rounded with a healthy blush etched years ago on school hockey fields. School, thinks Bea, was not a place she was allowed to go. Had she gone, would she, like this woman, be able to stand up and address such a crowd without flinching? The woman is continuing, '. . . a special welcome to Mary Fuller and Sarah Hodson, our comrades-in-arms, and "mice" most recently released from Holloway. Not only are they recovering but they are still managing to evade rearrest.'

One of the women with a bruised face whispers back: 'Still in fine fettle. Only our first time . . .'

Another voice, a familiar voice that makes Bea catch her breath, cuts in, 'What your bodies feel is irrelevant. Your spirits can always stay strong.'

It is Mrs Pankhurst, Emmeline, speaking out from her wing chair. She doesn't wait for a formal introduction, for determination and impatience are pushing against the walls of this room and there are other things that need to be done. While women are sitting here typewriters are empty, piles of envelopes untouched and suffragettes being force-fed.

'The government thinks it can ignore us,' she continues. 'We need to do something that it cannot forget.'

'Fire . . .' Bea can't see who the voice is from, but it is not such a strong voice, perhaps from one of the women weakened by a stay in Holloway.

Mrs Pankhurst does not wait. 'Another burning church won't do it. Those that need to have their minds changed must feel the heat a little closer to home.'

'Home?' Another voice, this one stronger.

'Women are laying down their lives. They need to be honoured. Nothing, nobody, is beyond bounds while we are not allowed a voice in this country. This is the only way to speak left open to us.'

As the words come out of Mrs Pankhurst's mouth, Bea looks round the room at the women with their straight backs and perfect hair, and bruises.

'Who then?' Another voice.

'It is the moment, not the person, that matters most. When that comes, the "who" will be clear.' Emmeline Pankhurst's voice croaks, and she is silent.

The hearty chairwoman takes over.

'Don't worry, ladies, Mrs Pankhurst simply has a slight chill. We all agree, I am sure, on the need for extreme action. I particularly agree that timing and planning are of the essence. In the meantime we need to continue with ordinary business. Any volunteers for handing out leaflets and chalking up pavements?'

'Remember,' says Mrs Pankhurst, 'even that has danger attached.'

What easy price danger, thinks Bea.

After two hours at Speakers' Corner, Bea is straining to remember what it was like not to be cold. She didn't feel the temperature at first, she was looking around, left, right and back again, as she had been told to. Not for the police; Bea isn't doing anything illegal. It was, and is, for the anti-suffragists that she's been told to watch out, especially the men, burly men, though even the small ones can be vicious. The women don't come right up to your face, they said in Lauderdale Mansions.

Bea feels flushed, and her breastbone is tingling. She's enjoying the sensation, and almost wishes for a small mob of aggressors.

Around her are the usual half-dozen soapbox speakers competing for attention. Religion, of course, the Salvation Army positioning itself the other side of the open area from the exhortations of the Evangelists. A Theosophist is reasoning calmly in between the Socialist Party of Great Britain demanding revolution and the anti-Home Rule propagandists arguing for no change at all in Ireland. No anti-suffragists this afternoon. Not even any of Mother's crowd. Thank God.

Bea's gloves are not thick enough to keep her fingers warm yet she cannot commit the cardinal sin of slipping them into the pockets on her coat, for her hands are still clutching the last few leaflets. Reticence, she has discovered, is not the key. Nor is announcing what the leaflet says before she hands it out, though her purple, green and white sash gives it away. Instead she has learnt the tactic of approaching a passer-by and smiling as she thrusts the paper into his or her hand. It makes the men, of course, more likely to take it, though they are hardly likely to read it. Still, it must be better to push out as many as possible, even if these men's sons simply make paper aeroplanes with them. In any case, Bea has to keep up with the battleaxe who came with her.

From here Bea can see home, just. With her binoculars trained spot on, Mother could possibly see her. Yet, instead of being frightened, after last night Bea feels a calm certainty that Mother would not actually throw Bea out of the house, leaving herself yet more alone.

Even if she did, Edie would take Bea in. Well, perhaps – newlyweds can be so conventional. Of course, on the outside it's all fun and games but challenge them a little and they are nervous of change. Or there's Celeste. But Celeste has other house guests. A perpetually rotating list of 'distressed' women and 'artistic' men. According to Celeste, the most reliable among them are the just-released hunger-strikers, of whom there are usually at least two languishing upstairs. She once picked up a woman off the streets whom she installed in the best spare and who charmed the other guests for a fortnight while yelping at any staff who tried to touch her possessions. After two weeks of complaining that 'those lot will have it all off me given half the chance', she vanished with two silver sugar shakers and a teapot.

'Funny,' said Celeste when she told the story to Bea. 'She didn't drink tea.'

This will not happen, however. People talk and Mother doesn't, she surely doesn't, want a scandal; she has enough to irritate her already and any more might weaken her standing with the Union. She cares about that more than anything, well, apart from Edward. Until Edward marries, Mother is the most important woman in his life. Even when he does marry, it is not a position, Bea suspects, that Mother will readily surrender.

It is five thirty before Bea has handed out the last of the leaflets. It's almost dark. The lamps are on and the park suddenly feels quite empty. She has to be at dinner by seven in order to make the theatre. It will take her more than a quarter of an hour to walk home – which of course she should not be doing after dark. Not the walk, nor the alone, nor the park. Bea smiles to herself as she sets off down the avenue of trees leading south.

It's funny how, after dark, even if there is still traffic, you can hear footsteps ring, especially the ones behind her right now. They come closer, making Bea feel a little uncomfortable, and she speeds up, but not as fast as they do, for a pair of silhouettes and pale faces pass on her right. She relaxes a little but moves to the centre of the path, as far as she can from the shadows of tree trunks. As she approaches the bottom of the avenue the path ahead empties of approaching figures and behind her she hears a steady knock keeping pace, a heavy one, too. She walks a little more briskly, but the steps copy hers. She glances to the left. Through the bars of the trees she sees her home, but there is a spiked wall of railings and a road in between. Fast now, Beatrice, but don't run, it would be far too impolite. Not to mention inelegant; she has never been a good runner.

Fifty yards to go. If the man behind her – and surely it is a man – is going to rob her, or 'even worse', as Clemmie used to whisper when Bea crawled into her bed at night, then he will grab her now. But, just in time, thank God, Bea can see someone turning into the park ahead of her, walking in her direction. Bea could run to this figure but just cannot bring herself to, and so she walks steadily and quickly ahead. As the bowler hat and ruddy face of the figure loom into view, she turns towards him and beams a smile. But the man does not smile back. Instead, he leans forward and hisses. Bea can feel the heat of his breath.

'Only a woman.'

It's not much, but Bea feels as though she has been slapped and her legs lose their direction. She wants to go forward but she finds herself slowing down right by this hissing, spitting person. Flecks of the half-rotten-meat smell from his mouth are landing, she is sure, on her face. As she stops she feels a heavy hand reach out from behind her and take her arm.

'Excuse me.'

It is a strong south London accent, one that, in the circumstances, does not make Bea relax. That's it, she's surrounded. The stranger behind her will ask her to hand her money over, quite rightly assuming that she must have some tucked in somewhere. Or worse, he could take her for the sort of woman who walks here alone. But that is not what he says at all. Instead he turns to the hisser, who has also stopped, and says, 'Would you mind leaving this young lady in peace.'

Bea tries to look the hisser in the eye imploringly. Don't go, she is trying to say, you may be rude, but you aren't about to rob me. It is, of course, too dark for him to see anything but the rim of her hat.

'She should be home,' splutters the hisser, 'asking her husband what he thinks.'

And he walks off, leaving Bea with this stranger behind her whom she can't yet see.

'Do you often walk alone through the park after dark?'

Bea gasps. He does think she is one of those women. How on earth is this happening to her? All she has done is hand out a few leaflets. Bea waits, dreading what he will say next, but he is telling her that she is still wearing her sash, perhaps asking for trouble. He's been trying to catch up with her for a while, but she's a galloper. Where is she going? Can she at least let him walk her out of the park?

Can she? Can she not? If she continues alone she may be accosted again, and she would rather have her belongings removed charmingly than roughly – if, if anything else, then she will run, properly this time. Bea slips her sash over her head, folds it and tucks it under her elbow. It can go under her coat before she reaches the house. Beside this stranger, she walks out of the park. This is, she thinks, becoming a habit and one which, though a little terrifying at stages, breaks at least half a dozen of the most serious rules she has been brought up with – satisfactorily so.

10

FOR THREE NIGHTS, SINCE MONDAY, THE LIBRARY BOOK under Grace's mattress has been burning a hole in her cheek. Each time she turns at night she fancies she can feel an edge, reminding her that she's not just having a bad dream. It's like one of those stories she reads in the newspaper – the maid who did the terrible thing, employers betrayed and hurt after such kindness . . . Maid's family shamed . . . She thinks of her ma and da and the little ones with no money from her, and no chance of working again, let alone in an office. Even Michael, he'd hardly be able to keep his career in the law with a sister locked up, and she was only trying to help him. You half-wit, Grace. Still, how's he to keep his career in the law with what he's up to? Grace is no fool. She knows what *The Condition of the Working Class in England* is about, and Karl Marx is one of the books he'd wanted with it – though she's not getting him that. She only has to glance at the newspaper to see that the 'Marxists' would destroy the lot of us if they could. Engels may sounds like the word 'angels' in comparison, but look at the subject matter for all that. It occurs to Grace that if she were caught with this book, the politics would be seen as much of a wrong as the thieving.

She could put it back, but when would she do that? She can hardly carry it down with the excuse that she'd found it somewhere and was returning it to the library. It's at that point, being in the library, putting it back, when she's most likely to be caught. No, she has to get it out of the house, and to Michael now. Whenever she's in her room she fancies she hears Mrs Wainwright's heels clip along the passage. Grace watches the door handle, waiting for it to turn. Even about the house she's waiting for a hand on her shoulder. What's the matter with you, asks Mary as they dress?

It's the china this morning, and with Joseph, too. Now they're up in the dining room together she should be smiling, shouldn't she? But she's looking away because she doesn't want him to see the wickedness written in her eyes, and because she's not looking and can't keep still, she walks into him and she jumps. He's in his shirtsleeves, cleaning the china; just a shirt it is between him and her, though she's her morning frock on, but that's thin cotton too. She clutches the plate she is holding close to her, and she hopes, to dear God, that Joseph hasn't dropped his dish. There's no shattering though, just his voice and she can't help but turn to it.

'Grace,' he says. Just Grace, but it's a hundred words for all its softness and pull and she purses her lips tight to stop them trembling. He looks at her, puzzled at her face, and so she turns away again.

'No,' she says. 'No, Joseph, no.'

Before he can reply, she has a stack of plates and is taking them downstairs for warming. She doesn't look back.

The family is out for luncheon and, after their own dinner, they'll have a break until four. Grace asks to be excused. Excused? says Mrs Wainwright. There'll be no food later. Today that's the last thing Grace is worried about, and at noon she hurries up the stairs to change into her black afternoon dress and white pinny so as to look right when she comes back in. She's not hungry, and wonders whether it's as much that she won't be sitting opposite Joseph at dinner as the book. When she buttons up her coat, it's awful tight, not much room for a book underneath. It'll have to be her tapestry handbag. Big enough it is too. Let's hope Mrs Wainwright won't go through it as Grace leaves. No thoughts like that, Grace Campbell, or your face'll be as guilty as the sin this is.

She moves quickly now, knocks back down the stairs but not too fast, nor too slow; she needs to catch Michael in the ten minutes she knows he's sent out to fetch soup and a slice. A pie for a treat, thought that's not often enough, not with those thin cheeks.

Up Park Lane she goes, fourpence in her pocket. She's to go five stops east from Marble Arch on the Tuppenny Tube, and it's the size of this city that scares her. It goes on and on east with no stopping.

The air even here, by the park, makes you cough. What with the motors and buses rattling enough to fill her ears and all their smoke, it's a wonder anybody can breathe at all. Not that the air was that clean in Carlisle. But it wasn't like this. It's worse the faster she walks, and she needs to be quick to catch him. She's not sure which ten minutes he'll have, varies every day, he says. The sooner she's there, waiting outside, the better. She checks off the mansions one by one as she walks along. She doesn't know them well yet. When she's out on a Sunday she's either rushing to church, or rushing back from seeing Michael. And she's hardly going to suggest to him that they take a look along the road. He has her address but she doesn't want him poking around, does she? Besides, he's told her he can't stand the people who live in places like these. Except me, she tells herself.

The houses are nearly all stone, but let darken to grey and brown. You'd've thought they've the money to clean them, the people who live here. But it seems the richer you are, the older your things look. The windows, too, look funny, all different, they are. Some have deep bays jutting out as if they're desperate for more space but if they wanted the rooms bigger, thinks Grace, why didn't they build square out to the front like Number Thirty-Five. It hasn't got the prettiest windows, though. Proud as she is, Grace is still honest about that. If she were to choose, she'd take windows with a triangle hat, but no raised stone borders down the side.

That's too much of a frill for her. Number Thirty-Five Park Lane does have grooves, pointed-edge dips between the blocks of stone for giant fingers to run through, but she doesn't mind them there.

The shutters on one of the houses are closed like nobody ever goes there. At dinner the other day the upper servants were talking about houses not visited for years at a time. Still get dusty, though. The furniture is covered in great white sheets and sits around the rooms like ghost beasts. 'That's what happened here,' James told her, 'when they all suddenly disappeared to Lady Masters' family's house in America for a year. Had to, they did, after Sir William Masters' gambling the house away and Lady Masters having to buy it back – for herself. She wasn't going to let him gamble it away again. And what with Sir William's dancing girl, and all that he'd given her, not to mention being so open about it and everyone knowing, well, the whole family needed to take themselves out of society for a bit. That's what people like the Masters do. If they stayed away for a year, everyone would be talking about something else by the time they returned. And so that's how it was – Number Thirty-Five full of life one week, with not a murmur of anything different, then like the grave the next.'

Am-er-ic-a, thinks Grace, savouring each syllable. Stories she's heard, that you can go from any street here and do well for yourself in America. Not a question of anyone being bothered about where you've come from, and a maid only being a maid; over there, they care more about what you can do. And the country stretches further than you can imagine, she's heard. Maybe she and Michael should go to America, and send back money from there. Go to America, though, and they might never see Ma, Da and the little ones, again. Not that she knows when she'll get herself back to Carlisle.

By the time Grace reaches the top of Park Lane she's becoming used to the noise and the road being so full of buses and motors, horses and carts picking their way between them. But it still feels as though all that engine dirt is layering itself on her. It's a funny thing, that the smartest place to live has so much of it. When she first arrived in the city she would have preferred a quiet street. She's not so sure now, the busy-ness makes her feel less lonely. And you get used to a bit of green all too quick.

At this end of Park Lane the houses are smaller, tall, thin and jammed together in a row of white plaster. Still, they're mansions themselves. On the other side of the road, in the top corner of the park, she sees a handful of men standing up on crates. Some even have crowds around them, so you can't see the crates and they just look like giants. She's at the end now, at Marble Arch, with steps down into the ground, and the Tube underneath.

She feared it'd be crowded. Grace has heard about the early mornings and late afternoons. Don't travel on it then, she was told in the boarding house, or you'll find yourself jammed in, breathing shoulderfuls of damp tweed. Then you feel the hands around your rear, though one girl claimed to have had hands around the front. But they don't dare touch your chest. You might see who it is, though there's not much you could do about it: you can't move, can't move an inch. Swivel your head and you'll lose an eye to the rim of a short man's bowler. So eyes forward and try to keep your mind off the fact that one of the men near you, his body squeezed against yours, is touching you there. The girls who aren't used to it go bright red. Take the omnibus, it may be slower, but it's safer, costs less, too. Grace took the omnibus when she was out searching for work up the city, down the city, right across London. Her world is much smaller now, she can walk to church, to the park. Today, though, she needs to be quick. She walks up to the ticket booth, hands over tuppence and in a minute she's underneath the city and in spitting distance, she must be, of all that rot that sinks down here. She can smell it, she's sure of it, for the same people built the Underground as built the sewers, including the first Mr Masters, Miss Beatrice's great-grandad. Funny to know so much about him, but then you can't miss it, not in that room at the back.

There's no air down here. How can there be? Yet she's still breathing, and that's not natural, is it? Nor is the speed at which the train is going along. She's counting the stops but she can't see much from the middle of this crowd, and who's to tell if they've been right through one she didn't see at all. What if she went to the end of the line and there wasn't a way out from there. But here it is, Chancery Lane, just like Michael said. The paper's in her pocket but she can remember his voice: 'Just at the bottom of Chancery Lane and in through one of the gateways. Then ask for this address. If you ever need me, that's where I am.'

Back outside it's drizzling a little; however, it's daylight again and any daylight will do but, my word, Chancery Hill they should call it, and she's at the top of it. Even the horses are leaning back as their hooves tilt forwards and the pavement's not much more than a couple of feet wide so you're knocked into the traffic. She has to hurry, even though her boots are skidding this way and that. It's a quarter to one and surely they'll send him out not much later. She makes her steps small, pushing down heavily to keep steady.

It's a passage, Michael said, at the bottom, through an arch, and Grace is looking. One looms on her left. Middle Temple Lane. Middle, was that it? No, no, that's not it. And she walks along. Outer Temple Lane, that's the next, yes, that was it, Outer. She walks down the high-walled alley barely wide enough for a wheelbarrow, wondering where her brother does work, whether it's a good place, after all those questions he had for her. But it doesn't smell, she'll give him that; and it's deathly quiet. Grace pauses, balancing on the cobbles, and closes her eyes. You want to drink it in, this sound, or not-sound, keep it in your head for when you're trying to sleep.

It's the ring of footsteps that opens her eyes. A pair of men dressed in wigs and with cloaks floating behind them are coming up the lane towards her like a pair of ghosts. Grace wonders what world it is that she has stepped into but on she goes, down another slope, through the archway at the end and into a silent square.

She's the only one in it, brick blocks with white-painted window frames rising around her, lists of names beside the doorways. A motor squeezes down a lane on the far side of the square. Grace walks towards it. Where there's a way to drive there's a way to walk. There'll be someone to ask.

She stops at the edge of the road and looks down the hill. She can see the Thames at the bottom, cold and grey. Is that what London is, she asks herself? Is that what it will feel like if I am caught?

An errand boy is running towards her, about to pass quicker than a word, but he smiles at her as he trots, and she calls to him, Hare Court? Through the archway. What archway? Thissun here. And he tilts his head towards a building on the other side of the road.

Through she goes, looking this way and that, but it's not Hare Court here and she waits at the far end for another boy to pass for they're tearing up and down these alleys like it's nobody's business. One boy and two turns more, and she's there.

It is dark, this building. The brick is dirtier than she's seen before, and there's a brown brick wall right opposite the door. Just inside the doorway is a young man, about Michael's age, arms full of paper tied with pink ribbon. Grace shrinks back. She'll stand by the wall, melt into it.

Grace keeps her eyes on her feet, glancing up at each echo of steps on cobbles, and down again. She doesn't want to be seen as staring. It's raining in any case, and her bonnet tilted forward is keeping the drops off her face. It'll be a mess, though, the bonnet; she should have brought an umbrella, but she didn't think, and now the tips of her boots are darkening in the wet.

And there he is, in his mackintosh, head forward. He doesn't see her, passes right by. Michael, she calls, and he jolts round.

'What are you doing here? What's wrong?' He looks worried.

'Nothing's wrong.'

Why should something be wrong? Does he think that's the only reason she'd come to see him? 'I've something for you.'

'Couldn't it wait till Sunday?' He begins to walk again and she falls in with him.

Rude, she thinks, and from her own brother, but she'll not let him push her away like that.

Doesn't he realise the trouble she's gone to?

'No, it couldn't, Michael.'

'Show me then, Grace. Quick.'

'No, Michael, not here, round the corner.'

'I've no time for that. I'm starving hungry, Grace. You'll have to walk with me.'

He's off and Grace is near trotting to keep up. She doesn't want to show him here, there are too many people, what if someone should see, though she can't think who. The bag is swinging side to side as she goes and she reaches in, grasps it and pulls, but the book is catching on the opening at the top. It's out now, she's handed it to him. He stops dead. Then he turns it over with such a strange expression on his face that Grace can't tell whether he's excited or disgusted, and this pricks her. She feels her skin drawing back across her face and she's having to fight more than little to go on looking so tender towards him.

'Where did you get this?'

'The library.'

'In the office?'

'No, in the house. We all live in the house, remember.'

'They lent it to you?' He turns it over in his hands and opens the first couple of pages, looking right over them. 'Grace, do you know what it's worth?'

He's telling her off. My Lord, all she's done, and he's telling her off. She's a mind to let him know . . . but she can't, can she? She can't say anything at all, and she's no idea what it's worth in money. To her it is worth her position and her ability to send money home.

'Don't you want to read it, Michael?' She can hear the anger in her own voice.

'Grace, it's signed by the man who wrote it. Did they know you were taking it out of the house? Why do you think they'd want you to read this?'

'Why shouldn't I read it, Michael? You weren't the only one to have lessons with Miss Sand, remember. And it's hardly a locked-up sort of book.'

'What's a locked-up sort of book?'

Grace blushes. Michael's eyes open wide, stare at her.

'What sort of family have you become involved with, Grace?'

What sort of family? They're a darn sight better than those he's working for, she's sure of that. She blurts out a bit too quick: 'Just talk, Michael.'

'Not talk you should be having, a girl like you. Did he ask you for anything?'

'No, Michael. It's not like that there.'

He turns the book over in his hands. 'You must be doing well, Grace. I'll wager he doesn't do this for his housemaids.'

On the corner of Chancery Lane and Fleet Street, Grace sees a shop window with barely a dozen books laid out. They're all sizes, one she could fit into the palm of her hand, another is the size of the Bible in church on Sunday, and this one is open, stretched wide. Grace looks at it through the glass; there are pictures in it, and thick, foreign writing. She thinks she can see a word or two she knows, but the rest, well, it's not English, not that she's seen. There's a book, too, which looks like the one she's given Michael. A thin binding, and leather, not so old, type like it should be. She doesn't want to know but she wants to find out, can't go past now without asking, even if it will make the worry worse. Now Michael's put the worry there, she can't get it out of her mind.

Grace hasn't much time left but she rings the bell. The door opens and the man in front of her is wearing a black jacket, with waistcoat and pinstripe trousers and seems too modern for the books, though he's losing his hair, most of it gone. He looks her up and down as though to say the cheek of it, to be coming into his shop.

'I'd like to enquire about a price,' she says in her best Park Lane posh, and, his eyebrows raised, the man lets her in.

Which? he asks. The one in the window, she replies. Across they go and Grace peers over the back of the display. She points.

'Just six pounds, madam.'

Just six pounds? It's half of what she earns in a year. She turns and goes so quickly that she's almost stumbling out of the door.

Still, Grace sleeps better that night, and Saturday too. She hasn't much fear that anybody will look for the book in the library, she's never seen any of upstairs go in. It's more the fear that somebody might find it on her. When she's not touching the book, it's not touching her. So when Michael gives it back to her on Sunday, and she feels the weight of it in her hands, the worry comes on her again.

'I've read it,' he says. 'Thank you.'

He's looking down at his feet as he hands it to her. Why, he's as sheepish as they come, but it's a thank you, and it's meant and it fills her up a little, makes her feel better about what she's done to get it.

'You'd better read it now, Grace.'

'Why, Michael' – she begins to say, but now he's looking at her like she's the riddle of the Sphinx – 'do you think I didn't read it already?'

'Did you?'

'Just teasing, Michael.'

'Better remember why Mr Townsend gave it to you, Grace. It wasn't to lend to me. He'll ask you what's in it.'

Mr Townsend, who's he, Grace is about to ask? Then she remembers it's the name of her employer that she gave to Michael.

'I've no time now, Michael.' She's quick today, and speaking straight ahead as though she's too grand to look at him. 'You've had it all week. You'll have to tell me what's in it. And, Michael?'

'Yes, Grace.'

'Don't speak to me as though I am a child.'

Now she turns, to be honest, to gloat a little, see him taken aback. But he's not listening. He's looking at her and the book is pouring out of his mouth, his words full of anger with the world. It's as if she's suddenly turned on a stiff hot-water tap that will never go back. She stares at her brother, dead proud of the way he can talk, and dead nervous as to where it will take him.

In the library the next morning Grace looks up, searches for the gap on the shelves to put the book back into, but the books appear to have expanded, filled it out. Or was that how she had arranged them? The steps are on the far side of the room and Grace remembers the rattle and the grind of moving them and the attention it might bring. Then she looks back up at the shelves and wonders if it would ever be noticed if she didn't put the book back. And when, after breakfast, she is cleaning the telephone booth on the ground floor around the back of the main stairs, she sees a directory on the shelf. Shutting herself in, small duster in hand as though she is scraping out the last grey grains, Grace opens the pages. If nobody's read the book she took for years, who's going to read it now, or ever again?

After dinner, for there's nobody for luncheon today, Grace heads south-east, her handbag over her arm. Hyde Park Corner; she'd like to walk through the arch some day. She hasn't time now as she doesn't know how long she will be. Perhaps on the way back. If she's quick enough maybe she'll have a chance to talk to Joseph too.

It's him that's turning away now. He looks at her like she's stuck a knife in his stomach and shows her his back, even when they're cleaning the silver together. She should be relieved, shouldn't she? But the silence is ringing in her ears and she just needs to explain to him, tell him how she doesn't want to give him ideas, seeing as she has plans of her own, and she's taken by her obligations. But she can't get close. And the house, it feels hollow now without his smile. But that hollowness makes it seem not so bad, what she's about to do.

Grace walks through Belgrave Square and its shiny black doors in tall white stucco, only dusty around the windows. Even the houses with three windows across, and large ones at that, look almost cramped compared to Park Lane. But how could she think that?

It's strange how quickly your perspective can change.

Elizabeth Street is narrow and pretty. The white is broken up by shopfront windows pushing out from the houses in blues, greens and browns. Grace finds the shop she is looking for halfway down on the right. The books in the window look more like the one she is carrying under her coat than those back on Fleet Street. A small man answers the door, a smile on his face she can't read. She follows him inside, where she draws the book out of her handbag and places it on the counter. He picks it up and opens it. His eyebrows flicker as he sees the signature.

Grace has no idea whether his offer is enough, but it's enough for her. Besides, if he's as good as stolen from her then he's not going to say anything, is he?

She leaves with five pounds in her pocket.

II

BEA IS ON HER WAY TO GLEBE PLACE IN CHELSEA AT half past three on a Saturday afternoon, in a taxi with a cough in its engine. The rally was announced this morning. It had been kept so quiet that she hadn't heard even a word of it in Lauderdale Mansions until she went in today, and by then it was already in the papers. The police, she was told quite directly, must have as little notice as possible as to where Emmeline might be. There are rearrest warrants out for her from one end of the country to the other, and she has to get into the house she is speaking from before they know where to look: they've no right to go in there. Still, Bea thought, am I so little trusted that I couldn't know?

Never mind, she's on her way and her pulse is quickening. She should not be as excited as this; she wasn't this jumpy when Celeste led her into Emmeline's room. Calm down, Beatrice, you're no longer a giddy debutante waiting for her first dance. You've been to one of these meetings before. So what's the bother about this one? She's just going, isn't she, because it would be pretty poor not to show.

Now she's standing in a wide street in Chelsea, one side low dark red-brick artists' studios, the other a neat white terrace. She's found a position bang opposite from where Mrs Pankhurst will emerge, and she's edged back up the steps to the front door of the house behind her to gain a little height, although it's not Mrs Pankhurst she's looking for but a familiar face from Lauderdale Mansions. The team, almost to a woman, is somewhere in front of her, yet how on earth is Bea to spot them? All she can see from here are backs of heads and so many banners she hasn't a chance of finding a soul. Blast, she should have asked where they were meeting up before they arrived. It's mid-afternoon, when there's no need even to pretend to have a chaperone, but for the first time Bea quite wishes she had somebody with her.

The crowd thickens and begins to heave. Bea remembers the chaos of Campden Hill Square and feels slightly nauseous at the thought. Backwards into this front door may be the only direction she can go until she is impaled upon the serpent doorknob digging into her.

The police are already several men deep around the house, and a few mounted. From her position on the steps, Bea can see over the helmets in front of her: there'll be plain-clothes in here too. Maybe this time a real one will arrest her. Her mind fills with the potential consequences. Who would she send for to pay her bail – if she was given it? Celeste first, though she is at a house party for a few days. Then Edie, if necessary. Edward's pockets are more likely to be empty than laden.

The crowd waits. Two more people, a man and a woman, are climbing on to the top step with Bea. She sticks firmly to her position in the centre, and finds herself wedged between them. At least, she thinks, this is warmer. Whispers hiss through the crowd in waves. Mrs Pankhurst is coming, she's about to come, she's been caught, that's why she's late, I hope there's an exit out the back this time. And they wait. Part of the drama, thinks Bea, and clever, for the people down here need to believe in Mrs Pankhurst. As Bea does . . . does she? She is mesmerised by Mrs Pankhurst – more so rather than less by having been within touching distance – and her breath is shortening as she waits to hear her speak again. But chaining herself to railings, throwing a brick? You don't have to believe in that to believe in Mrs Pankhurst, do you? As the crowd's rumble drops into silence, Bea holds her breath. The first-floor window across the street begins to open and she watches.

She jumps, almost yelps, as she feels a hand on her forearm, but catches the noise. Then slowly, not quite wanting to see, she looks down. It is the man from Campden Hill Square, as dark-faced, bowler-hatted and mackintoshed as before. Bea should want to shrink back, even if there is nowhere to shrink to, but she doesn't. My God, she can't be pleased to see him, can she, a man who has been so downright objectionable?

He nods up at her.

She nods back down at him and brusquely turns back to the balcony. A woman wearing a black hat with a large feather in it is standing out there alone. In the two seconds' silence that follows, Bea wonders whether she will have to speak to the man and what on earth she will say. But thank God, Mrs Pankhurst begins.

Mrs Pankhurst is less dramatic this time. Instead of urging people to lay down their lives, she declares that suffragettes will live. That those being released from prison as they are about to die, and being recaptured and force-fed again, will survive. However patient and long-suffering women may be, she declares, once they are set on a course they are 'more dangerous than any other opponent of the government', and nothing short of the vote will satisfy them. Nor will they rest until the 'horrible poison' of inequality that is dripped into little children is stemmed, and men and women are equal in the eyes of the law. Until then, why should women obey the law if they have no part in making it? And, so long as the juries judging women do not include women, they 'refuse to be punished'.

One of the reasons she was sentenced to three years' penal servitude, she continues, was because in court she spoke up for the women who behave 'through poverty as some men behave in pursuit of what they call pleasure'. A certain judge due to pronounce on such women, she had said, failed to appear in court that morning. The night before he 'had been found dead in a house of ill fame'.

The crowd roars with laughter. Bea laughs with it.

One name crops up again and again in her speech. Mr McKenna, the Home Secretary; Mr McKenna, who decides how the law will be applied; Mr McKenna, who decides that women will be imprisoned while political rebels in Ireland are not; Mr McKenna, who decides which women will be forcibly fed, twelve men and women holding each single prisoner down.

As Mrs Pankhurst disappears, the crowd surges. Within seconds it is a maelstrom. In the motion of hats, shoulders and umbrellas up and down, sideways and forwards, some are pushed backwards towards her, points in the air. That's it, thinks Bea, if it's not the doorknob, it's an umbrella; the headline will read 'GIRL IMPALED'. At least it will not be 'GIRL IMPALED WITH STRANGER' for that man has vanished again. The crowd pushes harder. Bea can feel the doorknob digging into her back. She shuffles to one side and is now against the door, in reach of the bell. She pushes it. But she's been standing outside for the past hour and there hasn't been a single light on. The crowd pushes harder and Bea is now frightened to the extent that the man she never wanted to see again is now the person she most wants to see in the world. Then a hand takes hers. She can't see the arm it is attached to, but it is a familiar hold. The man from Campden Hill Square squeezes through an invisible gap to stand next to her and puts his arm around her waist. Her waist! Just don't think about it, Bea, you need to escape this crowd.

He can make gaps appear, this man. He eases her through a press of bodies so tight she must be losing buttons all over the place. She lets her umbrella trail behind her for a moment until it becomes wedged and is pulled away from her.

They reach a right angle in the road, where it dog-legs down towards the river, before they have room to breathe again. He lets go of her waist and breaks into a quick pace, his footsteps echoing between the walls of red-brick houses on either side. The winter light is fading, and the street lamps cast a pale glow through which he is racing, his mackintosh, for some reason undone, flapping behind him.

Bea struggles to keep up. He's not stopping and waiting for her either, just striding on as if he were alone. This goads Bea on: she's damn well not going to be left behind. But by the time they reach the river the man is a couple of dozen yards ahead of her and Bea has had enough. To hell with him, she thinks, if he reckons I am going to run after him, and she simply stops dead by a lamp-post at the corner. A taxi will, she thinks, at some point appear. And good riddance, she whispers to herself; hadn't she wanted to give him the slip?

Beyond the road stretches the width of the Thames, its grey-greenness glistening in the light of the lamps along its edge. Almost makes the Thames look promising, thinks Bea, I must certainly be feeling pleased to think that. And then, again, a hand is upon her arm.

This is insufferable, she thinks. Is he coming or going, and if he can't make up his mind then she'll do it for him.

'The wind,' he says, 'will pick you up if you wait there any longer.' Bea doesn't reply; she hasn't noticed the breeze, and a stiff one at that, but as the man points it out she feels the chill on her face.

'This way,' he says. He must be joking, but there's something about 'this way' that makes her wonder where he is taking her. In any case, he's heading east, which is more or less the right direction for her home. Bea, only out of curiosity, she tells herself, follows. Just for a little longer. I'll take a taxi the moment I feel like it.

The man leads her across the road and they walk along beside the water. Bea fancies she can hear it lapping against the stone walls of its sides. He walks slower now, at her pace. So there is an iota of manners in him, she thinks, but as he opens his mouth it occurs to her that he simply wants to question her.

'So, what are you doing here?' The accent burrs through his speech and the question comes gruffly, as though he begrudges having to speak at all.

'What do you mean?' She still puffs a little, for they are, to be frank, walking as briskly as she can manage.

'Dressed like that I can't see you chained to a railing.'

Bea stops. For God's sake, the man really can't open his mouth and be anything but impolite, and downright provocatively so. How does he know that she wouldn't chain herself to a railing? Why, half of her would jolly well like to show him that she could. If she were to go back into the crowd it couldn't take long to find someone with a spare lock. But instead of telling him this, she lifts her chin and asks, 'So, what are *you* doing here?'

'Trying to change things.'

'What things?' She turns her head, as though she couldn't be less interested.

'Isn't it obvious?'

'Well, no, it isn't.' Of course it isn't. The people listening to Mrs Pankhurst want to change everything from the trade unions to religion.

'Not that you'd know.'

How dare he? And just when she thought that he was capable, in some way, of behaving like a gentleman.

'You are markedly uncivil, Mr . . . Mr?'

'Campbell.'

'Mr Campbell, you are speaking as though I have no idea of life outside of my own.'

'Do you?'

'I most certainly do.'

Mr Campbell does not reply, and Bea starts to doubt her own answer. Does she really have an idea, she wonders? What lives is she aware of besides her own and those of her friends, and the servants' – even then, has she any idea what it feels like to be them? With this she falls silent, too.

They are passing the Royal Hospital Gardens, its black bushes looming through the railings. Bea is walking on, chin pushed a little higher than before, when a taxi comes towards them. The words to ask Mr Campbell to hail it for her rise in her throat and she holds on to them as she watches the taxi come closer, and waits for this man to raise his arm for her. But he doesn't. When it has passed, empty, she is surprised to find herself a little relieved.

They walk by Chelsea Bridge, then under the railway to Victoria, and Mr Campbell crosses back over the road and turns left. And it is only at this point, as she enters entirely unfamiliar territory, it occurs to Bea that at no stage has he asked her whether this is the right direction for her.

'Where are we going?'

'I'm going home.'

'Home?'

'Digs in Pimlico.'

'Is this Pimlico?'

'Yes.'

'And . . . and . . . ?' For one of the few times in her life, Bea is lost for words.

'And what about you?'

She hesitates. 'Yes.'

'I was going to find you a cup of tea and then put you in a taxi.'

Bea finds she is very thirsty indeed.

There's a tea room around the corner. Not a Lyons, far from it. The walls were once white and tablecloths are a grey-tinged red check. Only one other table is occupied. Bea sits at the first table she sees, by the window and close to the door. Anything this man does will therefore be visible to all and sundry. And she can be out in a flash. Anything this man does . . . Is she really thinking that, still?

A middle-aged woman in a white dress and frilly apron is standing beside them almost as soon as they sit down. She is carrying a pair of plates bearing a base of grey squashed by a thick layer of white.

'Shepherd's pie,' says the woman. Any appetite Bea has vanishes. She glances across the table for a shared opinion but Mr Campbell's eyes are fixed on the plates. However, he orders only tea. When he turns to Bea, she nods.

'Two teas, then.'

The woman heads for the other table, shepherd's pies slopping to the sides of the plates as they tilt.

'You look hungry,' says Bea.

'What's that supposed to mean?'

Bea decides not to explain herself. Instead she starts to remove her coat, but it's chilly in here and she turns to look at the window and, as she breathes out, a patch of steam appears on it. When she turns back, she starts. Her companion is down to his shirtsleeves. Bea has never sat with a man doing this in a public place, and he is wearing armbands above his elbow, traces of ink on his shirt. At least he uses a pen for a living.

'Aren't you cold?'

He laughs, or that's what Bea wants to think it is, though it is more of a snort. He is looking at her as though he can't believe what he sees.

'You don't feel the cold, where I'm from.'

Bea considers ignoring this last remark and not asking him where he is from. But that accent really is familiar, and Mr Campbell is so irritatingly lacking in detail that she wants to know. If she is to score a point, it will be by showing up his remark by asking in the politest way possible.

'Where are you from, Mr Campbell?'

'Carlisle.'

'Oh.' Two people, Bea thinks, from Carlisle.

'On the Scottish border. West side of the country.'

'I know where Carlisle is.'

'Geography lessons, of course.'

'I know someone from there. What on earth is wrong with geography lessons?' And what, Bea wants to ask, is so wrong with me? If everything about me makes you so angry, then why have you brought me here?

'I think our schools were a little different.'

Bea doesn't tell him that she didn't go to school, that school was, like university, regarded by her family and their friends as being for solicitors' daughters. She was kept in an upstairs schoolroom, at the mercy of whichever governess was currently enduring her family. Most of them French or German. In fact, it is a miracle that she does know where Carlisle is, and it is only that she's passed it half a dozen times on the way to shooting parties in Scotland.

Bea looks across the table at the man in front of her. He is thickset and square-jawed, eyebrows a trifle too full and dark. Not pale-skinned, either. And his nose, yes, broken, or at least bashed. She is trying not to think that she is having tea with a stranger who might have broken his nose in a brawl of some kind. She is also struggling not to admit to herself that she finds this man in any way attractive. Pushing a boundary is one thing, this would be taking an axe and hacking a hole through the dividing lines. She pulls herself upright; she expects him to be a little cowed by her, if not her looks, then her accent, dress, the obvious existence of money. But he does not give the impression of being in the slightest impressed. He is a hard man to push, this one, and, annoyed by his apparent lack of interest in her, she says, 'Don't you want to ask any questions about me?'

'What would I learn that I can't already see?'

'You might want to ask me my position on suffrage.'

'Your position on suffrage is that it's all "a lark", as opposed to some luncheon engagement. It'll fill your time before you marry and immerse yourself in the causes of husband, children, dinner parties and servants.'

'Mr Campbell, that is unimpressively unoriginal. I had expected you to do better than that.' She had – that was straight out of some caricature in the papers. At least it can't be what he really thinks and, yes, she has now surprised him. His eyebrows are flickering, and there's not a trace of scorn in his face, so she continues. 'I can see you think yourself an expert on people whom you know not at all. I, in fact, am planning a book.'

This is almost true. Well, even though that was John's and her dream, there's no reason she shouldn't still do that, one day, if she can find a husband whom she can persuade to go abroad with her. Who knows, they might bump into John in some far-flung outpost and exchange cordial greetings before Bea, clearly radiantly happy, vanishes arm in arm with her husband.

'What type of book?'

'An account of travels.' She tells him that these will be travels abroad, to Siberia, she hopes. And this must have made something of an impression upon him for he leans back in his chair, looks at her and reaches across the table, hand open.

'Michael Campbell. Of Carlisle. And?'

'Beatrice.' And then she pauses before giving her surname but Masters is common enough and she cannot think of another to stick to so she goes on, 'Masters.'

He raises his eyebrows.

'Like the railwayman?'

'Who?' she replies.

Then she asks him what he believes in. Because, she says pointedly, one can be significantly more accurate in assumptions if one asks first.

Mr Campbell ignores the barb. Instead he leans forward and the words start pouring out of him. Inequality, poverty, injustice, turning the world on its head. The accent burrs through his speech and here and there she thinks she mishears a word but the more she listens, the fewer these words become. She doesn't want him to stop. This burning awakes something in her. There may be little place for the life Bea lives in the world Mr Campbell longs for, but that cannot be such a bad thing. For that's what she wants, something other than the future this Mr Campbell so dismissively mapped out for her. And isn't that what Mrs Pankhurst would want, what the whole purpose of Lauderdale Mansions is? Bea holds herself back from reaching across the table towards him. When he at last pauses long enough for her to utter a word, she hears herself promising to help him.

'You should write something,' she says. 'That way more people will hear.'

'In theory,' he says. 'But somebody like me can write all they like and there'll never be a soul to read it. Don't tell me, Miss Masters, that you are going to offer to send it to your friend, the editor of *The Times*?'

'I'll have to see what's in it first.' It comes out, a reflex of a reply that reveals more than she'd like, but which silences Mr Campbell. In this silence it occurs to Bea that there are indeed many things that she can see more clearly than he can. Perhaps he recognises this, too, for he still says nothing and just looks at her as if he's asking some all-encompassing question. *The Times*, she continues, is not the newspaper for all views. His might just, she believes, be more suited to the *Daily Herald*, where she knows the editor slightly better

This has certainly surprised him. The *Daily Herald*, the trade unionist newspaper; he clearly was not expecting that from a dressed-up girl looking for 'entertainment', as he called it in Campden Hill Square.

Mr Campbell looks down at the tea-stained tablecloth, then up again.

'Are you going to offer your writing skills to type it up for me? Do ladies type?'

Type for him? Is that the sum of what Bea can contribute to

changing the world – typing and envelope-stuffing? But, just as in Lauderdale Mansions, if she wants to help then this is how she has to start and so, she says to herself, this is where you, Beatrice, tell a barefaced lie.

'I'm not bad.'

Before she's drawn breath again he's asking her whether she has a machine. She hesitates. There's an old one in the library down at Beauhurst, dust just about kept off the keys. But Mr Campbell is definitely on the verge of laughter now, and this offends her. Why, their conversation has come so far – is it no more than a joke for him?

Her question as to what he finds so amusing comes out as interrogation. As well, perhaps, it should.

'The idea of such a young lady working as my secretary.' He calms down as he speaks but the mocking elation is still there. 'It's almost the revolution in itself,' he continues, 'but I could lend it to my sister. She can't borrow the machines at work, but she's fast. Right fast.'

'Oh, is she?' replies Bea. It occurs to her that she is unlikely to feel too friendly towards Michael's sister. His sister gets him books, he continues. They'll lend her those, her employers, in the office she works in. Well, one book. And he'd like to look at it again, but it's hard to ask in the circumstances.

I can do better than that, Bea says, and their conversation resumes. When she next raises her cup to her lips and finds the tea is cold, she realises how long she has been there.

Where on earth is it? Bea has searched E and F, just in case, then gone back to the catalogue again. It's there, it must be. It's not as though Edward or Mother will have Engels on their bedside table.

Bea surveys the yards of bookcases around her. E and F took her half an hour. That makes six more hours, at least, if she is to search the lot. Compared to S or M, E and F are rather thin.

One more time on E. She's up the ladder, this is where the damn thing should be. It's in the catalogue, for Christ's sake. She starts to pull out the books, for it might have been knocked into the gap behind. The books slide out easily, as though one of them has been taken away.

Well, it's not there, but there are two other books by Engels in the row. *The Communist Manifesto*, and *Socialism: Utopian and Scientific.* Bea takes them both down.

12

'ARE YOU ILL, BEATRICE,' BARKS MOTHER AT LUNCH ON Monday a fortnight later. 'You are barely out of your room. Can't have you looking only half there when, it appears, most of London will be turning up on the day after tomorrow. Still, I suppose if you stick to dancing and don't try to have a conversation nobody will notice.'

Mother is, as ever, presiding over the table and its offerings, her petite stature giving her chair a throne-like air. Even the tone of her voice has a regal quality to it. She studies, Edward claims, the speech of Queen Victoria, and he swears to Bea that he can therefore hear traces of a German accent. As Mother speaks Bea pulls herself upright, feeling again a twelve-year-old who has made some comment that Mother regards as naive.

If only she knew, thinks Bea, she would be appalled. Then Bea checks herself. Mother may disapprove of violence but Bea is only typing. And among Mr Campbell's views is a call for one of the very changes Mother is waging a campaign to bring about. Maybe, just maybe, Mother would be impressed.

Bea knows she is forcing the hand of optimism thinking this. For as much as the improvement of workers' rights is a recurring topic of conversation at Mother's Beauhurst house parties, the theme there does not include the overthrow of all the privileges enjoyed by Mother and her guests.

'What has happened to the friends who kept you so busy?' continues Mother. 'Given the rather unrecognised, I feel, quality of London air and the experience of life that it brings, to spend so much time at home and indoors is rather a waste. And you have no time to do that, particularly being still unmarried and, good Lord, having to turn twenty-one on the day of my first dance in years. However, whatever the coincidence, we are categorically not mentioning anything to do with birthdays; there is something rather inelegant about celebrating them. Anyhow, it is clear you need to get out, and I think you should come on my rounds this afternoon. A group of us are meeting at Sybilla Sandham's. Our spies tell us that, with Emmeline here, there's a new wave of violence coming. We must do what we can to stop it.'

Spies? What does Mother mean, spies? Is Bea being watched in Lauderdale Mansions? Will it be passed back to Mother that her daughter is a new recruit? She feels sick, and in her mind she goes around the faces in the typing room, the envelope-stuffers, the women in the room at the back of the flat. Which one, she thinks, which one is the spy? And does this mean she can't go back there? Her stomach turns again. Typing and stuffing envelopes, however menial, has, well, she's enjoyed it, it has given her a sense of, can she call it, 'purpose'? Oh, bother Celeste, surely Celeste knows about this, that Bea might be discovered by Mother. Damn selfish of her to draw Bea in so. Damn selfish for Bea, and damn selfish for Mother.

Bea sits there, and says nothing. Not that there is a need to say anything, for Mother, as usual, is continuing to speak and, being Mother, veers off into another line of conversation without a moment's notice.

'Oh, I saw Mrs Vinnicks last night at the Beltons'. Ghastly crush it was, reeked like a gymnasium. I was fanning myself with my dance card when she appeared from the crowd wearing pale pink satin like one of this year's debutantes and a corset she can hardly have been able to breathe in. Talk about mutton dressed as lamb. It took her a matter of seconds to tell me that she was "distraught". It appears that John has become engaged to a girl he met on the boat – some heiress. The jewellery the girl had with her made the newspapers as soon as they arrived in New York. Mrs Vinnicks is claiming distress that John will therefore not be returning to England – peculiar little woman.'

At least Beatrice thinks Mother ends like that. Her ears are ringing so loudly that it is hard to hear anything at all. She's not sure what she's more upset by, the news itself, or the fact that it's being passed to her so casually by someone whom Bea has been so worried about upsetting herself.

Ten minutes later, she is back at her typewriter. Her ears are still ringing but that isn't going to keep her fingers still. She hits the keys hard, bruising her fingertips and joints. The pain is jolting her into another man's words. Well, blast you, John Vinnicks, you would never write this. Blast you, Mother, for making me still care.

The next morning, she's up and out, no breakfast, no newspaper, barely a helping hand with her dress, and she's in a taxi heading for Lauderdale Road, telling herself to hell with Mother's spies. Every minute tomorrow will be focused around the dance. Mother will alternately incarcerate her so that she is not tired, and force her into the park so that she does not look as though she has been inside all day.

Today, however, is still Bea's. So what, so what if she were found out? Bea imagines a deputation coming to inform Mother that her own daughter has betrayed her. Well, then she would know what it feels like to be hurt. For Mother has, hasn't she, betrayed me, thinks Bea, scrabbling around in her mind for where exactly that betrayal was. It felt like a betrayal, to be told in such an offhand manner about John, as though it didn't even occur to

Mother that Bea might be upset. That, however, is Mother, none of that mollycoddling that other mothers give. All is set on not making too much of a song and dance about anything, simply leaving one to buck up and get on with it – as though belittling a situation makes it hurt less. But this doesn't hurt less. No doubt Mother believes that she was just treating Bea like a grown-up and assuming Bea had pulled herself together over it all. Well, if Mother wants a grown-up daughter, then, thinks Bea, I shall grow up however I please.

The apartment in Lauderdale Mansions is in a state of both uproar and industry. Doors are opening and closing, and women are striding along the passageway. Something is up, something that is obviously such common currency within these walls that Bea is simply assumed to know and therefore cannot possibly ask. At least everybody appears too preoccupied to wonder where she has been for the past two weeks. 'What Emmeline would want,' Bea overhears, 'is for us to keep on with it.' However, even merely keeping on with it, the smell of anger is competing with that of soap. In the typing room, where there's a space she's nodded towards, the keys seem to be clattering down louder than before.

Letting herself be caught up in the heat, Bea shunts the piles of papers into position and starts to tackle the machine in front of her. Her typing has improved, albeit marginally, over the past two weeks locked in her room – though perhaps not as much as it should have, given the hours she has spent transcribing Mr Campbell's spiky writing. Still, she goes on, she types and pauses, and types and pauses again, her fingers in the air as if listening out for whatever it is that has happened. If Bea is here long enough, the news must, surely, reach her ears. A hand touches her upon the shoulder and Bea jumps, sending her small pile of papers flying.

It's the woman with arched eyebrows. There's not an ounce of reproach in her, but Bea still shivers. 'Come with me,' she says. Bea dips her forehead and nods, before leaning over to pick up what she dropped on the floor. 'No, leave that,' says the woman. 'Come immediately. Now.'

The room is full, the beds are packed and women are lining the walls, but the first face Bea sees as she enters is Celeste's. Bea stalls slightly for, as nonchalant as she has convinced herself she is about Mother discovering what she is up to, she is not entirely happy with Celeste. 'Good chap,' says her aunt. 'Wanted you in on this.' Bea looks her aunt up and down. She is wearing plus fours, against which the crates and stones and machetes on the floor behind her almost pale into insignificance. Celeste notices Bea staring at her lower half. 'Hunting gear, my dear. We're back to battle here.'

To battle, and here Bea is, in the inner sanctum. Maybe Celeste is not so bad after all.

As Bea looks at the empty chair ahead of her and listens to the words ricocheting around her, she feels her heartbeat quicken and her eyes widen.

Mrs Pankhurst, she learns, was arrested yesterday in Glasgow. She'd been bundled up to Scotland in the back of a car – of course they couldn't take a chance of being spotted on the train. She'd spent the nights on the way up there at supporters' houses emptied of other guests. The rally was last night. Telephone calls and wires have been flying to and fro and they've all, apart from Bea, read the paper this morning, and voices are coming from every corner of the room:

'Nobody saw her come into the hall. They weren't even sure she had made it.'

'Half of them couldn't see the platform anyhow. It was packed. They were practically standing on each other's shoulders. Then when Isabel Margesson got up to introduce her, a cloaked figure stepped forward from the group at the back of the platform. She threw off her hood – and it was Emmeline! But it was then that the uniforms broke in through a side entrance. There'd been plain-clothes in the crowd, of course.'

'They put up a damn good fight from the platform. The flower pots worked. Small enough to chuck quite far. Still a smack. Soaked a couple too with the speakers' water. Then it was a riot. One of the best. Tables, chairs. The bodyguard and the police fencing with their clubs. We even had explosives prepared, though they didn't scare them off. Bloody determined they were. The pistol, too—'

'Pistol?'

'Blanks.'

'Cowards.' Three or four of the women are standing up or leaning into the centre of the room from the walls they have been leaning against. Now a thickset woman is waving her arms around as though she's doing a quickstep semaphore.

'No,' dissents a voice from a bruised woman sitting in front of Bea. 'One police martyr and we'd be set back years.'

'Wish I'd been there.' A gangly woman leaps up to say this, cheeks shining.

'We took several split heads.'

'Bravo, bravo.' Bea realises that the room is applauding. She turns to Celeste who is standing, clapping as hard as the rest of them. As if infected by the elation, Bea joins her. She is clapping the bashing of a policeman's head. And she is enjoying it.

Slowly, the women settle, even as the list of arrests continues. Ethel Smyth was taken on Sunday, and Sylvia Pankhurst at a Men's League demonstration in Trafalgar Square. Half the women here must think Sylvia's absence good riddance as her People's Army is taking the focus away from them. But she's still a Pankhurst and now two of them are in jail.

'We have to fight back now.' The gangly woman, perspiring a little more, is standing again, this time to a chorus of 'hear, hear'.

'Something big. They take us, we hit them. Something that stands out, won't be forgotten.' Bea can't see where this voice comes from. The gathering has turned into a free-for-all, with whoever feels like it giving their penny's worth. The chairwoman is just sitting there behind her table in front of the window, letting comments fly, and the temperature rises. Bea's is rising with it.

'Like Lloyd George's last year.'

'Yes.'

'Arson.'

'We can't do his house again.'

'Whose house then?'

'McKenna,' say half a dozen voices together.

'Bloody Home Secretary.'

'The bugger.'

'We've a right to petition the Throne.'

'He can't turn us down like that.'

'We're not fully fledged citizens, remember.'

'Not fully fledged humans. Can't think for ourselves.'

'And so, no vote.'

'Bastards.'

At last the chairwoman stands up. 'Ladies, are we all in agreement?' She is speaking as though she is introducing a guest at a church fete.

'That they're bastards?'

This is met with guffaws.

'That we need to take action as soon as possible.'

'Against whom?' This is Celeste's voice. Bea turns to find her aunt's eyes transfixed by the chairwoman as she speaks.

'McKenna,' says the chairwoman, and the heads around Bea are nodding, a few voices murmuring aye, aye, and Bea finds herself nodding, too.

'But,' the dissenter speaks again, 'what if somebody is hurt?'

'This is a war,' replies the chair. 'People get hurt. Think what are they doing to those of us in jail? What will they be doing to Emmeline, tonight?'

The thought curdles in Bea's stomach. Twelve men and women,

Mrs Pankhurst's arms strapped into a chair: Bea can almost feel the gagging reflex of having a tube stuck down her throat.

'As soon as we can, then. Tomorrow?'

'No, too rushed. We'll plan it today, get the kit in tomorrow. We go on Thursday. Who's in? We need a driver. With her own car.'

Bea can certainly drive. Faster than anyone here, she'll bet.

Her hand is the first to shoot up.

13

MARY WOKE GRACE UP AGAIN THIS MORNING WHEN rushing off to the lavatory. Green, she looks, though she won't say a word to Mrs W. She's begged Grace not to. Not with the dance and all, she says.

And it is the dance tonight. Mrs Wainwright is taking no prisoners in the morning's cleaning. As Grace stands to attention, all floral frock and mop, Mrs Wainwright's finger only leaves the surface she is walking alongside in order to examine it for dust. Grace thinks Mrs Wainwright barely needs to look, she can just feel the soft grains slow her down. They near spring-cleaned these rooms yesterday, and the day before and for as many days before that as Grace cares to think. But the furniture's been moved now. The men from Rumpelmayer's came in yesterday and pushed the chairs and sofas in the library and yellow drawing room to where they thought best. Of course there was dust underneath. They can't move every piece every day, and it gathers so fast, even in the rooms barely used. This morning Lady Masters is redirecting the furniture to where she thinks fit, and Mrs Wainwright has them at the spaces it occupied last night. Even Susan, though it's not strictly her job. We all have one job today, Mrs Wainwright tells them. Susan murmurs that she'll be blowed if Rumpelmayer's men don't move it all again when they put up the supper tables. And don't, she whispers, do anything more than tiptoe into the ballroom. The polisher's been frogging it up and down there for two days and it's an ice-pond so the dancers' feet can slide. But if one of us goes down, it's more work for the rest.

They're packing up the ornaments now. Nobody will admit to being at the end of their list today, and they're not, for the tasks are backing up: the snuffboxes, the china dishes, the photographs, all the silver. Even what's in those glass cabinets. It's for the pilfering, Grace is told, and she's shocked by this. What sorts is Lady Masters inviting? You'd've thought that with all they've got . . . 'Oh, they never have enough,' says James, 'and not when they see these pretty little things.' As Grace goes on wrapping, turning each piece as she lifts it, a flickering of relief, after all these weeks, begins to creep up on her. They're not going to wrap all the books, are they? And if they don't, then how're they to know when the book went, if they think one of the guests might take something. Grace is in the clear, isn't she, if they're expecting a room full of light fingers. But when, ten minutes later, Mrs Wainwright asks Grace to follow her into the library, the fear comes straight back at her in a big salty wave.

But she doesn't point anything out, Mrs Wainwright doesn't, and Grace doesn't dare look at that shelf. Then she asks Grace to run a duster along every bookshelf, again, and it's Grace's turn to feel tight in her belly; it'll be her running to the back of the house next like Mary. She reaches her fingers out to steady herself on the shelves, and Mrs Wainwright's eyes follow them, shaking her head. Then she glances upwards. 'This is your room, Grace, isn't it?' When Grace nods her head so as you can barely see it, it feels as though it'll wobble off.

She starts at A. She can glide the ladder with barely a sound, and it's easier than the steps. And she's quick. The books are as tight as a miser and none slips out of place as Grace runs the duster along. She's still sick with fear, eyes in a blur and head behind bars, so she doesn't see where she's at until the books fall to the side as she brushes along them. It's E. Top row. That row. But she's only taken one book. There's more gone from here.

Lord have mercy, thinks Grace. Then it occurs to her that whoever took the books might think that the gap is all theirs.

There's a clattering outside. It's Rumpelmayer's men coming in with the tables. They're putting the trestles around the room in pairs. They've done this so many times that they don't need to put the boards on top to know the space between each. When they reach the sofa and chairs they start to push them again. Grace hears the feet of the furniture squeak across the boards and watches dark lines appear on the floor. She hasn't spoken out since she's been in the house; she's held back every urge to throw a brush down on to the floor and say What Do You Take Me For, and that's been often. Or was; it's grown easier, the urges fewer recently, but now she's feeling sharp and the dark lines are spreading further and further across the floor she's polished clean not half an hour ago. Rumpelmayer's men look left, look right, up, down – down! They see the lines, but still go on, and at this, she cracks.

'You should lift that.' The two men stop, but don't turn. And then they continue.

'Excuse me!' They must think she's talking to herself. Now she's spoken she just wants to make them listen. The cheek of it, ignoring her. She walks around in front of the men and the sofa they're about to slide, and blocks their way.

'You need to lift it.' She points to the trails on the floor. 'Marks the boards.'

'It would need four of us.'

Grace doesn't move. Who's going to do the work? These men or Grace, when she's on her hands and knees, polishing the floor later.

'If I leave, it's to find Lady Masters.'

The three of them hold still, like the statues in the room at the back of the ballroom. She wants to get out of this library as soon as possible. Not to spend all afternoon here, scrubbing the floor. She's other rooms to do today. She turns to face them head on, moves her feet apart and folds her arms. The men look back at her, at each other, and then one leaves the room. And as she's still standing there, arms folded but glowing with victory, the florists come in with bushes of flowers, leaving a trail of leaves and petals across the boards.

'You can pick those up, too,' she says.

As they do so, Grace senses somebody behind her, standing very still. She looks round. There is Joseph, pinkening. He quickly turns away from her and leaves the room.

Grace's eyes are beginning to blur. Even though it's seven in the evening, she's again grinding the Ewbank sweeper across the carpet in the red drawing room, for according to Mrs Wainwright the day's traffic of men, flowers, caterers, even a team to arrange the candles, has left or may have left, a further, invisible layer of dirt. But there's the boot boy, running up to her, he's panting, speaking quickly. She's wanted, he says, by Miss Beatrice, and right away. Susan was to do it. She laid out the clothes earlier, but she couldn't help but imagine herself one of them ladies in the ballroom and she went right over. It's her ankle. Poor Susan, says Grace, and she might even mean it, but what she's thinking is why am I so pleased that I've been asked to help another woman dress?

Miss Beatrice's dress, tunic and sash are laid out on the bed and the pale satin and sky-blue chiffon leap out from the dark colours of the room. Miss Beatrice is sitting at her dressing table in a pale pink negligée. She stands up when Grace comes in, and it floats around her. Silk, Grace thinks it is. Like the sails on the Round Pond.

'Thank you for coming. How is Susan?'

Grace bobs. 'She's sprained her ankle, miss. Happy birthday, miss.'

'Oh, thank you. Thank you very much. Can you help me get into all this without destroying my hair. Though it's so damn tight that I'm not sure I'd be distraught.'

'Would you like me to have a look at it?' Grace surprises herself. She wasn't asked to speak. It had just come out. But Miss Beatrice chats back.

'Oh God, yes,' she replies, and asks whether Grace can make any sense of it – it's a new French Twist. Lady Masters sent Miss Suthers down to do it and Miss Beatrice felt as though she was being scalped as it was done. She's been in it since five this afternoon and it's killing her. Will Grace have a go at loosening it a little?

'But you want to look your best, miss.' Grace looks down at Beatrice's dressing table. Half a dozen silver-topped pots of powders and creams have been opened. A little rouge has been spilled to one side.

'I suppose so,' replies Miss Beatrice. 'But I'm not sure who for.'

'It's hard to choose, I imagine.' As Grace says this, she wonders whether it is as hard for Miss Beatrice to choose between what might lie ahead of her as it is for Grace.

14

BEA IS HOOKED, LACED AND PINNED, WITH A SATIN puddle train trailing behind her. As she twists to look in the glass, the beaded tassels on the long end of her tunic knock against her ankles. She pins on the diamond lace brooch Mother has given her for her unmentionable twenty-first birthday today. At tea there was a cake with only a vague half a dozen candles allowed, and barely enough time to blow them out before everyone dashed upstairs to start changing.

I look all right, she thinks, the pale blue is a little cool, but pretty enough. She doesn't mind looking coolish tonight. Rather fits the mood she wants to display, even if she is already in knots over what she is to do tomorrow. She tries to focus on the evening immediately ahead of her rather than the day that will follow it, but her head simply fills with the worry of how many conversations she will have to have without letting on that there is anything the slightest bit interesting in her life. Thank God nobody would dream of asking her what she is up to. In their eyes it is a pointless question. Unmarried girls are looking for husbands.

And no doubt they've heard about John. Mrs Vinnicks has probably taken out a half-page notice in the papers.

The dinner before the dance is at eight sharp. Officially a cosy, close family meal, the table is bending with silver and numbers have stretched to eighteen. Bea looks down the length of the table. Seated alongside each side, the party is a chequerboard of monochrome men and silk dresses that deepen in colour with the age of the wearer. Clemmie is in a green just darker than pastel, and Mother in a near-blinding mauve. It is not, however, the deepest colour there as, for the most part, the guests are not young. Bea is next to a member of the Cabinet so heavily moustachioed that she wonders whether its tips will leap the gap between them during the meal. On the other side she has a florid newspaper baron overflowing his seat. She has a friend, she tells him, writing this extraordinary essay, captures a political mood we cannot ignore. Food still in his mouth, he invites her to tea to discuss it further, with a look that makes her feel more than a little uncomfortable. Bea automatically smiles and nods in that way of saying yes to an invitation one has no intention of ever taking up, but as she does so she realises that maybe she should go, if she is serious about helping Mr Campbell. And of course she is: the idea of not doing so, not throwing herself behind someone who was speaking with such passion, that's the word, passion, is surely absurd.

It's ten o'clock, and the more elderly of the dance guests start to arrive. Bea is in a receiving line at the top of the stairs, sandwiched between Edward and Clemmie, who has joined them – even though she is married and has in theory left home – on the grounds that she has invited 'significant numbers'. 'I hope,' replies Mother, 'that we have enough to feed and water them with.'

'Don't worry, Mother,' says Edward, 'Tom can keep an eye out for the wrong sort of chap.'

'Is that a reference to my guests?' bites Clemmie.

'Well, quite honestly, none of you will have a clue whether he's the Duke of Bavaria or a law clerk,' he retorts. Bea flinches at this, and Edward turns towards her, eyebrows raised.

'What's up, Bea-Bea?' Edward can read her like a book, and her mind is filling with images of Mr Campbell and his mackintosh in midwinter.

'The wrong sort of chap,' she blusters out to cover her tracks, 'doesn't have the clothes.'

'Oh, Bea, they can be hired on Bond Street in half an hour. You know that. Look what happened at the Devonports'. The fellow danced with Lady D., and even the dowager, who'd hardly been off her chair for a decade.'

'Quiet, please. I am almost tempted to call you children again. You behave as such whenever you are together . . . '

' . . . with our mother, in our childhood home . . . '

'Edward, you are beginning to annoy your mother, too.'

'How did they find out he was a fraud?' asks Bea.

'What fraud?'

'The man at the Devonports'.'

'Ah,' says Edward. 'Everyone is always found out. There's no escaping the eye of society. In this case, however, the dowager was so entranced that she asked him to dine the following evening. She'd had a spread set up in the small dining room with so much shiny stuff on the table you needed to squint. As he sat down he asked if he could take off his "jacket", and she was so bemused both by the word and the taking off that she nodded. So he took off his coat and hung it over the back of one of those famous dining chairs that somebody had brought back from Italy a few generations ago. But it was the sleeve garters that gave him away. She says she hadn't spotted an accent, but she is as deaf as a post. When I asked her how she was the other day she replied, 'Princess Dorrie. A certainty for the Oaks.'

'Anyhow, once she'd realised her mistake she felt dreadfully sorry for the chap, says she copied all his interesting table manners to make him feel at home. Then she decided it was a jolly good excuse to behave as though the house was a museum and, would you believe it, gave him a tour. He gave her his arm quite charmingly. Apparently it was the Rodin he liked best.'

'You've made that up, Edward.'

'No, I have not.'

'All of it. In any case' – for why should she hide her views? – 'he sounds a perfectly good chap.'

'At your peril, my dear Bea. Beware of handsome strangers with feet of clay. Or perhaps I mean, tonight, feet of a dancer. I'd have to disown you for mixing with the wrong type.'

'There's nothing wrong with knowing the wrong type, children. In case it has escaped your notice, I have been seeking to help the wrong type for some years. They are poorly paid, disenfranchised, and have little choice in any matter of their lives.'

'I hope you have invited at least half a dozen, Mother.'

'I certainly should have.'

By eleven there is a swarm, and younger faces are beginning to appear. Edie, in tea-rose chiffon, loyally leads in an early bunch of their crowd.

'You look radiant, darling,' Edie declares as she reaches Bea in the line.

'Edie, you're making me sound like a bride.'

'Well, I gather it is strictly *verboten* to mention your birthday.'

'Then don't mention anything.'

'Bea! Be a little softer.'

But Bea doesn't want to be a little softer. Not tonight, not tomorrow, not until the day after that. Still, she replies, 'Sorry, darling. It's just not—'

'Don't worry. I know it's a nightmare.'

'What's a nightmare?' My God, she's not talking about John now, is she?

'Hosting a dance, Bea. Chin up.' And Edie blows a kiss at Bea as she leads her merry band into the thickening throng.

At half past eleven, Mother dismisses the line. 'To work, children,' she declares. 'No hanging about with just one small group when you've so many guests here. Except if there is a special reason,' and as she says this she looks at Edward. Edward! thinks Bea, and not me. Has Mother utterly given up on my ever finding a husband? No, Beatrice, she tells herself, you have far greater fish to fry now.

Most of the guests seem as interested in the house as in each other and, as at least in your own house you're allowed to make your way around the rooms alone without being accused of 'hunting', Beatrice starts to slip between the groups, skimming past conversations that dry up when she joins them.

'. . . and the American money.'

'My grandfather used to come here for the railway share tips. Only ones that weren't rotten, he used to say.'

'Quick. Talk about the *Rokeby Venus*, for God's sake.'

'Hullo, Beatrice, glad to see you haven't been wielding a machete in the National Gallery like that suffragette woman.'

'Oh, darling, she's hardly likely to.'

'Well, Eleanor must be one hell of an influence.'

'He doesn't mean it about your mother.'

'Mother might not need the machete,' replies Bea.

'Cut to ribbons, the painting was. A protest, apparently, about how women are regarded.'

'How they think they're going to get the vote that way.'

'Women might be banned, they're saying today.'

'Altogether?'

'From the galleries. Can't have the nation's works of art being destroyed over some fashionable enthusiasm.'

'Darling! You'll have me throwing firebombs if you go on like that. Anybody would think you were stuck in the last century, or the one before. Now, Beatrice, introduce me to some of your friends. I do so love the young.'

And still the rooms fill. The little groupings are pushed closer and closer to each other. Silk crushes against silk, puddle trains are stepped on, bare arms scratch against black wool evening coats. Those on the edges find themselves pushed against the walls. And the noise, even in these high-ceilinged rooms, is beginning to blur the conversations. Soon it will be a real crush and therefore a roaring success of a party. It will be hard to squeeze through the doorways, even to make it to the ballroom which is, Edward comes to whisper to her, still empty, much to Clemmie's intense frustration.

'Clemmie wants us to move people through.'

'With a loudspeaker? Good God, how embarrassing.'

'Better than starting the dancing.'

'Who?'

'You and me, sweet sister.'

'Why can't she do it herself?'

Bea is saved by Mother, mauve apparition that she is, descending upon her.

'Beatrice.'

'Yes.'

'Come with me. As you seem to be the only child of mine that agrees with me on this issue, you might learn something. We're going to have a word with the Prime Minister before he's squeezed out of the house. This way. Ah, Mr Asquith. What a treat to find my most distinguished guest.'

Standing in front of Bea and Mother is a man with a high forehead and a softening square jaw. He doesn't seem to be enjoying himself and is looking at Mother with a pair of deep-set and severe eyes. Nonetheless he takes Mother's hand and kisses it, bowing as he does so.

'You flatter me, Lady Masters.'

'I flatter everyone.'

Mother drops her chin, glancing up at him as she waves her fan in a short flutter. 'It's what my mother brought me up to do. You know my youngest daughter Beatrice?'

'Even more dazzling than the last time I laid eyes upon her.' Bea finds herself flushing. She has been preening to praise all evening but somehow such a compliment from the Prime Minister is a little different. Maybe he is not such an ogre after all.

'It's a little crowded in here, Mr Asquith, don't you think?'

'On the contrary, Lady Masters, your drawing room suits a crowd.'

'What I meant, Mr Asquith, is that I should very much like it if you would take a walk with us.'

'Lady Masters, I fully understand.'

Mother turns towards a pair of open double doors and the crowd in front of her rustles back to create a pathway. Bea smiles to herself at the thought that this may be more in fear of Mother than the Prime Minister. The gallery outside is crowded, every foot of the balustrade has a figure leaning against it, but eventually they reach the ballroom at the back. When they walk in they find the band valiantly playing to at most half a dozen, including Clemmie and Tom. Clemmie, to Bea's amusement, looks as if she is leading.

It is noisy in here, and the few couples dancing are nonetheless taking up the entire room, making standing anywhere in it hazardous. Mother leads the Prime Minister and Bea briskly across it, and through the doors to the museum on the far side, Mother closing them behind her. Candles flicker on almost every surface and a handful of empty champagne glasses are scattered about. The room feels halfway between a Greek temple and a saint's shrine, the portrait of Great-grandfather hanging in pride of place.

'Have you seen our Durbar Hall before, Mr Asquith?'

'Not looking like this, Lady Masters.'

'It's the candles, I tried ecclesiastical ones.' She walks him over to admire a pair. 'Bought without so much as a raised eyebrow. I must appear the very image of a verger.'

Mother keeps walking, giving him no chance to break away, and gets straight to the point.

'This Cat and Mouse of an Act to discharge the hunger-strikers until they are fit enough to take back is a mistake.'

'It will save lives, Lady Masters. How can you declare that a mistake?'

'Balderdash. Mr Asquith, for a man of your perception your vision appears worryingly short. The prisoner released may escape death in jail, but to keep on taking her back as she starts to recover will surely destroy her health and, in the end, take her life, even if she does not pass into the next world while actually in the government's capable hands.'

Mr Asquith stops and turns to face Mother. He is angry now, thinks Bea. His eyes are as hard as nails and his throat is flushed.

'Lady Masters, are you suggesting we give in to the militants and their violence?'

Mother remains wholly unruffled. 'No, I am trying to point out that if the violence grows you will appear to give in to them. And peaceful means must win, Mr Asquith.' She pauses in the centre of the room. 'Have you seen this map? The first Sir William Masters united the world. I wonder what he would think of it now. I fear for this world once violence is seen to work – this century already feels heavy with physical anger. We are not so far from the barbarians ourselves, I think. And, in our case, barbarians wielding machines.'

'Is there a trace of the Luddite in you, Lady Masters?'

'Perhaps. The children I see across the street in the park remind me of men and their motors and *mitrailleuses*. Have you travelled, Mr Asquith?'

'A little.'

'Have you seen one of these before?' Mother has stopped in front of a glass display case of feathered instruments. She opens the case and draws one out. It is about a foot long, one end looking like a razor-edged spoon ending in a point, the handle covered in red, green and yellow feathers.

'No, I have not, Lady Masters.'

'It is a tool used to gouge a man's eyes out. It would be interesting in the National Gallery, don't you think? Ah, not a flicker. Don't worry, Mr Asquith, I am not about to take the eyes out of the nation's statesmen. Neither in flesh nor portraiture.

'Now hopefully there are a few more in the ballroom. Shall we return? For the tango? Ah, you have heard of that one. Mr Asquith, don't look so horrified. I am teasing you. Now, look, you have a close colleague come to your rescue. The politician who turns down all honours offered.'

As they enter the ballroom a slender, mild-mannered-looking man is fast approaching. His face is oval rather than long, soft around the jawline and cheeks. Above them glow the reddish hints of his remaining, greying hair.

'Just the fellow,' Mother says to him as he joins them, 'though I sense your leader thinks he has well exercised the conversation. What a pleasure it is to see you. Mr McKenna, do you know my youngest daughter, Beatrice?'

'I haven't had the pleasure, Miss Masters.' He bows to her.

'Nor I.' The words patter out as they have innumerable times before, without any connection to Bea's brain, which feels as if a minor explosion has been set off in it. Where are this man's horns, his claws? Where are Mother and the Prime Minister to save her? They have both dissolved into the crowd.

'Is this not a terrific evening?'

'Yes.' Where is she to look? She can't meet his gaze, she can't stare at the floor. Avert your eyes shyly, girl, it comes to her. Slightly down and to the side.

'Or do these social fripperies bore you? You have the air of a woman with more depth than that, Miss Masters.' He knows, thinks Bea, he knows. He must have a list of everyone at Lauderdale Mansions. He must have a note of everything said there yesterday afternoon. Oh, don't be ridiculous, Beatrice, she tells herself, but ridiculous is what this situation surely is. How can he not see it in her?

'Are you,' he continues, 'a supporter of your mother's cause? A good deal better than the other crew, don't you think? But none of it, I must say, is much of a pleasure from my end of things.'

Bea holds her breath as he speaks. Is this some subtle challenge, a way of warning her off what she is about to do? She composes herself, ready to deny even her name, and looks straight at him to find him smiling at her with such genuine kindness that she almost flushes again. It dawns on her both that he cannot possibly know, and that, for the first time this evening, she is being asked what interests her. Bea's mouth opens but no words come out. Please, she thinks, go on talking, or something, anything. But thank God the orchestra strikes up a new tune. Surely he will go to dance with his wife. But he cannot, of course, leave Bea unless she is talking to somebody else.

'Ah, a waltz,' he says. 'Now that I can do. I risk a loss of dignity were I to have a go at one of those new-fangled things. And Mrs McKenna appears otherwise engaged.' He turns to his right and a young woman barely more than Clemmie's age is fully engaged in steering what must be a delicate line in conversation between a society portraitist with a certain reputation and the Bishop of London.

'May I have the pleasure, Miss Masters?' Bea's attention swings back to Mr McKenna. 'I have heard that you dance beautifully.'

Right now, Bea feels as if she must have at least two, if not three, left feet, but there is nothing she can do except nod and smile.

He escorts her on to the dance floor. Why the waltz? She would rather have a dance where you don't spend the entire time so clutched in the other's arms that it used to be banned. But the waltz it is, and up against McKenna she is, in a mix of chiffon and wool and starch crushed between them. She wants to pull in every muscle of her body, make herself as taut as a fishing line, but the pair of them would be over like skittles if she did and, well, she doesn't want ever to be seen dancing like a poker.

He dances well, too. She didn't expect that. But then, he's been dancing for a long time. He spins her around gently. Not so as she gets that rush into her head when a cavalry officer is taking it fast. Still, her head fizzes. There's only so many times you can be turned around before your balance threatens to leave you, that's what she's telling herself. Not that her head is spinning because she's dancing with a gentleman whose home will tomorrow be burnt with her help.

When the music stops, he beams at her and says, 'Miss Masters, the rumours are true.'

The compliment tightens itself around her throat.

Before the band strikes up again, she is rescued by Edward, who swoops in announcing that he needs to steal his sister. Bea looks back as he whisks her away. Mr McKenna is still looking at her. He gives a little bow, and Bea feels her insides twist. Might she have warned him? But now it is too late. Much as it is always a delight to be rescued by Edward, Mr McKenna, thinks Bea, is utterly charming, and she feels a little bereft.

Within seconds Edward has her surrounded by Edie and friends, quaffing ices at a supper table put up in the red drawing room. Edie has had more than the single glass of champagne that Miss Wolffe recommended to her pupils, and there is no sign of her husband.

'Where's Tony?' Bea asks as she squashes on to the other half of her friend's chair.

'God knows,' Edie replies. 'I have successfully lost my husband, and here's to that.' She raises a glass. 'Somebody else swept me on to the dance floor hours ago and I haven't seen Tony since. No doubt he's on the balcony flirting with the debutantes, only you haven't a balcony, have you? Well, it's rather twee to wonder where one's husband is, especially at a dance. I shall simply have to hope that he's worrying about me, and hasn't a clue who I've been dancing with. Chin-chin!'

Bea wraps an arm around her friend's back and squeezes it.

Next to Edie is a rather beautiful young man, eyes as dark-ringed as Edward's, and on the receiving end of much attention from Clemmie, who is on his far side, and has an expression on her face that manages to combine seriousness with amazement.

'Bea-Bea, you must let me introduce Peter. He's a friend of Edward's. He has been telling us how he once played cards for forty-eight hours at a stretch! Tom says he simply wouldn't last it, couldn't stay awake for so long.'

'I'll be blowed if I ever have to,' says Tom, who is sitting beside his wife. 'Enough to drive a chap mad.'

It is somewhere near four before Mother announces that their duties as hosts are over. Bea's head is still ringing and she is unclear as to how the last few hours have passed. She has also waltzed, she thinks, with the newspaper baron and her neighbour at dinner. There has been a bunny hug, a grizzly, a turkey trot and the new foxtrot. The effect of the one or two extra glasses of champagne that Bea has sipped her way through over the past half-dozen hours is now fading and her feet are beginning to ache. A few guests linger, but Bea leaves them to Edward and sneaks upstairs, quite exhausted. Luckily her corset is easier to escape than pull tight. Bea unhooks her front, her eyes closing as her fingers work their way down what must be two dozen tiny hooks. She climbs into her bed. But as her head touches the pillow, she realises she cannot sleep.

15

WHEN GRACE COMES DOWN IN THE MORNING, IT LOOKS like a riot has passed through. Candlewax has hardened on to table tops and cigarette ends have been trodden into the boards. Ashtrays, where used, have overflowed and the debris of food and stained, crumpled napkins litter the rooms. Almost every surface is packed with glasses. The rooms stink. Several chimneys' worth of cigars and the like have been smoked in here.

It's just as Susan, sitting upstairs with an ankle the size of a prize marrow, said. 'It's a rare sight; see what they really are, do you?' Yes, thinks Grace, she can see. To clean a room is to take pride in it and now weeks of work, every stroke of her duster, all those elbow-pushes of polish have been swept aside in a few hours. As she looks around her, she wants to cry.

It doesn't help that it's only six, an hour earlier than usual, even though none of the family, she's been told, will appear before noon. The orchestra broke her sleep until four, waking her each time the music started up again after a pause. Not as though she could sleep; not with Mrs Wainwright's words yesterday evening running through her head. Inventory, she said. Make sure what should be there, still is.

Grace puts her tray down beside a regiment of glasses. All those ones half full, and more. And the cost of it, she's heard, Lord knows why they pay all that. She picks up a glass and the liquid in it tilts from side to side. She sniffs it: it smells sweet, and rich, like those that drink it, Michael would say. She holds it up in front of her so that the daylight shines through. Does Miss Beatrice drink this, she wonders.

Grace lowers the glass. She glances behind her. Then she raises the glass to her lips and, as she sips, the gas from the glass tickles the insides of her nostrils. Her sneezes splatter the liquid over her hands. She licks it. Nectar, yes. The room is still empty. She takes a swig now, and her mouth buzzes, her nostrils filling with gas again. She had expected alcohol to taste more bitter but this does not, and she's thirsty, she's had no breakfast, not even a cup of tea. As she drains the glass, she hears footsteps behind her and she swings round, forgetting to put the glass down first. It's Mary, eyes wide open.

'Did you?'

'What?'

'Drink it.'

'Drink what?'

'The champagne. She'll smell it on your breath, Mrs Wainwright. They'll all smell it on you.'

'Don't be ridiculous.'

'They will.'

'I didn't drink it.'

'You're flushing. That's the alcohol.'

'I'm angry.'

'Because I said you drank it? Well, you did. I saw the glass there. Right at your lips.'

'I was smelling it.'

'You wait, it'll go to your head and you'll knock something over. Don't say I didn't tell you.' Mary leans in close. 'I can smell it on you now.'

Grace can smell it on herself, over her hands, cuffs even, where it splattered. But who's to say she didn't spill it? Who indeed? In any case, why should she care? She considers throwing a whole glass over herself, nobody would think she'd drunk some then. She laughs and the mess in this room seems bearable, the morning seems bearable.

Grace is still smiling when Joseph appears. He passes her without looking and heads straight for the doors to the saloon.

'Joseph,' she says. 'Good morning.'

He slows and stops, swivelling around on his heels to face her.

'Good morning, Grace,' he replies. And smiles.

Something gives in Grace. Part of her just falls away and she feels as full of tears as she feels full of herself.

'Joseph,' she says. 'It's not that . . . It's really not that . . . '

He looks back at her as though he doesn't know what to think. So Grace finds her arm going forward, something in her pushing it out towards him. Joseph is as still as death. Then he walks over to her and puts a hand on each of her shoulders, looking like he might cry himself.

'Do you mean that, Grace? Do you mean that?'

Grace thinks she nods.

They stop at twelve. Dinner, then they'll have an hour after. Grace tells Mrs Wainwright that she's not feeling well. You look a little pale, Grace, she says. Grace feels pale. The past two hours it's felt like the ceiling's coming down on her head. May she be excused dinner, she asks? She'd just like to put her feet up. No, she's not hungry at all. Mrs Wainwright nods. But we can't have this too often, she says. And I want you up again at two, we'll be doing the inventory then.

Inventory! thinks Grace, and her heart starts beating like soldiers on the march. Lord help her, all it'll need is for somebody to check the books, and they'll know. No matter that there's more taken out; she's no room for reason right now. All she can think of is a voice saying, 'Mrs Wainwright, one's missing,' and she's near ill with the thought.

Grace runs upstairs. When she's in her room she takes her overcoat out of her cupboard. She counts the minutes until they'll all be at the table. Then she goes back down, soft as velvet on the wooden stairs, coat over her arm so it doesn't look like she's going out.

Twenty minutes it'll take her. Not even that if she walks fast. Hyde Park Corner, Belgrave Square, along a bit and into Elizabeth Street.

It'll still be there, won't it, it hasn't been so long now. Well, it has to be there, just as Grace has to get it back before Mrs Wainwright's inventory. Grace can't count on it, can she, Mrs Wainwright, and Lady Masters and the lot of them, thinking that a guest last night filled his pocket with an old book like that.

If the bookseller recognises her, he hides it. Lets her stand there and explain the book she's looking for. Signed copy. Does he have one?

He hesitates, looks straight at her. Well, Grace looks straight back, doesn't she. Then he walks over to a cabinet and takes a key out of his pocket. He brings back a book that looks the same as she can remember it, if she's remembering quite right.

'Careful now,' he says, as she reaches out towards it.

She picks it up and opens the front pages and sees the signature. It's the same book, and relief floods into Grace. Thank the Lord she hadn't yet sent any of that five pounds home.

Tucking it under her right arm, she reaches into her pocket with her left hand and brings out the five-pound note she's been carrying with her. She puts it on the counter and turns to go.

'Young lady,' he says.

'Yes,' Grace replies over her shoulder.

'I think you'll find the door's locked. Unless you have another twenty pounds to pay for that book.'

16

GOOD GOD, THE CLOCK ON BEA'S BEDSIDE TABLE SAYS noon. Bea thinks she can remember seeing it at six, seven, eight and nine this morning. But she must have slept better than that, for her mind is electric, not in the slightest tired, but it's been like that since midnight.

In her head she can see a freshly dark-oak panelled and wall-papered drawing room. The sweet-smiling Mrs McKenna, who can be barely a couple of years older than Bea, is arranging her ornaments and photographs, picking up each one and admiring it before placing it. She moves on to the pale sofa, where she straightens a couple of cushions that have fallen out of place and as she walks to the door she turns and surveys the room. She nods to herself and smiles.

But the McKennas don't live there yet. Forget about the drawing room, Bea, the place is half built, and not a soul in it. Still, there's years of work put into it, of Mrs McKenna planning where the guests sleep, the children, how the main rooms should run into each other, but will not now. Oh, come on, put it out of your head, and think of what you are fighting for. And McKenna, last night he may have been a man as decent and kind as any other but this morning he'll be signing a force-feeding warrant. And he'll be ordering the release of one woman and the rearrest of another.

Bea, don't funk it. Don't even think of it. Just think of those bruised necks, of Emmeline and what they're doing to her now. He is a monster, you just couldn't see it last night. And, and, even if he isn't, then something, something, has to change, and this is simply the only way to do it.

And she's up, ringing the bell, striding into her dressing room. If she keeps moving then she won't have the time to think of buckling. It would be a damn poor show, and she'd find it hard to look at herself in the glass. She'll find it hard to look at herself either way. Get dressed, Beatrice, get on with the day.

It's Susan who comes in, bobbing as she steps through the door. Her skin is chalk, dark smudges under her eyes. Bea's never liked Susan that much, the woman has a hardness to her, and this morning Bea needs a gentle touch.

'Is Grace around?' asks Bea.

'She's gone up to bed, Miss Beatrice.'

'Bed?' Bea's eyebrows raise.

'Do you want me to fetch her?'

'No,' says Bea. 'Let the poor girl sleep. It's a wonder everyone isn't back there this morning.'

If Grace isn't here, Bea would rather do her own hair than set the other servants talking about what she might be up to on the Day After. It may not be 'done' to care about that sort of thing but, today, Bea doesn't want anyone talking. And she has to get downstairs before lunch if she needs the car at three.

At a quarter to one, Bea walks to the mews at the back of the house to check on the Calcott herself before joining the others upstairs. James is in the garage; how odd. Even odder, it looks as though Summers is having a go at him. The two men, man and boy, are staring at each other. They are almost two versions of the same man: how James will be in twenty years' time, and how Summers was twenty years earlier. Can people, wonders Bea, grow to look so similar?

Bea deliberately knocks a tin bucket sitting on the floor to draw attention to herself and the clatter breaks the conversation in front of her. James nods and excuses himself, stalking off like an animal that has lost territory. Summers brushes himself down with the relative self-composure of age. 'Good afternoon, Miss Beatrice, good to see you here.' And she tells him that she needs the Calcott, not on any account to take anyone in it, or let Edward or even Mother put their hands anywhere near the wheel. If necessary, say that it's not running well.

A look of horror appears on Summers' face.

'Or perhaps something more believable,' she gushes.

She turns to go, and reaches the door before she looks back.

'It might be a good thing to give the brakes a really good go. Oh, and the car, don't bother to wax it.' She doesn't want it to shine.

He shakes his head slowly from side to side, his eyebrows pushing his hairline.

Bea fidgets throughout lunch. And afterwards, as they have coffee in the still-furnished red drawing room, she is fidgeting still. For God's sake let nobody ask her what she is up to today. In her head she practises rattling off 'Oh, nothing much', though replying to a real out-loud question might be a different matter altogether. However, nobody has shown a jot of interest so far. Tom is silent, smoking, head miles away, no doubt in some Gowden antechamber. Edward, goaded, Bea guesses, by a sore head, is in a merciless mood and seems to have forgotten all pledges of friendship. 'Good Lord, Bea,' he says, 'you're dressed practically. You could run in that serge it has so many folds in it. And to a funeral, it looks like. I'm on for a more dignified form of exercise – behind the steering wheel. Just a little bit of shut-eye first.'

Bea is in the Calcott by half past two.

It doesn't start. Oh, God. Bea leans forwards on to the steering wheel and puts her head in her hands. One of the grooms is flinging his boy's arms around the handle while Summers stands beside him, reddening as he urges him on. Bea has refused to let Summers take the wheel. Nobody else is climbing into this driving seat before she's gone. And if she's sitting here, it will be damn rude of the engine not to respond.

'Wait,' she tells them. Bea knows cars. She's been into the bonnet and crawled under the engine of this machine half a dozen times. The Rolls and the Lagonda too. Down at Beauhurst, of course. Once she's in a riding dress in the country, nobody blinks an eyelid as to whether she's covered in mud or grease. But she can hardly do that here. In fact, she's not sure she could see anything straight, but it doesn't take much to know that these men are now so panicked they're not letting the engine rest before they try the next time. 'Wait a bit.'

'One, two, three . . . now.'

It starts.

Her going isn't perfect today. She stalls at Marble Arch and a riot of horn-blowing breaks out. As she goes on up the Edgware Road, she's still stopping every couple of minutes. Pray God that it's her and not the engine. Pray God she bucks up.

This afternoon she's not going to Lauderdale Mansions but to an address around the corner from it. Rather than a mansion block, it is a house. She pulls the bell, as instructed, twice, then pauses, then three more times. Bea can hear footsteps thumping their way down the stairs and a thickset woman whom she recognises from Lauderdale Mansions lets her in. Bea follows her up the narrow staircase and it occurs to her that she has never been in a house this narrow, or faded, before. When they reach the first floor there is a single locked door. The woman rat-a-tat-tats a sequence of long and short knocks, and the door opens to a smell of cat.

Bea is led past a door opening onto a small bedroom dominated by a faded rose-print bedspread, and into the flat's single sitting room. It too is small and the green flowered wallpaper above the dado rail browning. One of the several rugs on the floor has been knocked out of place to reveal the scratches in the floorboards it was hiding. Two other women, dressed in dark brown and navy blue, hats shielding their faces, are already occupying a pair of wooden chairs in silence. 'We look like a church ladies' walking group,' jokes Bea. None of them replies. She's seen them at meetings, but never heard them speak. Nor has Bea been given their names. She looks at them, and decides her own. Thickset, Skinny and Wiry. It is not clear to which of them these rooms belong, if any.

Half past three. They are to leave at six, but come here early, Bea was told, just in case you are followed. The police will only wait so long on a hunch. Unlike when they are waiting for Mrs Pankhurst; then they waited in Glebe Place for a day and a half, but they knew she was in there.

Bea brushes aside the cat hairs and sits in an empty armchair. There's a black Gladstone bag on the floor in the middle of the room and Wiry keeps leaning over and inspecting the contents. Apart from this, they sit and say nothing, and a silent tension rises.

Four o'clock. Yesterday's newspaper is lying on a table in the corner of the room. Bea has read it but considers going over to pick it up and read yet another time the story of the suffragette smuggling a machete into the National Gallery and slashing the *Rokeby Venus*. It might offer some excitement to distract from the nervousness building up inside her. But none of the others is doing anything at all and taking the newspaper might mark her out as different, and possibly therefore not feeling as they do. Bea is the new girl, she needs to fit in, yet she's not sure she can sit still for another minute for all she can think of is what she is about to do and whether she might funk it.

So she offers tea. That, at least, she can do, and Thickset and Skinny accept.

The kitchen is smaller than a downstairs lavatory in Park Lane. There's a gas burner in the corner, a kettle sitting on the top. Bea shakes her way along the tins until she finds some tea. China. Hope they like it. Well, that's all there is.

Five o'clock, and she's making her third pot. Even the action of raising the cup to her lips and down again has provided her with a degree of activity. The other women barely move. Bea feels far away from them, as though none of this is quite real. The tea, however, is scalding her mouth.

Thickset looks up and across at Bea. 'I wouldn't have too many of those,' she says. 'There's no stopping when we go. As you'll know from the route.'

No, Bea does not know the route. Where was she supposed to get it from? Has she, in the whirl of birthday and ball, or nervousness, simply forgotten? Thickset – Bea wonders whether she is in Mrs Pankhurst's bodyguard – does not look as though she would be sympathetic to Bea's situation. None of them in fact looks as if they might be sympathetic at all.

'Can I see it again?' Bea asks.

'Here.' Skinny pulls something out of her pocket and passes it over. 'Take another look, just to get the gist of it. But don't worry too much, I'll tell you when and where to turn. Just concentrate on getting us out like the clappers once we've done our bit.'

'What exactly are the plans?' She hasn't been told much, just the minimum, they said. The less that is known, the less the chance it'll come out. Not, of course, that they think she would . . . but just in case she trips up. That's why they don't drive the route first. A woman in a motor catches an eye or two.

'You're driving,' says Skinny. 'Keep to that. Don't worry about the rest.'

At a quarter to six, Thickset asks Bea and Wiry to leave the flat and drive three streets away. Thickset and Skinny will meet them there at six. They will walk there another way. Wiry carries the Gladstone bag. She sits in the rear of the car, and places it very gently at her feet. Bea drives off, trying to make herself think of nothing but the motor. She is, she reflects, so tired of waiting that now she simply wants to go and get it over with.

At six sharp the other two appear. Thickset climbs into the back behind Bea, and Skinny sits in the front passenger seat. Bea is sure she feels the side of the car dip as Thickset sits down. She wants to say something about balance and speed, but realises that the only way to improve the situation is for both women in the rear to move into the middle of the seat and for Wiry to sit on Thickset's lap.

Surrey, they are going to Surrey; Weybridge to be precise. This is where McKenna has chosen to have a retreat from the demands of high office. Bea begins to relax into being on the road but in Wimbledon she stalls, then almost as soon as she has started, stalls again. She feels disapproval dig into her from behind and she pushes her foot down more firmly on the accelerator. She does not stall from then on.

Bea thinks they have been driving for about an hour and a quarter when Skinny directs her up a side road that rapidly disappears into a rough track. Engine off, says Skinny. Headlamps too, and everyone out. Bea obeys and is handed a rope and a yard of black cloth which she can barely see in the dark. There's a moon up there somewhere this evening, but it is now behind a cloud. We'll do the back, Skinny continues, looking at Bea and tilting her head towards the bonnet, you others the front. Skinny begins to stretch the cloth over the number plate and asks Bea to hold it in position. Bea hadn't thought of this. Is that why they'll take a newcomer to drive, so if this falls off, it's Bea who will be tracked down?

They tie up the covers and climb back into the car. Wiry, Bea notices, has become a little more jumpy; she doesn't take her hand off the Gladstone.

'Shall we go?' Wiry asks Skinny.

'Quarter of an hour,' is the reply.

This is the worst wait. Bea feels as though she's pulled a tie too tight around her neck. What, what if part of the house is ready for occupation, and somebody is there? What if her car has been spotted? What if she stalls when trying to drive away, or the engine really is dicky? And what, what if, this is really a terribly wrong thing to do.

She looks around her. Skinny, Wiry and Thickset. She has very little choice.

A quarter of an hour later, the Calcott, lampless, rolls back on to the road.

Bea has not driven in the dark without headlamps before. 'Can you speed up,' asks Skinny. Not without, Bea wants to say, embracing a hedge. But her eyes are adjusting a little and she moves up a gear. As soon as she does so, Skinny barks in her ear. 'Left here.'

Bea turns and slams on the brakes. There is a pair of gates on the driveway, a thin chain wrapped around them. 'They're mine,' says Wiry, and leaps out clutching something pulled from the bag.

'What does she have?' asks Bea.

'Hedgecutters,' replies Thickset.

Wiry swings the gates open and the Calcott crunches up the gravel.

Not a light, not a single one. Bea thinks she can see a pile of bricks in front of the house. To the side rises the uneven shadow of a part-building without a roof. What can there be, Bea comforts herself with, to burn in here?

'Stop,' says Skinny. 'A little further forward.'

'Right,' says Thickset.

Pause, then 'Yes,' from Wiry.

The two of them clamber out.

Where are they going, asks Bea as the pair head to the back of the house. Why do they need to go round there to stick a petrol-soaked rag through a window? There are plenty of windows at the front.

'Turn the car around and stop,' says Skinny. 'But keep the engine running.'

As Bea does so, it seems that the gravel is suddenly crackling extraordinarily loudly and sharply. Then she realises it is the sound of breaking glass.

Wiry and Thickset come running back to the car.

'Drive, for God's sake,' screams Wiry. 'I think we've only got forty seconds on it.'

And Bea, a cloud thickening in her head, moves the car into full throttle and follows the pale gravel back to the gates.

As they reach them she hears a sound behind her as loud as a twelve-gun salute.

Forty seconds, that was the fuse.

'Headlamps on,' barks Skinny. 'And as fast as you can.'

And Bea drives, her head full of endings, and beginnings, and things that will never be quite the same again.

War

1915

17

DOWNSTAIRS IS DREADING THE ARRIVAL OF THE refugees and there's no other talk at dinner. Even when there's silence, the silence is talking too. Most of them are still here, it's only James and Joseph that are gone. The boot boy tried to go, too, but they sent him back from the recruiting station. 'You'd have to be a good mile taller to look eighteen,' said Susan when he came back in wearing his Sunday best, eyes to the floor. Now the maids – Grace, Susan and a slip of a girl who came when Mary left – have the footmen's jobs to do as well as their own. That's all the serving and clearing and the front door. Not that she minds doing it, Grace, for when women are doing men's jobs, who knows what comes after. Look at Miss Beatrice in her breeches, even if she has to wear that long jacket. What, they'll have Mrs Wainwright as butler next. Well, fancy that, Grace wants to giggle to herself as she pictures Mrs Wainwright in a tailcoat. But Grace is at table and she has to hold it in.

It's not long since he's gone, Joseph; he made the decision at Christmas. And though he was gone by the end of January, it's only April now. Ever so long, since it all began last summer, he'd been asking what Grace thought about him joining up, and what was she to say? Go, Joseph, so I can be proud of you? But it wasn't quite like that yet, between them, proud of you. You can't say proud of you unless you're family, or almost, and there was that question always hovering an inch or so behind his lips. There'd been more than one moment when she'd thought it was coming and when the moment passed, she'd let her breath out with relief. Same thing when he was asking, should I go? For, though she's soft on Joseph, and who wouldn't be, there's something in her that might like more than just married life, and she doesn't want to have to come to a decision yet. Anyways, it's not as though she sends home much, but she can't stop, can she? She couldn't have told Ma she was marrying, for what would Grace write when Ma asked her how she and Joseph had met? Michael would ask, too, and if he guessed, she can see his face thundercloud-dark before he turned and left. He doesn't like to be lied to, Michael. He'd be gone from all their lives, because Grace is the only member of the family that he is still speaking to.

When Grace sees that man, the editor of the *Daily Herald*, come into the house, her pride in her brother tastes sour. She doesn't have much of a chance to read what he writes, they'd not have any of a newspaper like that downstairs, Mr Bellows'd put it straight on the fire, he would. But if Grace has time upstairs and none's about, she'll look through for Michael's name and think how many's reading his articles. Well, enough for Da to have read it, too.

It was in Da's note at the end of Ma's letter to Grace. 'Tell Michael that I no longer want his letters. Not while he's still writing about the war like that. Other men's sons are making their fathers proud. Tell him not to write until it is to tell me he's going over.'

Michael nodded when Bea told him, just a gesture of a nod but a nod it was as though he wasn't surprised. He and Grace were sitting on one of the benches they liked in Kensington Gardens and she'd expected him to hang his head in his hands and say he'd stop writing, that he wished he'd never written. But he looked straight ahead, his face night. 'They'll learn,' he said, 'they'll learn.' And Grace didn't know what to think. She wants

Michael always to be right. But saying that the fighting's wrong sticks in her throat. What does that mean for Joseph out there? And James, and Susan's sweetheart, and Mr Bellows' nephew; there's no stopping the list. Mrs Wainwright must have someone out there too, not that she'd tell. Not that she ever tells anything about her life outside the house. It occurs to Grace that she may have none to talk of, and Grace hopes to God that it will never be her like that.

Da wouldn't have Michael's money either, so Michael gives it to Grace to send home with hers. 'Make something up, Grace,' he said, 'tell them you're in charge of the office, now that the man who was there has gone.' And it's then she wants to boast to him that there's no need to make it up, she's doing a man's job already.

Ma and Da are doing all right on the money. Last week Ma wrote that they've enough spare to do a trip over into Scotland to see Aunt Ethel in Glasgow, where she'd moved to find work. 'It'll be a day out for the girls.' Take the train first thing, they can, and be back the same evening. It's not the Continent, is it, thinks Grace, but it is to them.

Joseph's going over has been his chance to get there, the Continent. It's the opportunity of a lifetime, is the talk, when else will one of them have that? The way he writes you'd've thought it was an exciting lark; it makes Grace wonder about what's in the papers. Not the reports and the maps, Mr Bellows takes charge of those, reading what's happened and telling them all at tea as if it were his own idea. James and Joseph used to jostle for them once he was done, just to put their word in. Though now they're not here, their being over there is taking it away from Mr Bellows even more. No, it was the other things, like the one Bellows read out to them. *An Officer's Diary*. All mud and noise it was. 'I don't want to upset you young women,' he said, 'but I feel it's my role to make sure we all appreciate the bravery of our men.' Mr Summers, well, he says nothing, does he? ' I'm sure it's the last war,' says Mrs Wainwright when he's gone, 'with the Boers, he fought in that, and not everyone likes to remember .' Then it's her turn to fall silent.

Several families of Belgian refugees, they've been told, on the nursery floor. One family per room, and how many of them is that? They'll have the day nursery for sitting and what else are they to do, apart from sit, those that don't get jobs, and whose jobs will those be, Grace wonders? Mussyur Fouray, you'd've thought he'd be happy, what with them being Belgians. But he's not Belgian, is he, says Susan; them French don't want to be taken for Belgians. So he's murmuring away about how many he's to cook for, and what they'll eat and not eat. It's 'la gair' come to the house, he puffs; he might as well be in France.

Mrs Wainwright's putting a brave face on it, telling them all not to worry, they'll turn the library into a dining room, Gunters will bring in the tables, and they can hire another chef. Another chef! Well, you can imagine Mussyur Fouray at that. Like a chicken he is, strutting around the kitchen with that breast of a stomach pushed out and asking what's not good enough about my cooking? Or something like that, as it is in French. Mrs Wainwright, however, understands and says that it will be an assistant chef. Assistant, yes, he said. Many. Chef, no. And so Mrs Wainwright's looking. You'd've thought it'd be hard to find more help during a war, what with the men away. But, what with them being away and not needing looking after and so many houses shuttered up, there's more wanting to work than before and Mrs Wainwright says she's been 'deluged', all from one small notice, and maybe there's a chef among the refugees. Not that it's wise, she's said, to mention this to Mussyur Fouray. And she didn't say all this at dinner, but in the Pugs' Parlour, when she'd called all of the housemaids in.

'What about the cleaning?' Susan asked. 'Who's to clean up after however many dozens there'll be? We'll need our own army.'

'Well, it's service, isn't it,' says Grace.

'They'll clean up after themselves,' said Mrs Wainwright.

'Will they be any good at it, is the question,' continued Susan. 'We'll have mice back up there before we've said How d'you do. And the fires and the coal, what about that?'

Cheek! thought Grace. It's funny how just with Joseph and James gone, things aren't quite as they should be, in more ways than you'd expect. It's the war, must be. Who's who and when to speak and not, they seem to matter less.

'And the laundry.' Susan wouldn't let it rest. 'What about that?'

'Lady Masters will have it sent out.'

'Oh, it's all fine for them then. And the smalls, too, I don't doubt.'

'Susan!' Grace had never heard Mrs Wainwright so sharp. 'We are all finding things difficult. Be thankful that you are as safe as houses over here.'

'What about them Zeppelins?'

'Mr Bellows says they'll never make it this far,' said Grace.

It's the eating arrangements that trouble Grace. Not that the worry's ever gone away, just quiet, waking her only now and then. When it does, she turns to the side in bed, looking for Mary's shape, checking that Grace hasn't woken her by shouting out. But Mary's not there any more, is she, and Grace misses the way that Mary made her laugh. When it was just the two of them, Mary'd said what the others daren't, even if it were a trifle shocking.

But that was it with Mary, her breaking the rules. And that's how she left. Always went one step beyond what she should have, just as she went one word more. Grace has had a letter from her, though more of a note, for writing's not Mary's strong point. The baby's a fighter, little girl she is, called Grace. Mary asked if Grace didn't mind and Grace'd thought on it, being quite proud of the fact. Not to worry that the child's a bastard, giving her a name would at least be giving her something in life. So little Grace is weaned now, and quite happy being left with Mary's ma. She is a guardian angel she is,

Mary's ma. There was Mary, at her wits' end as to how she'd say it, half expecting to be turned out to the workhouse. Instead, she'd made the journey across London and been welcomed home, her ma saying it was lovely to have her back, whatever the reason that had brought her, and not to worry about her wage, they would do nicely. Mary's mother just invented a husband for the neighbours, run over by a coal cart, and half a dozen sacks on him, too. Mary even took a new name, Perkins she is now, and they'd put it on the birth certificate, a father, too. As good a name as any, she wrote. Now Baby Grace is weaned, Mary writes, so Mary's looking for work. Does Grace think she can talk to Mrs Wainwright for her?

Well, Mrs Wainwright kept it under her hat all right when Mary went. Not that Mary said, but Mrs Wainwright's no fool, didn't say a word and swallowed that Mary had to go home for her ma was sick. Mary was pale with the guilt, for if you say something like that, doesn't it make it happen? Grace thought of her own ma, and her stomach turned. Then it turned again as she already hadn't seen them for three months back then. Now it's a year and three. She has the photograph though to keep them in, and you can't tell the grey in Ma's hair. Grace won't see it, either, when she next sees Ma. She'll shut it out for she's not to get older, Ma. Still, the girls must have changed, what with Peggy going on from eleven and all that can happen from then. And Jenny and Baby Alice, nine now she is, stretching tall. Grace wants that, her sisters growing good and strong. No need to rush into adulthood, just making their ways steadily towards it. Though you'd've thought that the longer it was since she'd seen them, the worse it would feel, it doesn't. The longer your family's been getting on fine without you, the surer you are that they will stay that way.

So her stomach turns less now, when she thinks of them.

Grace isn't sure that Mrs Wainwright would take Mary back. It'd need just one of the others to know, and demand she's turned out. Besides, Sarah's taken her place, leaving only the kitchen, a come-down for Mary even if Mrs Wainwright could put her in above the others, and that's without asking how she can cook. Mary'd talk her way into it, even if she didn't know one end of a carrot from another. Grace stifles a laugh at the picture of it in her mind, only for an instant as her thoughts race back to the refugees eating and the library. What if they take the books out now that it's going to be a dining room? Surely they'll count them. Then they'll know, won't they, that one's missing?

18

IT IS WHEN BEA CLIMBS OFF THE MOTORCYCLE THAT her breeches start to itch. They're too jolly hot for this spring sunshine and the wool, no longer pressed flat onto leather and steel by her thighs, moves as she walks, its fibres sprung back to their scouring-cloth texture. A small price for the thrill of the ride, even if all she is doing is carting envelopes between an abundance of organisational HQs. She has considered shedding her WEC uniform and its obligatorily 'modest' sack of an overcoat down to her knees and having something run up instead, but there has been such a debate about what should be worn and who can afford it that it would just create a stink.

She's sure she heard a rattle as she came into the mews, it may just be the cobbles, but she needs to check. Shoddiness, however slight, is not tolerated in the Women's Emergency Corps. The engine is still hot to touch, even through her gauntlets, and she has to take them off, can't fiddle with a thing in these. She flinches as her fingers brush past the metal. Yes, that's it. Bea can't see her fingers now, but she's found a loose bolt. Need a wrench for this. She pulls her hands out quickly, burning them as she does so, and when she walks into the coach-house she has the side of her palm in her mouth.

Summers is sitting there, watching her. It's almost all he does now, sit alone in his cave that the coach-house has become. When the horses left, the grooms went with them. When he tried to sign up he was turned down. Too old. I wasn't too old for the Boers, he'll tell anyone who'll listen.

He has other things to say to Bea. These range from astonishment that she's doing 'a man's work', to 'Let me do that for you.' He never used to speak to her like that, but there aren't many drivers left to choose from. Bea wonders whether it's that she's wearing breeches and wishes he would be quiet. What would it prove, if they all relied on men to deal with the machines? She might as well join the knitting brigades.

Summers finds Bea a wrench. She returns to the motorcycle and fixes it, burning her hand in the same place as she does. Then she wheels it inside and throws a canvas tarpaulin over it.

If she's quick she may reach tea before it is taken away. No time to change, but as she passes the gentlemen's lavatory on the ground floor she dashes in to scrub what oil she can from her hands, and fix the pins on her hair. God, what a mess. She almost wishes she hadn't looked. Really, she should simply leave her cap on.

Edward is standing in front of the fireplace, his khaki neatly pressed and oil-free, although, Bea suspects, just as itchy as hers. His hands are behind his back and he is rocking forward on to the balls of his feet, the flames darting all over the place behind him, giving his steady rhythm a chaotic air.

'You look,' says Bea, 'too spanking new.'

'I am spanking new. Thank you for coming to my Last Tea on time.'

'I had a sack full of superfluous messages to deliver. Don't you know that there's a war on?'

'They're not superfluous, dear sis. We couldn't do it without you.'

'That is precisely the type of remark that makes me feel second rung.'

'Oh, come off it. Anyhow, you could have put a frock on, old gal. How's a brother supposed to go, not knowing whether his sister is really a chap?'

And then he is quiet.

He stops rocking and stands, feet still but head slowly moving from left to right. He is taking the room in, absorbing the image of every detail, Bea reckons, so he has it with him. The fire flares. Bea wonders whether his hidden hands are loose, or whether his fingers are knotted into each other, clenched tight.

It's damned unfair. As little as Edward wants to, he'll have a chance to fight. Whereas Bea, just because she has breasts, is left behind on the grounds that she isn't up to it. She's chucked grenades, hasn't she? Started fires? Where's the difference between that and sending a shell across the lines? She's a mind to tell them.

She misses it, misses every single raid she drove for, each one racking up both her chances of being caught and her excitement. It was the surprise of the explosion that did it for her, and the way that in even a simple fire the flames would suddenly crackle up several feet, making them all jump. They'd wait as long as they dared to see the glass, cracks flashed to the corners of the panes, holding still for an instant, then showering down.

But what now? Mrs Pankhurst raised Bea to the clouds, and then let her, let all of them, drop. The campaign has been abandoned for the duration of the war. Instead it is all Let's do War Work, giving in to the condescending novelty of the idea that women are doing men's jobs. Still, that's what Bea's doing it, isn't it.

Mother's voice is in her ear. 'Don't you think, Beatrice, that this afternoon, your brother could be allowed to be right? I hope you're changing for this evening.'

'Is Edward?'

'Of course not, he'll be in uniform.'

'In that case . . . '

'Proud as I am of you, it is my last At Home until the war is over.'

'Last?'

'There won't really be any point, will there?'

No point? Bea feels as though she has had the breath knocked out of her. She pulls herself up, appetite and thirst gone.

'Some of us' – she's trying not to bark it out but she's hardly going to be cooing over this – 'some of us, Mother, will still be living here.' Then she turns and as good as marches out on to the gallery, knowing even as she does that she shouldn't have stormed out on Edward's last afternoon. She's almost at the top of the stairs before she stops to look at her watch. It is a quarter past five and, dash it, Tuesday, almost time for Mr Campbell. Edward going over must have made her forget. She'll go as she is; anyhow it makes her feel Beatrice, war motorcyclist, and not Miss Masters of Park Lane, twenty-two and unmarried.

She'll take a cab to Pimlico and wait in their tea room; yes, their tea room she calls it now. Mr Campbell will be there by six, to avoid his landlady's 'gruel', and which, on Tuesdays and Fridays, he escapes by coming to meet Bea.

The red and white tablecloths in the tea room have yellowed further. She has had a great many teas here over the past year, teas that consist of a cup of the stuff for her, an evening meal for him, and a great deal of what Bea likes to think of as debate, much of it on the necessity of the war; Bea saying he is plain wrong, if not treacherous. But each Tuesday, once his tea is eaten and hers is drunk, he puts a small bundle of sheets of paper on the table. 'I really,' he says, 'need your help with this. Please, Miss Masters, in the interests of Free Speech, I know you care about that.' He bends his head a little then looks back up, straight at her, his dark eyes holding hers until she finds herself nodding. Then it's two evenings, or parts thereof, hidden away in her room and hammering it out with fingers still vibrating from the motorcycle. On Friday she hands the typed-up article back, ready for the Daily Herald, which prints it every week.

This evening there are only a couple of tables free, and their conversation will be drowned by the chatter of others. This is no bad thing, for Mrs White has ears on every bony joint. As Bea sits, the waitress swivels around and bustles over, a tray of half-eaten food hovering in front of her chest.

'Waiting for your sweetheart, miss?'

Bea forces herself to smile, albeit flatly, in return.

'I hope you don't have to wait too long.'

No empathy there, thinks Bea. She just wants to turn over customers as quickly as possible.

'You smell of grease,' says Mr Campbell as he sits down.

Bea remembers that she has not bathed. 'It's the latest fad.'

'As ever, a woman of fashion.'

Bea feels her nose wrinkle. Is that how he sees her? Even like this?

'Of course, that's all we women ever are.' It comes out as a retort. Christ, what's up with her today?

'Cut yourself on that.'

Bea ignores this and asks him when his next meeting is.

Mr Campbell is silent. He rolls his lips in, and looks to the side.

'Tomorrow.'

'I'll come.'

He flinches. Taps his fingers on the table. He always does this when she asks to come along.

'In your two-pound Women's Emergency Corps uniform?'

'And?'

'And you'd say you had come there with me? I think that might look a little odd, Miss Masters.'

Bea ignores this, too. He's right, that's why she ignores it, but she'll go on asking, and he'll go on saying no. It has become part of their Tuesday and Friday evening banter.

'You would be surprised,' she says, 'at how I could help.' He doesn't know which Miss Masters she is, does he? Nor the deep pockets she could find him. Surely he'd ask for money if he did. The strikers are crying out for money in the shipyards. But all she's given him are Celeste's address to contact her and a vague reference to her father being 'something in the City'.

'I'm not sure how you'd find Clydeside,' is his reply. 'Or a soup kitchen.'

'You'd be amazed at how fast I can ladle.'

Mr Campbell leans over and puts his hand on hers. Bea keeps her hand still. To move it would be rude, she tells herself, that's the only reason she's leaving it there. This is a purely practical working relationship: he writes, she types; there is nothing more to it than that. She doesn't even agree with half of what he writes, for God's sake. But Mr Campbell keeps his hand over hers and Bea can't push the idea out of her head any longer. Does he think that? Don't be an idiot, Bea, he can't possibly be thinking of kissing you, even if everyone seems to be kissing since the war began. Soldiers on their way out are being treated to kisses, and Bea herself has given more than one such treat, out of both generosity and curiosity. She has even been bold enough to offer them outright. The first time, she surprised herself, but her offer was so warmly received that the next offer slipped out of her mouth with barely a thought. There's only been one who held her tighter and closer than she might have liked and when she tried to pull away he pulled her tighter still. She bit his lip and he let go, cursing, wiping away the blood with the back of his hand. 'Vixen,' he said.

'Yes,' she replied.

But Mr Campbell isn't on his way over, is he? He does not approve of the war, he is a pacifist; he says it is against his religion, in his words, to raise a gun. What if they make you, Mr Campbell, what then, she wants to ask him? They'll shoot you if you try to leave. They're not going to make us all fight, he says, it's fool's talk, and saying that they'll send married men over.

Then the thought comes to her. Good God, is he married? Bea imagines a wife and children, two or three of them. More? Could he have spent a year without mentioning them? It is Bea's turn to flinch, even though why on earth, Beatrice Masters, should you care?

Mr Campbell takes his hand away.

'Good ladling hand,' he says. 'But no.'

Weeks on, Mr Campbell's 'No' is still irritating Bea as she drives over to Celeste's, all the more so because he, somewhat of a sudden, signed up and vanished to France, and she can no longer retort. She couldn't accuse him of a complete about-turn for he's not raising a gun, just ferrying the wounded about. Though, thinks Bea, isn't doing so somehow supporting the war, too? It's certainly a darn sight better than what Bea is up to with the WEC and all its Good Show, Old Chaps – and that's the closest she's found to Lauderdale Mansions since Mrs Pankhurst did her bunk.

The word now is that the Front's coming to London any day. Not that it will be the real thing. Then she wonders about Edward. Surely he's managing to find a bit of excitement, and that it's good for him. While she quietly hopes to God that he's not as scared as he was when he left.

Back here half the city is walking around with their faces tilted to the clouds, scouring the sky for Zeppelins. Makes talking a walk along the pavement perilous. Bea imagines Curzon Street engulfed in flames with a sort of fascination. It's still there, isn't it, that yearning for the rush of excitement? Revving the motorcycle's engine did it for her for a while, but it's not the same. Is it a wholly wicked thought to want the Zeppelins to come? Well, if she had a chance to get out there good and proper, she wouldn't have to be willing bombs to rain here. That's no excuse, she tells herself, for there's no getting around it, it is a terrible wish to have.

Why, this afternoon she had gone around to Edie's. There Edie was, sitting under her curving stone staircase in a billowing white dress and fanning her baby while fretting about sending him out of town to escape the bombs. 'I can hardly bear to let him go, Bea, yet it's so terribly selfish of me to think about what I feel when I should only be thinking of what's best for him.' Edie looked miserable, and Bea felt guilty enough over her desire for the war to come to London to be relieved when the conversation drifted into the pain of having to invite dull people to dinner. She even, in the course of it, agreed to come along. Which was certainly a mistake.

The rest of the day, a rare day off, had been intended for errands and dressmaker's. Apart from sweltering the two hundred yards to Edie's house, the heat– blistering and rather unexpected for May – defeated all; especially the visit to the dressmaker's, for she could hardly have muslin fitted with rivulets running down her back. Instead she had retreated to the cool of the museum at the rear of the house. It was tomb-stale. No sunlight or air, it seems, had entered for some time – one of the shrinkages in household duties since the footmen left. They were encouraged to go, Bea is sure, by Mother's offer to continue paying them their full wages in addition to army pay. Poor boys. At least they've missed the refugees, though for Bea, collecting car-loads of Belgian refugees from Charing Cross in the Rolls and delivering them to boarding houses and private homes had been a lark. Mother, however, became utterly carried away with it all and Bea had to exercise some restraint over her. Even when they were already up to three families, with four or five children apiece, Mother was still asking around for more and Bea told her they simply had enough. It wasn't Mother who was going to live with them. She had declared that now Edward was in France she would be spending most of her time down at Beauhurst, building up the dairy herd to feed the nation. She has, she announces to almost every visitor, already been milking the cows herself. Poor beasts, thinks Bea, will they ever recover?

Just as Bea pulls up outside Celeste's house, the sky above her cracks. Good God, that's it, a Zeppelin! She feels a surge of excitement and leaps out of the car to see a streak of light cut across the clouds. Then nothing. No Germans yet, simply the chance of rain. Sleep, too, if the temperature drops enough afterwards. The air is hellishly muggy and she is so damp that she might as well have walked over. She's a mind to beg an iced bath as soon as she's in.

She finds Celeste in her drawing room, standing by the fire, smoking, and floating in a cloud of lilac chiffon that looks as if it might combust with a single dropped ash. 'Champagne?' she asks Bea, waving her cigarette at the ice-bucket and a remaining glass beside it. 'South Pole temperature. Only thing to cool a fellow down. Help yourself. How's the cycle?'

'Oh, fine, fine. Running well. At least it was yesterday. I haven't been out on it today. Luckily, or its tyres might have melted. How are you?' Bea walks over to the bottle of champagne and pours herself a glass.

'Excellent. I'm up to nine refugees. And it's a wonder what they can do. Everything from haute cuisine to the accounts, though most of them are after jobs in the munitions', the men too, for which they are highly overqualified. I rather fear that they will desert me for the East End, poor buggers.'

Bea walks over to the window and half looks out at the slow-moving street melting below. She speaks with her back to Celeste.

'I think Mother is in competition with you.'

'That is not news, Beatrice.'

'Refugees.' Outside is now darkening as a black cloud arrives overhead. The walkers below are looking up, and quickening their pace.

'That's noble of her. How many does she have? What are you looking at out there?'

'Oh sorry, waiting for the rain. I rather enjoy it when the clouds burst; it always feels such a relief.' Bea turns back to face Celeste, and walks over to the cigarette box sitting on a side table. 'Anyhow, soon to be twenty-two refugees – if you count the small ones. Do you have a light?' Celeste nods, and throws Bea a large silver lighter, which Bea catches, then lights a cigarette with it.

'Good God, even in that house you can scarcely have room to breathe.'

It is Bea who can't breathe as she chokes on the cigarette she has taken. God, it's one of Celeste's Turkish ones. Quite disgusting. She stubs it out, and collapses back on to the sofa behind her. 'And Mother has fled the situation. I'm not quite sure who's in charge. Mrs Wainwright, I suppose.'

'And what is Mrs Wainwright doing?'

'What are we supposed to do?'

'Many of them are extremely well educated. I should try having a conversation with them and find out what they want. I should think that French was probably the only thing that all those highly strung mam'selles taught you.' Celeste is pointing at Bea with her cigarette.

'Our refugees speak Flemish.'

'That's no excuse,' says Celeste. 'You can always improvise a sign language. Or you could teach them English. Better still, learn Flemish from them and get yourself out to Flanders. After all, a skirt didn't stop Boadicea. Have some more champagne.'

Bea nods, pulls herself up and refills her glass. She remains standing and takes a large swig, which, on top of what she has already drunk, goes straight to her head, and she gestures with her glass as she speaks.

'It's not as though we're allowed to pick up a gun, Celeste. It's all "We couldn't do it without you" sort of work. I find it particularly condescending. And I'm not exactly cut out to be a nursing VAD who sits at a patient's bedside for hours on end.'

'Pretty weak excuse, old girl, and you know there's a good deal more to it than that. Besides, look at the FANYs, they're careering around on horseback, straight in the line of fire. And they're all scared, Beatrice. You don't imagine everyone over there is thinking that they quite fancy a good look at some wounds for a bit of entertainment. Where's your mettle, girl? Rather sounds like you're being a bit of a funk.'

Bea bristles at this. Her a funk? Has Celeste forgotten what Bea did before the war? How many raids she went on? Hardly a funk.

She crosses her arms, slightly spilling her champagne as she does so, but she ignores it.

'I don't think you can call me that, Celeste. Look what I did, and I would do it again. Near gasping to. Oh blast Mrs Pankhurst for giving it all up for the war. It makes me livid. God, I really miss it. Don't you?' Bea suddenly needs to know she is not alone in feeling this.

'We all miss it, but times have moved on.'

'Not for the vote.'

'There's a war on, Beatrice . . . '

'Oh, don't give me that . . .'

'We have to do what we can. If we help win this war, we may have a chance of voting against the next one. Besides, suffrage raids will pale in comparison to what you will see out there. Even if you don't lift a gun.'

With that, the sky thunders again, this time right over their heads. Bea walks over to the window and peers outside.

'I am sorry to disappoint you, but it is not the Zeppelins. You can't say you're as good as at the Front yet. You will need to go over for that. It will be the greatest thing you can do for the cause.'

Celeste's words are almost drowned out by the rattling of water on the window panes. The wood itself is shaking and the glass looks as if it might crack.

'It's the Flood,' shouts Bea. 'Come to wash away the war.'

'And it'll be taking the cowards with it,' mouths Celeste in return.

1916

19

GRACE IS IN THE SERVANTS' HALL WITH HER BEST summer frock on. The boot boy is trying not to look at her but Susan and Sarah, they're peeping all right, just pretending not to. They've all been waiting to see Joseph come for her this evening before he takes the train back. He called round more than a week ago and Grace wasn't in. Wasn't in, out just for an hour or so on an errand for Miss Beatrice. Fancy the luck of that. He couldn't wait, his note said, he knew he'd said it would be today in his letter but he had to go straight up to see his ma on the next train. Didn't know how long he'd be caught there, what there'd be to do. Harvest, he said, needs bringing in. He is sorry for letting her down.

Cheeky, thinks Grace. Let her down? He isn't the only thing she has to worry about. But that's not true, is it, Grace Campbell? Joseph and his big warm blondness are what's given her hope in the past year. It's strange, being so free to choose her own life now. She can go where she likes – but there's a nothingness to that, as though wherever she puts her feet, the ground beneath might slide away.

Not that she's seen him, it's all been in words, speaking out plain about the adventures he's been having but how all he's looking forward to, he writes, is his Grace, and her laugh and pretty face again. When she reads his letters, they make her feel that there's somebody who wants to look after her and she doesn't have to worry him about going off to marry somebody else. Joseph will hold her in his arms and tell her how much he likes her. It also makes her think that, even what with all that's happened, there is good somewhere, and her wickedness might not stop it coming to her.

Even though the world and his wife have now been in and out of the library and there's been not a flicker of notice about the book that is missing, Grace can't help but sometimes lay her head on the pillow and think she can still feel it under the mattress. At least she's as good as stopped the lying, for there's nobody left to lie to. And after Michael went to France she wrote to him to say that she's now working as a maid for her employer. Though she said that it's only because the business has shut, for there's not much trade overseas you can do with those U-boats skulking around. She told him that she'd rather be working in a nice house than a munitions factory, and it keeps her in place to go back to her old job as secretary when the war is over.

The war's changed now. It's not being all proud of our boys any more, it's worrying sick, and it makes Grace's insides tremble whenever her thoughts go there. This week the news has been so frightful: sixty thousand wounded in just one day, and a third of those dead. She can't not think of all those dead boys, and wondering whether it'll be Michael, Joseph, James even, next.

There are more in the newspaper every day. At least sweeping and cleaning you have to keep your eyes open and find the dirt; it's the jobs you don't need to think about that let your mind wander. So she's careful, Grace, when she's polishing silver and falling into a rhythm, for it's then that the pictures grow in her head. Young men, as far as she can see, lying there with bits blown off them, covered in other people's parts, too. That's Michael's job now, fetching the ones that aren't quite dead, and that's not a thought to have. Not just what it's like out there, turning them over to see what still moves, it's the guns, too. 'Conchie' they call him, Conscientious Objector it says on the forms. Won't fire a gun but will run in to pick up the dead and not an idea if it's safe. She hadn't wanted him to go, he had just told her he was leaving, now that the rest of the family was gone.

She can remember the last time they were together, before he left. More than a year ago, it was; they were sitting in Kensington Gardens, the sun warm on their faces and neither of them saying a word. Michael wasn't even tapping his feet on the ground, and Grace, well, she was far from sure she believed in God any more. Not after. No, not after . . .

Even though they were all to come by breakfast time that May morning, Aunt Ethel had done teacakes for Peggy and Jenny and Alice – a treat for Ma and Da too, for eggs, now, they weren't easy to find. When her lodger came back with the evening paper, she'd seen it, that three trains had come together on the line from Carlisle. The two of them looked at the teacakes and all the dinner gone cold, and she knew. She wrote to Michael in London. He hadn't had her letter until he was back from work on the Wednesday, then he'd written on to Grace. He was running, he wrote, to catch the evening train north, he'd find them, he promised. Then he'd send word, no, he'd come around to tell her it was all right. Even with everything, the thought of Michael turning up at the house and finding out how long she'd been in an apron and cap had given her a fright.

At morning break on the Friday, Michael's letter in her pocket, Grace had asked for the newspaper. Susan whispered to her in a way that is pretending to be on your side because it is a whisper, but puts you down. 'Mr Bellows has it. You'll wait your turn.' And, for the first time since Grace arrived, and, my word, it was something that she hadn't let them out before, tears were rolling down her face. She sniffed them up, kept breathing so as she could answer their questioning, but all that came out was: Michael, the letter being from him, even that he was in the law, and Gretna, and that all of them, the family, had been on one of those trains. Her voice ran out.

All of a sudden there was a fuss, and she thinks Mr Bellows said he'd look for her, and Summers was going through the old newspapers they used for lighting fires. 'It was Monday,' said Susan, 'that's when we first saw it, not that it'd happened then, Saturday it was. Thank the Lord none of us are Scots, I said.' Well Thursday's and Wednesday's had been burnt, and Tuesday's too, but Monday's *Times* was still there. Then Mrs Wainwright said, 'Let me,' and, 'For heaven's sake, someone give the girl a cup of tea.'

Mrs Wainwright opened the newspaper on the table and picked her spectacles up from the chain around her neck. She folded through the pages and then stopped, smoothing down the creases as though it were a dress. Grace could see her scanning the lines and she thought of Miss Sand and learning to read the Lesson out aloud. Read it through first, Miss Sand had said, so as you don't stumble on your words. Mrs Wainwright went on reading, more than just the first few lines. Then she looked up, took her glasses off and said, 'My dear, I can't read this out to you. I don't think you should read it, either.'

Grace's head was spinning with not wanting ever to see and wanting to read it right away. 'Now,' she said, 'if you don't mind, I'd like to look now.' They couldn't stop her, could they? The teacups were cleared and space made and the newspaper moved and folded out and pressed down in front of her and they all sat round her, as though ready to catch her if she fell.

She couldn't take it all in, just fragments like *worst ever*, and *more than a hundred dead.* And to think they'd been talking about it all week, Grace too. It had made her come over a little queer even then, before she knew. What with it being so close to Carlisle, the fire might creep all the way along the track to home.

'They'll be all right,' Mrs Wainwright was speaking dead soft, 'there are survivors, plenty of them, it'll just take a while for them to find their way home. Your brother's up there now and he'll find them in a trice. And some jumped clear.' Grace wasn't sure how far a nine-, ten- and twelve-year-old could jump.

Troop Train Disaster, five trains were in it, including the local one her family was on, she knows now. Her head was stew, words leapt out at her as she tried to read it. *Heavy death toll. Stated last night to be 158. The King has sent a telegram,* she read. Well, that's all right then, a telegram from the King must make things all right, but what's she thinking? It's the words that came after that which made her choke. More words. *Burnt alive. Scorched and charred. Little bundles of blackened bones and flesh.* And she turned to the side, right where Susan was beside her, and felt the contents of her stomach rising.

Grace was put to bed for the rest of that day, and told to stay there for the next. Yet when she woke up proper on that same afternoon, she dressed ever so carefully and went downstairs. She found Mrs Wainwright, who started to give her a telling-off for being up, not resting, but Grace begged to be given something to do. 'It'll keep those thoughts, Mrs Wainwright, from running all over my mind.' 'You're dressed for the morning, Grace,' Mrs Wainwright replied. 'Go and change before anyone sees you, and then you can sit down at the table and polish knives and forks.' Grace looked down at her skirt, blue print she'd put on, not black.

The following week the newspaper stopped mentioning it. Instead there were just lists of names of Mr Asquith's new Coalition Government, and the servants' hall changed to chatter about the politicians who came to the house. The Prime Minister of course. Mr Lloyd George too, with Mr Lansbury, even though he went to jail for women to vote. Lord Kitchener, that moustache, well, you couldn't miss him, not when he's on all those posters up and down the land, telling men to join up. Mr Bellows says she has them from all sides, Lady Masters. Grace took in not even half of it all. She couldn't think about Lady Masters' guests.

Still, they wouldn't let her alone on Sunday. 'You can't be worrying,' said Mrs Wainwright, 'I'll take you with me.' And they'd gone to church where Grace prayed so hard that she forgot to breathe, and had to steady herself on the pew in front, though she wasn't thinking of them as angels, wouldn't let herself do that.

Afterwards, she walked around the park with Sarah. When they came back, Grace pulled out the case from under her bed to go on with her sewing, a dress for Peggy, the eldest of her younger sisters, because if she goes on with the sewing for her then she must still be alive. Grace is making herself feel sure that they are, that Michael will find them, for Michael can do anything.

Next day Grace went to find Michael, to catch him before he came to her. There he was, eyes black like he'd not seen a wink of sleep. It was the train back down, he said, all night, and he'd given up his corner seat, the only one where you have a chance of sleeping, head leaning against the window. For a lady, he told Grace. Though, don't she dare call him a gentleman, he said, just because they do things like that. His chambers gave him an hour to see Grace; after three days off, he'd catching up to do.

Michael told her he had started in the hospitals in Carlisle, that's where they'd all been taken. He'd searched the beds for a woman, or a man without scraps of uniform, or a figure small enough. When he asked about those people he was told to go up the railway to Quintinshill; there was a farm building there and a village hall up the road at Gretna. Grace asked him whether they'd put together hospitals there like those field hospitals out in France. And Michael had looked away, the edge of his lip that she could still see curled in. When he turned back his eyes were like he'd caught flecks of dust, and he told her that everyone had been taken away by then. All the soldiers, they went to Edinburgh. There had been a woman and child, just one child, but a man had come to claim them. 'And they went with him?' Grace asked. Michael shook his head. They weren't going anywhere of their own accord any more.

The fire burnt for two days. The cries stopped, Michael's been told, not so long after the crash. Michael had been to the house, had to settle it, he said, before the month was up and the next rent was due. He asked the neighbours, just in case they'd all gone somewhere else. It was the early train, they all said, so as they'd be back by tea. The early train, and wasn't it a shame. Shame, too, that you need a body for a funeral.

Michael brought back for Grace Ma's silver-backed hairbrush that she'd been given as a wedding present and her glass bead necklaces, and the photographs for the two of them. The silver spoon too. He hadn't seen the point of anything else, no place to put the furniture. Besides, it was all he could carry on the train. She walked back to chambers with him and waited while he went in and came out again. Then Grace took the bus back to Park Lane, with all she had left of her ma and da and three baby sisters in a small brown paper bag.

And Grace's mind is again in the park with Michael the next Sunday after that.

They couldn't talk about anything that's not Them. But they couldn't talk about Them either, not without her eyes swimming. Her mind was off, drifting, wishing they had something practical to do, plans to make, a funeral, possessions not yet sorted. But it's all done, or will never be. She reached out her hand to find her brother's and rested it on his. It clenched into a fist below hers.

'I'll . . . I'll write,' she heard him say.

'Yes,' said Grace. Then she swallowed. She hadn't heard Michael stumble on his words since he came to London. But it wasn't that which was making her search for air, it was the realisation that she hadn't heard something he'd said. 'Best if I send what I can to you,' he continued. 'Leave you in charge, Office Girl.'

His fist still clenched, he turned to her stiffly and kissed a part of her cheek not shielded by her hat. Grace couldn't speak as it settled in her mind what he was doing. People kept passing; Michael didn't speak either. Then at last she found the breath to try. It felt as if she were reaching out to grab him and pull him back.

'What about all those things you've said, Michael? About the war?'

But her fingers caught only air.

He shook his head. 'I have to do something, after—'

'It wasn't the Germans that did it.'

'As good as. Anyways, what's the point in staying here now?'

Grace looked down. So what did she count for to Michael?

A year ago, it was, that Michael went, and now Joseph is coming to visit. Joseph who writes at least a dozen times as much as Michael, even though Grace sends so many letters to her brother.

Joseph's train goes in the morning, and he'll come by early this evening. Susan, bless her now only half-hard heart, told Mrs Wainwright that he'd been in such a hurry when he came last week that he hadn't had time to wait for Grace to return. So Mrs Wainwright has given Grace this evening off.

Let's hope he's not in a hurry for everything, Grace, Mrs Wainwright tells her. And Grace is a little taken aback. But it's with the best will that Mrs Wainwright's mothering her. Anyways, she's the only mother Grace has now.

Yes, Mrs Wainwright.

Thank heavens for Number Thirty-Five, for it's Grace's family now, even if the house is part dead, most of it dust-sheeted over. Miss Beatrice has been gone three months and Master Edward out there, too. Lady Masters comes up less and less, as though she doesn't want to see the house empty as it is. When she does, though, there's a dinner Of Great Importance, they are told, and the guests' names are only whispered around the servants' hall. It's us women, says Susan, she's trying to have more of us in the war, so that afterwards they can't say we didn't fight too.

As for the refugees, they've nearly all left; it was too far from the munitions', though Mussyur Durot, he's still here with his family, and well brought up they are. He was the one who could speak English and now the others have gone he doesn't look half so pale as he did when every word had to be turned by him. He was a businessman, he said, breweries, and more than one. You could tell that if you watched Madame Durot when she arrived, don't think she'd lifted a duster before. Now she's brandishing a broom in her fraying fine lady's clothes. Confusing the visitors, said Susan when she started. Makes it look like we can't do it ourselves. Her ladyship'll start moving us down to the country, and having us clean out the hospital as that strange house is now, and it's overflowing.

It's the telegrams that do the telling. Grace shouldn't have a kind thought towards Susan, not after all that business when she first arrived. But that's two years ago, more even, and though Susan still has the tongue of a snake, she has her own suffering now. The telegram didn't come to Susan; her sweetheart's mother was sent that. Then his sister came around to see Susan and she took to her bed for days, Grace sitting her up, making her eat, persuading her that it'll do her no good hiding away when there's all that life to distract her downstairs, Grace knows that. Though it's not as if Grace is much better. Sometimes she wakes up to sheets as though a river's run through her bed.

Then there's Summers; the boot boy found him out the back, curled over the piece of paper with James's name on it, which had come straight to him and it was only then that they realised James was his son. Explains why Summers was so mindful of him. Susan claimed that surely they all knew; it was obvious, just not worth mentioning. Grace doesn't believe that Susan didn't think it worth mentioning, not with James's mother not being married. Why Susan would've had it out in an instant, Grace tells Sarah. But perhaps, Sarah replied, Susan's sweet on him, don't you think? Was sweet, corrects Grace. No, says Sarah, sweet on Summers, I mean. Grace thinks about that, about an older man. Maybe they'll all be sweet on older men. There might not be any young ones left any more.

Whenever the doorbell goes and it's not the butcher's or the grocer's usual time, Grace stops and holds her breath. If it was about Joseph she knows she won't hear it straight. It's Mr Bellows, even Lady Masters, who'll get the news from his parents. It'll be a new hand on an envelope, thinks Grace. The post can make your stomach turn now.

*

Even Mrs Wainwright is to worry about at times. With Susan's sweetheart and James, Mrs W.'s face was so still, you'd've thought the news was for her. After James went she called Grace in, sat her down, and told her that Joseph was a good man, and gentle too. 'Not someone to turn your nose up at, Grace.' Grace puffed a bit at this. Turning her nose up? It was as though she should be grateful for anyone who showed a bit of interest. Mrs Wainwright watched her for a moment, then looked across the room at her sideboard and the picture-frame on it. 'I didn't,' she said, 'marry a man I should have once. And then it was too late.'

Whenever Grace is up in her room, she looks at the postcard Joseph sent her: the one of his troop ready to go. There he is, third row up, two in from the left, behind the ones sitting down.

Grace smooths down her dress. She's ironed it sheet-flat then shaken it into folds so as he won't be able to see the hand stitches she's had to put in up the side – for there's only so long you can have less worth eating without shrinking. He's seen the dress before, of course, but how's he to remember with all he sees? In his letters he says it's a fine thing to be playing a part, doing something for King and Country. And that's the doorbell – it's him and Grace feels a flutter of panic. She would have heard if he'd been wounded, but she still has a fear. She knows all about how different a man can look when he comes back to England, although she tells herself she's not one of those girls that might mind.

Susan and Sarah pull her up by the arms. Careful now, my dress, she says to them. They're not listening, they're bundling her into the hall and there he is. She looks up and sees that there's not a mark on him, thank the Lord, but there's something different about him all the same, and she's got a clenching in her chest.

He's as still as one of those statues down near Buckingham Palace, and looking at her as though tears are pushing to come out of his eyes with sadness so's you'd drown in it. No, thinks Grace. No, I can't have that. So she steps over to him, and touches his cheek. The skin is rough, and she flinches. He takes her hand in his.

'Grace?'

'Yes.'

'Am I really so different?'

There's a darkness behind his eyes, as though underneath that blue, the pupils just spread and spread.

'No,' she lies.

Then it's into the servants' hall for a cup of tea and news, and all the exclamations that go with it. After half an hour or so, the two of them are bundled out of the house with winks and nods. When they're standing on the street he says there's a tea room, near Victoria Station. And they walk along Park Lane, but with their eyes down, searching for the kerb. With no lights, says Grace, in case of the Zeppelins, you can't see whether you're in the road, and the motors can't see you in it. Not that there are many motors, streets are death quiet at night. As they walk Joseph keeps beside her and a foot away, like he's shy of touching her, and Grace wonders whether he won't put his arm around her, give her a squeeze that makes her feel a woman, and he should do that, especially as it's the first time he's seen her since Mrs Wainwright wrote to him about Grace's family. He wrote back to Grace time after time, saying as how the thought of it for her was near bringing him to tears, what with the sort of family they looked in their photograph, and how Grace spoke about them. Maybe it was all just words, thinks Grace, and she sinks a little. It can't be, though, she tells herself, it must be what's happened to him. Something's happened to him, for there's a silence between them makes the gap grow until, when they are by Buckingham Palace garden wall, Grace speaks into it. She wants to make a joke, but it's not there, so she asks a question, one that can cause no offence.

'Do you think it bothers him?'

'What bothering who?'

'Him. The war. The King.' Grace almost feels she should bob with the word, as they are so close to the palace.

'Yes,' replies Joseph. 'That's the point, isn't it, we're fighting for King and Country. Can't be any other reason to it.'

There's something harder, flatter, about the way he is speaking. Grace doesn't know what to reply.

He takes her to Pimlico. Just a place I've been once or twice before, he says, in the old days. He stops outside the tea room, and Grace's heart sinks a little for the paint is peeling off the sign hanging at the front, and there's a crack in the corner of a front pane. But she's with Joseph, she tells herself, what does it matter where they are? Only he isn't quite Joseph. Where Joseph's all soft, all boy, this man's like leather flapping in the wind. Grace isn't sure what she feels about this strange person beside her.

When he opens the door for her there's a rush of a smell that makes her hesitate. She's too used to Mussyur Fouray's cooking, even with all the potato flour he has to mix in with the wheat these days. They sit in a corner at the far end of the window. At least she and Joseph are facing each other now, and Grace stretches her feet out under the table so that they rest against his. Joseph doesn't move away. Then he talks to her about her family, that it's too terrible, but she's not to worry, she's a good future ahead of her, he'll make sure of that. Still this isn't quite what she'd hoped for, there's something that's missing from him, but when she turns a bit teary Joseph thinks it is for her family. Anyway, he starts to hold her hand, then he tells her that his elder brother has died, so the farm is his for going back to, and he hadn't written because he hadn't known how to tell her this terrible thing in the same letter as he told her about how different things would be. And he wasn't sure what she'd make of it, farming not being service and all that.

Grace sits there and thinks how sad Joseph must be, how she would be if it were news of Michael, but her mind can't go that far. At the same time she is thinking of sheep and cows and milk still warm without having to put it on the stove. That's all her hope in front of her now, and she tells him she is proud of him, which is true. A half-smile comes back to his face, then vanishes.

'Not much to be proud of.'

'One compliment, Joseph Salter, and you're asking for more.'

'There are a lot of' – he pauses – 'things I am not proud of at all.'

'Well, it's a fool can see his own virtues. You'll just have to take my word.'

'Your word, Grace?' He perks up.

'And what's wrong with my word, then?'

'Nothing, Grace. Nothing at all.'

It's like he's speaking a different language. But that's the war; when it's all over, the real Joseph'll come back to her. She can't hope for that baby face again, mind, there's part of him looks as old as Noah, and it's not just the moustache. But that's not going to stop her liking him. What's a little change to take away what she's been believing in, and what his mind must be full of, with that long journey to France tomorrow. So she tells him she's even proud of where he's taken her with its little tables, all wood, salt and pepper even, and just the two of them. Michael brought her here once before but she doesn't tell Joseph. Joseph knows about Michael, of course, but he's not met him. The war has given her that excuse.

'Can you afford this?' she asks, looking at the creased card in front of them.

'All three courses, Grace. There's no point being a rich man in Heaven.'

She turns her eyes down to the table. Just in case they fill at the thought of Heaven, who's in it, and who might be next. Joseph goes on talking.

'Thank you for wearing that dress, Grace. That's how I think of you when I'm out there. In that dress.'

After they scrape their plates, Joseph leans across the table and covers her hand in his again. It makes her feel safe. She's got him back, the Joseph she knows.

'Grace?'

'Yes.'

'Let's go for a walk.'

'Where would we go at this time of night?'

'The park.'

'We'll barely see our noses, let alone where we're putting our feet.'

'What a lark, then. Better not knock into a tree.'

Lord knows what she thinks, and what Joseph's thinking. But it can't be anything bad, for she knows Joseph, and she's to cheer him up, that's her bit now; that's what they're all supposed to do, make sure the men have a good time before they go back to fight for us. So if he wants a walk, then a walk it is, and she agrees it's a lark. They walk back up past the Buckingham Palace garden and into Hyde Park. There's enough of a moon to make it not totally dark.

He puts his arm around her waist. Nothing strange in that, he knows she likes him guiding her along by the waist, especially dressed as he is, all shiny belt and buttons. His arm is a little tighter than usual, though. Think nothing of it, Grace Campbell, she tells herself, but she starts to chatter as though she's putting the nerves out of her. She tells him about the kitchen maid with a nose like a potato marrying a man who came back without an inch of sight in his eyes. Now she's in Croydon, nursing him, though he can find his way round with a cane right enough. The two of them joined the servants for Christmas, her with a smile near broke her face.

But Joseph's read this all before in her letters, and her voice fades as she remembers. He's walking steadily and they're alongside bushes now. Grace doesn't look too close to the side, she doesn't want to see the branches move and people come out like she's heard they do. It's less bad here, though, than it was with them all on the streets, where they were before the patrols came. Then Joseph suddenly swings her round until she's facing him, and kisses her.

It's not their first kiss, but as a footman he couldn't have a moustache. The hair tickles her lips. Soft hair it is; some men look as though they've a scrubbing brush and their sweethearts must have faces raw as tomatoes. The kiss makes her feel warm and light-headed and she lets her shoulders go. Then he stops.

'Come on, Grace.' And he takes her hand and rushes forward, pulling her along behind. 'Let's cut through here.'

They're in a bush, and Grace isn't sure about this. The Joseph she knows wouldn't have taken her in here, it's not where proper people go, and Grace finds proper reassuring for it's set in its ways, so that you know where you are. He's kissing her again but this time she's not enjoying it for he's squeezing her shoulders as though there should be only an inch in between, and he's ramrod against her. Grace is feeling more of him than she should and his tongue is at the back of her throat. It'll have hers out with it in a moment. He pulls his face off hers and Grace feels a wave of relief but his body's still pushing, his head just over her shoulder, whispering in Grace's ear. 'Please, Grace, please. You can't imagine what it's like out there.' As he speaks she feels as though it's a stranger with her. This isn't Joseph, it's just some man come back from the war wanting what they all want, not wanting Grace in particular. Why she could be anybody, and Joseph, the Joseph that has kept her hoping isn't here any more. He goes on whispering, 'Please, please, Grace, for me, let me, just this once. Next time we'll marry, promise you that.'

Grace doesn't know that she wants to marry him, for the man in front of her isn't the strong one she'd hoped to spend her life with; he's a shell of a man who needs her more than she needs him. Now Grace is thinking of him as a poor soldier, and they're told to comfort them, the women here at home. And that's the only purpose Grace seems to have as she stands there, that's all she can give this man, she realises, not her hand, not her life, just the instant that he is breaking for. And this could be his, their, only moment, she thinks, tears beginning to come out of her again as she reasons how, how can I refuse him this?

20

IT'S SEVEN IN THE MORNING AND IT LOOKS TO GRACE like a riot's been in the billiard room. Good Lord, there's bottles on the edge of the table. What of the baize, if one of them fell? Better not knock one, Grace Campbell, and pick them off quick. She darts to the side of the billiard table but as she reaches it, she trips on a cue and catches the edge of the table with her hand, steadying herself. It's an accident waiting to happen, balls and the like left on the floor. What a state they must have been in. Still, it was Master Edward's last night, and a mess is better than a rain of gloom. She can whip through anything so long as there's no misery to it. They're all working hard now, to keep sadness away.

Joseph wrote to her soon as he was back over. A long letter it was, talking about their life together, and the farm and how wonderful it will be and how she, Grace, makes up for everything else. He doesn't make up for everything else for her. She wanted a rock, not sinking sand. War has taken Joseph from her, even without putting a piece of shrapnel in his head. Park Lane, with all its fireplaces and china and silver, is all she has to cling to. Grace has become one of those servants now, like Mrs Wainwright, their whole life turning round their employers.

The coals are not just hot, they're red still, and where's the shovel to sort things? There are waves of black dust on the hearth, and on the carpet, too. That'll need the Ewbank and some. Good Lord, the dust is halfway across the floor, maybe the shovel's at the end of it, thrown under the table.

The trail disappears under the valance hanging along the edge of the billiard table. Grace kneels on the floor and reaches under the velvet.

Somebody grabs her arm.

She screams, not a loud scream, more of a gasp. The grip is tight on her forearm. Grace doesn't move, hoping that if she's still as a mouse he – for it's a he for certain, with that strength – will let her go. Instead he pulls her arm further in under the valance.

She keeps her eyes shut as though it will shut out what is happening. Don't move, Grace, she says to herself, perhaps he'll think you've fainted. And what can a man do with a woman who's dead to the world? So she's still, and waits what seems like an age.

'Grace.'

It's Master Edward, and a part of her relaxes a little for she knows him. She opens her eyes.

'It is Grace, isn't it? Help me. Help me, Grace.' His voice is shaking as though he's weeping and then she hears the sobbing itself, for he is crying like a baby. His grip loosens. She could in fact break free from this man now, yet she doesn't. Some days it takes all Grace has got to stop herself sobbing like this too. Master Edward goes on shaking the words out, 'There's no one, there's no one who will understand!' Grace is suddenly frightened, not frightened as though she will be hurt, but frightened

'Stop it!' she shouts, then bites her tongue. You'll make him angry, Grace, and what will he do to you then?

Instead what comes are words so plaintive and desperate that they near make her cry with him.

'I can't do it any more. I can't go back.'

Grace doesn't want him to go back, she doesn't want a single one of them to go back, and not this person who is as alone as her. But he has to go back or he'll be shot. Why that should be suddenly makes her angry. This is a senseless, senseless world in which even children hundreds of miles away from the guns, on trains somewhere between Carlisle and Glasgow, die.

'Please help me,' he goes on. 'Help me to find the, the . . . '

'Courage,' she says. And now Grace is crying too.

'Hold me, Grace. Please.' He lets go of her arm and she finds herself reaching back out for his. She wants him to hold her almost as much, she thinks, as he does. His arm is limp and Grace feels a flutter of panic. She rolls on to her stomach and crawls, on her elbows, under the table. The curtain tassels knock against her as she crosses their boundary. She can feel his arms, his chest, but it is still, and panic flutters again in her. She runs her fingers up his breastbone, up his throat, curving over his Adam's apple and turning the corner of his chin.

Then she reaches up to his head, wraps her arms around his neck and pulls him towards her.

His cheek rests on hers and she feels the warmth of his tears. Then she turns her lips on to his skin and moves them gently across his face. It's comfort he wants. And it's what she wants too. She finds his lips and kisses them hard.

21

IT IS HOT IN BEA'S FLEABAG AND HOWEVER PROUD SHE is of her strength at the steering wheel, her arms and shoulders ache as though they've been pummelled. Her underclothes are soaked through. They'll just have to dry off during the day – it gets damn hot enough for them to, even here, on the northern coast of France. The heat makes everything smell worse, including herself. Ladies didn't sweat at the start of this war, but then they didn't dash around in thick wool uniforms at the height of summer. Now, well, she won't say what it's like, but you can hardly simply whisper 'perspiration' any more. It's the fear as much as the exertion that brings it on, though it's not always easy to distinguish between the two. Some jaunt this is.

Ladies' pretty bodies weren't livid with flea bites before the war either, especially ones where they have to sit on their hands to prevent themselves scratching the tops off. You can hardly sleep in that position, not unless you're on your stomach, fingers trapped under your hipbones, which is hellish hard to achieve given the sag on the canvas bed under her. She might as well be sleeping in a hammock. Bea examines her fingernails for traces of blood from scratched bites. There is a brownish gunk under her fingernails, and some smeared around the side; it could be from her, or . . . she doesn't want to think about that.

And there's no time to dawdle; she was woken by the whistle. She's had a full three hours' sleep and now she has five minutes until roll-call at seven thirty. Sharp. One slip and she'll be scrubbing the lavatory again. At first they all tried pulling their uniforms on over their nightdresses and pyjamas, but the commandant saw right through that. You could see your face on the lavatory floor for weeks afterwards, so many of them had been ordered to scrub it. Now they just fall asleep in their combinations so they're ready to go in the morning. They often fall asleep in everything they've got on. Too damn tired to do anything else.

Four minutes to go. Teeth. Bitter, bitter taste. Three minutes. Uniform, cold water again, get that red-brown mark out of the front of her skirt, if it hasn't set in there. Two minutes, hair and just enough time for the end of last night's cigarette as she finishes off. Smoking, that's one thing she's come to enjoy more out here. It kills appetite which, given what is on offer, is no bad thing. Now she has a cigarette between her lips as often as she can. In fact, she's downright irritable, they all are, when they're short of them. One minute left, make her bed. God, she longs to get back into it, and fat chance of that. How can it be this hard to straighten a fleabag? She shouldn't be in the warmth of a fleabag in summer anyway, but she needs it, she needs, for whatever small part of the day she can, to draw up a barrier between her and the outside world.

Bea glances across at the bed next door. The blankets are crooked, a hairbrush and pins strewn on them. She moves across to whisk them off before they are seen by the commandant. Watching somebody else being given some heart-grinding task is almost, but not quite, as bad as it happening to you. Bea hesitates. But it's not going to happen to Peggy, is it? That's what her real name was, though, snub-nosed and bright-eyed, she was known out here as Bunny. They all have nicknames, preserving their real ones for the life they will, hopefully, return to. Bunny, a decent sort, from Bromley, still eighteen.

Her truck turned over on the mudslide that passes for a road up to Hospital Number Eight. Just as good as being hit by a shell turfed out of the cockpit of a Hun plane, having to pelt lampless down that road in the dark to pick up the next lot. Plucky girl, they're all saying, as though it wasn't every one of them being damn plucky. Every damn night.

As Bea stands to attention, she can feel the bites on her thighs itch but she can hardly lean over and have a go at them now. Death is just about the only way out. That and septicaemia, dysentery or measles. Even spotted fever has its appeal. The next time Bea has somebody infected with it in the back of her truck, she'll climb in and embrace him good and long. And when she and the truck are disinfected, she'll simply pray the disinfectant doesn't do its trick.

Bea laughs to herself. So this, this is the big adventure she'd been longing for, the one that she had envied Edward, Tom, Edie's Tony and the rest of all those chaps who'd been khaki-ed and brown-belted and sailed over here. Even poor Mr Campbell, who had eventually written to her to explain why he had suddenly signed up. Poor man. Bea would be in pieces even if just Edward went. Now Mr Campbell is fetching and carrying on stretchers, and Bea doesn't envy him one bit; she sees quite enough of the mash of men who are ferried into the back of the truck. How had she thought that ambulance-driving would be glamorous? She'd had a vision of herself careering between shell-holes and swaggering back to the cosiness and camaraderie of barracks. At least that's the picture she'd put together from her love of driving and Edward's letters, all football and polo and jolly dinners in the mess.

The only faint resemblance this bears to what Bea expected is the driving at top speed along rutted tracks, and Bea has made sure that she is the fastest at this. Where the others slow down to take a pothole, Bea just goes hard at it, and flies her truck over the top. Her truck, Mildred she's called it, they're one and the same creature when they're on the road, Bea tries to let herself think of nothing else, not of the men in the back, who have names and families. That one of them might be somebody she knows. Might be Edward.

The loss of Bunny makes her feel hollow. Not any more wobbly than she is already, rather that a piece of the gang has been cut away and it could be anyone next. No matter that she's only ferrying the parts of men that are still breathing from the convoy trains up to the camp hospitals – the Hun'll get you if he can, even if it's only by willing a flat tyre at the wrong moment in the road.

For the men, death is the only way out. The men volunteer and are then sent back and back again until they are too ruined to fight any more. No funking for them or they'll be shot as deserters and cowards. When she hears the words 'This one's gone' as she reaches the hospital, she wonders whether she has done them the kindest favour she could.

She could be a funk, have herself written off as a spectator and say goodbye to all that baking heat and hunger and dirt. There is something demoralising about being dirty; you can't for one second imagine anyone, let alone any man, would want to come near you. It makes her feel she has lost the power she once had. She could be warm, dry, clean and being admired as she thwacks a tennis ball over a net, but that would be giving in. And not just on her own part. Every woman who gives in is another not making the grade, showing that women aren't up to it. However irritating it is that Mrs Pankhurst isn't campaigning for the vote any more, there's something in what she says, that we should all be mucking in, showing that women can do what men can do. It's more than just 'a fantastic job' they're doing out here, they could be killed at any moment. That, Celeste wrote to her, is what makes it worthwhile. When Bea first read this, she laughed, thinking, Damn you, Celeste. But Bea's found it again, that rush from doing something that has some effect on the world outside her old, petty life. Curiously, Bea driving ambulances is the one thing that Celeste and Mother have, unknowingly, agreed upon, even down to the same words. Bea has been bouncing between 'I'm so proud' coming from both directions, and Mother has sent over a surprising onslaught of letters.

Breakfast is reassuringly not good. This means that Bea is not dreaming. She can't work out whether she's strengthening her teeth on the bread or grinding them down. Whichever it is, she's too damn thin, she knows her breasts are shrinking. But out here they're not really women, are they, rather staging posts on the way between the two sexes. And always so damn hungry, unless what they've just seen is still making them feel green. Actually, breakfast itself can be enough to make you feel green. No matter, they'll be at the parcel contents afterwards, though food parcels have been thinnish recently, but not, however, parcels of carbolic belts sent by relatives to ward off body lice and other evils. Celeste provides enough to Bea for her to supply two of her room-mates. This is not entirely altruistic, for the fewer lice in their room the better. They say it's hellish difficult getting rid of the buggers, and that they're doing the rounds of London as well, among those who are being 'foolish', as Clemmie calls it. Though Bea suspects that this is rumour fabricated to try and deter the increasing loss of what Mother's generation call 'virtue'.

So Bea has carbolic belts a-plenty, but all too few bottles of Bovril and ginger biscuits. Not that any of them 'has' anything once it arrives. Everything is thrown into the ring and divided up, apart from the cigarettes. Bunny had two packets of cigarettes. They all know that and none of them are mentioning it. By the time somebody does, they will have been pilfered.

It is Mrs Wainwright who sends Bea food. Bea wonders if she realises that she is supplying almost all of Bea's diet. There are no army rations for volunteers. Although Bea is not sure that volunteer is an accurate description of young women who have to pay for the privilege of being out here. They just have Mrs Bell, whom Bea is sure scratches the flea bites on her arms over the mixing bowl, into whatever food she is pounding beyond recognition.

When Mrs Wainwright's parcels reach Bea they come up trumps every time, with the Bovril-to-drink standard fare, the biscuits Huntley and Palmers Best Assorted, together with roof tiles of chocolate. The top-notch stuff is the potted meat, which is served out among them 'like caviar', Razor cut in when Bea's first package arrived. Razor, her one-liners as sharp as her nose and chin. Bea was sure the caviar allusion was a dig at her and her family.

Masters is hardly a triple-barrelled rarity. But Blister – one complaint was all it had taken for the girl to be given that name, Bea learnt – had asked it straight out, in that reflex, cocktail-party-chat way. Bea, off-guard, must have reddened for there was a chorus of 'Ohs' and 'Are you?' and 'Hardly Park Lane here'. Razor was on to her straight away, 'Rails'. And it stuck.

Bea is first out into the yard. The ambulances still have last night's muck and a putrid stink inside them and when Bea opens the rear of her truck the smell of urine hits her first, and she draws away. Then she steels herself and climbs in, chucking buckets into the corners and trying to step out of the way of the stream running back out. It brings the vomit from the floor with it, the rest she will have to scrub off the sides. If it is vomit, it is bile, for by the time the poor souls reach Bea, bile is all they have left inside them. Lumps are something altogether different and there is a pile on the floor this morning that will not wash off as she sluices it. The water nudges it a little, unsticking the edges, but the centre does not move. Bea cannot tell its colour in the gloom inside the truck. She has little wish to tell its colour. Some poor bugger coughed his gas-ridden lungs up, or tore off his bandages on the way, letting the bits fall out. Bea is amazed at how much a human body contains: it's so densely packed that when the skin opens, all bursts forth.

Really this job should be done before breakfast. Bea wouldn't have anything in her to vomit then.

Her engine is still playing up. She's cleaned everything, put her arms right down inside and felt the satisfaction of reaching the nuts with long fingers that are nonetheless strong enough to turn them. But it still splutters, just when you need the oomph to push out of a hole. There's no point in saying anything; she'd be told to fix it, which she can't. She doubts anybody can, engines don't always work to rules. Instead she has become used to taking the dips a little faster. If you keep on going it's not too bad. It's the braking afterwards that throws it back.

The commandant is here. She climbs right into the back of Bea's ambulance, poking her nose where Bea barely dares to venture. Then she goes around to inspect the front. Bea's grille is, luckily, like a looking-glass this morning. The commandant pauses, as if she's caught sight of herself in it, and moves on. Pass. Bea goes back to her dormitory. There's a pause now, though they've not a clue how long it's for as more trains than ever have been coming in for the past month. The worst was at the beginning of July. It's almost the only way they know what's going on in the war. That, and out-of-date copies of the papers whose descriptions bear so little resemblance to what passes beneath their own eyes that, sometimes, they simply laugh.

One of the beds has a pair of scissors on it. Next to them sits a brown-haired girl who looks as if she'd pout given half the chance and is, as ever, pulling and pushing her locks about her ears. They laugh at her for this. She does this every day and more than once a day. She is therefore known as Hairnet. It's one thing if you're going into the town for the evening, but another altogether when you're driving the near-dead in the dark. What a waste, thinks Bea watching her, what a waste of time, and Bea checks herself. A year ago, she, too, would have done hers more than once a day. She gets the knots out some days, though mostly when she finally crawls into her bed she hasn't the energy to wield a hairbrush, and in the morning she just stuffs it up under her cap for roll-call.

She runs her fingers through her hair. Four inches out, they jam. She picks away with a comb but her hair, dried out by summer and dust, starts to break. Hairnet's scissors gleam at her. Bea wouldn't be the first, it's almost a badge of honour, provided that you don't think about the main reason for doing so. Nobody back home would put head lice and young ladies together in a sentence. No, they take short hair as *le dernier cri* for a devil-may-care gal who's game. Bea still hesitates; the shorter her hair, the harder she'd have to work at making herself feel feminine, and femininity is not a concept she feels close to at the moment. When she runs her hands over her face and body at night, she finds not the idolised softness of female flesh but a dry tautness, and those flea bites. Her hair is perhaps all she has left. She digs the comb in deeper, hoping that she doesn't scalp herself in the process. Christ, Beatrice, what the hell are you doing out here?

The evening's business starts early, straight after lunch, with an evacuation down to the harbour at Boulogne. The tide is kind today and it's not a four thirty in the morning start to catch it high. Bea's given Hospital Number Four as she leaves the yard; that's not too bad. Four isn't far, though there are a couple of hairy bits along the way. There's something to look forward to, the satisfaction of driving and the back-to-frontness of evacuations lightens the journeys. At least these men are going home – you just have to keep your mind off the wives and mothers who will be welcoming back their mauled bodies.

Bea drives up to the hospital empty, her behind settled into its familiar dips in the leather, evidence of all the hours she's spent on this seat. It's not quite rock, unlike the steering wheel, which is as hard as nails and thin as a rail. If it weren't for the cushioning of her driving gloves, there'd be little to hold on to. But she's off, and when she's on the road she can lose herself completely in the mere action of driving. She almost feels as though she's riding a mare with a perfect gait as she bounds up and down, steering hard to keep the truck on the track. Driving empty, and light, is pure pleasure, not as though she's doing any work at all. She wills her ambulance forward, and feels a surge of elation when it makes it over a particularly vicious hillock or rut in the road.

The voices are almost sing-song as they are loaded in, even if they are missing a limb or two. They're well enough to make the journey, and they're on their way back to Blighty. Anything is less bleak than being here. A growing number of craters pockmark the browning fields, like an unpleasant skin condition breaking out across them. Bea has grown used to the smell of fireworks. It lingers for days, it seems, after a raid. And the men bring it with them, explosive embedded into their wounds and uniform.

When they reach the ship, Bea walks to the rear of the truck, and is whistled at. Kisses are blown in her direction. She waves back, laughing with them at their gallows humour. Evacuations are definitely the best of the lot.

By the time she's back in the yard, a convoy is coming in and it's down to the station. When she arrives there, the train has ground to a halt half a mile along the line. Bea starts to mill around among the ambulances lined up, rears open to where the carriages will draw in. The stretcher-bearers are talking about being moved further forward. 'Could be our last evening with you,' says a weather-beaten man, a crescent grin spreading the width of his face as he grabs Bea by the arm and waist and pulls her into a mock waltz. Playing up to the scene, Bea tilts her head back and closes her eyes. The voice that comes, she thinks, is perhaps all the louder for the fact that she cannot see the speaker and it bites into her ears. 'Masters! Let go of that man. This isn't some dance hall' – she pauses – 'or a debutante ball. As you seem to have so much spare time on your hands, you can clean out my ambulance for a week.'

Bea manages a half smile at her dancing partner as she backs away. Goodbyes are best not said. See you soon is perhaps the worst: even in good times it can mean that you'll not see each other again. She clambers back up into her cab. New stretcher-bearers.

Who will replace them? The image of Mr Campbell comes into her mind. But what's the chance of that? And would she have heard, if he knew? He doesn't write often – even less than he did before she came out, when he was still sending letters to Celeste's. Then why should he write, it's not as though they are sweethearts. Maybe he has one, someone younger than Bea, fresh out, her face not yet ravaged by lack of sleep and the wind blowing through the front of a windscreen-less truck. With this thought Bea's elation subsides and she starts to look forward to the grim but distracting business of the train's arrival.

Even at the snail's pace with which the train crawls into the station, the screech of the brakes hammers in her ears. It's barely stopped when her ambulance begins to rock with the stretchers being loaded in. From what she sees it's hard to believe that many of them were ever alive in the first place, butcher's shop that they have become, served up on stretchers slotted into the sides of the truck. Bea's stomach turns. It turns with every convoy. When she arrived, a girl called Ginger – raven-haired, but ate a pack of the biscuits in one go – told her it would wear off after a couple of weeks. It will never wear off. For as long as Bea lives she will, she is sure, wake at night to memories of bloodied parts of men. She is sick at the whole damn war – and she can't let on; at twenty-three she's one of the older ones and the others look up to her. So she has to bottle it up, but it festers. Other things fester in her mind, too. Explosions have lost their glamour. She never wants to hear one again and she feels, well, downright shameful to think that she ever enjoyed it.

She's loaded, she's away. Number Six she's given at the gate, and it's down the track, the weight of the stretcher cases in the back adding swing to the bumps. She's already growing tired today, and she can feel each jolt hitting the base of her spine, or is it just the screaming from the back that is sharpening her senses? Even the wool pressed against her is grating her bites as the truck lolls forward and back and from side to side in jerky fits and starts.

She's trying not to listen – she must get the man now sitting beside her to talk to distract her. Body lice, thinks Bea, then tells herself off. But that's how we catch them, isn't it, wedged up against someone straight out of the trenches.

She glances beside her and the wind presses a loose strand of hair into the side of her eye as a splatter of grit stings her jaw. Bea is beyond wincing; at least, she thinks, it wasn't in my mouth. From what she can see of his uniform he is a corporal. He has one arm in a sling, the end of it looks thin for a hand, and his head is hanging down, chin practically on his chest. Screaming again from the back. They're a noisy bunch, this lot, except this man who looks as though he may never talk. But this trip she needs to crack him, and she is well provisioned to do so.

'Cigarette?' she asks. 'I've a packet.'

She glances to her side again. He nods, or rather she thinks it's a nod, it could just be a jolt in the road.

'They're wedged into the back of the seat. Behind you. Matches, too.' Thank God, she thinks, that his good arm is on this side, for he's fumbling for them as it is. He lifts the packet to his lips and taps a cigarette out into his mouth. Bea slows down so that he has a chance of lighting it. She shouldn't, she should be doing everything she can to reach the hospital as soon as possible, but if they'd damn well give her a windscreen she wouldn't have to. With impressive dexterity, the man manages to hold the matchbox between two fingers and the match between two others. He gets the cigarette alight and then offers it to Bea. Strictly forbidden, and Bea hesitates, then the noises racket up again, that last bump no doubt. She takes the cigarette, and he lights another.

He exhales, and with the smoke come words.

She doesn't mind any more how terrible his story will be, she's heard it all. She knows how a body can disintegrate in dozens of ways. Just keep on talking, she wills him, as the noises rise again. Makes her long for a funeral transport. A noiseless run, then five minutes' calm standing there, head bowed, as the service runs its short course and Bea wishes the poor man well in the peace he has found.

The sitter falls silent and she is listening to the screams again. Listening to them makes her want to slash the Hun. After all, that's what she came out here for, to do her bit in one of the few ways she could. Only she's not slashing the Hun, is she? She's as good as feeding it with the men she takes to be repaired so that they can be sent back to be fired at. Don't think like that, Beatrice, she tells herself. It's war, it's about being brave and taking risks, being as daring as you can, it always has been, hasn't it? She half laughs. Right now, being as daring as you can consists of smoking while she's driving, but the track ahead is smoother for a while and she puts her foot down. Sooner she can get this lot into hospital beds the better.

Number Six; she's arrived. Stretchers off, groans fading as the men are carried inside, and then she's back to the station as fast as she can, there'll be another load off this convoy.

It's about half past five in the afternoon when they filter back into the dorm. Blister is heating up Bovril on the gas burner. Bea lies down on her bed; every drop of strength has been shaken out of her limbs. Christ, is her fleabag still damp with last night's sweat? She closes her eyes.

That voice cuts in again. Sharp and shrill.

'Masters.' Oh God, the commandant's ambulance. So soon? But it hasn't been ambulance-cleaning time. Perhaps she's done something else wrong? It'll be another week now, and no doubt a week after that. She'll still be cleaning it at Christmas at this rate. Bea pulls herself upright, sitting, then standing. Her nose is almost touching the top of the commandant's cap.

'Masters.'

Bea nods.

'Out here.'

Bea follows her outside.

'It seems that you do have your debutante ball after all. You've been invited to dinner. His Highness the Prince of Wales needs some company to help him do his good works, visiting his subjects at war. Someone, unsurprisingly, picked your name off the list. You will be fetched at seven.'

The commandant turns to leave but comes back.

'You'll be on duty afterwards.'

Bea nods again. She is too tired to speak, let alone be company at dinner.

The others are still on their beds, nursing Bovril, and Bea hopes that none of them overheard. No potted meat will cure that envy, as misguided as it may be.

Bea is going to have dinner with the Prince of Wales in her uniform and boots big enough to break a wall. She starts to beat the dust from her jacket.

'Not in here!' Ginger yells.

Bea takes her dust clouds outside. She is not sure about dinners in the officers' mess. Last one, an older officer she knew from London – he'd been at Park Lane more than once – drove her back himself. As they passed what remained of the farm on the road between the town and here, he pulled off to the side, lights out, and without so much as a May I, leant over and kissed her. His mouth tasted of whisky and ash and she pushed away, but he pulled her tighter with one arm and started unbuttoning her jacket before clamping his mouth on hers. She screamed but that only opened her mouth wider. So she hit him, with the one arm not pinned to her side. Hit him harder and harder, on the chest, then the shoulder, the neck. At last she winded him and he drew back, gasping for air. When he pulled himself upright he looked at her as though she were the Hun.

'Well, not quite like mother, like daughter.'

Bea didn't reply.

He started up the engine again and drove her home, not looking at her once.

Bea sat smarting, as much at the slight of Mother as at his attempt to kiss her.

When they reached Bea's hut, he climbed out and walked round to open the door for Bea. She gave him a curt nod as she slipped by.

Thus, when Bea is driven back after her dinner with the Prince, she wedges herself at the far side of the seat from her escort. This time, she makes it to her hut intact. As she reaches the yard, the girls are starting up the ambulances. Bea is straight into hers and out towards the station.

Once she's going, the fresh air coming at her in the cab is an improvement on the fug and smoke of the mess. She does three rounds before she realises it is half past one. Her truck feels heavy, as though she's pushing against an ox and she'd really just like to fall asleep on its shoulder. Well, dinner was jolly. There were a couple of FANYs there as well and as she walked in, bottles of wine were beckoning from the table. My God, she was gasping for some and clearly so, for the Prince noticed, smiled and, with a flourish of his arm, said, 'Give Miss Masters a glass. She looks as if she might expire.' Bea felt as though she hadn't been shown gentlemanly good manners like that – the steady I-will-look-after-you sort – in an age. He was as charming as Edward at his best.

'Do you enjoy your work?' the Prince asked all three women. 'It's damn good of you all to come out here. Though it seems as though you manage a fine time, too.'

Six months ago these comments would have infuriated Bea, but tonight, indeed any night or time of day, she was simply grateful for being thanked. Perhaps it's because it has become clear that what she is doing is something genuinely worth being thanked for, rather than some fatuous task meriting fatuous praise.

Her glass was filled, and refilled each time she emptied it. She had forgotten how delicious a good red wine could be. But it was the food, it was the food that did it for her. Only beef stew, but meat distinguishable from its sauce, and what a sauce. Monsieur Fouret would be sacked on the spot if he sent this up, but it tasted better than anything Bea had eaten in months. How can you use the same word, eating, for that and what they're served up back in their hamlet of board huts?

By the time the meal was over, it was already nine thirty and Bea felt her eyes were going to close. It was stiflingly warm in there, and any breath she managed was filling with cigar smoke; quite a different proposition to Bea's cigarettes. Please let him go, she sat wishing, so that we can, too, and I have a chance of even just the shortest shut-eye before the night runs. Blast the tradition of not being able to leave before a member of the Royal Family, even out here. The more dire the circumstances, the more it appears people cling to etiquette. Just as she was thinking this, a trio of troopers entered, song sheets in hand. Oh no, how could she have forgotten: of course there was going to be an after-dinner show.

As Bea struggled to keep awake through half a dozen tunes, her mind turned to Edward. He claimed to spend his evenings like this, but it wouldn't make him safe, would it? Some of the men she has transported spent their evenings like this, too. It didn't mean they hadn't ended up on a stretcher. Dear God, she sat silently praying, dear God, please don't let that happen to him.

And then her thoughts are interrupted as a new train comes in to the station. Bea feels herself revving up, her sleepiness metamorphosing into a buzz as she reverses her ambulance in beside Blister's, turning to wave at her. The girl's face is drawn back over her cheek and jaw bones, as though she has taken a sharp intake of breath and it has stuck. She isn't looking to the side; she's rigidly facing forwards, as though she wants to see as little as possible of what is going on. Bea, thank God, is not there yet. She's loaded up faster than she's been before and the side of her truck is rapped to tell her to be off. 'Busy tonight,' yells a stretcher-bearer. And, relieved to be away from the terror on Blister's face, she is gone.

No sitters on this one, just Bea, out alone with half a dozen strange men. And no chaperone; she laughs to herself in the way that you only can when you're losing your reason, and things seem lighter, funnier, tonight.

A thud shakes the truck's rear axle, and a screaming starts up in the back. Hell, it's that ditch. No, it's not that ditch; the truck isn't stuck, it's still going. Bea's certainly got that awakening fear now; she can feel the sweat soaking into her hair under her cap. Had the ambulance fallen into that hole, there'd've been no pumping it out. The screaming is still going too, though it's not a scream, it's a yell, with words, the same words coming again and again. 'He's down, he's down. Stop, for God's sake.' Someone half off his head. You can't stop, you're not allowed to stop, you have to get them to a hospital as quick as you can for the sake of those who might still make it. More words are coming. 'He's off the rail, rolling around the floor.' Bea goes on driving but the yells worsen. 'He's down, I tell you he's down.' It's the same voice. 'Stop the bloody ambulance.' Bloody ambulance, thinks Bea, yes, in every imaginable way. 'Stop! Stop! Stop.' It occurs to Bea that maybe she should stop and, as gruesome as the prospect of manhandling a near corpse back on to its stretcher might be, she could save a life. It would not be so terrible to be sent home, either. Isn't that what she wants, a decent excuse? But she knows they can't spare her, rumours of what this job is really like are seeping back and the girls are sticking to Blighty now, working in hospitals. Lead-swingers. What would Bea say to her burstingly proud mother, Celeste, even Edward, if she went home?

The calls from the rear of her truck are going on, 'He's on top of one of us. Get him off!' They're all at it now, and what, what if they're right? There are hellish turns ahead. No matter what's been drilled into her, she can't carry on knowing that her driving is killing a man behind her.

She's passed the turning to Six and Seven and there's a flat patch on the side of the road. The commandant can't see Bea here. She won't be going this far for she always gets the nearest hospitals, and expects you to be just as quick even if you've been three times the distance. Bea pulls over, she takes a deep breath, climbs down, goes to the back and opens up. She hates this, looking in. Remember to keep your eyes away from the faces, Beatrice, for there's always that fear – that you've danced with one.

A stretcher in the middle row is empty. The man has rolled off it and is lying against one of the bottom stretchers, which is only just far enough off the floor to avoid the blood and urine. It is not far enough to stop the fallen man's torso covering the face of the man lying on this bottom rung. The latter's legs are flailing as though he's gasping for air. Bea's mind, slowly it seems, is taking it in. Then she leaps up inside and grabs an arm of the fallen man to pull him away. The arm comes off in her hands. She retches as she drops it, adding her own vomit to the cesspool around her feet.

The legs have stopped flailing. The man on the bottom stretcher is quite still. Bea can't look up at where she thinks the voice came from. Whichever he is, he's fallen silent, too. There's just one still groaning 'Help me, Mother' up there.

Bea turns and jumps out, jarring her knees, and rushes back to the cab. She left the engine running, thank God, she's not going to be a damn fool who finds it can't start again. For hell's sake, Beatrice, get moving.

It's fallen quiet as she leaves Nine. But empty she can drive faster, as fast as she dares, keep that fear going, keep her awake. After all she's Beatrice Masters, proving that she's not just some little rich girl by being the fastest on the road. She knows every bump, she could do it blindfold, and she might as well be blindfold when there's no moon and she's driving in the dark without her lamps on. She shuts her eyes for an instant, just to see what it is like. There is, she concludes, little difference, even if there is a flicker of a moon tonight. Cigarette, yes, she'll have a cigarette. She slows down to light it and as she draws breath she feels a rush and exhales as though she is a dragon breathing fire. The cigarette sits in her right hand, which is only barely resting on the wheel. Now put your foot down, Beatrice, to make up the time. There's that pit she detests coming up. Dammit, she thinks, I'll have the better of you and she ups the throttle. But she's fumbling almost, what is wrong with her? Blast, that's too much. The ambulance bucks and skids forward on its rear wheels. One catches in the pit. At least she thinks that is what is happening as the truck turns on to its side and off the track.

Blackness.

1917

22

BEA IS PACING THE BALLROOM OF DARTMOUTH HOUSE brandishing a mop which so reeks of disinfectant that it makes the back of her nose feel like a well-scrubbed bath. Little wonder, she thinks, that the men are coughing in their rows of iron beds. It's not just the gas over there that's got to them.

Mopping is at least physically active, even if she's not the best at it. She thought it would take only a couple of months for her arm to heal, and she'd be back over the Channel. But not a chance that she could take the weight of the steering if she's still one-handed with a mop after a year. At least the arm's there, though, and thank God it's her left. Jolly close shave, old girl, they said when she woke in Number Nine. That's funny, she thought when they told her where she was, I left here. I'm sure I was driving away. Maybe they've called me back for an evacuation. Once they've loaded my truck they'll put me back in the cab. Then she lost consciousness again.

Sometimes she tries to persuade herself that it was damned bad luck. After all, it was just one of those dents in the road. Oh, the excuses were there. The engine wasn't up to it . . . But serves her right for not owning up to the fact it wasn't in perfect nick. That was just it, Beatrice Masters, you thought nothing could touch you, and now you are paying the price. Cripple, that's what you've made yourself, and you might as well be a funk and a coward.

The only way to make sure that she hasn't been a funk is going back. In a couple of months some of these chaps will be bandages off and on the boat over, having been cleaned for, washed-up for, even fed by Bea, former woman of action and now ever-patient member of the Voluntary Aid Detachment. She misses each one. Not least because they're too grateful for the forkfuls she slips into their mouths to care if she's now holding the fork like a spoon.

Bea starts to sweep the mop across the floor in grandiose gestures. She's almost humming. Today is a good day: Edward is coming home on leave. Only on leave, but still home. And he always makes her feel a dazzler, whatever form she's on. Just the afternoon to get through first.

It's the limbs that simply aren't there any more that are the worst here. Don't look or you'll see the saw marks, Ada Milton rattled out on Bea's first day. Ada, who'd learnt the social niceties with Bea and Edie at Miss Wolffe's, and who had once fainted there when Edie cut herself on the flower scissors, now doesn't flinch at a thing.

Bea flinches, not just with the gruesomeness, but the terrible, terrible sadness, especially each time she's asked to see what she can do about an itch on a leg that is no longer there. At first Bea lifted the sheets and scratched away at where a foot should have been. They couldn't feel her hands; well, of course they couldn't, what was she thinking of? They'd ask her to move her fingers this way and that, and scratch harder until either they realised, or Bea's eyes gave it away. Then they'd fall still, looking so deep inwards that Bea thought their eyes would suck her in too. Now, when she's asked to scratch, she just squeezes a hand and promises that it will go away.

The holes come in every part of the body. She's seen a man who has lost his behind; the other VADs joked about being asked to scratch it, though nobody laughed aloud. No point in their conversation giving the nurses something else to complain about.

They seem to delight as it is in sending the VADs after the bedpans. Bea tries not to think about what she's cleared up, but there's no time for prudery, it's all matter-of-fact. Bea sees parts of men she hasn't seen before, inside and out, and many in a state that she hopes she'll not see again.

As she manoeuvres the mop she taps a bedframe and the occupant reaches forward with his hand. Nurse, nurse. Bea walks around, taking mop and bucket – Sister would murder her if she left it at the end of the bed. She gives the man her hand, her good hand, and he grips it.

'I'm not a nurse, Captain Peters, just a VAD.' Need to put that in quick. She doesn't want to be done for masquerading.

'Oh, yes, I know your voice. It's Masters, isn't it?'

'Yes,' says Bea, 'yes, it is.'

Nothing wrong with his eyes, the doctor says, yet he can't open them. Sister Adams suggested packing him off to one of those hospitals where none of them are quite right in the head any more, but Lady L. came straight down on her. If he goes home, he can be looked after perfectly well, blind or not. But the letter sent to that home was returned, *No longer at this address* scrawled across it. He can't stay for ever, can he, said Sister Adams. It's my house, replied Lady L. So he has stayed. He's a handsome man, Captain Peters, if only he would open his eyes.

'Miss Masters and the pianist's hands. Will you play for me one day?'

'Yes, I will,' lies Bea, thinking that he would have to be deaf, rather than blind, for her to pass muster on any instrument.

'It's wonderful, isn't it?'

'Yes.'

'The smell . . . '

'Yes.'

'Cut grass. Dampened by the morning dew. Is there anyone on the lawn? They'll have to wait until it dries before they rake it up.'

Bea hesitates, but gentle lying seems to be a part of nursing.

'Yes, they will.' She gives his hand a squeeze.

'But the sun's out, isn't it? It's on my face. It'll dry quickly this morning. Mind you don't let your pretty skin burn. You're fair, aren't you? Your skin feels like that. Tell me what birds you can see. I hear them, but I'm no expert.'

'Nor am I, and they are hidden.'

'Hidden?'

'In the bushes.'

'Rhododendron?'

'Yes,' she answers.

'They must be in flower, now that it's late May. What colours? White is my favourite. Rather unoriginal, I know. And a little funereal.'

But Bea can't reply to this. Not even to tell him that it is September.

When Bea walks back into the hallway of Park Lane at six, Edward is already there. At least the shadow standing in the middle of the wide hall has the name of Edward, the same height, and resembles him as much as a shadow can resemble anyone. The circles under his eyes and his complexion match the black and white of the marble he is standing on bolt upright, looking brittle enough to fall with the touch of a forefinger. His voice, when it comes, is surprisingly full. A little too full, as though he is used to shouting to be heard.

'Lit-tle sis!'

The old joke, from when he passed her in height as they grew.

She doesn't rush up to him, fearing that she might crush him. So he walks towards her, puts his arms under her shoulders, lifts her up and, his neck taut, swings her round, her feet skimming the kit bag on the floor beside him.

'We shall make merry, dear sis.'

Then he pulls her up to him and squeezes his cheek into hers. The stubble grates on her skin, but it is him, not her, who pulls away.

'Sorry, forgot to shave this morning, damned rush for the boat, and a trench habit. They seem to have us down there more than on our horses, well, what horses are left. What do you think of the tash?' He puts her down, takes a couple of paces back and poses on each side. 'Pretty fine, eh?'

It must be that which is making him look so much older. But then he is hardly a boy any more. Sir Edward, even, since their father keeled over somewhere between roulette and vingt-et-un in the South of France.

'Yes, pretty fine.'

'A man needs a moustache at twenty-two, my dear, and in charge of his own merry crew.'

'How long have they given you?'

'Two joyous weeks. I shall dance until the early hours, and see every show in town. And you shall come with me.' He takes her hands in his and starts to sway her round the room. 'Will they spare you, all your patients?'

'I don't think . . . no, it's not the moment. Edward, you need a bath.'

'I'll take that as it was meant. What are we up to tonight?'

'Tonight? I thought—'

'Fourteen days, Bea. Can't afford to waste even one.'

'There's dinner with Mother, she's coming up to town to see you. Clemmie will be up tomorrow.'

'Mother's here, I've seen her, and good it was. Near squeezed me to suffocation and I must have been dreaming it but I thought she was going to cry. Mother's never cried in her life, I don't think. Half expected her to appear with straw in her hair in her new farmer life but I suppose she's holding sway over the hospital in the house too, and she looked as though she'd never left a drawing room. What about after dinner? Come on, sis, you can't put a soldier early to bed.'

He looks half dead but there's a desperate energy to her brother that is infectious. An hour ago, when she was still cleaning up at the nursing home, the last thing she felt like doing was dancing. Now the look on Edward's face makes her feel a jittery need to go out for the evening.

'There's one of George Moore's—'

'Dances of Death?'

'If you must call it that.'

'It'll be the last show for some – and it's not what it used to be.'

'What?'

'Death.'

Bea calls for a maid to help her dress. She misses Grace. Blast her for having vanished overnight last year. Bea needs help until her arm is better, at least with all the evening's hooks and laces. The dress she's had airing is far too plain for a dance, even in wartime; perhaps the emerald tunic instead. It is autumn after all, though everyone's behaving as though the news of the latest surge forward means they're skipping winter altogether this year. Oh, Beatrice, jolly well fix on what to wear so you can show your brother a good time. Bea settles on a dark peacock tunic but hesitates over her pantaloons. In fact, she always hesitates over her pantaloons. Bought with a flourish, and brought out almost every time she is deciding what to wear, they have all but once been put back. She bought them as soon as she was up and about after the accident; a statement that, even though she was out of the action, she could still do what the men were doing, in her own way. However, they don't want that, the men, when they come home: they want women to be as pretty and feminine as possible. Moreover, Bea needs to make up for having a bad arm. She settles on a long chiffon skirt to wear underneath the tunic. Sarah hooks her in, and Bea goes downstairs to join Edward and Mother.

The Ritz dining room is full of young people. The three of them squeeze on to a table for two between the windows, as if emphasising the awkwardness of having Mother with them in a place so full of youth. Edward pushes out jollities in between visits from other diners. It's ripping, he says. Just you think, what an adventure I'm having. Never know what's up from one day to the next. Just when you reckon you might be bored – though when we're not in the Line we keep ourselves damn busy with all sorts of matches – we're all turned around again to go back in. Tests every bit of my wits, keeps my head ticking over.

'Well, it's terrific,' says Mother, 'that you are out . . . ' Bea thinks she hears Mother's voice falter, but surely she is imagining it for Mother is steaming on, 'there. If I didn't have a farm to run to feed the country, I'd be up to my knees in dirt, helping pull wounds together.'

They work their way through dinner and step back out on to Piccadilly, scarcely lit by the dim, blue-painted streetlamps. A couple of cars pass, looking lost in the width of the road. Then it is quiet again.

Summers is waiting patiently in the Rolls. Mother hesitates on the pavement. Where are you going, she asks? George Moore's. Oh. For a moment Bea thinks Mother is going to declare that she would like to accompany them, and a dread of being thrust in front of single men by her rises in Bea.

'Coming too?' asks Edward.

'Oh, no,' Mother replies, 'I, I . . . '

'Where are you off to, Mother dearest?' asks Edward. 'Perhaps it is more exciting than where we are going.'

'No,' replies Mother, almost too quickly and firmly, then brusquely, 'I'm just going home, Edward.' She moves towards the Rolls, and Summers is out and holding the door open for her. She climbs in and Bea sees her tapping the rear of the passenger seat with her umbrella, and Summers steadily, but immediately, drives off.

'She could have offered us a lift,' says Edward. 'She was awfully short just then, don't you think?'

'Perhaps she was late.'

'To go home?'

Bea is silent. She doesn't know whether to be amused or irritated by her brother's naivety.

'Not a taxi in sight,' he continues.

'Never is. Gold dust.'

As they turn off Piccadilly into the side streets, the streetlamps thin and it darkens further. The two of them fall into a contented silence as they walk, Bea keeping her eyes on the kerb. How long will it be, she wonders, before this all brightens up again?

'By God.' Edward suddenly breaks the quiet. 'Isn't this Celeste's?'

Bea stops and looks up. Her mind must have been miles away. They are, indeed, opposite Celeste's front door, and Bea's by here almost once a fortnight, if only to see whether Mr Campbell has written to her. Slivers of light are peeking through the black-out curtains.

'Haven't seen the old girl in an age. Wonder what she's up to?' And before Bea can make any other suggestion, Edward is across the road and ringing the bell. Bea follows him, hoping to God that her aunt is not in. She wants Edward to herself until they reach the dance.

Celeste's front door is answered not by a maid but by a clearly drunk young woman, cigarette holder in her hand. She looks them up and down, her eyes resting upon Edward. 'Come in, darlings,' she says. 'Haven't a clue who you are, but you are most invited to join the fun.' And from upstairs, Celeste's drawing room, comes the sound of dance music and guffaws. Bea's heart sinks. Edward will want to go up there, and then they will be stuck. At least you can move around George Moore's dances. And then it occurs to her that, quite possibly, Celeste might not be at home.

'Is Celeste here?' she asks.

'Not yet, darlings, not yet, but she has absolutely prrromised to come later.' The woman rolls her 'r's. 'At least,' she continues, 'I suppose it's her bed she'll come back to.' Then she shrieks with laughter at her own joke. Bea, to her relief, sees Edward recoil. They make their excuses and back away into the dark calm of the streets.

Even though they walk, they arrive early and the band hasn't started yet. They watch the other guests drift in fragments of familiar groups, more women than men, most of the latter either in uniform or clearly scarred. More than one is missing a limb. The tables are as usual covered in white lilies that could be a little less wreath-like; the talk is, however, upbeat. Well, it always is, for nobody can say the words they actually think. That is, if they can't stop themselves thinking.

'What ho. Why, if it isn't Beatrice, Clemmie's younger sister.' The voice comes from over her shoulder and she turns. The skin on the right half of the man's face looks as though it has been stewed and his nose is at an angle. She does not recognise him, something else she can't say.

'Hullo,' she says.

He holds out a hand.

'It's Flipper Braithwaite. D'you remember? Down at Gowden and, well, about the place.'

He's half the size he was. His remaining cheek is still as red, though, this time as if it has been burnt and then frozen that way.

'Of course I remember you, Flipper. It's good to see you.' This she means, for it is good to see any of them; you can hardly think a man an oaf any more.

'So how's your sister?' He pulls out a silver case, takes out a cigarette and offers Bea one. She shakes her head, for it will keep her there for as long as she takes to smoke it, and replies, 'Oh, Clemmie's fine. Turned one wing of Gowden into a Land Army base, and another into a hospital, sheets flapping from the windows. Spends a good deal of her time keeping the almost recovered patients and the girls apart.'

'And Tom?' Flipper taps his cigarette on the case.

'Still going strong. How long are you here for?'

He looks down, and now rat-a-tats the cigarette on the box.

'Been here the usual couple of weeks.' As he moves the cigarette to his mouth, his hand is wobbling. 'Back at the crack of dawn.' He pulls, equally shakily, a lighter out of a pocket, lights the cigarette and takes a deep draw before exhaling and looking back up. 'Of course it'll be good to get back to the action. Now the Boche is on its rear foot, and with Americans on their way, it'll be hard to get a look-in soon. Better make the most of it.' He smiles at her, and Bea feels herself soften. She wonders how much it hurts his face to smile.

'So, how's your horse?' he continues.

Bea laughs. She hadn't thought of him as droll before, there's hardly a horse left in the country. 'Replaced by one of the donkeys not yet whisked away to France,' she replies. Head tilted, he laughs at her joke. Bea feels a surge of confidence. 'Come on,' she says, nodding towards the ballroom, 'the band's going. Let's have a turn before you flee.' Maybe Clemmie was right all those years ago, Bea thinks, Tom's friends weren't so terrible. Although maybe it's not that, it's just that they are not so terrible now. Even so, she's not sure she could ever bring herself to kiss what remains of Flipper's face.

On the way back, and flushed from turkey-trotting, Bea passes Edward. He isn't dancing. Nor is he flirting with the throngs of women. Instead he appears locked in conversation with a young officer in a corner of the room. A couple of girls hover nearby hopefully, which is not surprising for Edward's friend is the spit of one of those muscular statues in the museum back at home. As, perhaps – and of course Bea would think this, and a little proudly – is Edward, even as the ghost he has become. However, it doesn't look as if there's going to be any gentle butting-in for the girls. The two men are fixed on each other, in some shared world of warfare, no doubt. Well, dammit, she's going in, she's his sister and he can't spend his leave talking about being back there. Bea strides over and takes her brother by the arm.

'I could ask politely but instead I think I'll just insist you dance with me.'

The conversation stops suddenly. Bea turns to Edward's friend. His eyes look at her, hard. Go away, he seems to be saying, you are not wanted here. Bea looks straight back at him. How dare you, she thinks. It is Edward who breaks the silence.

'I'm sorry, old chap. Women nowadays. We only have to turn our backs for an instant and they transform into huntresses . . . '

'Edward!' She glares at him, but he is laughing.

'Just kidding, sis. Beatrice, may I introduce my dear friend Captain Charles Finers to you? He's been here a fortnight. Back over in a couple of days. Charles, this is my sister, Beatrice. And I'd keep a wide—'

Bea, quite deliberately, steps on Edward's toe just as Captain Finers' right hand reaches out for hers, taking it. His look has now softened, and he places his left on top.

'Enchanted.'

'We were saying,' says Edward, 'that even the wrong sort of chap is showing his mettle over there. Makes you feel a sight differently about those fellows.'

There's something to this line of conversation that Bea finds sticks with her. It would be easier if she could, but she simply cannot bring herself just to nod along with it. She looks down at the floorboards.

'Well, Bea?'

'I don't know what you mean by the "wrong sort of chap". What exactly do you mean, Edward?'

'You know exactly what I mean, Bea. Somebody you wouldn't invite to the house. Except on their business, of course.'

'So Mother has been filling her drawing rooms with the "wrong sort of chap"?'

'Politics is their business, Bea.'

'But it's not always politics,' she blurts out, and then wishes she could swallow the words back in, for Edward is looking at her a little confused. 'Sometimes,' she rushes to continue, and not as confidently as she might like, 'it's just a good meal.'

Edward doesn't flag. By two, Bea's eyes are closing and she is counting the hours until she has to be up again, uniformed and at Dartmouth House. Really, she should take a break from it while Edward is home. Sister Adams, however, might simply replace her with one of the VADs who are near lining up around the block to work there, and Bea would be out of having anything to do at all.

'You look all done in, sis. Let's get you home.'

'You're still raring.'

'Used to it, old chap. The Hun starts up his concert performance at bedtime.'

When they are in the street, he crouches down, beckoning her behind him. 'Want a ride on my shoulders, sis?' She laughs, and swings her evening pouch at him.

'Whoa, stop assaulting an officer. What's in there?'

'Oh, powder. You know.'

'So we're quite the painted lady now? I was thinking you looked rather soignée.'

'Fine time in the evening for the compliment.'

'Well, don't take it then.'

The streets feel even sadder than before. As they wander on, Bea slips her arm through her brother's and falls quiet.

'What's up, Sweet Bea? All well at the nursing home?'

'Oh, yes, fine. Absolutely ripping.'

'Don't trouble yourself over it.'

'Over what?'

'Not going back. Nobody thinks you're a lead-swinger. And look what you're doing now. We couldn't do it without you.'

And even though she's a country away from the Front and just mopping floors, these words no longer bother Bea.

They reach the door. Bea takes out a key. 'Look, wartime living. I let myself in at night.'

'Not even a maid to do it any more? Where've they all gone?'

'They're here, Edward, just fewer of them.'

'That's what I mean. What's happened to the ones that are missing, like that girl you liked, Grace?'

'Oh, I don't know, she simply vanished one day last autumn, didn't even leave a note.'

'Nothing?'

'Nothing.'

'Oh,' he replies, and falls silent for a moment, which strikes Bea as a little odd.

She turns the key and puts her shoulder to the door.

'Heavy as iron,' she murmurs. 'I bet it would send the shells bouncing back. Always a challenge at the end of the evening.'

She walks into the hall. A light has been left on for them. As she goes ahead she realises that Edward's footsteps aren't following her and she turns back to him.

'Might pop back, old girl. There's still some life in me yet. No time to miss a minute of fun.'

He blows her a kiss, and closes the door behind him.

23

BEA IS THERE FIRST. SHE HASN'T BEEN IN THIS TEA room for two years, and never before at lunchtime. There are cracks in the window panes that have not been mended, and the tablecloths, the walls, appear more stained than she remembers. Even after her months in France, the smell steaming through the kitchen door is damper and less appetising than before. Well, hardly a soul has anything decent to cook with nowadays; not that the food was ever anything but grim here.

Will Mr Campbell have changed? Everyone changes out there, including her, the Beatrice Masters who can now sit silently by a man's bed without itching to move. But it's not something to think about, oneself, you can't look at yourself any more apart from in the context of the war and what you are doing for it. Maybe that's all Bea has become, just a part of the war effort, its exhaustion and suffering and grief, and the simply going on, even when she's in the Ritz dining room with silk flapping on her ankles. Every time she's been there in the past month, memories of her dinners there with Edward flood her mind. Come back soon, she almost wishes out loud.

She doesn't see him come in, and suddenly Mr Campbell is sitting opposite her. He is still black-haired, strong-jawed, but his uniform bags across his chest as though he is melting away. When she looks into his eyes expecting to find that old darkness, it is gone. Instead they are sharp and worried.

They don't speak. They just look across the table at each other, his hands knotted on the top of it, Bea's underneath, on her lap, and neither of them asking How are you? For the answer will certainly be a lie.

Then Bea talks.

'It's good to see you.'

At first he doesn't reply, just nods. Embarrassed by the silence, Bea looks down and to the side. Then he speaks.

'Been a long time.' His voice hasn't changed, and its deepness sends a familiar rumble through her.

'Two years.'

'Decade, could be.'

She doesn't understand, and looks back at his face. The decade is there, lines fan out from his eyes and run in creases across his forehead. Edward and the other men she knows have not grown this much older.

'Is it so bad what you do, so different? From the others, I mean.'

Again he is still, then pulls over a smeared menu card lying on the table and looks straight down at it. As Bea watches him, his face whitens. Then he pushes the card away.

'Not a conversation good for the appetite.'

Their cups of tea come, and Beatrice's is placed to her left. She can't reach across with her good right hand, so thinking fingers, fingers, keep the wrist straight, she raises it with her left. It's not strong enough, and the cup wobbles, tea-stained milk adding to the growing map on the tablecloth.

'What's wrong with your arm?'

'It's just for a little while,' she says, too quickly, forcing a smile on to her face, but his eyes have sharpened further.

'I don't believe you. Show me.'

Bea doesn't want to show him, but he's staring at her, telling her with his eyes just to do it. She puts her gloved hand on the table, trying to straighten her wrist and fingers. He takes it in both of his hands and turns it over surprisingly tenderly, and Bea feels the stiffness in her melt a little.

'You wrote that it was a small thing.'

'Compared to' – she hesitates – 'compared to out there. In any case, a hand is small.' She smiles at her wit, and glances at him for approval. Mr Campbell is looking at her almost as though he has tears in his eyes.

The park, he says when they finish, let's go to the park. Not a museum, nor the cinema. Not back into darkness. What he wants to see is green, and up to Hyde Park Corner and to the park they go.

They walk alongside each other and she tells herself that she's relaxed with him, even if she flushes a little each time they pass a couple with their arms locked. Out of embarrassment, Bea keeps hers pinned to her sides. Not that Mr Campbell is the type to offer his arm. But Mr Campbell today, she feels, might do anything.

As they enter the park, Bea pulls west towards Kensington but Michael is marching straight on and up towards Marble Arch, alongside Park Lane. This way, he says, better view of the houses from here, like great ships they are, floating along while everyone else is drowning. Yes, says Bea. It must seem like that.

'Not that you live far away. That address of yours.'

'It's not my address.' This at least is true. It is Celeste's house. 'It's just my mother,' she continues. 'Such a hoo-ha about the prospect—'

'Are there many prospects?' he butts in. 'Young gentlemen with an income and the possibility of a future.'

'According to you, young gentlemen will have no future at all.'

'Remember that, Miss Masters.'

Still she worries whether he does know where she lives and is just testing her, or whether she'll flinch as they pass her home and he will guess. She must be a little unsteady for as they draw up alongside Number Thirty-Five, she slips on a wet leaf and for the first time in over three years, since Glebe Place, his hand is on her arm again.

He pulls her upright, and she feels the warmth of his body, and a strange light-headedness with it. When she has steadied her feet, she looks up. Mr Campbell's face is but half a dozen inches from hers, looking down at her more tenderly than she has ever thought he could feel. It is Bea's turn to be still, for a moment. Later she will tell herself that her head must have still been spinning from her skid, and that's why she kissed him.

His lips don't move and Bea jerks back, her eyes already wet with embarrassment, but he catches her again, holds her and kisses her as angrily as she should have expected.

There are voices in the drawing room when she passes. She walks in to find Clemmie, and the back of a head with short fair hair next to hers on the small green sofa.

It is Clemmie who sees her first.

'Bea-Bea!' she exclaims as she pulls herself up.

The man, now upright too, swivels round to face Bea. He is slightly flushed. Bea does not recognise him.

'I didn't think—' continues Clemmie.

'No,' interrupts Bea. 'You didn't think. Either of you.' And she stands there, eyes fixed on the pair of them as the man straightens himself and mumbles, 'See you at dinner, I suppose,' and walks out, nodding to Bea as he passes.

Clemmie has already lit a cigarette.

'Don't look so horrified, darling. It's wartime. The war effort, you could say. Tom's been away such ages. They need something, you know, not to mention we do . . . ' Clemmie pauses and stares back at her. 'Oh, Bea, don't be such a prig. You're behaving as though you're still a virgin.'

*

Bea lies on her bed, surrounded by green creeper and red velvet, and thinks about Clemmie's remarks. Is Bea really being sanctimonious, do the rules change that much in wartime? Think about it, Beatrice, think how much they have already changed for you. When, before the war, would she have leant forward and kissed a man before he had tried to kiss her? She may like to think that she had it in her, but she didn't do it. Yet this afternoon she had not been embarrassed by kissing Mr Campbell, well, not once he responded.

Yet, God, what has she done? Mr Campbell is a law clerk, the sort of man whom she should not even know, let alone kiss. The more enjoyable it was, thinks Bea, the more hideous her situation is. Clemmie may talk about breaking the rules but Bea will wager she hasn't even imagined anyone going this far. She wants to say Never see him again, and that would obviously be the simplest. Or maybe it would be enough that Mr Campbell will say, as he surely will when she sees him on Thursday – and how can she not turn up now – that Monday was the most terrible mistake and they should forget it immediately. And that was what, in the very least, they would do.

Bea is pushing open the glass-panelled tea-room door at twenty past eleven in the morning, feeling nauseous even before the smell has hit her. The memory of what she did is becoming more, rather than less, embarrassing. He had wanted to kiss her, hadn't he? After all, he did kiss her back, and it had hardly been a politely surprised kiss back. Yet that anger – she had taken it for a degree of passion, but it could have been anger at her for daring to change their friendship. And what will he say to her now? Bea is trying to think of the conversational practicalities or, rather, impossibilities of two people so divided by social station that they still address each other by their surnames, yet have kissed, and her cheeks simply grow hotter.

Mr Campbell is over there, by the window on the far side of the room. When she sees the back of his hatless head, her stomach clenches and she forces herself to take a deep breath.

She sits down opposite him, her eyes fixed on his interwoven fingers, which are whitening at the knuckles as they squeeze his palms.

'Hullo,' he says.

'Hullo.' Beatrice, you cannot have a conversation with a man's knuckles, she tells herself. So she looks up and there they are, those chocolate eyes, fixed on her and steadier than they were two days ago.

'It's good to see you,' he says, more tenderly than he has ever spoken to her, and Bea feels herself flushing.

'Yes. Yes,' she replies, then stops. What does she say now? Say something, anything, Bea. What conversation are people flogging to death at present? And, almost automatically, Bea finds herself asking Mr Campbell a question that has rolled off her tongue several dozen times during the past fortnight: whether he reckons that the arrival of the American troops any day now means that the war will be over soon.

Means nothing, he replies, clearly a little surprised by her change in tack. 'Until they are actually here. At the rate it's going, it may be too late for your lot.'

'My lot?'

'The men won't have much more of it.'

'You're making it sound like Russia.'

'It's bad enough.'

Christ, she walked into that one.

'How's your sister?' she asks quickly.

Mr Campbell looks away, and Bea is almost sure she sees him biting his lips.

'She's gone,' he says. 'She vanished a year ago. Not a trace of her.'

Bea doesn't know what to reply. His sister was the only one he had left. God, poor man, she thinks. And as she looks at him, his aloneness appears so evident that, without thinking, she reaches across the table and puts her gloved hand on his bare one. He hesitates, then pushes his fingers up through hers, interlocking them.

Bea looks down at the tablecloth. It is torn. Underneath she can see cheap wood scarred by knives and forks.

'I'm sorry,' she says.

'At least my ma's not here to see. And it's them that this bloody war is supposed to be for,' he continues.

'I think I should do more,' she says.

'I think you've done your bit.' He nods towards her left arm, crooked hand fixed underneath the table.

'All I've done is help ease the pieces back together, or try to.'

His grip releases. 'That's all I do.'

God, how could she have said that? Angry with herself, she feels sick again, and then she realises, relieved, that at least the question of where 'this' is going has been resolved. But the conversation can't suddenly end now, so Bea tries to bring it to a graceful close.

'But we're helping, aren't we? Just getting them ready to go back out again.'

'We,' he says, 'we. Isn't it funny, that it was violence that brought us together.'

'You pulling me out of it,' she replies.

He is silent. He just looks at her and shakes his head. Then he grips her hand again, tighter than before. Hers doesn't move. 'Come with me,' he says into her silence. She follows him out of the tea room.

The front of the house is a dirty white, window panes almost the same colour. She follows Mr Campbell inside. He steps into the landlady's room and engages her in loud conversation as Bea tiptoes up the stairs. Top floor, he's told her, at the front.

The stairs smell of rotting wood and Bea, chest pulled in as though that's the only way she'll fit between the banisters and the wall, tests each step before she puts her weight on it. She didn't expect the house to be this grey, even the wood has a greyness to it. Bea runs her finger along the handrail as she climbs. There's no dust, at least it's clean; the colour is just from the years of penumbra that have saturated the building and its contents.

The floorboards in Michael's room are grey, too, rough and unpolished. Bea wonders whether she will be more or less likely to pick up splinters in stockings or bare feet. Did one, in any case, remove one's stockings in these situations? There has to be some sort of convention, everything else seems to be governed by one set of rules or another, even if the principal rule seems to be that they should be broken. Though perhaps not this far. It's not just that Bea is in a man's bedroom, but what sort of man's bedroom she is in.

The walls are not much better, a browning yellow. In the far corner is a clothes horse with two pairs of socks hanging from it. Does he do his own laundry? Who else would he have to do it for him? Would she, once they had done this, be expected to do it for him herself?

Mr Campbell is upstairs with her now. His steadiness has gone and he is mumbling about the years he's been here, that the landlady is a good sort, her son's in Flanders. He's looking everywhere but straight ahead of him at Bea and the bed beyond. It occurs to her that maybe he is a virgin, too, and what a farce that would be, if he knew no better than her. She suddenly wants the whole matter to be over and done with as soon as possible.

Deciding to take some sort of initiative, she takes two steps backwards and sits on the edge of the bed. The springs sink, and the mattress with it. The sharp hospital iron of the bedstead digs into her calves.

Mr Campbell walks to the far side of the bed and sits on it, she imagines, facing the window. The mattress rocks from side to side as he does whatever he is doing. He has stopped talking. After an hour-long minute of movement and silence, Bea turns to look behind her. Mr Campbell has removed his shirt and is sitting in his vest, chin to the window and the tendons on his neck taut. Against the plaster of his skin his vest is grey. Laundry again. Bea puts her purse on the floor and unbuttons her coat. She stands up to slip it off, and once she is holding it in her hand she realises that she is unsure of where to put it. On her side of the bed there is only the clothes horse, and she doesn't quite have the guts to start striding about half naked. She moves the damp socks to one side and drapes the coat over it. Stepping backwards, she returns to the edge of the bed and starts to unbutton the top of her shirt and stops. Surely she can do better than this. She slides her hands behind her and, even with fingers half clotted, manages to unhook her skirt, letting it fall to the floor. Almost before her waistband has reached the splintering floorboards, she is in the narrow bed, stockings still on.

She is now tucked up to her collarbone between a pair of sheets thinned to the slipperiness of an ice-rink and under a faded pink blanket. She leans her head back, searching for a pillow. There is only one, roughly in the centre, and Bea is firmly holding her position to one side. It seems churlish to take the pillow and impossible to lie half on and half off it, so she shuffles her shoulders further to the side, leaving the rest of her where it has landed, putting her in an awkward diagonal.

Mr Campbell is clearing his throat.

Ready now? he asks, his voice reed-thin.

Afterwards, Bea doesn't know whether to be relieved or shocked that he had a preservative. Had he been planning the event? And was it for her, or, or . . . A far from romantic thought comes into her mind and she checks herself; is there always this much hypocrisy around making love? If that's what this was. They are lying in silence but Bea is still short of breath, she feels as though her insides have leapt out of her and back in again. She had no idea that 'this' would be so energetic. From the way she had heard it whispered of, it was a distanced affair.

Distanced is not what she feels. She wants to reach out and touch Mr Campbell's face but is unsure whether it would be too forward, even now. She smiles to herself. But what struck her more than anything was the extraordinary vulnerability that men are reduced to, it hadn't occurred to her that Mr Campbell could ever be so at her mercy, and she suddenly feels a burst of gratitude towards him. Thank you, she wants to say, thank you for doing this for me. Instead she turns towards him having now decided to stroke his forehead, and finds his big, dark eyes drinking her in. He reaches for her hand and kisses the heel of her palm.

'Beatrice? May I call you Beatrice now?'

'God. Yes.' She hesitates. She's never called him by his Christian name before, and it is slow to form in her mouth. 'Michael.'

He reaches for her hand closest to him, the bad hand.

'Will you marry me?'

Her hand freezes on his forehead. She pulls her fingers back.

'Beatrice, will you marry me?'

'Michael.' It still feels strange to say his first name. 'I don't understand.'

'Understand what?' Anger is flashing back into him, and Bea feels her pulse quicken. But what does he mean? Move into this room and wash his clothes? She pushes away from him and sits up. He watches her, puzzled.

'What's wrong? Are you all right?'

Bea doesn't reply. She stands up and starts to dress quickly. She's fumbling, but she can just pull her coat on over her clothes.

It's Michael's turn to sit up, and his voice is irritable now. 'Where are you going?' He says, as if telling her to come back.

'Mr Ca— I'm sorry, Michael—'

'Sorry?' He's out of bed now, stark naked, without even the manners or care to cover himself. 'Why, what was this to you? Some charity fuck?'

As Beatrice runs down the stairs and pushes past the small woman standing at the bottom, she bursts into tears.

She's still a wreck when she falls in through the front door of Number Thirty-Five. Clemmie is in the hallway, looking shrunken.

She casts a glance at Bea, up and down. I see you've heard, she says. Heard what, Bea replies, and Clem can't meet her eyes. And with this look, or not-look, Bea knows. She shuts her eyes, holds her breath. She wants to block the words out.

Clem holds her elbow as they go up the stairs. A stone statue that is Mother is sitting on the far sofa in the red drawing room, her neck livid and her face white. A piece of paper is in her hand. Her eyes are as red as the wallpaper.

'Poor Edward,' she says.

Bea opens her mouth to speak but no words come out. Not that Mother will hear anything. Bea stares at Mother, Clemmie, the paper, the brown envelope, and she turns to the door.

'Beatrice, where are you going?' asks Clemmie.

'Out on the motorcycle,' she says. 'It was still in the garage when I last looked.'

And Clemmie is chasing her, whispering don't do that as though she wants to shout it out. You'll kill yourself. But Clemmie can't shout that out.

'Your arm, Bea,' she pants. 'How will you hold—'

'Fuck my arm.'

Aftermath

1918

24

THE HOUSE IS BEING SHROUDED. WHEN BEA WALKS PAST the yellow drawing room on her way back from breakfast she finds Mrs Wainwright directing Sarah and Susan in the laying of sheets over furniture, as if for its own burial. Bea stops at the doorway: she's had a thousand, no, thousands of conversations in this room, and, among them, goodbyes. Her chest tightens. Edward, she thinks, it's the last place I saw Edward. There's a shadow in the corner of her eye, in front of the chimney piece, and for an instant she thinks she sees him there but as soon as she is facing the fireplace, he vanishes.

The fireplace is cold and bare. Every fluff of ash has been brushed out and only the blackened brick behind it admits that there was ever warmth there; even the furniture has been deadened. Bea surveys the room. The sofas are like corpses on stretchers, their ruined bodies hidden from sight. The last sheet has been thrown over the last chair. Susan and Sarah have slipped away – to turn the next room into a tomb, thinks Bea – but Mrs Wainwright is hovering, a question on her lips. No, Bea wants to say, we're all still here, it is only Mother who is being buried today. But Bea can't get these words out past the lump in her throat. She has no spare emotion to give this morning; instead what emerges is, 'We're coming back for lunch.'

Mrs Wainwright nods as though Bea has a desire to play out for as long as possible something that is clearly over. Bea almost says that she hasn't any intention of leaving this house in the near future. Which is, in a way, true, for intending is not the same as possibly having to. How odd, she thinks, that I have spent so long wanting to escape all that this house stands for, and now that I might have to go, all I want to do is stay.

The rest of the country, Europe, the rest of the world, seems to be celebrating peace as though there were no war before it. Yet for Bea the past week has been a wake for every single face that will not return. If you are not going to see them again now, then you really never will.

Nor will you see Mother, though the question was raised by Clemmie, extremely briefly, as to whether the coffin should be open at any stage in the ceremony. 'I know it's a little strange, and you probably can't, what with it being the flu and all that,' she said when they met with the funeral director. 'But she would so hate to be shut out of things. She must be furious at going the day the war ended.' Bea can't imagine what Mother would have done with peace. She had surged through the war on such a wave of the gallons of milk she produced from Beauhurst that it is almost impossible to imagine her ever having slowed down again.

Even from her mortuary slab, she is still being controversial. While Bea's and Clemmie's friends are engulfed in a wave of almost spontaneous weddings, Mother is having a funeral. Yes, Mother, marriage seems to be what they want, the men, when they're back. A wife, home, hearth, a certainty of some kind; so they're rushing up the aisle as though at any minute the whole bloody thing will start again. What you should have done now, Mother, was to tie the knot. You could have welcomed some war-weary general home, installed him amidst the healthy sea vapours of Beauhurst and given him glassfuls of fat milk from your cows. But you didn't do that. You went and died, on purpose, it almost seems. When you were told to rest, you were up and about far too soon after your fever broke, and so it came back, pushing you away in its place. It was really very inconsiderate of you, Mother, to die. Of course, now that you've gone – or are almost gone, because you are still here, making your way over from the cold stone mortuary to the church in a polished oak box. Now that you've gone, we are realising how much you held us all together, even if it was by irritating us with those hypocrisies you called practicalities.

The practicality now is that we are all unravelling. Two daughters, acres of crumbling brick in the countryside, few funds and precious little means of gaining any more. Unless one of us were to marry well. Us? That's only me, thinks Bea. And, Beatrice, who is there to marry? She can't think of any rich man she'd want to see at breakfast every day. In fact she can't think of any man she'd like to see at breakfast every day. Then she checks herself, for that's not quite true. All too often the moment she ran from Mr Campbell's room comes back to her mind. Though she still hasn't managed to picture the life she and Mr Campbell would have lived together.

In any case, it's too late. Every letter you sent him afterwards was returned, and you've no idea whether you will ever see him again or whether he is still kicking, or in pieces. Is that why you are thinking about him so much, because the fact that you are extremely unlikely ever to see him again makes him a safe dream to have? And safe because even if she did, it could never, however much she might puzzle to find a way, lead to anything.

Safest of all, however, because she'd blown it. More fool you, Beatrice.

The red drawing room, the only one on the first floor not dust-sheeted over, is still cold when Clemmie, Bea and Edie come back for lunch. Edie is staying with them for 'moral support', though who is supporting whom is a trifle unclear. There is no fire and Bea walks towards the bell but Clemmie interrupts her. 'Darling, I can't.

Not after this morning. It'll be a funeral pyre. That's what they must have thought. Have a drink. Or a cig. Some fire in that. Throw me the box, darling.'

'Nonsense, the servants are just annoyed that the drinks were at Claridge's.'

'It was, may I say,' ventures Edie, 'a little inhospitable.'

'Oh, God, Edes,' Clemmie drops into an armchair and flings her head back, blowing smoke at the ceiling, 'I don't think I could have stood having it here. People would never have left. I mean, they haven't left there, yet, have they? It was turning into some sort of political rally. We all needed somewhere to escape to.'

Escape, thinks Bea, from Mother. Perhaps that's what we've all been trying to do, perhaps that's what all daughters do. But mothers reach far, even from beyond the grave.

Clemmie continues. 'At least we are able to bury Mother.'

'Oh, Clem, don't.'

'And the half of Tom I haven't buried yet.'

'He'll come back to himself, Clemmie. He just needs a rest.' Given her recent form, Edie sounds almost worryingly calm.

'A life-long rest. How's Tony, Edie?'

Edie shrugs her shoulders. 'I guess he's back,' she says.

'Hasn't he come to see Archie?' Clemmie is now leaning forward in her seat.

'He's not too interested in Archie.'

'How peculiar,' says Clemmie and, her mind clearly on children, excuses herself to go and check on the nursery. 'I'm rather hoping,' she says as she leaves the room, 'that they understood enough of it to be shedding at least one tear between them.'

'Shouldn't think so,' says Edie when Clemmie has left the room. 'Children don't notice these things.'

None of them eats lunch. They just push it around on a fork enough to keep the servants happy. Nor do they manage any conversation beyond the listing and confirming of the born, married and dead. As they reach pudding, Celeste turns up in a somewhat melodramatic silk and lace mourning dress.

'Half the nation's suffragists are still,' she says, 'at Claridge's, making speeches for the vote for women under thirty. I should imagine they will remain until the law is changed again. Rather like the idea of an occupation of Claridge's, even if all that lot'll do is talk until they're out of breath. Your mother would be furious to have missed out. Can't say I don't miss the old girl. There's nothing like a good feud to keep one going.'

Bea is surprised by Celeste's words. Not just her affection for Mother but, Bea realises, it is the first time that either of them have admitted that battle lines were so clearly drawn.

The solicitor arrives at half past two. Clemmie, Celeste and Bea return to the red drawing room, and Edie diplomatically excuses herself 'to be rather self-indulgent and spend some time upstairs with Archie'. The solicitor is a bowler-hatted and slight, quick-moving man whose discomfort seems to increase as he is asked to sit down. As he reads the will, his eyes dart from side to side, as if noting the expressions he sees. Clemmie and Bea shift positions as his gaze crosses them. Celeste sits, arms crossed, and with the motionlessness of certainty, thinks Bea, that she will not receive a thing from Mother.

'Typical Mother,' says Clemmie when he has left. 'Not choosing quite the right sort of man. Seemed damn sharp to me.'

'That's only,' Bea replies, 'because he told us that there wasn't much money left.'

'I think that may be rather understating the situation, Bea.'

After a surprising, but modest, bequest to Celeste, there are several to trades unions and, of course, a substantial one to the National Union of Women's Suffrage Societies. What remains is to be divided between Clemmie and Bea. However, Mother, for reasons that will now only be known to herself, left no indication of just how the houses, pictures, plates even, should be divided.

'Blast her,' says Clemmie, and it is Celeste who looks shocked at this. 'After all those years,' Clemmie continues, 'of telling us to be practical and now what are we supposed to do, saw everything in two?'

'I think you are both,' cut in Celeste, 'old enough to make a few decisions. She clearly thought you were capable of it. In any case, you should be damn grateful.'

How odd, thinks Bea, Celeste is batting for Mother. A little late, perhaps. It would have been a bit more convenient if they had managed to ride the same train while they were both alive.

'Thank God there's no heir,' says Clemmie, then chokes. 'I didn't mean it that way, just not some wretched cousin that everyone else usually suffers. We're too happily nouveau riche, if you can bear the irony of the riche bit, to have entails and distant male cousins who inherit, and things like that.'

'They'd be dead anyhow,' replies Bea.

'Beauhurst,' interrupts Celeste.

'Lord knows when the soldiers will be out of there,' replies Clemmie. And Bea finds herself saying, 'Why don't they just have it? You never liked it anyway, Clem, and it's not as if anybody is going to buy it now. We'll be lucky enough if they agree to take it.' Clemmie purses her lips. The room is still for a moment, then she nods. Celeste looks up and smiles. Item one crossed off the agenda. Item one simply crossed out of their lives.

'You don't suppose,' says Clemmie, 'that anyone will want to buy Park Lane?'

And Bea, who didn't cry this morning, finds herself fighting back the tears.

'All settled?' asks Edie as she totters into the room. Bea shrugs her shoulders. The house is Clemmie's, too, and she wants, says she needs, the money for it, 'Or Gowden's roof will quite simply cave in.' For a second Bea wonders whether she and Celeste could club together to buy Clemmie out. If only the pictures weren't all, as

Edward had so rightly said, fakes. But a house like this without pictures, and dozens of servants if not inhabitants, would feel deserted. So no, it's obvious, Bea will go to live with Celeste, and Park Lane will be put up for sale.

'Will probably be snapped up by an awful sort,' says Clemmie. 'Doesn't bear thinking about.'

Edie is out of her chair and straightening her clothes. She looks around the room and at Celeste, Clemmie and Bea, curiously slowly. Then she pulls herself up sharply.

'Well, I'm just popping off,' she says, and struts towards the door. She stops on the threshold and turns to blow a kiss to the room. 'Goodbye, darlings.' And a minute later they hear the clip of her heels echo up from the hall.

'How odd,' remarks Clemmie.

'What's odd, Clem?' asks Bea.

'Not quite sure, just something.'

Uncertain of what else to do, the three of them sit there for an hour or so, going through more 'practicalities' as their tea grows cold and the light outside even greyer.

'How long have I got,' Bea asks, 'to say goodbye to this place?'

'You'll be much better off with me,' Celeste butts in. 'Think you should hop over this afternoon. You don't want to be living here with people poking their noses and purses into every corner. Besides, it's a bit of a mausoleum, isn't it, Beatrice, my dear?'

'She only died here, Celeste, we haven't buried her under the floorboards.'

'That doesn't mean to say that she has, in every sense, gone. It will do you good to—'

'It still annoys me,' Clemmie breaks in.

'What, Clementine?'

'That she came up to London just at the beginning of another wave of the flu, having hardly been here for years. I can't help feeling it was somehow negligent of her. She was always too damned busy with her causes to think about any of us.'

A small creature runs into the room in a blur of blond, starch and tweed, and buries itself in Clemmie's lap.

'Good God, Clementine,' says Celeste. 'Is that one of yours?'

'No,' she replies, stroking the boy's hair. 'It's Edie's Archie.'

'I'll see if any of them know what Edie's up to,' says Bea, and rings the bell.

When Susan appears Bea asks her when Edie is expected back.

'Back?' says Susan.

'Yes, back.'

'Oh.'

'Oh, what?'

'Well, I didn't think she was coming back, Miss Beatrice, not with—'

'With what, Susan?'

'With her trunk, and all.'

'Her trunk?'

'Yes. Labelled it was, too. Mombasa it said.'

25

GRACE'S WAR ISN'T OVER. THE FIGHTING MAY HAVE finished in France and Flanders, Russia, too, but here, in this runt of a farmhouse outside the village of Gowden, Grace is still a prisoner. Grace and Baby, and all the little words and softness of his not quite two years.

Not that Grace hears many of his words, for she only has him to herself at night, and then she has just his breath to listen to behind the locks put on her door. Even when, in the daytime, Mrs Blunt doesn't have Baby in her farmer's-wife arms that'll crush him if she holds him any tighter, she doesn't take her eyes off him for a minute, and Grace can hardly get close. Mrs Blunt bars the door into that gloomy kitchen with a chair, making Grace have to knock and beg through the wood-planks to be allowed into the same room as her own child. She has to shout, too, to make herself heard, what with the clattering and washing flapping, and every machine that grinds too loud as you turn it. When she's shouting, and Mrs Blunt's not hearing, or just not answering, Grace's heart pounds so high in her chest that it might pop out of her mouth.

She should have run the moment she first came. She had been as fresh as she could be from volunteering for the Women's National Land Service Corps: two weeks on a training farm and new boots that laced almost as high as her knees, breeches even. Though she's a loose belted coat over these. Regulation. For modesty. The WNLS had sent the girl with no apparent friends or family straight down here. The first thing she saw was the grey-walled house. It was blackened with dirt on the rump of a building out the back; the privy standing in a sea of as much animal doings as there were inside it. All round in the stinking mud were near man-traps of nails and rusting barrels that she'd tripped over as she made her way through. By the time she reached the front door she hadn't been able to see a scrap of that leather she'd polished on her new boots.

Grace knew then, didn't she: even before the door was opened by Mrs Blunt clutching her spear of a broom as though she'd give an ox a run for its money. Even before Grace saw Mr Blunt bent, hook-lean, over the table, scraping at a block of wood with a knife, and not looking up or saying a word. But Grace could hardly go back to the Land Army and say it wasn't to her liking, not to mention that she didn't want to draw attention to herself, not in the circumstances. And where else was she to go? She'd walked out of Park Lane one afternoon with not much more than the clothes on her back – for none would fit more than a month. She had imagined how she might leave the house, handing back her uniform and sailing off in her office clothes, but it could hardly have been more different. She hadn't even left a note, just vanished into the war with her shame. And now she's had Baby, she can barely get near him. For Mr and Mrs Blunt say they are sure, as sure as day, that Baby is the son of their own son, Robert. And Mrs Blunt isn't letting Baby out of her sight.

Robert hadn't yet gone to France when Grace arrived. He wasn't a handsome man, just a tall, skinny boy with pitted skin and shoulders not yet broadened; he looked as though he'd crack when he put his shoulder to the horses. But steel wire, he was: he'd ease the plough through gatherings of stones, put there by the pixies at night, he'd joke, and when he leant down to listen to you it was like a gentle giant, sweet as honey, just as Joseph had been before he went off to the war. But Grace wasn't that type of girl, who'd do that in the state she was already in; though Mrs Blunt had fair pushed her at him, as though if Robert were taken with Grace, he might decide to stay.

Robert took Grace out into the fields before he left, and showed her how to shake the horses on, how to sometimes pull them from the front. Grace pulled hard. You'll hurt yourself, Miss Campbell, he'd said. But she wanted to hurt herself, hadn't she, wanted to make what was in there come unstuck, that was why she'd run to a farm. Every night Grace touched her belly with her fingers, hoping there'd be nothing there any more, then she'd put the palm of her hand on it and when she felt Baby move she'd hate herself. Another life, she'd think, all that goodness, even with her being so bad.

It was Grace's fault for not keeping Robert when he went, so Mrs Blunt said. But Robert had been going to France before Grace came, even if a thunderbolt had had him. He hadn't limped into the recruiting station like Mrs Blunt had told him to. Mrs Blunt behaved as though she blamed Grace for that, too. All the extra Grace had to do then, as if Mrs Blunt was making a point.

The telegram came so quick you could still smell Robert in the house. Missing, nothing found, and all those stories of boys drowning in mud. Once, when it rained, Grace saw Mrs Blunt staring out of the window at the swamp in the yard, chickens slipping in it, falling over, and struggling back up. Then she turned to Grace and shouted at her, pushed her out of the door with that broom spear, saying that's what it was like for Robert, you know.

It was November that Grace couldn't hide it any longer. There Grace was, the portions she was being given on her plate growing smaller; there's less for everyone, Mrs Blunt had been saying, like there were rations on a farm of all places. And less for you than us. Though you could just see there was more of Grace by then, and

Mrs Blunt, her eyes running down over Grace's stomach, stopped. Grace waited for it, the roar, being shouted at to pack her bags, that this house wasn't a place for that sort of thing. It didn't come. Mrs Blunt stood stock still, eyes inward, mind slowly turning. Then she stuck out her fingers to count the months. Grace was told to sit down quickly, and was asked what was she doing with all that sowing, let alone those buckets, and it wasn't up to her any more. Robert'd be sure to come back now. Grace had to make sure all was right for him. No thinking of herself, said Mrs Blunt, there's everybody to consider now. And what it means to Mr Blunt, to have a little Robert on the way.

As the portions on Grace's plate grew again, she couldn't see the harm in it. So she sat down and shut her mouth, feeling right thankful that they were going to look after her and Baby, especially given that, even with all she had been doing, Baby was still there. She didn't want to go about for the next few months, either, not with Miss Beatrice's sister, Miss Clementine, no, Lady Dagbert, Grace should call her, not two miles off. Imagine the luck of it, Grace to be posted so close. No doubt there'd be all sorts from Park Lane wandering about and one sight of Grace and it'd be all out then. No, Grace wasn't going near the village until she could go way beyond it, and for that she'd need her baby in her arms, not lolling in her stomach.

When Baby came, it was too late to go. Mrs Blunt had Baby up and in her arms as soon as he appeared. Grace only held him when she nursed him, and Mrs Blunt was right strict about that from the start. Not that Grace has been nursing him awhile. All she has is her night-times, when she curls up tight with Baby in her bed and runs her fingers through the blond locks she can't see in the dark. 'It's not long,' she whispers to Baby, 'not long until we're away.' But it's herself she's saying this to, and she hasn't the rest of it to tell.

Any day Grace could leave the field, hitch a ride to Birmingham and vanish into the city, but she wouldn't be able to take Baby with her, not with him walled into the kitchen, Mrs Blunt's apron strings tied round his waist. Sometimes Grace wonders whether she could snatch him away. Then she thinks of Mrs Blunt's arms clamping him tight, and Baby screaming as he is being torn this way and that. As for night-time, Mr Blunt sleeps with that ring of keys under his pillow, Mrs Blunt has told her straight, and Grace's window is barred. She could take a file from the stable and saw away at a bar bit by bit. But she couldn't do it in a single night, and Mr Blunt's eyes are sharp as pins. Where've you to go anyway, says Mrs Blunt. For in the more than two years Grace has been with them, not a single letter has she had.

Maybe Grace could go to Aunt Ethel, invent a husband who's dead in the war, and there's no shortage of those. Some invention it would have to be, though, for Aunt Ethel's the sort who's too interested, asks questions like the schoolmistress she is. No, the only other place Grace could go is to one of those homes for unmarried mothers who have nobody to give their babies to. And they're not places anybody would want to be.

Sometimes Grace even thinks through what if she left Baby; she can't say they don't care for him here. All the food he could eat and more. In the evenings Mrs Blunt sits stitching for him, and the needle could be going through Grace, the more for Grace hasn't a needle or cotton to sew for him herself. There's the farm, too. It would all be Baby's, so long as they think he is Robert's. Maybe Grace mustn't think of herself but what's best for him, and she's not a thing to offer. But her insides are turned out of her at the thought. She'd never be able to smell a thing but for his sweetness, and what would her cheeks feel if they were pressed against an empty pillow at night. It only takes a second's more thought to remember that the Blunts are March mad. Grace could never leave Baby with them, not even with all he might get. Why, they might coo over him now but who's to say it wouldn't be him barred in next?

Still, some wicked days she wishes he hadn't been born yet. If it weren't for Baby, she'd still be back at Park Lane, waiting for Joseph to come home. Then her taste turns sour, and she thinks she'll fry for that thought. Though she'll be frying anyway for what she's already done, all of it, for God's not merciful any more, they all know that. Even a vicar must stumble over those words in the service. Though Grace hasn't been let near a church.

Grace wonders what Mrs Blunt'll do with Grace when Baby's big enough to need to run around outside more, for that's when Grace could take him. Grace looks at how he is walking, and counts the months before Mrs Blunt will have to let him out of reach. Maybe they'll lock Grace up whenever Baby is playing out there, but Mrs Blunt is still talking as though Robert's coming home. 'Them telegrams are wrong half the time,' she says, and repeats the story she read in the newspaper of the boy who came home to find his name already up on the church wall. 'You'd've thought them in charge don't have an idea what's going on out there.' Though she can't believe it, Grace keeps mum. For so long as Mrs Blunt thinks Robert's coming home, she'll keep Grace and Baby well for him.

Grace is sitting at breakfast and Mrs Blunt is talking again about how Robert might have been lost and could still be found: taken prisoner, joined another regiment, become confused. Grace is all nerves because now the war's over, it'll be clear soon, won't it, that Robert is none of these things, and she so wants Mrs Blunt to go on believing Robert is coming that her mouth goes off of its own accord. 'Perhaps,' she says, for it's all she can think of doing at the moment, 'perhaps he might have just run away.'

As soon as she's said it, she realises what she's done, but it's too late to catch the words back again. Mr Blunt lifts his head and stares straight at her with eyes that look as though the colour's washed out of them, and his hands twitch up.

Better be dead than a deserter; or the parents of one.

*

Mrs Blunt has hung black about her photograph of Robert, and yesterday she said that Baby is their memory of Robert. It's how he's come back to us. Almost as fast as Grace can think, something has changed. Grace can see it in the way Mr Blunt looks at her sideways long and hard till she catches his eye and he turns away. Clear as day, now that the Blunts have decided Robert's not coming back, Grace is just in their way.

Grace has to leave with Baby, and she's no time for pride any more. She'll have to ask for help wherever she can, and that's from the one person she's told herself she could never go to. As little as Grace might not be able to open her eyes for the shame of it, and there's not a chance he'd let her keep Baby, he would at least give Baby a future. Not send him to the workhouse as a bastard child. And now, now there's a chance he'd be allowed the time to come and find the two of them.

He would never forgive her, and Grace wants to weep at the thought he'll know how she's let him down. So long as he didn't know she could pretend that he loved her still. But she has to put Baby first. Even if she might as well put a knife in her gut as she hands him over to Michael, and he asks her to leave.

She slips two pieces of paper and envelopes from Mrs Blunt's desk, pen too. And stamps. Hides them under her pillow for when she goes up at night. It's only when the wall is rattling from Mr Blunt's snoring, and Baby's breath is soft and deep, that Grace slides them out. She lights the candle, whispering a prayer that nothing will bring either of the Blunts out of their room. And she writes.

It's so long since she's written that she scarce knows how to move her hand across the page, and what'll Michael make of a scrawl like that. Still, she's no paper to spare, for she has to write twice. One to the old lodgings, just in case. One to the service address – there's a hope they'll find him. She's not thinking about where else he might be.

She writes to come and find her, that she's been trapped here, not able to send a letter out before, and she needs him to look after her now. We'll be a family, she writes. That's not telling him so much he won't come, she thinks, but he won't be able to say that she lied to him.

Next morning she's out the far end of the field and down to the road to catch the postman as he passes. She stands in the middle of the road and waves him down like there's an accident around the corner. He has to pull the horse up so sharp that its hooves are near on Grace's chest.

She's still enough of a smile on her to get a nod and wink back. And a promise not to tell the Blunts, as it's for a surprise, and who would want to ruin it? As the cart rattles off, Grace sends a prayer with it. Please God, she begs, if you'll still listen to me, send me Michael. Then you can do what you want with me.

26

IT'S EVEN RAINING INSIDE, THINKS BEA. THE restaurant's windows have steamed up, and small droplets are beginning to run down the panes, streaking the view of Piccadilly. She looks back across the table at Bill Fitzroy, all pale brown hair and reasonable, well, quite attractive, blue eyes fixed on her intently. A little too intently. She should perhaps not have kissed him ten days ago.

Last week, last week she was liable to kissing. The day after Mother's funeral, she drove the Calcott to Pimlico, her stomach turning with embarrassment and excitement and a heave of memories, not all of which she wished she had. The house looked as grey on the outside as she'd remembered it being inside. The door was answered by a short, wide-shouldered woman with dyed black hair piled up into a bun on the top of her head. Below, the skin on her face sagged from wartime rations. The woman looked her up and down. Mr Campbell, she said, dear, you're not his sister, are you? He only left word for her, didn't mention anybody else. He's one of the ones that hasn't been back for over a year, dear. Bea's head whirred, of all the things she'd been steeling herself for, this had not been one, the dread of him no longer wanting her drowning out that possibility.

She took the tea offered. Don't be silly, she told herself, of course he isn't dead. To her, though, he was perhaps as good as, for he had not even thought that she might have wanted to find him.

A couple of days later, her head still spinning, and fired up by half a bottle of champagne, she had, extremely willingly, kissed Bill Fitzroy.

Since then there have been two bunches of flowers and three calls. The first two calls, mercifully, she was out. On the third, she'd been running downstairs, practically buttoning her coat as late as ever. This time for the family solicitor, for Bea has been left to supervise the sinking of the ship. Clemmie has retreated to Gowden and the half-baked Tom, Edie's little Archie scooped up under her arm. I wanted another, she said, and I don't think I'll be getting one out of Tom. Thus Bea has been left to pack away the world they grew up in.

What then? VAD nursing will trickle on for a while, for the wounded don't recover the moment the bells ring. However, it will end soon and Lauderdale Mansions has been empty since the war began. Now there's the vote at thirty, Emmeline has retreated. The Women's Party in the election last year was such a damp squib that she, Mrs Pankhurst that is, is going to lecture abroad. This Celeste despises. 'Damn fickle woman, should have spotted it a mile off. Come on, Beatrice, are you really going to wait another five years for the ballot? You might even miss the next General Election.' Bea's not sure how much she cares any more. It's a detail, a fingernail compared to everything else that has happened since the war began. She's almost back to where she was beforehand, floating along between social engagements with Celeste trying to stir her up to something.

Bea leans back, taking her elbows off the restaurant table and mistakenly letting her bad hand fall on to the tablecloth in front of her. Before she can withdraw it, Bill's one remaining hand is on hers. His other wrist hovers below the table top. He has managed quite well to keep it out of sight, which has only made her the more curious. She has grown used to trying not to gaze at the injuries that pass on the street. Some, the legs, or rather lack of legs, she can hardly bear to see. It's the powerlessness, she thinks, on a body that is otherwise so strong.

'Beatrice,' begins Bill, and Bea feels a prod of panic. It is clearly a 'begins' and she somewhat dreads where he is going next. He can't be going to, is he soft in the head, a touch of what Tom has? She thought it was just Bill's hand that he'd not come back with. She wants to say Good God, is that the time, but they've not even been there an hour and are somewhere between the main course and pudding – which they went for instead of a starter. Won't lunch, thinks Bea, become inconveniently long when rationing ends and they can stuff themselves on three courses in the middle of the day again?

She interrupts, stop him, Beatrice, dead in his tracks. 'Bill?'

'Yes.' His eyes light up. Hell.

'Will you excuse me?' She picks up her purse and winds her way through the tables towards a glass door leading into the hallway. As she enters the hallway, she steps around the ladder of the man recruited to de-fog the windows and thinks that, were she with someone she wanted to be with, she would have rather liked the fogged glass to cut her off from the world outside. But everything familiar to Bea seems to be falling apart in a way it wasn't during the war. Is that another reason why she kissed Bill? To take herself back to the old days? He was a face from that past, and she might have kissed him then.

There's also that glaring word being muttered around all the dregs of drawing rooms in town. Shortage. Good God, it's so tasteless, like the harvest was poor while the other harvest, over there, was so damn rich. Take what you can, says Clemmie, who is all for accepting a spontaneous proposal. And in the absence of Mother, Bea finds that she is behaving in just the manner that, out of pure stubbornness, she refused to do when Mother was around. She is contemplating marriage for the hell of it because Mother may just have been right when she said life is easier with a husband; however little you are in love with them, at least then nobody thinks you are looking, especially if you are twenty-five.

Bea glances through the now cleared window and stops stock-still. Looking back in and straight at her is a face she recognises. It stares at her hard for a second or two, then turns and walks away quickly.

Her ribcage is squeezing into itself and she's catching her breath. It's like that image of Edward she caught in the yellow drawing room. It can't really be Mr Campbell, can it? Not walking down Piccadilly at half past one in the afternoon. And what are the chances he'd be back so soon? Unless, like the others, he's on a brief leave before going back to clear up the mess. Mind you, stretcher-bearers, all they have to do now is help those who can still travel return home. Mr Campbell, no, Michael. Her anger at herself makes her feel sick. But would she not just do the same thing again? No, she could still slip away from the shining bars of marriage and country-house life that she is but half a dozen words from right now, and do something quite different, couldn't she? But it was a ghost, wasn't it, a figment of her imagination appearing at the final hour, just in time to make her realise she might have a choice.

She rushes to the door and out into the street. That bowler hat and trench coat, thick young neck between, is ahead of her but moving away fast. It is damp and chilly and she hasn't a coat, and she's left poor one-handed Fitzroy to wonder whether she's quite well, but she's trotting to keep up. She needs to trot faster, all he'll have to do is vanish into the crowd at Piccadilly Circus and she'll have lost him. Ahead there's a small crowd blocking his way and he stalls to step aside. It's long enough, and her hand reaches his sleeve, as she gasps for lack of breath.

'Michael!'

He stops, turns and looks straight at her as though she's a bridge away.

'Miss Masters,' he says.

Lead pie in her stomach. Miss Masters? Where's the 'Beatrice' that he asked to call her last time they met? Does he hate her that much? His eyes are pitch-dark enough to make her run. Stand your ground, Beatrice. If he goes now, then he's gone.

She's been through this moment in her head more times than anyone can count. Next time, next time, this is what I'll say, she told herself, but now there are no words there for her.

He's talking, though. How funny, it always used to be her who spoke more.

'Not like a lady to run down the street.'

Bea finds herself shaking her head. No, she says. Not like a lady.

'Shouldn't you be returning to your lunch companion?'

Damn you, Michael Campbell, she wants to say. You're so damn ungentlemanly – but the Bills of this world dull in comparison. Does he realise that the angrier he is, the more determined it makes her to stay?

Same place, he challenged her to. The tea room. What if the Zeppelins had it, she replied. Then it's since breakfast this morning, he said. But, she began, and then she stopped. How could she say, But you're not back in your old lodgings. Or at least you weren't last week.

She is in her bedroom, still debating whether to change her outfit again. There's not been much new since the war began, just a lot of taking-in, and only half of her clothes fit into the cupboards in Celeste's surprisingly feminine spare room, which, though barely a quarter of the size of her room on Park Lane, feels four times as airy. The other half of her clothes are on the unused nursery floor upstairs and for the past hour Bea has been pattering between the two, hunting down skirts and dresses and blouses that flap at the edge of her memory. She wants to look different to the woman who ran away from him after they'd made love.

The front doorbell clangs and Bea starts. Celeste's visitors rarely put in an appearance at such a civilised time of day. Bea can't help but walk to the door of her room and open it just to listen.

Whoever has arrived is planting weighted footsteps across the marble floor of the hall. Now he has stopped and is speaking measuredly, as if considering each word before it is delivered in a voice strange to this house, but very familiar to Bea.

She doesn't run downstairs. She can't move, can barely breathe, and she is waiting for the room to spin. Somewhere outside her head she can hear steps padding up the stairs to the drawing room on the first floor. Bea sits down at her dressing table and leans on her elbows. A pot of powder falls over and she watches the grains spread on to the carpet, light as dust. That's how I feel, she thinks.

The knock at her door still startles her. One of Celeste's maids stands in the doorway, all crisp in her black and white, her face soft with concern. Christ, does she know, too? She's been with Celeste long enough. Before the woman has had the chance to speak, Bea nods. As she starts to stand up from the dressing table, the maid moves towards her as if to help her, but Bea shakes her head, pulls herself upright, wrestling her feet back into her shoes, and then heads for the door.

'Miss Beatrice?'

Bea stops. She really doesn't want to stop, in case her legs don't work when she starts moving again. But there is concern in the woman's voice, and Bea pauses. What is she going to say? That he's missing an eye, an arm, a leg?

'You've a couple of hooks still open, Miss Beatrice.'

'Oh.' And Bea lets her do them for her and, without asking, smooth down one side of Bea's hair and add a pin. Then Bea goes out on to the landing and down the two flights to the drawing room.

He is in uniform, and five years have aged him ten. His eyes are calmer, almost dulled, as he looks at her, but he is still John, all slim and high-cheek-boned and somehow boyish. She turns away so he can't see whatever look it is she has on her face, which feels flushed and freezing and watery, all at once. Her insides are knotting themselves. You can't, thinks Bea, just shut off everything you have once felt, blow it away in a puff as if it were never there at all. The world must be filled with people whose hearts do not fully belong to one person. Blast it. How damn annoying, how annoying of him to be here, now, waking the kraken she had long put to sleep. It's not true, is it, that if you let wounds heal well enough, the scars can never be pulled open.

'Thank you,' he says.

'For what exactly, Mr Vinnicks?' and she feels a little stab of pleasure as he starts at the froideur of being called by his surname. Thank her? She's angry now – it has taken her five years to be angry. She tells herself it's with him, for being pulled along by the hand for all those months and then so suddenly let go. But it's not: she's angry with herself for the fool she was for believing him, and the fool she might still be.

'For seeing me.'

'I could hardly pass you on the stairs as I left.'

'Beatrice, I'm sorry.'

'It's too late, John.' This was at least true until five minutes ago.

'Bea, I made a mistake.'

'A lot of mistakes have been made over the past few years. You shouldn't marry people you meet on a boat.'

'I didn't.'

'Oh, you knew her beforehand?' Take the anger out of your voice, Beatrice. You're giving yourself away.

'No, we didn't marry.'

Bea flinches, she can't help it, and she knows he's seen. She should be sympathetic now but she can't do it. She can't lie like that, it would be too damn obvious what she really thought. So she says exactly that, what she really thinks.

'Don't expect my commiserations.'

He pauses, swallows, looks at the carpet and then back up again. 'Will you—'

This time she's not going to stand and wait for the words not to be the ones she wants to hear. Five years, a war, a quarter of the men she used to dance with dead, and holes left in the rest patched up with her own hands, and she's still not up to being disappointed by John again. And the thought that he hurt her that much gives her a rush of desire to hurt him back.

'Good God,' she interrupts him, 'you're not going to propose now, are you?'

He doesn't reply to this. He just looks straight at her. 'I've two tickets for *Carmen*,' he says. 'For the day after tomorrow . . .'

Bea nods.

She feels sick in the taxi to Pimlico. She's late. Of course she's late. Not that John stayed long, not even beyond simply arranging to meet, but afterwards she'd had to go and sit down upstairs, wait for the flush to subside, and wonder what she was going to say to Mr Campbell.

What is she doing with him, with John, with Bill, with any of them? That she's such a far cry now from war-wounded Bea who felt she barely merited a second glance should make her feel pleased, but she is simply uncertain as to how she should behave. There are no rules for all this sort of thing now, it's not how it was.

It's guilt that she's bringing with her: she's barely seen Mr Campbell, and she's going to let him down again. Of course she couldn't have stood him up after last time. She'd certainly never see him again then. And she doesn't want that, even though John is back.

There's nothing between Mr Campbell and me, she tells herself. Not after no letter for a year and just five minutes on the street. When she'd returned to the table Bill had still been sitting there, looking nowhere. An old friend, Bea said. We lost contact during the war. Yes, Bill said. Bea glanced down and saw that he had already settled up. Let's go, he said. And they went. She sent a short note to thank him for lunch. He has not replied.

*

Pimlico is sadder than ever. The tea room more so, and Bea hesitates outside. The paint has all but vanished from the sign and there's a board across one of the front windows. She pulls her coat tighter around her as she walks in.

He's not there. Good God, she can't be so late that he has come and gone already. She looks at her watch. Half past, hell. It's started to rain, her taxi's gone and the street is empty. She sits down at a far table and considers how angry he must still be with her to have left.

Bea is still sitting there five minutes later when a figure in the doorway catches her eye. It is Mr Campbell, mackintosh undone, the hem swinging around his knees. She gets a half-smile across the room, but no apology. I know, he says, when he reaches her table, that you have hardly been waiting. The waitress approaches, half the age and size of the one who was here before. As she puts a card on the table Bea notices, they both notice, the indentation of a wedding ring. That's not been gone long, he says when she walks away. No, replies Bea.

He's different to how he was in Piccadilly. The dislike has gone and in its place is a distraction; he's tapped that cigarette on the table over a dozen times. He's looking at her, though, with what, Bea thinks, is a look of regret – and this gives her hope. He is moving the cigarette towards his mouth when he glances at Bea and hesitates.

'Yes,' she says, 'I do.'

He passes it to her and she puts it in her mouth, holding it high and to the side. He takes out a box of matches, strikes one and leans over the table towards her and she can feel the size of him swallowing her up. Hold fast, Beatrice, she tells herself, and break this silence.

'No lighter?' she teases.

'No holder?'

'There weren't so many in France,' she replies.

'Bloody mess. The whole thing, a bloody mess.'

'Isn't slaughter always bloody, Michael,' she says, using his Christian name pointedly, as if to pull him to her.

'Sadly, it is not,' he replies, 'always pointless.'

'So, where has it not been pointless?'

'When it makes men free.'

'Still the idealist. Where will your ideals take you after all this?' They're sparring now, she must surely be winning him back.

'Only as far as my circumstances allow me.'

He brings it straight up, the chasm of class between them, that his circumstances are less than Bea's. He is saying he has neither her money nor her connections, and has to pound away at the law, while Bea can do what she likes.

Does he think, she wonders, that is why she turned him down? She wants to tell him he is wrong.

'That is the sort of pragmatism that suffocates ideals,' she hits back.

'A man must do the right thing. For four years, I, and every man around me, have been searching for the right thing to do amidst a morass of wrong. It is habit-forming.'

But not happy-making, thinks Bea, for she can feel a heaviness in him as he speaks.

'How do you know what the right thing to do is?'

'It makes itself very clear.'

'You sound obliged.'

'Obligation, Miss Masters, comes in many forms.'

Thoughts of possible obligations start to race around Bea's mind, taking various female shapes. Pale-faced women, sickly women, seductresses. She almost asks him whether he has someone in the f.w., but stops herself. Would he even know that meant the family way and, in any case, she can't bring herself to ask. Then she wonders whether that was all his proposal to her was, an obligation to a woman to whom he had just made love? She can feel him slipping away from her. Dammit, Bea, you can't let him go now, and, instinctively, almost unconsciously, because it is her bad hand that leads the rest of her, it reaches forward and places itself upon his clenched fist before she can think to draw it back.

Even through her gloves his fingers are warm. Mr Campbell's fist collapses beneath her hand. A second later, his fingers are locked through hers, and he leads her back to his old digs.

Afterwards, they lie smoking in bed as well as they can, for there isn't the width for them side by side, and they laugh as they pull each other back up as they start to fall. In the end they cling on to each other, his thick arm around her back, turning them into a single, balancing mass.

There was no tentativeness this time on his part. There is no resemblance, she thinks, thank God, between now and last time. She blocks out of her head what may have happened in between. Not that Bea's been, well, there's been nobody she liked that much, not worth the bore of worrying about whether she were pregnant. However, there've been a few inconclusive long evenings with the Bills of this world, who would not have been, she imagines, as openly hungry.

Bea never did this with John. They didn't even spend a long evening together; that part of their relationship was left entirely to a combination of idealised hopes and ignorance. It wasn't supposed to be done then, certainly not before you were engaged. But few bother with 'supposed-tos' now.

Bea thinks about how John's slender frame would fit beside her easily in this bed, and how she can't imagine him holding up the pair of them with one arm, and she's not sure she would want him to. All she wants now is for John to ask her what he failed to before – so she can turn him down. For she will, won't she? You can't marry two people at once.

Bea looks to her side and can't quite say it, so she turns to blow smoke rings at the wall opposite the bed. It's the same room, same floorboards, same greyness, even a couple of socks hanging on a rail in the corner. But apart from these, barely a personal possession in view, just a small battered suitcase, firmly closed and, on the table in the corner, a hairbrush half hidden by the cheap paper of a couple of open letters. At last she finds the ability to speak.

'Michael?' Will he answer to 'Michael' again now.

'Yes.'

They couldn't stay in England, they'd have to take her remaining money and his accent somewhere it wouldn't matter any more. They would vanish, like Edie, into a new and exciting place. America, she thinks; now John is back in London, they could go. It would be an adventure, and there they could make what they wanted of their lives – surely he would like that. And it comes,

'Michael, I will marry you, you know.'

His arm slackens, and she begins to fall. He catches her and it feels as if he is holding her from necessity, his face is pointing away as he speaks. My God, he can't bring himself to look at her. They're coming again, aren't they, those words that are the opposite of what she is expecting to hear.

'Beatrice,' he says, 'I can't marry you now.'

And Bea feels a darkness clouding her head. She closes her eyes and takes a deep breath, trying to push it out. Then a couple of fat teardrops fall on to the outside of her eyelids. She wipes them away with a clumsy fist of a hand, and opens her eyes.

He is leaning over her, his eyes damp with more tears. 'I can't,' he says again. 'Not now.'

Then he curves himself right over her and kisses her, so slowly and deeply that he could be taking her very soul with him.

She's run away, gone down to Clemmie at Gowden. She doesn't understand what can have changed so – apart from her hand. And it couldn't be – she's sure it isn't that. The war, or rather the end of it, has changed him. At least, that is what Bea is forcing herself to think, that now 'It' is all is over, his urgency for life has faded and class is dividing them again. So much for being brought up to avoid fortune-hunters. Michael needs what money she has more than most; it's more than enough to put him in Parliament, but he would rather go without it than have her.

His kiss had suddenly stopped. He had drawn back and stayed looking at her with sadness in his eyes. 'I have to go,' he'd said. Bea had nodded, realising that he meant quite the opposite, that she should go. So she'd pushed herself up with an 'I'm late', as though she had an appointment. Yet she was late, a year late in coming to her decision. The moment had passed and she'd missed her chance.

She and Clemmie are packing up the war. Most of the hospital beds are still full but they are putting what they can into the back wing until someone comes to take it away. Though who, says Clemmie, would want a hundred bedpans? Moreover the cupboards, even entire back rooms, are already full of family possessions emptied from the house when it was turned into a hospital. Shall we take all this out first, asks Bea? Some day, Clemmie replies, I'm not sure I can stare at all those dead animals again.

So they pile blankets and pillows around leopards' and lions' heads, slowly drowning the creatures in wool and feathers. Let's move the moose. Don't be ridiculous, Bea, it needs a dozen men to move one of those heads. With at least two legs each. Then do you think, asks Bea, we can hang some of these bedpans off the antlers?

Clem falls silent, and the two sisters go on folding. Then it comes. At least Tom isn't alone, she says, though it's a different type of hospital he needs. Bea almost drops the corners of the sheet she is holding.

'Clemmie, how can you say that about your husband?'

Clemmie isn't looking at her; she's still folding her end of the sheet.

'It's been a terrible problem,' she says, 'with the nurses. At times he doesn't know where he is. Or what he's wearing. I've started to lock him in at night.'

'Clem . . . '

'Don't tell me it'll get better with time, Bea. Good God, look at the colour of these sheets. Shall we burn them?'

After lunch, they walk over to the woods at a slow pace, the children running between them and around them, almost tripping them up. Among the trees it's all silver bark and a palette of oranges of autumn leaves. She and Clemmie catch up with the children, who are tracing their fingers over lines scratched into the bark. It's the soldiers, says Clemmie, their initials, and the dates they were here. They've decorated almost all the wood. I like the hearts best, though some of those stories must have turned out terribly sad. Some of them, though, some of them, I like to think, may have ended up together. In any case these hearts will keep on growing with the trees. That's something, isn't it? In fifty years' time, children will be fitting their fingers right into the grooves.

'Clem?'

'Yes.'

'You haven't nagged me about finding a husband. It's not like you.'

'Well, now there are so few . . . it must be a sore point, Bea, mustn't it, and I didn't want to . . . How are you, you look like you've been ridden over. It's Mother, isn't it? We all feel—'

'No, it's not. Well, perhaps a little.' Of course it is. Though, Mother, mothers generally, never really go, their voice is always in your ear. More so when they're dead – at least being corporeal limits where they can be. 'It's just that I am beginning to think I rather should get married.'

'Good God, that sounds jolly vague. To anyone in particular?'

'I thought you approved of vague. A sort of choose-from-the-list-of suitable candidates.'

'Well, that's what most of us do.'

'Clem! I thought you and Tom . . . '

'Oh yes, of course. You can't help being in love when you're getting married. There's all the fuss, and the clothes, and the pantomime. Really for six weeks you're in such a whirl it's a miracle that not everyone falls over with exhaustion at the altar. But it's not necessarily in love with the person you're marrying. Besides, what a bar it was to live up to in Tom's case. His parents' perfect marriage, he said, dying in each other's arms as the ship went down. So who's in sight? Anyone I know?'

'No.'

'I thought Bill Fitzroy was sniffing around.'

'Yes, he is, or was. I'm not sure any more.'

'Well, don't let him slip through your fingers.'

'It's back to the old Clem . . . '

'Well, I'm sorry.'

'John came back.'

Clemmie stops still. She turns to face Bea, immediately angry.

'What did he want?'

'He wanted to take me to a show.'

'And?'

'I agreed, then chucked and came here instead.'

'You've done the right thing.'

'Because I was so fixed on him?'

'Because John Vinnicks is a cad.' Clemmie pauses. 'Now he's back, Bea . . . you can go to America.'

Yes, thinks Bea, I could. I have nothing to stay here for now.

They are on the club fender in the small sitting room, watching flames the same colour as the leaves outside. Bea's face is burning in the heat from the fire and she's sure her stockings are about to singe. The two of them have picked at a supper of not-quite-the-worst of Mrs Cleaver's offerings.

'Don't tell me to replace her, Bea. There are no replacements left. Honestly, even housemaids are as sought after as doctors. Women either only know how to pack shells, or want to work in an office.

Half of them ran off in the war. Didn't you have a couple who left Park Lane?'

'Well, in the war, Grace. I rather liked her.'

'There you are. She couldn't give two hoots for you, vanishing in a flash when you were so short-staffed.'

'I don't think it was like that.'

'What do you mean? Trouble? We had one here. Obviously one of the patients wasn't quite so wounded. Anyhow, it can stay with her mother, and I'm tempted to have her back, but the other servants here would throw a fit, they mind so much about these things. You still haven't told me whom you are thinking of marrying.'

'No, well. I thought he wanted to marry me, but now he says he doesn't.'

'What rot. Gosh, you must know by now that men can never make up their own minds, we have to make them up for them. And once they have been made up, they don't change. They can say terrible things, but they always come back round to where they were in the first place, otherwise they would have to admit they were wrong. Is he . . . ? No, d'you know, after everything, I don't think it matters. Is he as boring as Bill Fitzroy?'

'No.'

'As caddish as John?'

'No.'

'Then for God's sake what are you waiting for? I'm packing you off on the first train in the morning.'

'No, Clemmie, I really think it's too late.'

'Until he's down the aisle with somebody else, it is never too late.'

'Clem, I need some air. It's too damn hot here. Let's go for a walk.'

'Can't see much in the garden at night.'

'Let's walk down to the King's Arms.'

It has stopped raining. The sky is moon-bright, and so clear that it feels as if a frost is coming down. In the silence, their heels ring on the road.

'Are you not going to tell me anything about your mysterious beau? Is he a fox or a dog? Is he tall? A dwarf? If you don't tell me anything, I shall have to assume that he is a dwarf.'

'He is physically perfect.'

'Even after the war?'

'A few scars.'

'That's rather detailed knowledge. I hope you're not being foolish. Does he have any prospects?'

'Yes, Clem. I think he does.'

They have reached the King's Arms, a picture-book glow coming from its windows.

'Let's go in, Clem.'

'It will be full of officers.'

'They're your patients, and it will be good for you.'

'What do you mean?'

'Let them make you feel good.'

'Is that what you want for me, my wicked little sis?'

'For both of us. We need it. All women do.'

'It feels as though it might rain again.'

'So let's call it shelter, Clem.'

27

HE COMES IN THE EVENING, IN THE DARK. THEY haven't thought that there is anyone to come for her, haven't thought to push her out of the way when Mr Blunt opens the door. It was Mrs Blunt who called to him to do it, even before there was a knock. She must have seen the mackintosh and bowler hat from the upstairs window and thought that's news, money even.

The steady rain is dripping over his hat and the part of his face she can see, but Grace only needs an inch to know her brother, the way he holds himself hasn't changed. He's upright and wide, pushing his shoulders out to fill as much of the doorway as he can. His chin is raised as if to avoid the blows he must be expecting, to give as much as to receive. If Mr Blunt has his eyes open, he'll duck.

A draught's coming in. The cold air cuts between the armchairs, heading straight for the fire, and Baby, and they're all shivering. Michael doesn't speak, and even though she's quaking at the thought of it, Grace feels a surge of strength as she waits for what he might tell her to do.

Grace can't see his eyes beneath the rim of his bowler and the shadow of the door, but she can see the direction his chin is pointing and the hardness to him. He is staring at Baby sitting on the rug in front of the fire, and Grace's heart feels like it's trying to escape her ribs with just the thought of what might be going through his head. Baby's all he needs to see to understand her letter, though. Grace, don't be a fool, she tells herself, of course he knew. Whether he's going to ask her to hand Baby over, or invite her to come with him, she doesn't know. She's not going to wait, either, for she's between Mrs Blunt and Baby, and she moves towards her child as Mrs B. is still facing Michael, waiting for him to speak.

Mr Blunt's eyes are following Michael's gaze from Baby to Grace, and he starts to lift his arm back to the door. Grace has packed a bag ready, Baby's too, and hidden them both far under her bed. But there's no time for that, not unless she wants a fight, and what about Baby in that, and Michael? Grace doesn't want to think what Mrs Blunt might have in her hand.

Michael's put his foot in the door quick as silver, and Mr Blunt can see Michael moves faster than he can, and for a moment Mr Blunt isn't pushing it any further. Grace is like lightning, she grabs Baby up quick and he cries out at the suddenness of it all. She pulls him tighter, he's feeling soft and hard with the struggling, but she takes a hold and pushes his soft wet cheeks against her. She runs through the gap that Michael has left between his back and the door, and into the watery blackness outside, her boots squelching into the reeking mud.

She goes on running. There's a moon and she can see where she's going, can spot the glints of metal lying in wait for her feet, but her feet are sticking in the thickness of the mud, making her stumble. She won't fall, though; you can't fall when you're carrying your baby, there's something stops you doing that. She holds Baby tight, she'll keep him warmer that way, for though the rain has stopped his blanket is damp, and it's not the time of year for an infant to catch a chill. Not that Grace can feel the weather herself. It could be baking July, could be snow. If she shut her eyes she couldn't tell which. She squeezes Baby tighter, then loosens her arms a little, to make sure he can still breathe.

When she hears the squelches behind her she keeps on running,

Baby light in her arms. Don't look behind you, Grace Campbell, stop to look and they'll have you, and back you will go. It's only when she hears Michael's voice telling her to calm it, that she slows to a walk, a fast one, mind. She's still waiting for the squeak of the Blunts' trap, though it'd take them a little while to harness up first. And there's the mud to slow them down too.

Grace and Michael walk on. No more words. Two and a half years, and each of them could have been dead. Grace can't look at him, what does he think of her? He came to her, though, even if he'll leave her and never speak to her again. She's waiting for him to ask her how it came about, how she could be so short-brained. He says nothing, there's no scolding, no demand to know who the father is and that he should take Grace straight to him. Although Grace should be relieved that he's not telling her how angry he is, the silence is worse, because she's still waiting. Perhaps this is it, silence because he's so angry with her that he can't bring himself to speak. He reaches his arms out for Baby but Grace pulls her child tighter to her.

Michael takes off his overcoat and hooks it around her shoulders. She pauses to let him button it up the front, Baby in her arms in the warmth underneath.

'Where are we going, Grace?' Flat as a pancake.

Why's he asking her? For two years she hasn't been able to see beyond a half-dozen fields.

'Wherever you're taking me.'

'I don't know where you want to go, Grace.'

She stops walking and he stops beside her. She turns to look up at him, under his hat. It has stopped raining, but she can feel warm wet lines running down her face. 'With you,' she says. 'I want to go with you.'

Tonight, he says, we'll stop at the village. Gowden? she asks, though it is the only village around here. There's an inn there, he says. The King's Arms. But Grace doesn't like the thought of going into the village. Can you afford it, Michael? He doesn't reply.

Don't be silly, Grace Campbell, she tells herself. What's Miss Beatrice's sister going to be doing wandering about the village at night, and not that she'd recognise Grace anyway.

'Don't you think it's too close, Michael?'

'It's as far as we'll get tonight.' Don't worry, he continues, I'm here now. There's something about Michael that makes her not worry. Nonetheless, as they approach the King's Arms, they see a couple of slight figures walking away in the dark. Grace turns her head in the opposite direction. You never know, she thinks.

As they reach the inn, a pack of uniforms, bandages and crutches hobble out of the door and start to climb into a couple of cars.

'Back to the monarchy of Matron,' one calls out, and the others chuckle.

'Those who can walk, do so,' says a voice that sounds as if it is used to being obeyed. 'We need space,' he continues, 'to pick up the two ladies who were with us this evening.'

'They were insistent,' says another, 'that they wished to walk. Good Lord, who's this? Joseph and the Virgin Mary? No offence, my good man, but you do look like refugees.'

'What's up with you?' Michael asks Grace when they're in their room. They are to share a bed, Baby between them like a married couple. 'Can't you calm down now,' he asks, 'now that you're free of them?' Now that she's free? Of course Grace can't. Freedom's one thing for a man like Michael, for Grace and Baby it's simply uncertainty. 'It's just,' she tells him, 'that I haven't been anywhere new in so long.'

Bread, soup, she is managing that. 'You must eat,' he tells her. 'I've not come all the way here for you to starve to death. We have to go on tomorrow.'

When she's eaten, she can't keep her eyes open. 'Get into bed,' says Michael. 'I'm going downstairs to see if they'll still give me a drink.'

'Take the key, Michael,' she says. Still, her head is full of worries, but her eyelids are too heavy to think them through. As he makes for the door, he hesitates and turns to her.

'What's his name, Grace?'

Her stomach tightens.

'The child's name, Grace.'

'Edward,' she replies.

A week now, and Grace still isn't used to seeing that this is how Michael lived. She never came here, they just met out somewhere, and now she can see why. To think where she was living all that time she was in London. Not that her room was anything but plain, but at least it was white instead of grey, and she didn't have her washing hanging in the corner.

It's her doing Michael's clothes now, and a struggle it is, for his and Baby's whites seem to be absorbing the colour of this room. What would Ma have said, to see them living so? Coming down south was supposed to be the opportunity of their lives, but their home was a palace compared to this. Let's hope Ma can't see them from wherever she is up there. Though at least she'd be pleased to see them together, Grace and Michael. And that's how it will be, Grace knows that.

He'll go back to the law and rise to head clerk. She'll keep house for him and, yes, she's found the will again: she'll have a business of her own and stay as far from the kitchen as Ma would have wanted. Baby will grow, and make up for the fact they've no other children between them. And how would either of them want a husband or wife then?

The landlady looked a little queer at first when Grace and Baby arrived and mumbled something about Piccadilly Circus. Then her eyes ran over Grace's face again, and back to Michael's, but when Michael asked for a camp bed, she calmed down. Michael'd given a wedding band to Grace, and the landlady looked a little tender when she spotted it on her finger and said, 'So you're still wearing it, love?' Grace nodded. Michael hadn't yet asked who

Baby's father was. That first night in Pimlico he just passed Grace a letter written to him by Mrs Wainwright. She was returning to Michael's unit a letter that Michael had sent to Grace at Park Lane more than a year ago. Mrs Wainwright explained that Grace had departed suddenly, leaving no forwarding address, and that Mrs Wainwright would be grateful for news of her as they were all concerned. Further, she had to pass on the sad news that Grace's friend Joseph was reported Missing In Action two weeks since. Would Michael be good enough to pass this on as he saw fit? With many thanks, Elsa Wainwright.

As she read this, Grace's head spun. She pictured Joseph, and it was as though he was disappearing out of sight. She didn't know what to feel, for she'd so long put out of her mind that she would ever see him again. But nobody would see him again, would they? She imagines him lying there quite still, his arms unable to give one of his hugs again. Then came the shakiness and tears.

Michael watched her read the letter, then sat down right next to her, wrapped an arm around her and squeezed. 'I'm here now,' he said.

They do the same every night, and that's what they're doing this evening. She and Michael have a chair each by the stove, and baby asleep on Grace's bed. There have been few words, their thoughts echoing around the room. We have each other, thinks Grace. It'll be what I wanted and we'll make a happy life. Thank the Lord that we're both still here.

There's a sadness to Michael that makes Grace's stomach tight. It's almost as if he's not pleased to have her here. It can't be that, she tells herself. She may have given him woman and child without as much as a by-your-leave, but she's looking after him and that gives her ground to hold. This is the way it has to be, she wants to tell him. Family comes first. For Grace isn't giving Michael up, not ever.

Then there's a knock at the door and it breaks her thoughts. It is a gentle, reluctant-to-disturb-you knock. Michael stands up, equally gently, straightens his trousers and walks to open it.

'Michael,' Grace says. 'You don't know . . . ' for she's still scared that the Blunts will have found her, and be standing there, sticks in hand.

'Stop worrying, Grace. You'll be all right. And the boy.'

Still, she stands up, too, and crosses to the corner of the room shielded by the open door. How long will she do this for? She hates this, when he opens the door. No, nobody snatches anything from Michael, she tells herself. One of his looks and they'll back away.

Then she hears the voice. Hullo. It's a woman's voice, and cut-glass, and Grace wonders what a woman like that is doing coming to see her brother. A woman like that, though, think what she could offer Michael, and a worry comes into Grace, her ears turn razor sharp. The voice doesn't go far. Just, 'Hullo, how are you? I've come to . . . ' And it stops, as though it was going to say more.

But there's something about that voice, isn't there? Hard on the outside, soft in the middle, she hasn't heard it for more than two years now but she's half dreamt of doing so, of being back in those gold and coloured rooms, thick oil paintings all over the walls. It's the voice she felt worst about leaving, and now she's come to find her. My word, Grace hadn't thought anyone back there, let alone Miss Beatrice, might care about her that much. And how had she found her? It was Michael, wasn't it? Said he'd written back to Mrs Wainwright with this address, just the day before he received Grace's letter, just in case Grace went back there. So now she's here, Miss Beatrice, and what's she going to say to Grace? That she's getting married and can Grace come to be her lady's maid? A little surge of excitement rises in Grace, she starts to smooth down her apron and straighten her collar, readying herself to come round and bob to Miss Beatrice.

Grace hasn't quite stepped out when Baby cries, or rather whimpers, and her dream wavers. Miss Beatrice would never have her if she knew. But what's to stop Grace saying he's a nephew, and going back to his mother before the day is out. She'll find someone to take him. It'll be the best thing for Baby; she could have him taken in near enough to see on Sundays, and think of the future she could give him, on a lady's maid's wage.

As Baby cries, Grace, though she can't see a thing from behind the door, is waiting for the exclamation, the how divine, what a cherub, waiting for it, a little hesitant for she doesn't want Miss Beatrice to look at Baby too closely. That's not what comes. Instead she hears a gasp and an 'Oh my God, Michael. Oh my God.' Then soles and heels clatter down the stairs as if they're being chased by the Devil, which must be Michael, because he's vanished down after Miss Beatrice. Grace is left listening to Baby's cries mount as her mind races as to how well Miss Beatrice must know her brother to call him by his first name. She stares at the empty doorway and realises she is now hoping that, for all she's thought about Miss Beatrice, she will never see her again.

When Michael comes back into the room and sits down heavily and quickly in the chair nearest the door, and puts his head in his hands and shakes, Grace hopes that even more.

1923

28

BEA'S TAXI IS PASSING THE BRITISH MUSEUM WHEN IT occurs to her to buy some flowers to take to lunch after all, even though they are unlikely to be much of a match for what she could find in her own garden. But Bea's garden is three thousand miles away, in New York, at the house by the Hudson in which she had spent a year of her childhood. It has been hers for all of four years, since one of Mother's aunts died and left it to Bea, along with the funds to live in it. Bea finds it a little sad not to be there in May of all months, but she will be back there soon.

She has spent the winter in Cairo, and is now passing through on her way back, staying with the still-campaigning Celeste, whose friends are growing stranger. Next time Bea will stay at Claridge's. She went to see Edie in Paris where, having given up on farming in Kenya, she is now living a nocturnal life fuelled, it appears, by champagne, cigarettes and God knows what else. Tomorrow Bea goes north to Clemmie's where, Clemmie has written, garden and children (including Edie's Archie) are all growing strong – but not Tom's mind.

This afternoon, Bea has decided, she will visit Park Lane, or rather drive by. On her last trip through London the traffic jammed not a hundred yards away. There she was, in a juddering taxi, in sight of the house – and of the demolition ball that was swinging into the side of it, right where that lengthening crack had been. As the ball smashed on to the stone, Bea winced and turned away, but looked back to see the wall split along the line. All the house's secrets were suddenly opened up to the world outside. The ball swung again and, just as Bea had once imagined, the dining room exterior collapsed. The walls inside, Bea could see, were bare. Then the traffic moved on.

They've built a hotel there now, Clemmie told her.

Bea raps on the taxi window to stop, and steps out in front of a delightfully pretty shop. The window frame is painted a grey-blue, with the name Museum Flowers curled across the top in navy, and outside are bunches of freesias, lilac, stock, all her favourites, and good ones too. A crowd of magnificent hydrangea heads fill what must be two buckets. She was wrong about not finding a match for her own garden. These are exquisite. Even the roses are of such a delicate salmon pink that she hesitates over them for a moment – but not roses, not today. Bea walks into the shop and stands at the counter watching the florist, who has her back to her as she finishes a bouquet. Bea watches her work, catching flashes of fingers and ribbon and scissors. I wonder what she's like with hair, she thinks.

By the time the florist returns to the front desk, Bea has wandered behind the central plant display.

'Can I help, madam?' the florist calls.

'The sweet peas are perfectly lovely.' Bea always surprises herself when she speaks in England. Although back home she is told that she sounds starkly British, her voice has softened enough so that she sounds quite American over here. 'They remind me of the borders in Sussex,' she continues, 'when I was a child.'

'Oh, Sussex,' says the florist, sounding a little surprised. 'They come from Sussex, madam. How many would you like?'

'Oh, two dozen, blue and white. Don't make too much of a fuss in wrapping them. Shall I pick some out?'

'I have some here, madam.'

Bea circumvents the potted palms and returns to the desk. As she approaches she notices that the florist is looking at her strangely and Bea, in return, is feeling a little disturbed that she knows this woman from somewhere and she can't quite place her. Her mind starts to run through the continents she has visited. But don't be ridiculous, Beatrice, you haven't met this woman in Cairo. France, though, it could have been, in the war. She's just old enough to have been out there with Bea, if she had been able to pay her way on the ambulances. The woman is now avoiding Bea's gaze, but this makes Bea all the more curious until at last she says, 'Don't I know you from somewhere?'

The woman flushes down the side of her face and neck that Bea can see.

'Yes, I know you,' says Bea. 'Where do I know you from? Good God, it's Grace. The vanishing maid. I've found you. How extraordinary.'

'I'm sorry, ma . . . ' The florist is flushed pink from her collar, and she dips her head and bobs and stammers out, 'Yes, Miss Beatrice.' Then, 'No, sorry, it's probably Mrs or Lady now.'

No, Bea thinks, just Miss, and thirty years old. However, an independent life is just what Bea once said she wanted. And if you have a house and land yourself, then you are not so clearly looking for a husband.

Before Bea has time to find a reply, a small boy runs in from the back of the shop. He is no more than five or six years old and near white-blond curls flop onto his face. Bea stops speaking. The boy stops and looks up at Bea. Bea holds her breath as her mind tumbles back twenty years and more, to small ponies and nursery pillow fights and knees scraped green by bushes and trees.

Grace is staring at this little boy as though she too has seen a ghost, but the ghost runs over to the far side of the counter and wraps his arms around Grace's legs. Having squeezed them tight, he steps backwards and points to his chest. 'Look at what Uncle Mikey gave me, Mummy.'

Beatrice cannot help but look, too. It is a campaigning rosette. *Michael Campbell*, it says, *Independent Labour Party*.

She doesn't know which to be more stunned by. There are too many connections being made at once to make sense of them, and her head is spinning as she struggles to remember whether she ever knew Grace's surname.

Uncle Mikey. Grace is looking straight at Bea, reading the confusion and shock that is clearly showing on her face. As Bea puts her good hand on the counter to steady herself, she sees Grace turn to hush the little boy as though she is brushing his words away into a corner.

Almost five years have passed but Bea now has her answer, all her answers. Her stomach clenches. If it was not to be five years ago then how, how could it be now?

Bea needs to leave this shop, Grace and little Edward as soon as she can. She opens her purse and takes out the money to pay for the sweet peas and turns to go. She hesitates, and pulls a card case out of the clutch bag not yet under her arm and takes a card out and presses it down on the counter.

'For the boy,' she says, 'if ever . . .' Then she takes a deep breath and adds, 'There's no need to pass on . . .'

Grace nods.

Bea picks up the sweet peas and walks back out on to the London street.

HISTORICAL NOTE

Park Lane is a novel but its story is inseparable from its historical setting:

Mrs Pankhurst held rallies in Campden Hill Square and Glebe Place, and the evening and afternoon unfolded exactly as described here. The Suffragists and Suffragettes disliked each other and the WSPU's HQ was in Mrs Pattie Hall's flat in Maida Vale, though not necessarily in Lauderdale Mansions. When the flat was raided by the police in May 1914, stones and machetes were found there. Lloyd George's house was bombed, and the Cat and Mouse Act was continuously being passed over in favour of the question of Home Rule for Ireland. The Gretna Green rail disaster was the worst rail crash in the United Kingdom, involved five trains, and a total of 226 people died. And Dartmouth House, now the English Speaking Union in Mayfair, was a nursing home run by the Countess of Lytton who, as Pamela Plowden, had been Winston Churchill's first great love.

The first Sir William Masters, Bea's great grandfather, was inspired by Thomas Brassey, regarded by many as the greatest railway builder the world has seen. And the Brasseys, like the fictional Masters, lived in a house on Park Lane which was sold at the end of the First World War. The Brasseys' house had attached to it an Indian Durbar Hall that was filled with ethnographical trophies brought back from travels abroad. The family were ardent, and influential, Suffragists – in particular one Muriel Brassey, who was tiny in stature but huge in character. She had a daughter (rather than a daughter's friend) who 'bolted' to Kenya, but that is the subject of another book . . .

London, October 2011

ACKNOWLEDGEMENTS

This is my first novel. It has been an immensely enjoyable but very different writing experience from non-fiction and I should like to thank my talented editor Lennie Goodings for all her guidance along this new path. She is not alone at Virago and Little, Brown in her help. Vivien Redman copyedited the manuscript with great care, along with Mari Roberts and Jenny Page. Susan de Soissons, Judith Greenberg and Naomi Doerge have helped launch *Park Lane* into the world. Thanks, too, to Victoria Pepe for her views. The encouragement of my agent, the wonderful Gill Coleridge, has been with me from the start and thank you also to her assistant Cara Jones. In the US, both *Park Lane* and I have been equally well agented by Melanie Jackson, who has again delivered me into the talented hands of Vicky Wilson and I am thrilled to be working with her once more. As I am with the immensely capable Andrea Robinson and Russell Perreault of Vintage, both of whom worked with me on *The Bolter*. Finally, *Park Lane* could not have been written without the support and love of my friends, and my family. Thank you George for helping me find the time and space to finish. And thank you Luke and Liberty. I promise I will try to write a children's book before you are too old to read it.

ALSO BY FRANCES OSBORNE

THE BOLTER

In an age of bolters—women who broke the rules and fled their marriages—Idina Sackville was the most celebrated of them all. Her relentless affairs, wild sex parties, and brazen flouting of convention shocked high society and inspired countless writers and artists, from Nancy Mitford to Greta Garbo. But Idina's compelling charm masked the pain of betrayal and heartbreak. Now Frances Osborne explores the life of Idina, her enigmatic great-grandmother, using letters, diaries, and family legend, following her from Edwardian London to the hills of Kenya, where she reigned over the scandalous antics of the "Happy Valley Set." Dazzlingly chic yet warmly intimate, *The Bolter* is a fascinating look at a woman whose energy still burns bright almost a century later.

Biography